AIRSHOW ILEX

Mary B. Lyons

WORDPOWER™

AIRSHOW ILEX

Copyright © Mary B. Lyons BSc(Hons) 2010

First Edition 2010
Firstclass Fiction series

Published in England by Wordpower™
P.O. Box 1190, SANDHURST, GU47 7BW

www.wordpower.u-net.com

The Author asserts her moral right to be identified
as the author of this work. All characters, companies, official
organisations and trade names in this book are fictitious. Any
resemblance to these items or to real persons, living or dead,
is coincidental. Technical and legal procedures and
equipment are fictitious and should not be relied upon. Some
true geographical locations are specified in the appendix.

All rights reserved.
No part of this publication may be reproduced, stored in a retrieval
system, or be transmitted in any form or by any means, electronic,
mechanical, photocopying, recording, spoken aloud or otherwise,
without the prior permission in writing of the author and publisher.

A CIP catalogue record for this book
Is available from the British Library

ISBN 978-0950821238

Cover Design by Mary B. Lyons BSc(Hons)

Typeset by Wordpower™

Printed and bound in England by
The Midas Press PLC

AIRSHOW ILEX

About the Author

Mary B. Lyons, an established writer in several genres, was born in Surrey, England and has been writing since the age of eight years. Those who know her will agree that she pours boundless energy, innovative creativity, positive thinking and attention to detail into any project that she undertakes. AIRSHOW ILEX is, no doubt, the first of many blockbuster novels to pour from the fingers of this talented writer who deserves every success.

Writing a first novel is a huge undertaking. The journey has been fascinating and, at times, utterly amazing as my characters progressively interacted. I set out to write an entertaining and interesting book, not realising that the process would be so excruciatingly, creatively productive.

I could not have achieved it without the unstinting support and encouragement of my husband Pitt and my son, William, together with my friends and colleagues. I owe a special debt of gratitude to my dear daughter Cassandra and to my friend and fellow writer H. Harrington who both, in addition to Pitt, painstakingly proof read and critiqued for me. They always found time to discuss the work and debate the nuances of syntax. If I never see another hyphen it will be too soon!

Mary B. Lyons
Hampshire, England, 2010

Also by Mary B. Lyons

The Lonely Shade © 2008
Original bereavement poetry

A5 booklet with monochrome photographs
ISBN 9780950821214

CD of *The Lonely Shade* spoken by the author
ISBN 9780950821221

Available from the Wordpower™ website:
www.wordpower.u-net.com

Published by
Wordpower™, PO Box 1190,
SANDHURST, GU47 7BW

and

Poetry for Pregnancy
Quirky humour with line drawings.
Soon to be republished.

Study Buddy® reading stand in cool white.
Invented by the author for those who love to read.
Available from the Wordpower™ website.
www.wordpower.u-net.com

For all the people I love.
You know who you are.

AIRSHOW ILEX,

Chapter 1

**Phillipstone Airport. England
Sunday, 12th June.**

'Your tripod's sticking in me.'

'Come here and stop complaining!'

Roland Dilger, airshow photographer, pulled the woman in the shocking pink, flying-suit nearer to him, the naked light bulb only inches from his balding head and the aroma of disinfectant assailing his nostrils.

'You could have found somewhere better than a broom cupboard?' she muttered as he nuzzled her, fumbling with the silver zip that ran unhindered from her neck to left knee.

'It's worse than trying to get into a packet of biscuits,' he commented.

'I didn't have time to change. You knew I had a practice this afternoon. Then there was a briefing. Being chief pilot of the *Pink Perils* is no walk in the park. Hey! Pack it in!'

'Come on Debbie. You know you like it. Remember the Rouderoi Airshow? That little place behind the magazine displays?'

'That was a bit different from having to stand up like this,' she grumbled, reluctantly wriggling out of the suit and surveying the serried ranks of cleaning materials, toilet rolls and boxes. 'Why can't we get a proper hotel room or something?'

'We will. I promise.' His hands were all over her. She sighed at the re-awakening of their long-term, opportunistic romance. 'When the airshow's finished at the end of next week, I'll book us a suite at *The Supreme* on the ring road. You know there's nothing to be had for miles around right now,' ... adding mentally, 'except you'.

*

Gig Cattermole paced around the circular first floor corridor of the Press Centre, the thud of his legendary feet, characterised by the dragging sound of the left one, echoing in the unfinished building. Taking out a handkerchief, he wiped it across his forehead and paused to look out from the curved, panoramic window onto the darkening airfield. In one week's time, the chaotic scene spread out in the deepening dusk below would be in pristine order, ready to welcome the thousands of exhibitors, trade visitors and, on the final weekend, the great, unwashed public to the Phillipstone International Airshow, set in the heart of East Anglia.

Gone would be the men on ladders, the painters renewing road lines and the transporters carrying equipment for aircraft, exhibition halls and catering. Internal bus stops would be in place and courtesy cars over-heating in the traffic jams on the road that looped in a figure of eight around the flatland that was the airfield site.

Gig had seen it all many times before but there was always something of a thrill about the preparation and anticipation... like Christmas but in the summer. There were secrets on a grand scale, as exhibitors kept their wares under wraps until the last minute. Every kind of aircraft had flown or been carried into Phillipstone airfield over the past ten days and the halls were crammed with multifarious articles either directly or remotely connected to aeronautical and military hardware, seductively lit and presented.

The temporary town that sprang up every June with its patchwork of halls, marquees, caravans, hard-standings and walkways would soon be peopled by denizens of industry, entrepreneurs, wealthy buyers and government representatives from all over the world.

Tons of fast food and *cordon bleu* cuisine would fuel the frantic week of meetings, presentations, deals and disasters.

AIRSHOW ILEX

Hundreds of floral arrangements and potted plants would soon start to arrive. Acres of carpet would be laid in the halls. The skies were already ringing with the sound of various aircraft... everything from the vintage, phutting *Crotter* to the chest-rattling *Volto* would weave or thunder down onto one of the two runways before being conducted to their allocated exterior show places. From his vantage point in the Press Centre corridor, he had watched earlier as a super-sized cargo carrier had been coaxed slowly backwards onto its site, like a metal elephant being persuaded into a circus van, its broad wings reminiscent of big, flapping ears.

Gig stuffed the handkerchief back into his pocket and turned to see a plump, black, cleaning woman waddling towards him. She was clasping a mop and had the handle of the bucket hooked over her arm. As usual, she wore a big, toothy smile and her hair was tied up in a multi-coloured scarf.

'Good evenin', Mr. Cattermole,' she chanted in her singsong, Caribbean voice.

'Hello Zelara. Finished for the night?'

'Yes sah. All done. Toilets gleamin', floor shinin', paper towels in dispensers and the man is comin' to put up dem wall mirrors in de mornin' if he can find de time.'

The tall, waxy-faced guard smiled down at her.

'I dunno what we'd do without you ladies to help us.'

'Aw, we enjoys it, sah. Good money. Nice people. Shame about dem loud aeroplanes though!' She chuckled with a dismissive flap of her free hand as she ambled on her way along the curved corridor to the cleaning cupboard near the top of the stairs. She put down the bucket and opened the door of the store.

'Oh my grandmother's curlers!' She exclaimed, dropping the mop with a clatter. Debbie looked over Roland's shoulder into the surprised eyes of the cleaner.

'I ain't never seen *that* before!' exclaimed Zelara, shutting the door quietly.

*

'No. I'm sorry. I've told you already. You simply cannot have a parking space on site this year Miss Framp.'
Celeste Blagden, the Press Centre Controller, stood by her desk holding the phone away from her ear as the voice of Eleanor Framp, frightfully cultured and insistent, poured from the earpiece in a torrent.

'I have to go now, Miss Framp. Please forgive me.' She slammed the receiver down and quickly put her fingers in her ears as the *Drig-Vb* roared overhead, fulfilling its test flight for the show. Everything in the Press Centre shook and rattled. Celeste ran her elegant, manicured nails through her shoulder-length black hair, sighed in exasperation and reached for a pencil.

On a sticky-back notelet she wrote, 'That irritating Framp woman journalist has been on at me again today. If she rings for a parking space, refuse. We've got tons but tell her there aren't any.' She stuck it on her assistant's monitor. Then, flopping down into her, cream leather, executive chair, she smugly surveyed the headquarters of her empire, before swinging around and clicking the mouse to check her emails.

She replied and printed out the copies, paper-clipped them together and dropped them into her assistant's tray before clicking open the next message from the *Primrose Surgery*. It read, *Further to your recent communication, an appointment has been made for you on Wed 15th June at 11 a.m. Please confirm or rebook.'*

Celeste sat back in her chair, palms over her eyes. That wretched *Drig-Vb* made another pass over the airfield at full throttle.

'Shut up!' she said aloud through gritted teeth as the spring-loaded table-lamp buzzed in sympathy with the vibration of the huge windows. She took a deep breath and was on the point of opening the next message when the phone rang, startling her into snatching up the receiver.

'Hi, Honeybun,' said a smooth, male voice. 'How's my girl?'
'Oh,' she replied. 'Daddy. How good to hear from you.'
'You sound a bit tired, darling. Everything alright?'
'I'm just very busy. You know how these things are.'

AIRSHOW ILEX

'You're working late,' he commented. 'Do you realise it's getting on for ten o'clock? I tried the flat but nobody's home.'

'Yes. I'm in free-fall time at the moment and Rupert's in Hamburg. There are just not enough hours in the day.'

'Have you bitten off more than you can chew, eh?' She could hear the gentle teasing in his voice.

'I couldn't refuse, could I? A career opportunity not to be missed.' She drummed her fingers silently on the mouse mat. As he talked on about the garden, her mother, next year's planned holiday and other trivia, her eyes latched onto the pile of work still awaiting her attention. He certainly chose his moments!

'Well, how about it then?'

'What Daddy?'

'Haven't you been listening? Come to the concert with us on Friday night. It'll do you good to relax.'

'Oh Daddy, I simply can't. I'm up to my ears here.'

'Look, pussycat, I got you that job to make you happy, not give you a nervous breakdown.'

'I'm very, very grateful,' she said dutifully, 'and I do love it here but I really can't do anything else while the show and preparations are on. They're paying me very nicely for this, you know, and it'll look great on my CV.'

'Sure I can't persuade my little girl?'

'Not this time Daddy.'

'Alright then. I'll let you off the hook just this once. I'm going down to join Mummy at the cottage for a couple of days from tomorrow but we'll be back for the concert before the weekend. Toodle-oo!'

'Bye Daddy. Take care!' The line went dead.

She hung up and laid her hands, palms down and fingers spread, purposefully on the desk.

'I am twenty-nine years old. When's he going to stop treating me like a child?' She hissed, grabbing the receiver again, dialling Germany, drumming her fingers, waiting for the connection.

'Hotel Weiss-Schwanbrook. Guten Abend.'

'Good evening. Please can you put me through to Mr. Rupert Skinner?'

The receptionist switched to perfect English, with a hint of superiority.

'Your name please madam?'

'It's Ms. Blagden.'

'One moment please.'

Silence.

'There is no reply from Herr Skinner's room, madam.'

'Are you sure?'

'Yes, madam, of course. Would you like to leave a message?'

'No. No thank you. Goodbye.'

Celeste looked at her watch. Where was he? After his flight back from Paris today and with a meeting early tomorrow morning, not to mention the one-hour time difference, he ought to have been back at the hotel by now. She took out her mobile phone and texted him, *'Sorry missed U. Call me 2mor lunchtime. Luv U. C. xxx'*

She'd had enough for today and turned off the workstation, leaving the string of emails dangling in space for the morning. Standing up and stretching, she turned and cast her eyes around the office, taking in the wall-charts filled with coloured oblongs like some modern painting, the huge posters of aircraft and helicopters, the message board scribbled with urgency and the giant trolley, its pigeonholes bulging with mail for the media personnel who were already flooding in from the capital and abroad. Hundreds of foreign exhibitors lost no time in churning out hospitality invitations to those who might just give them a mention. Indeed, with judicious planning, it was possible to eat your way around the show for the entire week with nothing more than a press pass.

The huge, black voids of the night-time windows beckoned to her and she went across to look out. The airfield was in darkness, save for the glare from security gantries and the stabbing points of the runway lights, flamboyant in red, white and green, like some frozen firework display ready to welcome the incoming exhibition aircraft that would cruise in under cover of darkness.

AIRSHOW ILEX

Where was Rupert? Why wasn't he back at his hotel? She breathed onto the pane and drew a heart in the misty surface, then added a frill all the way round it, followed by an arrow across the centre. Angry with herself for being so sentimental, she obliterated her artwork with the palm of her hand and wiped away the moisture on the thigh of her *Du Prève* trousers. She needed him.

She went out of the office and into the relaxation area, swiped her electronic card that opened the door to the viewing balcony and stepped outside onto the carpet. The cool air was heavy with the scent of meadowsweet. There was just a hint of moisture on the breeze that bathed her face. She took a deep breath.

Then suddenly and unexpectedly, her eyes filled with tears that over-spilled and ran down her hot cheeks into the corners of her mouth from where she instinctively licked them away, surprised at their saltiness. She fumbled for a tissue from her jacket pocket and dabbed at her face in the darkness. For crying out loud! She was a grown-up with a responsible job and status. Smacking herself on the wrist, she said aloud, 'Stop it! Stop it! Pull yourself together! He's probably at a business dinner with somebody important.'

Celeste didn't believe it though. He was too handsome, too charming and too rich to be loose in a foreign city on his own on a beautiful June night with the stars piercing the sky like tiny, sparkling, snowflakes through a velvet roof. She went back into her Press Centre office, gathered up her bag and coat and headed out, flicking off the lights, calling it a day. It was late and she was bushed.

'Goodnight Zelara,' she said disinterestedly, keeping her head down, pretending to search for her car keys, making her way across reception, opening the electronic doors and stepping down onto the wide, curved staircase that led to the ground-floor foyer. 'Clear away those cleaning things.'

'Miss Blagden, ma'am... just a moment please... Miss...' but the Press Centre Controller was gone and the cleaner was stuck with nowhere to put her bucket and mop. She cast a rolling eye towards the broom cupboard and grimaced to herself. No sound emanated from the closet. The key was still on the outside. Dare she turn it? It would serve them right if she did. She scratched at the edge of her corset through the white, nylon overall. It was awful being fat. She pushed back her sleeve and checked the time. Then she parked the bucket and mop in front of the cupboard door. That should give them a fright when they came out!

'An' don't you go knickin' none of my supplies!' She said in a low voice before going across to the locker room to get her vacuum cleaner.

*

The self-imposed prisoners stood and waited.
'Do you think she's gone, Roland?' whispered Debbie.
He pressed his ear against the crack.
'It sounds quiet out there. Make yourself decent and I'll have a peek.'
He quietly and gently pressed the lever handle and peered out.
'Seems all clear,' he said as the bucket and mop went over with a clatter. 'Stupid woman's left her gear outside.'

*

Head of Security, Gig Cattermole, having completed his circuit of the floor, came back along the corridor in time to hear the noise.
'Quick! Gig's coming,' Roland hissed. 'I know his footsteps.'
With a flash of forethought, he put the key on the inside and turned it, quickly hitting the light switch so that the pair stood in total darkness amid the smell of bleach bottles, packs of toilet rolls and their own sweat from recent activities. They heard Gig's quickened, limping gait approaching. By the time the head of security reached the closet, all was quiet.
'What the heck's Zelara playing at, leaving this stuff all over the place?' Gig muttered to himself, bending with difficulty as he

picked up the wet mop, propped it against the door and rattled the handle in vain.

Roland put his finger to his lips in the darkness... a wasted gesture... but he could hear Debbie trying to breathe quietly in that airless place. Gig's footsteps retreated. It seemed like forever before Roland was brave enough to open the door again. Now all the Press Centre lights were out. The mop tried to fall over again but he had his hand around the door and caught it.

'We're stuck here for a bit longer,' he cursed, as he heard the electronically operated security doors at the top of the staircase slide open, then 'whoosh' shut. He guessed that Gig was now making his way downstairs to check the halls.

'That cleaner's still clattering about out there,' he added.

*

Zelara struggled to get the heavy vacuum cleaner out of the locker room and across reception. She pushed open the teak effect door bearing the gold-coloured plate stating: 'Press Centre Controller.' It was always a pigsty in there. They'd been in for three months, Miss Snotty Nose and her team of dolly clones. The floor was always littered with sweet wrappers. 'Pthah!' she spat, under her breath, kicking the machine through the doorway and unravelling the lead.

The roar of the mechanism was deafening and blotted out the sound of the late night arrivals on the runway. The cleaner pushed and shoved it around, hitting the furniture and giving the cream, leather chair a particularly good clout. Job done, she took out her yellow duster and started to wipe around the surfaces... window ledges, computer key-boards, shelves and desks. Desks. That looked interesting. She peered at the note on Celeste's. *'Ring doc in morning.'*

'I wonder what that's all about?' she mused, stooping to empty the waste paper basket into a black, plastic sack. 'Now, what's this?' She read the note stuck on the assistant's monitor and tutted. 'You spiteful little madam,' she said, shaking her head in puzzlement.

Time to go home. With the vacuum cleaner safely back in the locker room, Zelara peeled off her sticky, nylon overall and took her outsize, lemon, cotton coat from the hook and put it on. Carrying her crocheted shopping bag, she made her way to the top of the stairs. Card in the slot. 'Swish' of sliding doors. 'Whoosh' as they closed behind her.

*

In the broom cupboard, Roland whispered 'She's gone but I think we're here in the Press Centre for the night though.' The sound of his face being slapped was followed by a scuffle, a key rattling and the emergence of two perspiring and dishevelled people from incarceration

'Aw Debbie,' he pleaded. 'Give a fella a break. It wasn't my fault.' His paramour was already on her way to the ice-cold water dispenser.

'Don't speak to me,' she hissed, her voice laced with anger.

*

Brecht drove the hire-car smoothly into the check-in area of Gate Alpha, the quartz headlamps piercing the Sunday night darkness as the engine purred quietly to a stop. The window went down. The guard on duty said, 'Pass please.'
Brecht held up his security card that he wore suspended on a braid around his neck.
The guard read, 'Brecht Slipkopj'.

'That's a funny name. Where you from?'

'From Former Kridiblikt Republic. Got work permit.' He produced it.

'Who's that in the back?'

'I don'ta know, sirr. I voss asked to collect her-a and take her-a to the maintenance reception.' His foreign accent was heavy. The guard looked down at him suspiciously, taking in the curly black hair, the tanned face and the single gold earring before shining his torch into the rear of the car. A woman with long red hair and a very low-cut, sequinned green dress, leaned forward, looking candidly into the blinding torch beam. Her eyes matched her dress.

'Please get out miss,' the guard said, opening the car's rear door.

She swung her long, black-stockinged legs around, placed her feet elegantly on the ground and stood up, her white, lace stole slipping from her very beautiful shoulders.

'Where's your pass?' he asked.

'Call your supervisor,' she replied coolly.

'Look, miss, you can't come onto this high security site without a proper pass. What's your business here at the airfield at this time of night?' Brecht drummed his fingers on the wheel.

'Canna I go now?' he called out.

'Only if you take her with you,' came the reply.

The woman stood shifting her weight seductively from one leg to the other on her very high, red, patent leather heels and pulled at the glistening strands of russet hair that cascaded over her creamy, smooth skin. Brecht turned off the engine.

'Everything alright over there?' called the other guard from the kiosk.

'Got some woman wanting to come in without a pass,' replied his colleague.

The second guard emerged from the well-lit warmth into the cool, black of the June night, shining his torch towards the visitor.

'Synth!' he exclaimed. 'Good to see you again! How've you been doing?'

'Busy, busy,' she replied, with a dazzling smile. 'How's the family?'

'Good, thanks for asking. My boy's off to join the army in the autumn. What about that batty old mother of yours?'

'Still driving me round the bend,' she smiled.

Then he turned to the first guard and said, 'Let this lady through. She's an old friend of the airshow.'

'What about searching her bag?'

'I don't think that's a very good idea,' replied his colleague as the woman winked at him and got into the back of the car.

'Off you go Synth. Have a good night!' and he waved the car away.

Brecht started up the engine and the vehicle purred up the approach road, taking the left fork towards the bothies... a collection of temporary huts used by the airshow maintenance staff. A cheer went up from the men sitting around the glowing brazier as they saw the headlights. There was a smell of barbecue in the air and the glint of fluorescent jackets shone like beacons of hope for what they knew to be the start of a really great night.

Synth called from the open car window, 'Hello boys! Party time!'

Two or three rushed forward to help her out of the car and carry the hold-all that the regulars knew was full of promise.

Brecht said, 'Vot abouta my money?'

'Sorry mate. Forgot about that,' replied a burly guy with a half-eaten pie in his hand. 'Come back at six in the morning!' He dropped a twenty-pound note through the open car window.

Chapter 2

Monday, 13th June

'Good morning Zelara!'

The cleaning woman looked up and saw the tall reflection of the glamorous restaurant manager in the cloakroom mirror.

'Oh, Miss Paula you sure give me a fright! Didn't knows nobody was in jus' yet. It's not even eight o'clock. You's lookin' mighty swish in dat get-up.'

'I've got to make an early start. There's a rehearsal for the VIPs coming in for lunch on Thursday.' She paused. 'Thank goodness we've got mirrors in here at last! How are we girls supposed to beautify ourselves without them?'

She plonked her ample handbag at the side of the basin, took out her styling brush and bent her knees.

Zelara continued filling the swivel soap dispensers while Paula prattled on in that husky voice of hers. The cleaner wasn't in a good mood. She'd had an ear bashing from her supervisor this morning about the mop and bucket episode last night. The Press Centre Manager had reported her first thing.

Paula turned, looked around her and laid her hand on Zelara's shoulder. 'Check the cubicles!' She commanded. Without question, the cleaner pushed open the row of doors one by one.

'All clear,' she said, in an upmarket voice entirely devoid of Caribbean tones.

The restaurant manager drew her to one side. 'Information. Details in there.' She thrust a folded piece of paper at the chubby, black woman. Zelara tucked it into her ample bra, remarking with a hint of chagrin that Paula had by far the better job.

'Ah yes,' the restaurant manager agreed, 'but then I've got real responsibilities. Health and safety, hygiene, menus to plan and all that.'

'Don't speak to me about hygiene. If I see another mop or toilet roll I shall quite literally scream myself silly.'

'You knew what you were taking on. You'll be well paid. It'll set you up for life.'

'I appreciate that. It's just so boring establishing this alias.'

'Look, nobody's going to remember you. You're just an overweight Caribbean cleaner. They'll never suspect what you really are.'

Zelara's warning glance in the mirror alerted Paula to the arrival of the Press Centre Manager, Celeste Blagden, who quickly made her way to the farthest cubicle, ignoring the cleaner who had hastily started tap polishing and declaring loudly in a voice rich with cane sugar and coconut palms, 'Why's thank you, Miz Paula. That's mighty kind of you to show yours appreciation .' Paula grimaced a smile and left.

A minute later, Celeste was at the basins twiddling her fingers under the stream of tepid water.

'I hope there won't be a repetition of your slovenly behaviour again, Zelara,' she barked. 'It was really quite unacceptable to leave your cleaning things laying around in reception like that last night.'

Zelara tried to look contrite and humble but had to scratch her cheek to hide the smile.

'Yes ma'am, Miss Blagden,' she said. 'It won't happen again. I sure don't knows what come over me.'

'Well don't let it come over you again! Temporary jobs at this airshow are in great demand and you are easily replaced.' She primped her hair in the mirror. 'I'm working here from seven in the morning until ten o'clock at night for weeks on end and I expect my staff to give one hundred and ten percent too.'

'Yes, Miss Blagden, ma'am.'

'That mirror's got a smear on it,' she said as she left. 'See to it!'

Zelara stuck her tongue out at the back of the retreating figure and cussed under her breath, giving the soap dispenser a smack that made it spin like a top on its spindle causing the liquid soap to spew all up the tiles.

AIRSHOW ILEX

'Your card is marked, you arrogant pinhead!' she spat.

'What was that you said?" enquired Debbie as she came into the ladies' room, freshly attired in a newly laundered, shocking pink flying suit. She carried a fringed, tan leather bag over her shoulder and her auburn highlighted hair looked a mess. She made for the cubicles.

'I wants a word with you, missy!' called Zelara in her thick accent.

'Oh yes?' came the reply. The cleaner wandered over to the cubicle, twisting her cleaning cloth in her hands.

'You and your fancy man got me into big trouble wiv yous antics in ma broom cupboard last night,' she accused, wagging her finger like a metronome at the closed door.

'I don't know what you mean,' Debbie called back above the noise of trickling water.

'Don't you come all innocent with me, you Jezebel! I knows how many beans makes five.'

'Mind your own business.'

'It is my business when my job's in jeopardy 'cos o' your shenanigans.'

'Little bit of harmless fun.' There was the sound of loo roll being torn off.

'What's fun to you nearly cost me ma livin' and I had to put up with an ear bashing from that miss hoity-toity Press Centre Manager and ma supervisor.'

The toilet flushed. Zelara raised her voice. 'Why should I'se have to eat crow for yours carryin's on?'

Debbie appeared, brushed past her and marched over to the basins, pausing for a moment, hands halfway to the soap.

'So, suddenly you're in charge of airshow moral behaviour, are you? Oh yes,' she continued, carrying on with her ablutions. 'I suppose you come from one of those 'converted' islands somewhere.'

Zelara struggled to hide a smile.

'Jus' you watch it, my lady, jus' watch it or I'se gonna be tellin' tales out of school.'

Debbie shook the droplets from her fingers and took a paper towel, dried her hands, scrunched it up and dropped it on the floor. Then she thrust her hand into the pocket of her flying suit and pulled out a five pound note, slapping it into Zelara's brown palm.

'Will that shut your mouth for you? The woman pilot queried.

'Sure will,' replied the cleaner, stuffing the note into the other cup of her bra. 'Jus' let me know if yous wants to use ma facilities again and we'll arrange a special rate.'

*

Eleanor Framp, journalist extraordinaire, tramped her way along the concourse wearing a grey mackintosh and carrying a brown briefcase. Her short, straight, iron-grey hair was parted on the side and held out of her eyes with a hair grip. The press pass hanging limply from its cord around her neck gave the impression that it too was fed up with life as it half-heartedly attempted to mate with the string of her instant camera. She made her way to the outside aircraft exhibits, many of which were already in place.

What could she say about the plethora of military jets, passenger planes and helicopters that hadn't been said a million times before in newspapers and magazines all over the world? The *Saturnian* always gave her this commission, perhaps mistakenly thinking that it would be a nice fortnight for her, out in the air, meeting lots of interesting people.

She stopped and put her briefcase down on the wooden walkway that led to the static displays. The mac had to come off. These hot flushes were becoming unbearable. She folded it over her arm, picked up the briefcase and trudged on. Now, where to start? Her eye was drawn by a rather pretty, twin-engined, executive jet in lilac and white livery. She went over and peeped up into the interior of the cabin through the open door.

'Would you like to come in and have a look, madam?' said a smart, young man, popping his head around.

'Thank you. That would be most interesting.' She went up the steps and into the stuffy, leather-scented interior. Her host was

AIRSHOW ILEX

most enthusiastic, dodging about pointing out the luxurious features, statistics about fuel consumption and range tripping from his tongue, although he seemed rather reticent about price. She put her briefcase down and took out a notepad.

Twenty minutes later, ears ringing with technical information, she thanked him kindly and climbed down the steps out into the hot sunshine again.

'It's always a pleasure to greet members of the press,' he said, deferring to her departure with a fixed smile. She stood a short distance away and took a picture with her little camera. Then she was off to the military section to sit in a cockpit and be bored to tears with information about radar, missile ranges and pressure suits. She dutifully noted it all down and graciously took leave of the uniformed personnel who seemed to have been through charm school.

Further on, there was a big American transporter.

'Come on up, ma'am,' called the cheerful airman on duty, extending his hand to hoist her up the ramp and into the poorly lit interior of the aircraft.

'Well, I expect you'd like to know all about how we do parachute drops from this little beauty,' he said, before expounding on his favourite subject until she felt she could have been dropped behind enemy lines anywhere on the planet.

'Of course, we don't just deploy personnel. Oh no, ma'am. We got room in here for jeeps and small tanks and even gliders. You can stick a parachute on anything.'

'Really?' said Eleanor, writing it all down.

'Did you know, ma'am, that they even parachute dogs in sometimes?'

'How very interesting,' said Eleanor, silently wishing that she could volunteer her neighbour's yapping poodle.

Time for a helicopter. Why did she feel that the crew was on the edge of laughing at her as she posed her erudite questions and marvelled at the technology.

'We can fit four stretchers in here,' one of them told her, looking down sceptically at her lisle stockings and brown, lace-up shoes.

'So, do you have a toilet for the crew?' she asked, straight-faced.

'No. I'm afraid we do not but our squadron is renowned for its control.'

'Thank you,' she said as she left, trying herself not to smile at the thought of a basic need not being met at three thousand feet. She supposed it must be the same for light aircraft too.

So the morning wore on, up and down the steps, in and out of the cabins, perusing flight decks, trying out seats, admiring whatever was indicated, asking questions with perspicuity and all the time formulating the article in her head that must be emailed to her editor this very afternoon.

*

It was just before noon when the large, flatbed lorry manoeuvred carefully into the maintenance area, bearing big crates strapped securely in place.

'Where the 'eck 'ave you been? You wuz s'posed ter be 'ere yesterday.'

The young driver wound his window down further, leaned out on his elbow and yelled 'Sorry mate. Gasket went up near Darlington.'

The maintenance manager hadn't had a lot of sleep last night. Synth's party had gone on until dawn.

'Why didn't you ring me? '

'Well, guv, I tried but your mobile was switched off or summit.'

A scowl and kind of muted snarl emanated from the sleep-deprived man.

'Well, yer 'ere now, so park over there by that stack of orange drums and mind you don't 'it them.'

The youth manoeuvred the vehicle into place and switched off the ignition. The lorry gave a shudder of relief as the driver grabbed his clipboard and climbed down. He followed the grumpy maintenance yard manager into the bothy.

'Any chance of a cuppa?' he queried hopefully, wiping the sweat from under the arms of his tee-shirt.

AIRSHOW ILEX

'Yeah, yeah,' he said, taking the clipboard from him and flipping over the top two sheets. 'I'll get one of the lads onto it in a minute. What's this?'

'What's what?'

'It says, 'Two Maximillion independent air-conditioning machines, model number JS49b/220XG.' He stabbed his finger against the whiteboard on the wall. 'Can't your supplies department read? This is what we ordered,' he said. 'We need the 5,000XGs. Those things out there won't cool down a dog kennel! We've got an 'eat wave coming. Take 'em back!'

'Aw guv...' spluttered the youth.

'You 'eard me.' He shoved the clipboard back at the exasperated driver. ' Go on. I want the right ones 'ere by tomorrow.'

'Can't yer find me a cup of summit before I go? It's been a...'

'On yer bike, sonny!'

The young driver went out, climbed up into the lorry, started up and hauled at the steering wheel angrily, not listening to the constant reversal beeping in his rage. There was the sound of a crash and the maintenance manager appeared immediately in the doorway of the bothy.

'I told you to be careful of them drums,' he bawled. 'Them's very expensive ballast drums for an important aircraft...' but the youth was beyond caring and swung out of the yard leaving only a V-sign in the air behind him.

'I'm going to ring your boss and tell 'im, you young whipper snapper. You just wait...' but his final words were drowned by a continuous hooting as the flat bed lorry swung away and onto the perimeter road.

*

Immaculately dressed in a figure-hugging black dress and matching jacket, Paula, knowing that her voice didn't carry far, beckoned her staff to come closer for their daily briefing. She lifted her chin, somehow balancing her massive coiffure and long, false eye-lashes.

'We are standing here in the stainless steel kitchen of *Clouds* restaurant at Phillipstone Airshow.' The staff looked at each other, puzzled. Of course they knew where they were. Why was she telling them this?

'You may wonder why I am reminding you.' A few crossed their arms and nodded sagely.

She continued, 'This is the most prestigious restaurant at the most prestigious airshow in the world. Our standards are of the very highest. As a team, we have worked together for six weeks in preparation for this event.' They nodded in unison in agreement.

'My reputation and your future careers depend on immaculate presentation and customer service of the highest calibre. Do I make myself clear?'

A mumbled, 'Yes Paula' went around the group of twenty like a low-level Mexican wave.

'Today,' she continued, 'is our first real test. Practising on the show staff all last week was one thing, but now we must raise our game to cater to the wishes of our first group of VIPs who will come on Thursday. Today is our dress rehearsal.'

One or two put up a hand to ask who the VIPs were but Paula waved aside their unspoken question. Jack, resplendent in waiter's outfit of frilled, white shirt, black bow tie, dinner jacket and long, red apron was one who really wanted to know. He persisted.

'Miss Paula, please tell us who's coming to eat in this supremely elegant restaurant?'

His twin brother, Marcus, a mere kitchen hand in whites, elbowed him in the ribs, eliciting a torrent of abuse and ribald jibes. Paula glared at them.

'As fully trained restaurant employees under my tuition, you will not bat an eye-lid as you prepare food for, and serve, the illustrious people who will come here in three days' time. It goes without saying that security will be tight, as elsewhere in the show. So I am now going to introduce you to some extra staff.

A group of high-level security personnel dressed as waiters, kitchen staff and luncheon guests had quietly joined them.

AIRSHOW ILEX

'You will ignore these people. They don't know the first thing about cooking or serving. You should understand, however, that they are all fully armed, so don't surprise them!'
There was a titter and some knowing grins from some of the newcomers.

'Right. Everyone else to your posts. We'll begin service at twelve noon. Main, sous and pastry chefs to my cubby-hole now please... oh, and by the way, no gratuities will be offered or taken on the day. Is that clear?' If Jack and Marcus exchanged a disappointed glance, nobody seemed to notice.

*

The Press Centre computer room was there for the sole convenience of the press. Eleanor, the only occupant during the lunch-hour, chose a station over in the corner by the water cooler, put her belongings on an adjacent chair and plugged her memory stick into the back of the tower. It was deliciously cool in there. Well, the machines had to be comfortable. She propped up her notes one of the complimentary Study Buddy™, fold-away, reading stands and called up her template. One thousand words were expected from her but the show photographer would provide the pictures. A title? A heading? She racked her brains. Perhaps she should have eaten something, she thought, as she struggled to concentrate in a room that seemed to be floating. Water. Yes, water. She took a plastic cup and filled it from the cooler, dipping her fingers in and splashing it over her face and neck. Then she drank, long and deep, with her eyes closed. The flush subsided and she took some deep breaths. Flaming menopause! It was so unfair! Men didn't have to put up with all this.

Then she turned to the monitor and watched with mounting pleasure as the words began to flow. *'Flying into the Future,'* she wrote and then started the article.

> *'Nothing can prepare the visitor to the Phillipstone International Airshow for the utterly astounding array of*

aircraft and helicopters spread out on the tarmac for their delight. The very latest technology is on display from countries all around the world.

Next week, for seven days, local people may enjoy the afternoon flying displays free of charge as aircraft zoom over their homes, businesses and schools, for several hours a day. This is in addition to the normal flights coming into the airfield all year round from early morning until late at night, a bone of contention for those living under the flight path. It has been remarked before, however, that if people don't like aircraft, then why choose to live near an airport? There is no doubt that airports generate industry that benefits the local and national economy.

From Monday 20th until Friday 24th June, trade visitors will be allowed into the show but the following Saturday and Sunday will be open to the public. People will flock in their thousands to enjoy days out wallowing in candyfloss, climbing walls and flying technology. This is Phillipstone Airport's sweetener to the local population.

It was with some reservations that our local councillors passed the application for the building of the second runway specifically so that larger and more powerful aircraft could land at the show. It does not take a great stretch of imagination to realise that it is the thin end of the wedge and that Phillipstone will soon be expanding to become a major air hub for East Anglia.'

She checked what she had written and saved it. It was less than two hundred and fifty words and only a quarter of the way through. Would the editor stand for the angle? Well, Eleanor was heartily fed up with the inconvenience and politics that impinged on normal life in the area at this time of year. Take today, for instance; there was a convoluted one-way traffic system winding around the borough ensuring that anybody local who wanted to go anywhere at all had to travel at least four times as far as usual, using a concomitant amount of petrol. There wasn't a taxi to be had for miles except to and from the airshow, even during this preparation week.

Of course shopkeepers were rubbing their hands together in glee as they welcomed in the air-show personnel who threw money like confetti at the tills. Many locals stocked up in advance so they didn't have to shop during the crucial fortnight. Some took their custom elsewhere. Could she write all this? No, because didn't the paper rely on all the copy and advertising that the show provided? Didn't the airfield and its ancillary industries keep the town afloat?

An hour later she had tidied up the piece, reached the thousand words mark, coated it in honey, and emailed it through, with a sigh of relief. Wouldn't it be lovely to write something instead about her beloved embroidery one day? Removing the memory stick, she popped it into her briefcase and then sat there feeling drained. It was time to go home for a meal and a nap before setting off for her evening appointment.

*

Grant Landscar sat in the foyer of the *Old Turret Hotel* on the outskirts of Phillipstone. The white stetson was on the table beside him, together with a tonic water... doctor's orders. Relaxed, with his white-booted foot carefully placed across his left knee, he peered through the gold half-spectacles resting on the bridge of his nose and perused last week's edition of the local paper, the *Saturnian*. It was full of air-show speculation, traffic management routes and the prospect of a huge income for the local economy. That's what it was all about. Making a buck or two. It never ceased to thrill him... the prospect of yet another big deal... and he intended to live long enough to enjoy his wealth.

The hotel was fairly buzzing with excitement as high ranking media personnel, top grade pilots and VIPs settled in for a few days of eclectic camaraderie. Nobody came to this great airshow who wasn't besotted with the industry.

'Do you mind if I sit here for a moment?' asked Debbie, taking a stance like a model in front of the silver-haired man. He put down his newspaper and looked over his half-glasses at the attractive woman before him. 'Please do,' he said. 'Excuse me, but aren't you the famous lady pilot who runs the stunt team?'

'Thank you for the accolade,' she smiled. 'Yes, I'm Deborah Foxon. My friends call me Debbie. May I have the pleasure of knowing your name?'

'I'm very honoured to meet you,' he replied, rising slowly and removing his spectacles, clipping them in the top pocket of his very smart suit. He shook her hand. 'Delighted. I'm Grant Landscar. Let's sit down, shall we?'

Her diminutive figure was dwarfed by his height. She looked up at him and her glance was captured by his lively blue eyes, wrinkled at the corners but vivid in a bronzed face.

'Are you meeting somebody?' he said, as they made themselves comfortable on the sofa.

'Oh, no,' she replied. 'My team and I are staying here. I thought I'd relax for a moment before turning in for the night.'

'You're all here in the hotel? he asked.

'Well, not exactly. There are eight of us and we're sharing two family rooms in the annexe. My agent rather let us down and left the booking until too late. You know how it is around show time.'

'That must be a little inconvenient.'

'You can say that again! Eight women, two bathrooms. It's a scrum, I can tell you!'

Grant smiled knowingly. He understood women.

'Why are you smiling?' she quizzed.

'Oh, just that I grew up as the only boy in a family of girls. So I know about the bathroom thing.'

Debbie played with the clasp of her black, leather handbag without looking up. She'd heard about his wealth.

'I expect you have plenty of bathroom space now.'

'Fourteen.'

'Fourteen?' Her eyes were wide with amazement.

'It's a matter of convenience,' he joked, taking a sip from his glass.

AIRSHOW ILEX

'Is your house near the airfield?

'Not too far away. I have a little spread west of here. It backs onto the river. The place is called *Casslands*. It's very handy, the river, I mean.'

'Do you sail or something?'

'I've got a motor launch that I take out on the Broads, The *Lucky Lady*. You must come and see her when you're not so busy. Let me know when you'd like to.' He reached in his pocket for a business card and handed it to her.

'Thank you,' she said, 'I might take you up on it.' He was easy to talk to but their conversation was interrupted by the tone of his mobile phone.

'Excuse me for one moment,' he said, getting up and moving a few paces away. She heard him say, 'Yes. No. All according to plan. They're here. Catch you later.' Then he put the phone back in his pocket and rejoined her.

'May I offer you some refreshment?' he said.

'Thank you but no. I've got an early call. We have a routine to run through.'

'Stay for just a while longer,' he demurred, patting the Regency stripes and moving the cushion. He spread his arm along the back of the sofa. She couldn't resist.

'Tell me about your aerobatics team. How did it get started?' He was very persuasive.

'My father's a pilot. He let me go up with him from an early age and I just sort of took to it. I got my licence at eighteen.'

'That's young. Who backed you in the first place?'

He sensed her reluctance to talk about money in his presence.

'Do you really want to know?'

He nodded. She settled back comfortably.

'I delivered single seaters for a small company up north until I'd earned enough for a deposit on my first plane. It was only a *Cubbette* turbo-prop but I learned my skills on it. Dad guaranteed the repayments and I met them by putting on solo displays and skywriting... that sort of thing. Now I've got six aircraft... *CR-Cadets*... plus a spare, and there are eight of us who are pilots. We're the *Pink Perils* aerobatics team.'

'Impressive,' Grant said admiringly.

'I once had to trail a marriage proposal above a polo match. I think it scared the horses!' she laughed.

'Did the lady accept?'

'I don't know but the trailing banner was hell when I landed. It all seems a long time ago.' She stifled a yawn. 'Sorry,' she said, 'but I think I have to turn in now. I need to be alert for tomorrow.'

'Oh! Please don't let me interrupt!' said an up-market voice.

The pair raised their heads to meet the cool gaze of the slim, gaunt woman in a belted, grey raincoat and carrying a briefcase. 'Glamour' was clearly a word that had passed her by.

Grant Landscar got to his feet and extended his hand firmly in greeting.

'Miss Framp. I'm so glad you could make it!'

The lady pilot gazed in amazement.

'May I introduce Debbie Foxon, leader of the *Pink Perils* ladies' aerobatics team?'

Miss Framp leaned over and shook hands with the epitome of attractive womanhood.

'Charmed,' she said, unenthusiastically. If a fleeting thought of how men always went for crumpet flitted across her mind, she hid it well. Debbie's eyes darted from Grant to Miss Framp and back again. Surely not? These two?

'I was just about to go. I have an early start,' the younger woman said, getting up.

'I sure hope you have a real good rehearsal in the morning,' said Grant with a warm smile.

'Thank you,' she replied, making her exit as fast as decently possible, feeling like a child who had just caught her parents at it.

'Where?' asked Eleanor Framp.

'I've booked a little room for us where we won't be interrupted. Just one moment. If you'd like to wait over there by the elevator, I'll just go to reception.' Grant Landscar took his stetson and went over to collect a key-card. An inviting tilt of the head brought Eleanor to his side and they walked to the open lift doors and stepped in. 'Floor three,' he said.

Chapter 3

Tuesday, 14th June

Tuesday morning dawned dry and fair with a light wind from the east that soon dispelled the hot weather haze that hung across the airfield. The flags of many nations lining the concourse roadway flapped as if they too were excited at the prospect of the next week to come. From everywhere emanated the sound of frantic work. Engines whined as outside exhibits were manoeuvred into their allotted spaces. Signs were hammered up and litter bins delivered to strategic spots as bus and taxi drivers did 'the knowledge' of the airshow layout. The site was large and complex, incorporating a relentless one-way system.

In a queue of traffic approaching Hall Three, Brecht idly twiddled the knobs on the car radio. One station came up loud and clear.

'Good morning airshow addicts! This is Radio Runway, working to keep you informed about all the Phillipstone International Airshow events over this fantastic fortnight. Tune in this week to hear all about the plans for next week. Tune in next week to keep up to date on EVERYTHING that's happening at the PIA. This is Radio Runway!'

The station jingle came up after the sound effect '*zoom*' of an aircraft : *'Radio Runway... Airshow news and views,'* followed by another '*zoom*'.

The announcer continued, *'After the news and weather we have an exclusive interview with local councillor Percival Springstock, but first, the traffic. A lorry has shifted its load of animal feed on the motorway and two lanes are closed southbound at junctions eight to ten. We understand that flocks of pigeons are also a hazard here. It seems they can't resist a free meal.*

The accident is leading to long delays so avoid the motorway if you can. Over at Singhurst there is a fire in the woodland behind the castle. Ten fire appliances are in attendance and the fire chief says that, despite water shortages, the blaze is nearly under control. Smoke is still pouring onto the surrounding roads so try and avoid that area too, if you can. Elsewhere on our patch, traffic is moving smoothly. Now we are going over to the main news.'

'Here is the eleven o'clock news. Foreign dignitaries are arriving for a luncheon with the Prime Minister. It is believed that discussions will be held ahead of the energy summit next month. A demonstration by The Anti-Airshow Action Society is taking place nearby but protestors have so far been kept behind barriers. The half-yearly export figures are lower than expected but it is anticipated that the forthcoming International Airshow at Phillipstone will boost the economy. A pop festival due to be held on the Isle of Splendour on Miffin Broad this weekend has been cancelled due to the drought. Fifty thousand ticket holders will get refunds. The organisers said they couldn't guarantee health and safety standards and it was hoped to re-schedule in the autumn. This is the end of the news. Here is the weather forecast: The sunny period is set to continue throughout the week with pollen counts high. Temperatures are expected to climb to thirty degrees by Friday in all parts of the United Kingdom.'

Brecht hit the radio 'off' button and leaned back indolently in the leather seat, tapping his fingers on the steering wheel. The map of the site lay beside him on the passenger seat. His air conditioning was sucking in fumes from the car in front, so he turned that off too. He undid the seatbelt and removed his jacket, dumping it on top of the map. It was stinking hot. He took the water bottle out of the door compartment and swigged from it. It tasted tepid. He screwed the cap thoughtfully back on, wondering when he would be contacted.

'Tap-tap.' Somebody was knocking on the passenger side window. He pressed the button and it wound down.

AIRSHOW ILEX

'Yes?' he questioned. 'I need to go through the tunnel,' said a cultured female voice. The woman was tall and bent nearly double in order to see through the window.

'Can you take me? I don't mind paying.'

'It's-a free, lady,' he replied. 'Get in. I take-a you... WHEN we go.

Eleanor Framp opened the rear passenger door and deposited her briefcase and mackintosh on the back seat. Then, like a grasshopper trying to squeeze itself into a matchbox, she crammed herself in.

'Goodness knows how it will be next week,' she exclaimed, putting her sunglasses away and adjusting the artificial white flower on the lapel of her navy-blue jacket. 'Have you done the airshow before?' she queried by way of conversation as she secured her seatbelt.

'No, lady. This is-a my first-a time. I have work permit and, see...' He held up his pass on its sweaty cord.

'Yes, I'm sure you have,' Eleanor replied. She'd seen the sticker in the car window. This was a show taxi.

'Ah!' said Brecht. Here-a we go!' and he jammed his foot down on the accelerator and zoomed forward into a narrow gap, causing his passenger to lurch violently back and then forth so that her elegant neck was in danger of whiplash.

'Oh!' she exclaimed, clasping the briefcase.

'You OK-a there?' he grinned into the rear-view mirror.

'Fine. Fine,' she responded as the bothies sped past her, the flags became a blur and the stench of Brecht's after-shave made her feel slightly faint.

'Can we have a little air, please?'

'Yes. Of-a course, dear lady,' he replied, turning the air conditioning on full so that the car was filled with a blast like a sauna.

Was she the contact? She didn't look much of a fighter. Perhaps he'd better try the password. Now, what was it? Ah yes. He paused and then said 'Ingenious, don't you think?'

'Yes,' she replied. 'Ingenious.' She looked puzzled. What did he mean? The air-conditioning, obviously. 'Yes, it's very clever.'

'Ingenious. InGENious,' he said again. Why wasn't she giving the correct reply?

'Amazing,' she said.

He swung quickly to the left and took the side-road that led to the tunnel exit. Perhaps she'd forgotten the response. She was wearing the white flower on her jacket after all. He'd try one more time.

'Quite ingenious,' he laboured.

'Absolutely,' she replied.

He gave up and roared into the tunnel, its overhead amber lights momentarily dazzling him as they flicked rhythmically past, changing the face of the woman in the mirror to a dull bronze.

Then the anchors went on. Another jam. Eleanor's breathing quickened. She felt trapped and hot and a little light-headed. She wanted to be somewhere else. Her early morning interviewee hadn't materialised in the Press Centre. She'd got up at six for nothing. She was hungry. A jolt. The traffic was on the move again. She sighed and started to get her things together. There was the light at the end of the tunnel. The amber glow gave way to brilliant sunlight again and Brecht pulled over so that she could get out in the transit car park.

'Thank you,' she said, gathering her belongings. 'See you again probably.'

'Yes, lady.' He paused. 'Tella you whata. I not supposed to do tha tours off-site but for you I do it.' There was a queue for the free bus to the station and Eleanor viewed it dismally.

'How much to take me to St. Bede's?'

'Ten-a pounds,' Brecht replied instantly. This was all extra, easy money.

'Very well,' she said.

As the vehicle moved forward, she fumbled in her pocket for the folded letter, took it out and, after putting her reading glasses on, started to peruse it but the air in the taxi was clammy and the seats felt sticky. Eleanor pressed the window button.

'I think-a it-a better to keep it shut please lady. Tha fumes-a, you know.'

'Oh, very well.' She returned to her reading.

AIRSHOW ILEX

St. Bede's Convent, Phillipstone. Friday.

My Dearest Eleanor,
I have been meaning to write to you but have been so busy lately with the retreats and the fund-raising for the new teaching wing. The girls have also been sitting their examinations, of course. It's that time of year.

Your name often appears in the local paper, always in connection with some cause or other. Your dear mother would be so proud of you, as indeed am I. It is, with some delicacy, that I approach you on a related matter. You may recall that the convent owns a large parcel of land that abuts to the airfield, on the south side. At present, as you probably know, we farm it and are mainly self-sufficient.

I have received a rather distressing letter from a solicitor. It seems that some American person is challenging our ownership of the land and buildings and is citing some old documents in this regard. You can imagine how lost we would be without our farm. Not only does it allow the sisters to produce excellent fruit and vegetables for the convent kitchen but we also do so organically. Even the animals are fed organics. We attend the monthly farmers' markets and have started growing asparagus.

If you feel you can advise me on this matter, I would be very pleased to see you for tea one day soon. I know you are very busy with the airshow (and we have suffered the noise of the flight tests all this past week) but I would really appreciate it if you could find time to come to the convent. I wanted to talk it over with you before writing to the mother house but do not wish to take legal advice at this stage because of costs. Sister Catherine sends her best wishes to you and, like me, hopes you will come soon.
Your Affectionate Aunt,
Veronica, Reverend Mother.

*

'Mum, turn that down, will you!' Synth screamed from the upstairs bathroom.

'What?' called the old lady, pretending not to hear.

'Turn it down!' yelled her daughter, thundering down the stairs wearing a white towelling robe and hair rollers.

'Ow!' she exclaimed, tripping over one of the cats as she lowered the volume on the plastic-cased radio.

'My little Timmy. Come to Mummy,' crooned old Maud, snatching up the yowling pet.

'Where's he come from?' demanded her daughter, folding her arms and glaring at the interloper.

'The people were moving. They wanted a good home for him,' said her mother, nuzzling and stroking the sleek black and white tom.

'Mum, I told you we couldn't have any more. Don't you think fourteen is enough? There are hairs everywhere and the place smells like a gents' toilet.'

'Well, dear, they're old and their bladders not so good... like mine!' She cackled with laughter. The cat struggled to get down.

'Anyways, I was listening to that councillor fella. You know, the one what came knocking here for our votes last year.'

'Since when were you interested in politics?' her daughter retorted.

'It's very interesting, as a matter of fact. He says they're going to build a wind farm on the airport. You know, all them big windmills. I'm a fan of free energy,' she added.

'They'll never allow it.'

'Yes they will.'

'No they won't.'

'Course they will. He says we've got an energy crisis and the lights are going to go out. You'll be tripping over the cats all the time, you will, if that happens,' and she roared with uncontrollable laughter.

'Mum, have you fed them this morning?'

'There's nothing in the cupboard,' Maud said adamantly, folding her arms and gazing at the ceiling. Synth struggled to keep her temper.

'Of course there is. I went to the supermarket yesterday. There are loads of tins stacked up and three chickens in the fridge.'

'Are there dear?'

'Look, you wanted all these wretched cats. Just look at them!' Her gaze swept around the sitting room. 'I can see six in here... there are two on the sofa, one on each chair and a couple more on the window ledge in the sun, not to mention that one you had. It has to stop. I don't have time for all this. I'm trying to earn a living and keep a roof over our heads.'

'Would you take a little bit of pleasure away from an old woman?' wheedled Maud.

'There's pleasure and there's obsession. They cost money to feed and then there are the vet's bills.'

'They're company for me when you're out all night,' said her mother reproachfully.

'I'm out all night trying to earn enough to keep us. Once you've had your sleeping pill I can go to work knowing that you won't be doing daft things around the place. Don't you think I'd like a day job with a nice pension?'

'You bring enough from the night shift at the factory.'

Synth hesitated. 'Yes, the factory pays just about enough but it's hard work.' If a transient hint of guilt traversed the younger woman's face, her mother didn't see it. Nobody ever said that life was perfect. She had to do what she had to do.

Still carrying the cat, Maud followed her daughter through to the little kitchen at the back of the cottage. There were dirt trays all along the badly lit corridor leading to it and, on the draining board, stacks of feeding dishes waiting to be washed up.

'You said you'd do these before I got up. I didn't get in until six-thirty this morning and I've had four hours sleep. How do you expect me to keep going like this?'

'You can have a nap when I do, after lunch.'

'Lunch.' Synth threw open the fridge door and a cascade of water hit the floor.

'Mum! The fridge has defrosted.'

Synth clenched her hands in exasperation.

'Has it dear? I unplugged it just for a little bit because it seemed very cold in there.'

Synth screamed through gritted teeth. 'I can't take any more of this.

'Oh no! You can't put me away. I've looked after you ever since your Dad died. I've always been here for you. Look, I even made some cakes for you this morning.' She indicated the side where a baking tin of fairy cakes sat there, uncooked. Synth took in a deep breath.

'I think I forgot to put them in the oven,' Maud confessed like a naughty child.

Synth suppressed a sigh of exasperation and put her arm around her mother's shoulders. 'I know. I know. You try. Why don't you go and look through the cat magazine while I get us something to eat?' Maud nodded dumbly and shuffled off, her unmatched ankle socks sagging over her slippers.

*

The taxi drove up the track past the cottage where several cats snoozed on the porch roof in the sun. When it reached the imposing, old building that was St. Bede's Convent, where the edifice's yellow sandstone façade glowed in the late morning sun, Eleanor gathered her belongings, paid the driver and got out.

'Thank you,' she said. 'See you again, probably.'

'Yes, lady. I think so.' Then he drove away fast, leaving her to crunch her way across the scorching gravel to the arched portico. She pulled the bell and a distant jangle could be heard from deep in the bowels of the building.

A meek little novice whom Eleanor didn't recognise slid back the small, square, barred hatch and looked out like a furtive robin peeping over the side of its nest.

'It's me... Reverend Mother's niece, Eleanor Framp.'

There was the sound of heavy bolts being drawn back and the weighty door creaked open to release that peculiar atmospheric combination of floor wax, candles and incense with which all convents are imbued.

AIRSHOW ILEX

The nun bowed stiffly from the waist and indicated that the guest should enter, pointing at the wall clock. Of course, it was the silence time. Eleanor nodded in understanding, then followed the *religiouse* along the parquet corridor and up the grand, wooden staircase to the first floor, passing statues and crucifixes in alcoves, paintings of saints and stands of flowers. There was always something so peaceful and orderly about coming here, despite the sound of aircraft ripping through the skies above.

The door of Reverend Mother's study opened as they approached and Eleanor's aunt, a rounded, elderly woman in navy blue artificial serge habit and a white coif, came out and embraced her warmly. She put her finger to her lips and beckoned her niece in, closing the door quietly behind them. The clock above the Adams fireplace showed three minutes to the hour. Eleanor again took out and read her aunt's letter. When she had finished she looked up and Reverend Mother Veronica pushed a sheaf of documents across the desk and waved her hand as if to say, 'Read!'.

Eleanor's gaze flew immediately to the leading line of the first page. 'Our client Mr. Grant Landscar...' She looked up and said 'I know this man.' The clock struck one.

*

'It's the local paper on the line for you.' Celeste's assistant put her hand over the mouthpiece.

'They want a comment from you about the airport plans.'

'I can't speak to them now. Say I'll call back.'

'The Press Centre Controller will call you back.' There was a pause. 'They say they are happy to wait,' said the assistant.

'I said I will call them back,' barked Celeste, snatching the receiver and banging it down on its cradle. 'Now, where is that flaming stapler? I've got four hundred of these briefs to get out this afternoon.'

'Here it is,' said her colleague, handing it over. 'Sorry. I borrowed it earlier.'

'Don't touch my things!'

'Mine's broken. I indented for a new one two weeks ago.'
'Well go and BUY one and give me the receipt!'
'OK. Can I go to lunch now? It's half past two.'
'Yes. Go. Don't be long.'
'I'll grab a sandwich and eat it here.'
As soon as she was alone, Celeste dialled the surgery.
'*Primrose Clinic.*'
'Celeste Blagden here. I need an appointment as soon as possible. Yes, tomorrow morning at eleven will be fine. Yes, I'll bring a sample.'

She hung up, then swivelled her chair and rolled the mouse around on the mat. She selected the search engine and put in "Phillipstone Airport' and 'Wind farm.' Up came a cluster of links to web-sites belonging to the council. The first click produced the report of a council meeting last week.

'Good grief!' she muttered. ' If it goes through it'll put paid to this airport and any future airshows. This is unbelievable.' How could she comment? How come nobody had told her? Half the airport land was being claimed by some American. She saw her high-powered, anticipated career crumbling and dissolving before her eyes. She unclipped her mobile from her belt and speed-dialled Rupert in Hamburg.

'Hi!' he said, not sounding mightily pleased to hear from her.

'Hello,' she replied. 'Where were you last night?'

'Oh just out with the rest of the team. We did a few clubs and ended up at one of their apartments over by Dormsdorf. Why? What's wrong? You sound down.'

'I just needed to hear your voice,' she faltered, catching a sob.

'Not like you to be grizzling, old thing,' he cajoled. 'Tell Rupert all about it.'

'I'm just tired.' There was no point in relaying her medical fears to him just yet, let alone the wind farm debate. Would he care?

'Well, when this rotten airshow of yours if over, we'll nip off to the Maldives or somewhere and relax. Nice swim, dozing on the beach, bit of nooky.'

Celeste sighed.

AIRSHOW ILEX

'There will be weeks of work after it's finished,' she said. I can't get away until the autumn.'

'Oh well, we'll steal a weekend in Prague or somewhere.'

'Yes, maybe.'

'Gotta go. We're all off to the golf tournament and to meet the players. I just love being in P.R., don't you? So interesting. Take care my little juicy fruit. Keep yourself ready for me. Talk tomorrow. Cheers!'

'Bye Darl…' but he had gone. She clipped the mobile back onto her belt and sat down.

A packet of sandwiches landed on her desk as from heaven.

'I got one for you too,' said her assistant. 'Cheese, ham and tomato. OK?'

Celeste said a weak 'Thanks' and picked uncertainly at the plastic wrapping.

*

Gig Cattermole was on night duty again. Half of him liked it and the other half didn't. Split shifts like this ten until six effort played havoc with the old body clock. His bad leg dragged him down as the hours ticked by.

'You've got to make hay while the sun shines,' his wife used to say. Well, it made him feel better not to be at home in that vast empty bed at night. He still missed her. The peace and quiet of night duty made him feel as if he was lord of the manor, pacing his estate. The halls were still open tonight as carpenters and contractors worked around the clock to get everything done by Saturday morning. Then the sniffer dogs would come in. After that, the sea-green carpets would be laid. The huge rolls were already standing at the ends of the halls. It all had to be finished by Sunday, ready for the big day on Monday. The usual frenzy always resulted in a perfect presentation.

There were seven halls of varying sizes, all with incomprehensible themes apart from Hall Six which held some of the larger indoor exhibits He came out of Hall Five, relieved to get away from the smell of paint and adhesive, and walked along the outside, sheltered by the convoluted, clear, plastic roof that covered all the exterior, brick-paved ways connecting the halls to each other.

It was a warm night and he eased open the collar of his blue shirt and loosened his tie. Nobody would notice. There weren't many people about. His feet ached. Dropped arches and hammer toes, the legacy of a lifetime on the march, first in the army and then with the security industry.

'Beep beep beep.' The insistent tone of a reversing delivery truck alerted him from his reverie. It was carrying a huge silver nosecone destined for the central display area. The massive swing doors were fixed open and he slipped into Hall Six.

'Golf Charlie just entering Hall Six,' he said into his walky-talky.

'Roger,' replied the duty officer in the security room.

Gig started along the left-hand aisle, trained eyes scanning the stands, ears straining for the sound of anything that might be amiss. Millions of pounds worth of equipment were already installed… technology from all over the world arrayed in settings that had cost thousands to build. Most were in darkness but some had low lighting on. The overhead spots were on up in the roof, illuminating the space so that it seemed almost cathedral-like, making the exhibits take on the aura of statues, casting deep shadows that crept like black treacle across the chip-board flooring.

As he paced further away from the delivery truck, Gig's shoulders tensed. This was a very big hall. His footsteps echoed. He stopped to listen. What was that? A sort of scraping noise. There were no fitters up this end. It seemed to be coming from behind the false wall that ran along at the back of the stands. Trying to walk quietly, he made his way to the junction of the aisles, where the displays ended, and went around to the side of it where a maintenance door was cut in.

Suddenly and without warning, the door flew open and a dishevelled figure fell out, staggering towards him. Gig pressed the emergency button on his walkie-talkie and jumped back out of the way.

'Control here. Everything alright Golf Charlie?'

AIRSHOW ILEX

It was then that Gig recognised Roland Dilger, flustered and very embarrassed.

'It's me, Gig. It's OK. Tell your control room it's only me.'

'Golf Charlie to Control.'

'Control here.'

'Everything's fine. Over and out.'

'Roger, Golf Charlie.'

There was a 'click'.

'What the heck are you doing in here at this hour of the night and what do you think you were up to round the back of the stands like that?'

'There's, there's a… ladder… yes, a ladder round there. I needed it. Thought I could go up it and take a bird's eye-view snap from the rafters when the P.M. does his official tour, ' he gabbled.

'Hm,' said Gig suspiciously.

'No, really, it's true,' he nodded knowingly. 'I have to work out my viewpoints.'

'Why so late?'

'Ah,' said Roland.

'Well?' said Gig.

'This is a really good time to walk about and decide on the shots for next week as well. It's quiet and I can think.'

'Couldn't you think in the daytime?'

'Too much noise. I'm an artist. Photographers are artists. We need quiet to think…' His voice trailed off, as he exhausted his well of story telling.

'I don't think much of you creeping around behind the scenery,' Gig complained.

'I've already explained…'

Gig drew himself up to his full height and looked at the gibbering show photographer.

'I think it would be a good idea if you called it a night,' he said firmly.

'Yes, you're right. It's been a long day. I'd better go and get my beauty sleep. Goodnight Gig,' and he made his way towards the exit.

The Head of Security waited until he was out of sight and then peered into the cavity behind the stands. There was no ladder, just a cloying whiff of perfume.

Chapter 4

Wednesday 15th June
Early Morning

Windscreens glittered in the sunlight as the low mist evaporated to reveal the airshow site already a-buzz with pre-show activity. From his vantage point in the Press Centre corridor, Gig Cattermole surveyed his kingdom. The *ILEX* had come in under cover of darkness and had already been manoeuvred into position on the apron. She certainly looked different from anything else he'd seen over the years. She was entirely black and seemed to be coated in glass. Four gun-toting guards in dark leather and helmets, stood sentinel around her.

His radio buzzed.

'Control to Golf Charlie.'

'Golf Charlie to Control.'

'Anything to report?'

'Nothing unusual, except I see the *ILEX* is in.'

'Yes, it is. Control over and out.'

There was a click.

'Bit short with me today,' he mused.

'Talking to yourself already?' interrupted Roland, swaggering towards him loaded with equipment. Gig looked at the show photographer scathingly.

'You want to watch it, my lad. All that messing about in Hall Six last night.'

Roland paused. 'Give me a break old timer! Weren't you ever young or were you born with that parrot on your shoulder?' As if prompted by its mention, the 'parrot' squawked into life.

'Control to Golf Charlie.'

'Copy Control.'

'You're needed over at the *ILEX*. The Press Centre Controller is already down there and waiting for you.'

'Roger. On my way. Over and out.' Gig gave Roland the benefit of his cool stare, sniffed deeply and limped away.

Roland called after him, 'Can get you some birdseed cheap...'

The *ILEX*'s massive, vulture-like profile looked threatening on the tarmac apron where the Wednesday morning heat was already building. The armed guards stood robotic and motionless, barring Gig's way, their reflective visors sinister in the absence of eye contact but he knew that he was being scrutinised thoroughly.

'Morning chaps,' he ventured.

Celeste stepped out from the shadow of the fuselage. 'They have been instructed not to speak. Please let him through.' The guard swivelled to one side on his heels.

'Blimey,' said Gig. 'We are in select company.'

'The *ILEX* guards are a crack team of specialists in security and counter-terrorism,' she continued. 'They come under the auspices of the Department.'

'Never heard of them and I've been in the business ever since I was invalided out of the army after Aden.'

'This is confidential information. You are being given it because tomorrow we will have a surprise visit by the P.M. He will be coming to see this aircraft for the first time after the luncheon, at which there will be members of the Royal Family. So you can see that we have a very tight ship to run.'

Gig half-closed his eyes and peered up at the highly reflective plane above him. Its surface swam with images of psychedelic intensity.

'Apart from looking like a melted liquorice toffee, what's special about it?'

'Just watch what you say, please. The development and production budget of this revolutionary new passenger aircraft would make the outlay for the Olympics look like a fleabite. This is the only operational one in the world and there are many nations that would like to get their hands on the revolutionary technology.'

'So, what does it do then? I've seen pretty well everything down the years. They're going to run out of ideas soon.'

'I don't think so. This plane is going to change how we think about flight in the future.'

AIRSHOW ILEX

'How come you know so much about it then?'

'As Press Centre Controller, I am privy to much embargoed information. There will be a press release tomorrow and, trust me, it will make all the front pages. You will be able to tell your grandchildren that you were there when they announced it.'

'I haven't got any,' he muttered.

'Well, you get the idea of how important it is anyway. Come on back with me to the office and we'll draw up a security deployment plan for tomorrow.'

'What about my rounds?'

'Delegate.'

'OK.' He touched the 'parrot's button and Control responded.

As they walked away from the *ILEX*, Gig felt the eyes of the leatherjacket guards boring into his back. Celeste, smart in a muted lilac trouser-suit and crocodile sling-backs, matched her pace to his as they made their way along the outside exhibits, pausing to let service vehicles and towing trucks beep their way past. Some of the executive aircraft already had their steps down as staff burnished the fittings and put out signage. Many of the smaller leisure planes still wore their nose covers. The military contingents were lounging around their fighters in summer fatigues, enjoying a comparative rest from time spent patrolling the world's hotspots.

The pair drew level with the food outlets and even though the kiosks and mobile burger-vans were there for the benefit of the public and trade visitors due next week, they were already doing a roaring trade with maintenance and delivery people. The stink of fried onions at this hour made Celeste wrinkle her nose and even turned her stomach. Her companion was busy talking into the mouthpiece.

'Come on Gig. Get a move on!'

'One moment, Control. What's the matter Celeste?'

'Let's get away from this awful smell.'

'I'm doing the best I can. War wound, you know,' he said, indicating his bad leg. 'Sorry about that, Control. Civilian.' He gave a sideways glance at the Press Centre Controller who was holding a tissue over her mouth and nose.

They ambled on, past the pantechnicons containing simulators and geo-rotating experience equipment. To one side was the climbing wall for family weekend at the end of the fortnight and to the other, a playground crammed with kiddies' entertainments, including a Punch and Judy tent and a small stage. There was something tacky about all this stuff at a serious airshow, but, supposed Celeste to herself, they had to keep the locals sweet. Not everybody liked the inconvenience engendered by the show and some even hated any activity at the airport. There had been a real rumpus recently about a possible extension of landing hours.

Soon the tarmac gave way to a boardwalk and her heels clattered on the wood. The 'parrot' and its master chattered on. The Press Centre Controller was thinking about tomorrow's guests, how they would reach the *ILEX* and the photo-opportunities that would be possible en route. Great pictures would only reflect well on her. She would speak with Roland later.

'Good morning Miss Blagden.'
Eleanor Framp stood in front of them, still toting her grey mackintosh and a heavy bag.

'Good morning Miss Framp,' said Celeste curtly, stepping aside to go around her.

'I was wondering,' said Eleanor, also niftily sashaying sideways and looking down at the diminutive woman, 'how I get a pass for tomorrow's tour of the *ILEX*.'

'How do you know...? I mean there are no passes.'

'I think you will find that I can have one, as an accredited member of the press with top security clearance going back twenty years.' She put her bag down on the boardwalk and laid her mackintosh over it. Gig, sensing trouble, said, 'Over and out'.

'Morning Miss Framp. Problem?'
Celeste butted in. 'We're just on our way back to the Press Centre for an important meeting, so if you would kindly move out of the way...'

'Oh, that's good. I'll join you and we can sort it out up there,' Eleanor said indicating the first floor complex across the road.

AIRSHOW ILEX

Gig had seen the middle-aged journalist many times over the years, not only at the airshows but at other important events. She was no beauty with her gaunt face, side-parted grey hair and inevitable mackintosh, but she had contributed hugely to the local and national press and his admiration of her was evident.

'That seems like a good idea,' he said. 'Shall we?' He picked up Eleanor's accoutrements and shepherded the ladies forward. Celeste was too astounded to respond. After all, she was used to being told what to do by her father.

*

'Good morning airshow addicts! This is Radio Runway, bringing you all the news and views of the fabulous Phillipstone International Airshow.'

Synth groaned and raised herself onto her elbows, her red hair catching on the pink, velvet, deeply buttoned headboard. What was that thumping noise she could hear above the sound of that perishing radio station?

'Mum!' she yelled. No response, so she hauled her naked body out of the rumpled sheets and grabbed a blue satin kimono. Down the stairs she went, barefoot and tousled. It was the postman, in for a treat.

'Alright! Alright! I'm coming.' Was there no peace for a working girl? She flung open the door.

'Oh!' said the postman.

'Couldn't you have just left it outside? It's hardly likely to get lifted here.' Her eyes followed her sweeping hand as it offered the landscape of convent land beyond which lay the airfield.

'Too big for the letterbox and you have to sign for it anyway.' He was torn between looking into her green eyes and her cleavage.

'Give it here,' she said and grabbed the bulky envelope and tucking it under her arm, severely compromising her modesty as the kimono reached its limits. She signed and shut the door.

'Turn that wireless down Mum!' She shouted up the stairs. 'Your *Cat Fancying Year Book* has come.'

The radio still raged on so she made her way through to the sitting room where about ten cats were draped on every available surface. They looked up and greeted her with half-closed eyes. A shaggy Persian was even laying on the radio itself. She pushed it with the edge of her hand and it hissed. In desperation, she yanked the plug out of the socket. The silence was deafening. Maud was nowhere to be seen. A search of the bedroom and bathroom revealed no clues but the kitchen door to the garden was wide open. She dumped the envelope on the kitchen table.

'Oh knickers! She's gone walkabout again.'

Synth shrugged on a coat and wellingtons that she kept in the kitchen corridor, and set off in search of her demented mother, calling as she went. A half-hour tour of the nearby fields produced no sighting, so she went back to the cottage to call the police. As soon as she got in, she could hear the phone ringing. She picked up.

'This is Reverend Mother Veronica at St. Bede's Convent.'

'Oh,' responded Synth, gathering her coat across her chest.

'We have your mother here. Perhaps you would like to come up and collect her? She's down in the refectory having tea and toast. She said she was hungry and there was no food in your house. We didn't believe it for a minute but thought we'd humour her.'

'Thank you so much. Sorry for the inconvenience. I'll be up directly. Thank you.' Synth put the receiver down.

She went up to her wardrobe and picked out something casual and low key, a sort of homage to the nuns' habits in that it consisted of dull brown trousers and a beige pullover. No matter how plainly she dressed when she went up there, she always felt sort of dirty in the presence of such holiness. Reverend Mother's gaze was so innocent and pure, like a child's, that she felt her innermost thoughts and lifestyle could be read. If they knew what she did for a living, they'd have her out of the cottage in a trice!

Once in the turquoise *Verva*, she set off along the track that joined the cottage to St. Bede's Convent and parked to the side of the gravel forecourt. Unaware of her unkempt hair she went around to the back and rang the kitchen doorbell. Down in the half-cellar refectory, Maud was sitting at a corner table, gorging on toast, telling her stories to a circle of Filipino novices who smiled and half-covered their mouths. Goodness knows what she had been saying to them!

'Mother! I'm here.' Maud looked up nonchalantly.

'This is my daughter, Synth. She lives with me. Say 'hello' to the sisters.'

Synth half-bowed because it somehow seemed appropriate and made her way over to her mother.

'Time to go, Mum.'

'Oh, must we? I was having such a lovely time.'

Then Synth caught sight of what her mother was wearing... a dark blue habit. She touched the sleeve and turned to ask the novices who collapsed into giggles.

'Excuse me, lady,' said the nearest. 'Your mother, she have no clothes on.'

Synth's hand flew to her mouth.

'Where was she?' (Hoping that she hadn't been within sight of the road.)

'In the orchard, picking green apples.'

'I am SO sorry...'

'No problem. Your mother nice lady. Just seen many years of life. We understand.'

Synth took her mother firmly under the elbow and raised her to her feet.

'We're going. Say your goodbyes.'

Maud sensed that the party was over and grabbed a couple more slices of toast for the journey.

'Byeee! Byeee!' they called after her as Synth steered her up the short staircase and out into the morning sun.

'Thank you!' Synth called back, and 'just wait until I get you home, you exhibitionist you!'

'...but I had my boots on,' Maud protested as Synth pushed her into the back seat of the car.

*

An unlikely trio walked across the upstairs foyer of the Press Centre to Celeste's office.

'Come in,' she said, grudgingly to Eleanor and Gig as they followed her in.

'Shall I put these on here for you Miss Framp?'

'Yes, thank you Mr. Cattermole.' The bulky bag and grey mackintosh were placed on a chair.

'It's after ten and I need my mid-morning perk-up, so I'll just pop along and get myself a coffee while you ladies sort out the pass business. Back in ten minutes.' Then he disappeared. If he'd learned one thing in the army, it was when to make himself scarce. As soon as he'd left, Celeste let rip.

'Look here, Miss Framp, I am the Press Centre Controller and I decide who gets passes for sensitive visits. I don't know how you got to know…'

'No,' said Eleanor in a measured tone, 'you listen to me Miss Blagden.'

'Well! Really!' Celeste spluttered.

'I've been covering this airshow ever since it moved here and I could be your best friend in press terms. There is nobody who knows the area, local government officers and officials, Members of Parliament, military personnel and local businesses better than I do.'

Celeste tried to interrupt but the journalist was a mistress of words and she had her platform.

'You, Miss Blagden, are out of line…'

'Well! I'm calling security…'

'Mr. Cattermole will be back in a moment anyway, so hear me out. Why don't you sit down? You look a little green.' Celeste sat tentatively on the edge of the cream leather executive chair. Eleanor reached into her bag and took out a mini-album of photographs.

'Take a look at that.' She tossed it into the glaring Controller's lap.

'Go on!' Reluctantly Celeste undid the snap fastener of the little leather book and flipped through the plastic pockets. Her involuntary intake of breath was not lost on the journalist. Page after page of Eleanor standing smiling with everybody who was anybody, from politicians and royalty through to magnates and film-stars.

'I've been in this business for a very long time and I have many friends in high places. You, with your youth and glamour think that the world is your oyster but if you don't change your attitude, you will come to a sad end. Now, do I get my pass for the *ILEX* tomorrow?'

She held out her hand and Celeste passed the album back to her. Defiantly she looked up at the skinny, middle-aged journalist and said, 'No.'

Eleanor strode across to her bag and put the pictures away. Then she gathered up her mac and went out without a word, passing Gig on his way back into the office.

'Bye Mr. Cattermole,' she said.

He nodded affably, slightly puzzled at the atmosphere.

'Sorted then?'

Celeste said 'Come in Gig. Here's what I propose photography and media-wise for tomorrow.' She pulled out a folded plan from her desk drawer and opened it.

'Sit down. The press contingent will be small and handpicked. We are allowing in three photographers. One is from Fleet Street, one will syndicate the photographs to our friends abroad and then, of course, we have our own show photographer, Roland Dilger. We decided not to permit the foreign press because of the risk factor, apart from one from the European Parliamentary Press Corps. After all, it's not every day we have the Prime Minister and a level two Royal all on the same spot.'

Gig took out his spectacles, supermarket best, and perched them on his thread-veined nose. He perused the plan, running his stubby finger over the dotted route.

'Not keen on the proximity to the burger stands,' he said, stabbing at the map.

'Well you'd better get them moved for the duration. I need a clear space there for the journalists who'll be coming in. There are three of them too. Top notch, of course.'

Gig sucked air in through his teeth and tutted a little.

'The burger people won't like it but they'll have to shift. I'll get it sorted.'

Celeste looked down at her marcasite watch. 'I've got to go now, Gig. Appointment off-site. Here's your *ILEX* pass. Guard it with your life. Oh, and you'll need a password and a body gesture.' She moved conspiratorially towards him and whispered something in his ear. He looked a little surprised but shrugged in acquiescence.

'Finally,' she said, pulling what looked like a handheld computer game out of her top drawer, 'just give me your right thumb print on there.' He did so.

*

The *Primrose Surgery* was aptly named for its exterior walls were colour-washed in bright yellow. It was in an old house, a mile from the airport and set in a good residential area. Celeste parked in the road outside and went through the automatically opening door into reception. At the far end, there was a child with a hacking cough being read to by its bedraggled mother. By the white-painted reception bar, several old people sat waiting for their transport. Celeste stood there patiently. The receptionist appeared not to notice her.

'Excuse me...' she ventured.

'One moment please,' the bleached blonde replied before disappearing through the doorway at the back. Then another, more friendly, woman arrived and asked, 'Can I help you?' through an ingratiating smile like an advert.

'I have an appointment with my doctor at 11 o'clock.'

'Name?'

'Celeste Blagden.'

'Please take a seat Miss Blagden. Do you have your sample with you?'

The pensioners perked up at the prospect of seeing a jam-jar of somebody else's specimen but they were disappointed because Celeste had put the container inside a brown paper bag. She handed it over, scarlet in the face and walked across to sit down. She picked up a glossy magazine from the low table and tried to ignore the singsong voice of the scruffy woman at the end who was giving her all to a banal story. 'And what did the big bad wolf do then?' The child hacked away. 'He ate the little piggy, didn't he? Now that wasn't very kind of him, was it?'

'Hypocrite!' thought Celeste. ' You look as if you've eaten enough pork chops to feed any army.'

She crossed her feet demurely. It was great not to be baggy and untidy or tall and wrinkly. She smiled smugly to herself.

'Celeste Blagden. Doctor will see you now.'

She dropped the magazine back on the table, stared with hostility at the room full of NHS hopefuls and made her way to the consulting room. She tapped on the door and went in.

'Good morning. Do sit down. Well, what seems to be the problem Miss Blagden?'

The doctor was a very tidy sort of man with hair plastered down by hair-cream. He wore check shirts and knitted ties and had very white teeth. He smiled encouragingly at her.

'Good morning Doctor. There's something not right..

'Well, I've had nurse check your urine sample and it looks clear of infection and diabetes indications but there is something else I'd like to be sure about.

'I see that you are twenty-nine years of age.' She nodded.

'I presume you are sexually active.' She nodded again.

'When was your last menstruation please?' She racked her brains. Life had been so busy lately.

'I don't know,' she admitted. 'Probably a couple of months ago, but I'm on the pill.'

'Have you had any gastric upsets in the past few months?'

'Well, yes, actually. I had a very nasty night following some Vindaloo that was off around Easter bank holiday. We had been to...'

'You know, Miss Blagden, the pill only works if taken regularly. If you failed to keep it down, even for one day, that cycle would have been compromised. I also got nurse to run a pregnancy test for you. I don't know how you're going to take this, but I think you are pregnant.'

'Celeste looked up at him, eyes wide with amazement. 'I can't be. I can't be. I have a career. I'm not married. I'm not the maternal kind.' She fumbled for a tissue. He leaned forward in an avuncular way.

'The urine sample test was positive but we can run another one if you wish.' He paused. 'Look, I know it's a shock for you but we can provide some counselling.'

'How far am I...?' She blinked rapidly, her heart pounding.

'I'd say about three months but we can be more accurate once you've had your scan. I'll see if the hospital can squeeze you in next week. There's still a little time if you decide not to go with the pregnancy. '

'I need to think about it,' she said, rising to her feet. 'Thank you doctor.' She made for the door.

'Just a moment.' He hastily scribbled a prescription and handed it to her. 'This is folic acid. It helps prevent spina bifida and other possible problems. There are some vitamins and minerals in there too.' She took it from him, mumbled, 'thank-you' and rushed out, her eyes blinded with tears.

'The midwives will be in touch with you,' he called after her, '...and we'll let you know when the scan is.'

The pensioners were still sitting by the reception bar, watching as she shot past, probably knowing that she had received bad news. Outside, she stood on the surgery garden path and breathed in deeply. This couldn't be happening to her. Rupert! She had to tell him, now! The mobile phone said that the SIM card wasn't ready. Why wasn't it? Why a temperamental SIM card? She pressed speed-dial and heard his voice-mail kick in.

'Hi. You have reached the voicemail of Rupert Skinner. I'm unable to take your call at present but if you'd like to leave a message after the tone, I'll call you back as soon as I'm available again. Beeeeeep.'

Celeste stared at the little screen in disbelief. She couldn't tell her parents. Rupert had to know.

Trying to sound nonchalant, she recorded, *'Hi Darling, it's me. I need to talk to you as soon as possible. I'll be working late again tonight if you want to try and get me in the Press Centre.*

Otherwise, I'll leave my mobile on. Love you. Byeee.' There was nothing further she could do. She felt the rustle of the prescription in her pocket and looked down at it. It was just the start of the take-over, the eclipse of self, beautiful body, career, sex-life... and she would end up like that awful mumsy type in the waiting room.

As if summoned by angels, the woman and child appeared on the path behind her.

'Now let's pop over and get you some nice cough mixture from the chemist's and then we'll go home and watch children's telly together. How about that then? Fun, eh?' The child hacked away beside her. As they passed Celeste, she held her breath. The woman smiled. 'Lovely day,' she said. Celeste nodded weakly and followed them out of the gate where they parted company. She went to her car to find it had been clamped.

Chapter 5

Wednesday 15th June
Noon

Grant Landscar relaxed under the gazebo on the terrace of his mansion west of Phillipstone. His white Stetson lay on a sunchair beside him. The river at the bottom of the garden glistened in the noonday sun as leisure craft lazily made their way to the canal and thence to the Broads. The *Lucky Lady* bobbed at her mooring, the orange cork buffers tapping the landing stage as sporadic washes disturbed her equilibrium.

'More caviar?' He waved his well-manicured hand in the direction of the refrigerated trolley beside him. Councillor Springstock swallowed and desisted. 'Delicious but I've had enough, thank-you Mr. Landscar.'

'How about a little lemon sorbet?'

'Tempting.' He paused. 'Yes, why not?'

Grant helped them both to a portion. 'Try that,' he drawled

'Well I must say you have a delightful estate, Mr. Landscar.'

'Please call me Grant.'

'Grant.' He smiled ingratiatingly. 'How long have you lived here?'

'Well I bought *Casslands* in the nineties slump and had it entirely renovated apart from a few rooms upstairs. It used to belong to some pop star. I've got about two hundred acres, plus the river frontage, of course.'

Councillor Springstock dug into the sorbet with a long-handled spoon. The 'supping with the devil' connection flashed through his mind. 'No, no,' he remonstrated with himself. There was nothing devious about Grant Landscar.

'So,' said the Councillor without taking his eyes off the sweet, 'what can I do for you?'

'Now, now Councillor,' cajoled the American. 'Why should I want you to do anything for me?'

'People mostly do.'

AIRSHOW ILEX

'Aren't you being a trifle cynical?'

'When you've been in local politics as long as I have, you soon learn that there's no such thing as a free lunch.'

'O.K. I'll come clean with you.'

'Here we go,' thought the Councillor.

Grant reached into his pocket and produced a small, leather note-book. He flipped through several pages and then said, 'Ah.' Councillor Springstock put the sorbet down beside him and blotted his clipped, grey, toothbrush of a moustache with the white napkin. He was now paying attention and Grant was aware of a stiffening of his guest's frame. Indeed, if he didn't know better, he'd have said the man was holding his breath.

'It has come to my notice, Councillor Springstock... or may I call you Percival?'

'Percival's fine.' How he hated that name. It had haunted him throughout his career. Why hadn't he changed it by deed poll before he'd become well known?

'...that we could be mutually useful.'

'Back-scratching,' thought the councillor but he said, 'please do tell me more.'

'I had the pleasure of an interview with the, shall we say, 'straight-laced' lady journalist Eleanor Framp last Monday night at the hotel. When the *Saturnian* comes out tomorrow, details of my next project will be in there...'

'...but,' interrupted the Councillor, 'I was on the radio only yesterday morning talking about your proposed wind farm. It's well known that you'd like to put up thirty wind generators on the land next to the airport. The plans came in last week and we've already had a couple of council meetings about them. As chairman of the planning committee, I'm well up to speed on all this.'

'That's as may be,' said his host, 'but there are one or two other details that might just rattle a few cages. I need your help.'

The councillor blotted his chin and forehead with the napkin. 'I can't see what I can possibly do to influence a planning decision. We are a democratically elected council and it's up to the members to vote. '

Grant Landscar leaned forward confidentially, elbows on his open knees and touching the tips of his fingers together.

'I've had my lawyers look into some little matters concerning land ownership around the airport.'

Percival sat up more. 'Really?'

'Yes indeed, and some very interesting facts have come to light. For example, that convent... *St. Bede's* I believe it's called... is occupying land that belonged to my kindly but rebellious, English grandmother. It seems that she, being something of a religious freak, lent the building to the nuns way back in the nineteen-twenties on some sort of free lease that also included the fields around it. She was in the states with her new husband, you see, where she later died and the whole matter was just left to moulder because she hadn't told my grandfather anything about it. I expect she knew only too well that he would have objected, being an Atheist as he was. Maybe she didn't want him to know that she had inherited a fortune... that would be for personal family reasons... and why she'd abandoned England. However, I have certain of her diaries referring to the property. They came to light when we were clearing her house in the States. The nuns are trespassing.'

Percival looked to right and left. 'What? You're going to turn those poor nuns out of their home?'

'Well, that's just part of the problem because it seems that some fifty percent of the airport land also belonged to my grandmother. The aviation authority is, in fact, trespassing on our property. I intend to reclaim it and build my wind farm there. It gets a great air stream from the east coast.

'The council leases the land to the airport authority.'

'That sure is interesting.'

'What's all this got to do with me?'

'Well, I know that you know that the airfield and the airshow are not universally welcome around here.'

'True, but it brings in a lot of revenue to local companies and retail businesses. In fact, the annual show generates a large proportion of the borough's income. It's not just that. There are ancillary industries that have grown up around the airfield...

maintenance, parts, transporters, taxi services, hotels… you name it.'

'I don't much care about all that. I'm intent on reclaiming what is rightfully mine. In any case, planes are so wretchedly, environmentally unfriendly. A wind-farm is good for the world. Lovely, gentle energy. Rotors turning, quietly making electricity.'

'Not everybody would agree with you on the 'quietly' side of that. They can make a whooshing noise and there have been complaints about bird strike and interference with television signals, not to mention the reflections. The Broads' twitchers won't like it. We have enough trouble with their objections to aircraft flight patterns anyway.'

'Mere details. As, you say, they don't like the planes either.' He brought the side of his hand down firmly in a succession of rhythmic jolts as he spelled out: 'Successive governments have been shilly-shallying about renewable energy for decades. Look at the wave power experiments that got nowhere. Why hasn't every home in this country got a solar panel to heat the water from spring to autumn? Why isn't it obligatory for every new build to have photovoltaic tiles to generate its own electricity? I'll tell you why. This government is addicted to oil. It's got its arms in the oil can right up to the elbows what with personal investments and reciprocal agreements over arms and liquid gold. It's so far in, it can't get out. It needs somebody like me to shake them into reality.'

Percival ran his hands through his non-existent hair. His face was florid and the veins on his nose stood out. 'Yes, but I ask you again, what do you want me to do?'

Grant picked up his tonic water, took a sip and put the glass down again. He wagged his finger at his guest in a beat that kept time with his words. 'You, Councillor Percival, are going to ease the path of my one hundred wind generators, through your procedures.'

Percival sat bolt upright. 'One hundred!' He exclaimed. 'When did thirty become one hundred?'

'Two reasons. The first was when I considered the economics of the project. I decided that this part of East Anglia is full of traditional windmills, both active and derelict and that I'd be following in a fine tradition.'

'The other reason?'

'When I found out that you, Councillor Percival, have been rather a naughty boy.'

'I'm sure I don't know what you mean.' The anticipation of receiving bad news caused him to wriggle uncomfortably in his seat, fidgeting with his hands. Grant Landscar reached into the pocket of his tailored, summer shirt and languidly drew out a folded cutting from a newspaper. He handed it to the councillor who took the slightly crinkled sheet nervously and then cast his eyes over it. He bit his lip.

'Happy reminder of a misspent youth?'

'Where did you get this from? It's old, from a paper up north.'

'Life is quite amazing sometimes, Councillor.' Grant waved his hand carelessly towards the house. 'I happen to be a collector of fine porcelain. I bought a particularly interesting piece of *Strandwood* on the internet some years ago and guess what?'

'What?'

'It came, all the way out to the U.S. wrapped in that very piece of newspaper. When I was unpacking a box of china recently, there this was, like manna from heaven.'

The duly elected council official blustered, quite lost for words, finally rolling the item into a ball and throwing it at Grant in a rage.

'I'm not frightened of you,' he said, starting to get up.

Grant retrieved the paper and smoothed it out again.

'Twenty year old student Percival Springstock, received a four-week custodial sentence for non-payment of rates and resisting arrest at North Stinton magistrates' court last week.'

'I was making a protest. They refused to fix our pavements. I've always cared about the community I've lived in.'

'Wouldn't look good coming out now though, would it? Local elections due again in the spring.'

The councillor slumped back in his chair. 'Tell me what you want,' he said dejectedly.

*

AIRSHOW ILEX

Gig Cattermole approached the *ILEX* via the walkway that went past the food outlets. He paused by BurgerBaron and noted the roaring early lunchtime trade as carpenters and delivery men queued up for their calories. The other two burger vans were well attended too. The air was still thick with the stench of fried onions. His meeting with Celeste Blagden earlier hadn't been too difficult although there'd been something odd going on between her and the woman journalist. What was this thing with women getting their claws out at each other? He'd never understood it.

'Morning, you guys!' he called across to the serving staff, resplendent in striped aprons and boaters.

' How're you doing?' one called back, waving a tube of tomato paste at him. 'Want one?'

'Watching my waistline. No ta.' He patted his stomach and grinned. 'Need a word with you in a minute. Just going up here.' He pointed to the glistening black *ILEX*, crouching like a monster fifty yards away. He strolled on, taking in the fairground-style ambience, glad to be part of the party.

There was a barrier all around the plane. He stood the other side of it and called across to the leather-bound guards shining like beetles, standing motionless, guns at half-mast. 'Hi fellas. I need access. OK if I come through here?' He indicated the low gate. Nobody moved so he started to undo the catch. In a second, all four special guards pivoted on their heels towards him and raised their weapons in unison.

'Halt!' one called. The visitor paused and raised his hands in the air.

'It's me. Gig Cattermole. Head of Security. Look! I've got an *ILEX* pass pinned on my uniform.'

The guard nearest to him motioned with the weapon that he should take his hands off the gate. It seemed expedient to do so. Then the faceless robot strode over slowly to him, taking a palm-pc out of his jacket pocket and raising his visor to peruse the pass.

'Password.'

'Password?'

'You heard what I said.' Gig looked into the narrow slit where a pair of cold, dark eyes stared back at him without blinking.

'Oh yes, password. Now let me think.' He racked his brains and then remembered that he'd written it down and put it in his breast pocket.

'May I?' He nodded towards his chest. The guard assented silently and Gig, very slowly, unbuttoned the flap of his tunic pocket and withdrew a small piece of paper.

'The password is: 'Convolution'. Yes, that's it.'

'And the sign?'

Gig looked at the paper again and read to himself 'scratch left ear with left hand.' So he did.

The guard seemed satisfied and unhitched the gate, jerking his head to indicate that the visitor should advance.

'What do you want here?'

Gig inflated his chest and adopted a facial expression of dignity and superiority. 'I need to reconnoitre inside the *ILEX* ahead of tomorrow's important visit. As Head of Security it is imperative that I am cognisant of the interior layout of the aeroplane.' He silently congratulated himself on the vocabulary he had picked up on duty at trade union conferences.

'Special Guard Alpha to Captain of *ILEX*.' The guard spoke into his built-in microphone. Somebody was obviously replying.'

'Head of Security, Gig Cattermole, requests tour for security planning ahead of tomorrow's VIP visit.' Another silence.

'Roger, Captain.' Then he turned to the visitor and said 'Somebody's coming to fetch you. Please wait. Stand clear.' The sun beat down. The peaked hat was a blessing.

After a couple of minutes a whining noise proved to come from a shutter door that was being raised in the side of the *ILEX* forward of the wing. Then, a hatch below the door opened and out came a folding staircase, like a lizard's tongue unrolling. It touched the ground surprisingly quietly and then the handrails sprang up and there was the sound of bolts going home as it became rigid and ready for use.

A uniformed flight officer appeared at the top of the stairs, and gave a cheery wave.

AIRSHOW ILEX

'Come on up Mr. Cattermole. Captain will see you now.' With some trepidation, Gig walked slowly over and put his foot on the first step. It seemed firm enough. As he gripped the rail with his right hand, a loud tone of four beeps rang out.

'Don't worry,' called the man. 'It's just checking your thumb print. You're through!'

As he mounted the steps, Gig looked up at the fuselage. It was completely blank. No sign of windows, not even on the flight deck, and the entire surface shining like new black tarmac. When he reached the top, the man shook his hand warmly and welcomed him aboard. There was a loud whining as the staircase rolled up behind him and the shutter door closed.

'This way please.' He ushered the visitor into the body of the plane where the Captain joined them from the flight deck.

'You are very welcome,' he said in crisp, upper crust English. 'My flight officer will be delighted to show you around the *ILEX*. I take it you do not have a camera with you.'

Gig shook his head.

'Good. Needless to say, everything you see here is top secret and not to be discussed with anybody. Although, as Head of Security at this highly acclaimed airshow with so much military hardware about, you have signed the Official Secrets Act.'

Gig nodded.

'Enjoy your tour.'

'Thank you Captain.' Both nodded and parted.

It was extraordinarily hot inside the plane. Gig took off his hat and surveyed the chaos before him. Every centimetre of the cabin was packed with electronic test equipment. Cabinets, monitors and cables were everywhere. Along the walls, insulation hung in tatters like seaweed at a rock-face, drifting gently in the hot breeze from the air conditioners, making shadows on the lashed-together bundles of cables of every hue that ran fore and aft as far as the eye could see. Above his head, partitions were open and lights flickered as the omniscient hum periodically changed tone.

He stood agog. How could something that looked so perfect on the outside be such a mess inside?

'You're wondering what all this stuff is for, right?' The flight officer didn't wait for a reply. 'This is a test aircraft. It is several years away from being capable of carrying its payload of 1000 passengers. However, we have brought it to Phillipstone Airshow this year to encourage orders and to reveal to our customers the new, green technology that has to be the way forward for air travel.'

'But why's it so hot in here? I thought it would have state of the art air conditioning.'

'We have to test the equipment to its limits. You may have noticed that the entire outside of the aircraft is covered in a special, shiny, black material.'

'Is it glass?'

'I'm afraid I cannot confirm or deny that. However, the surface area of the aircraft is one huge photovoltaic collector.'

'What, like a solar panel that makes electricity?'

'Yes, that's right.'

He walked steadily backwards along the central aisle that ran between banks of large, orange-coloured drums.

'What are those for?' Gig asked.

'We use these as ballast instead of real seats, passengers and luggage during the trials.'

'What's inside them?'

'I suggest you wait until tomorrow for some of the answers.'

Gig nodded and then wiped his forehead with the palm of his hand. It was sweltering in the plane.

'Er, I need to look at the security aspects of the forthcoming VIP visit,' he said.

'Yes, yes. No probs. Just watch they don't trip over the cables and mind their heads on the turn of the stairs to the top deck. We'll go up there in a moment.' He paused.

The flight officer gave him a conspiratorial look and opened a luggage hatch halfway along.

'Fancy a lolly? We've got a mini-fridge in here, rigged up to the PV system.'

'You rascal, you,' said Gig.

The flight officer opened the fridge door.

AIRSHOW ILEX

'Well, there have to be some perks to the job. Choc-ice on a stick or Fruity Favourite?'

The two of them sat down on a couple of rather scruffy passenger seats bolted ignominiously to the floor. The flight officer leaned back and pulled off the wrapping. Gig did the same.

'Cheers.'

'Cheers.'

Feeling like a cub scout on a sleep-over, having a midnight feast somewhere spooky, Gig licked the lolly and felt slightly ridiculous, sitting opposite this smartly turned out flight officer in his crisp white shirt and shoulder stripes.

'You must have seen a lot of interesting things in your time in security,' the host said by way of conversation.

'Well, nothing very exciting really. That's how I like it. I just want to get through to my pension next year, although goodness knows what I'll do when I retire.'

'Fishing? Golf?'

'Nah. Don't appeal to me, what with my gammy leg and all.'

Noting the wedding ring on his guest's podgy hand, the other replied, 'Your wife'll be pleased to have you home all day though.'

''She's gone. Died five years back. Cancer.'

'Oh, I'm sorry to hear that. You must miss her.'

'It's quiet in the flat without her. That's why I do so many extra duties. Your job's probably been a lot more interesting than mine. Apart from my army days, where I copped this, it's all been rather dull.'

'Every job has its routine, I suppose, but I have seen a lot of the world. Been all over the place, test-flying for various governments. I only assist, you understand.'

The lollies were melting fast and the men simultaneously licked the sticks clean and held them up saying, 'Snap!'

'Drop it in here,' said the flight officer, indicating a rubbish bag next to the seat. 'The cleaners will be in later.'

'What? In here? What's to clean?'

'We have our own bathroom and galley and they try to keep the dust down for us. We virtually live on here, bunks and everything. This is a very valuable aircraft and it is never left unattended.'

'I hadn't thought of that,' said Gig.

His host slapped his hands on the frayed arms of the passenger chair and said 'Now, what do you want to discuss with regard to security? It's pretty tight on here. All comings and goings are recorded. Visitors have to jump through hoops to get on the *ILEX*.'

'My concern is not this plane but the VIPs tomorrow.'

'I assure you that no unauthorised persons will be aboard for the tour. The sniffer dogs will have done a sweep. The visitors are more at risk from tripping over a cable than anything else. They'll all be searched on entry, apart from the royal and the PM and we'll close the door once they're in.'

'Sounds satisfactory.'

'Well, I think that's it. Shall we go?'

The pair went downstairs again and the flight officer pressed a button on the panel near the door.

They stood, suddenly short of conversation, waiting for the hatch to slide up and the staircase to unroll. Air from outside gusted into the cabin and Gig gulped it in, grateful to be almost away from the claustrophobic, humid atmosphere of the *ILEX*'s interior.

'See you tomorrow then,' said the flight officer.

'Tomorrow, and thank you for the tour.' They shook hands. The staircase handrails sprang up and the bolts shot into place. The robotic guards stood glistening below on the apron. Gig made his way down. Just as he reached the bottom step, he heard two loud beeps. His host called out, 'It's just noting that you are leaving.'

*

It was time for Gig to talk to the burger van people. The queues had dwindled and the Head of Security approached BurgerBaron first, followed by Blissful Burgers and then Bappy Burgers. He got the same response from them all, a barrage of abuse and rude gestures.

AIRSHOW ILEX

Cries of, 'This is my living mate' and 'Little Hitler!' rang out.

'It's not my fault fellas,' he moaned.

'Why've we gotta move. Go on! Tell us!'

'Can't.'

One said 'I've got a licence to stop 'ere for two weeks. It's the best income I get all year and no pumped up little twit in an 'at is goin' to tell me what to do.'

'Watch it,' said Gig.

'We want compensation.' They gathered around him. 'Yes, compensation. Where are we supposed ter move to?'

'Lower car park.'

'There's no business down there.'

'Sorry mates. You can come back up here tomorrow at three o'clock but I want you off this patch by ten o'clock tonight. We'll come and check, so make sure you've gone.'

Another tirade of expletives bounced off Gig's back as he made his way to the boardwalk. His 'parrot' squawked. He responded by pressing the button.

'Golf Charlie to Control. Over.'

'Control here, Golf Charlie. Got a message for you. Press Centre Controller has been trying to contact you for an hour. She sounds upset'

'I've been switched on. Must be a fault. Anyway, I'll catch up with her now.'

'Roger. Over and out.' He was so near the Press Centre that it seemed to make sense to go straight up there.

*

'Where the heck have you been, Gig? You've been impossible to contact.' The Press Centre Controller glared at the Head of Security who looked down at his 'parrot'.

'It was on. Hang about a sec. I was in the *ILEX*. Possibly their set-up blocks the system.'

'And what's that chocolate stain on your tunic, may I ask?'

'Oh crikey,' he thought. 'Choc-ice,' he said. 'It's hot out there.'

She rolled her eyes.

'Gig,' she said, 'I need one of your men to go and get my car unclamped.'

'Off-site?' he queried.

'Yes, off-site.'

'No chance.'

'What do you mean?'

'Private car, off-site. Not our responsibility.'

'Look, I had to get a taxi back here because some lunatic clamping company decided to make a quick killing. There were no signs anywhere and I've been thoroughly had. I just don't have time to go and pay the fine.' With that, she sat down and burst into tears. Quite unprecedented.

Gig cleared his throat. 'Miss Blagden, Celeste, don't take on so. I'm sure we can sort something out. How much is the fine likely to be?'

'Fifty pounds.'

'Have you got the money?'

'I left my cards at home. Hardly any cash on me. I came out in a hurry this morning,' she snuffled, blotting her mascara neatly into panda circles.

His hands itched to pat her on the shoulders but caution told him to stay clear.

'Alright. I'll help you out, just this once. Where's the car?'

'Near the *Primrose Surgery*.'

She didn't see his eyebrows go up as she looked at him through her smudges.

He hesitated. 'Is that all?'

'Yes. Of course that's all. I just need to get my car unclamped.'

'Give me the details and I'll go and sort it out for you now. Got the keys?'

She wrote down her registration number and gave it to him with the fob.

'Thanks Gig. I won't forget this.'

He gave her a sympathetic half-smile.

*

Back at the *ILEX*, the officer rejoined the Captain on the flight deck.

'Asks a lot of questions, doesn't he?' he said.

'Too many,' replied the Captain.

Chapter 6

Wednesday 15th June
Early Afternoon

The hangers on the far side of the airfield crouched like grey sea monsters in an ocean of shimmering green. Outside their massive doors, parked on the tarmac, two fire appliances and two police cars stood at the ready. Inside hanger B, shafts of sunlight filtered through from the roof and lit up columns of dust that sparkled and swirled in the huge space that contained the seven *Pink Peril* stunt planes belonging to team leader, Debbie Foxon.

In a side room to the right, on a pile of packed parachutes, Roland Dilger, show photographer, and his long-term sexual partner, Debbie, lay on their backs, stark naked, and linked toes in mid-air. His sandy-haired legs waved about as he playfully and mischievously tried to capture her pretty little feet between his own.

'Gotcha!' he exclaimed in triumph, engaging her in a leg-lock.

'Hey, don't hurt me. I've got a rehearsal this afternoon.' She glanced hastily at her gold wristwatch. 'The girls'll be here in an hour.'

'Just got time to do it again then,' he said, pulling her towards him.

'Dream on, lover boy! Are you never satisfied?'

'Never.'

'There's a name for people like you.' She sat up, moodily perusing her own leg. 'I've got a buckle-mark on my thigh.'

'So you have. Let me kiss it away.' He leaned over to start work on it but Debbie'd had enough for one day.

'Leave off, Roland. It's all been lovely but I need to get myself ready for the practice display. What have you got to do the rest of this afternoon?'

AIRSHOW ILEX

'Not a lot. I thought I might go up on the Press Centre balcony and take some of you and your team.'

He screwed up his eyes and looked upwards.

'The sun's to the left, clear blue sky, nice pink planes. Are you smoke-trailing today?'

'Do you want me to? It costs, you know.'

'Depends which figures you're doing. I like that one where you do a starburst with pink and white smoke. Then, of course, the head-on near-miss with purple and fuschia always looks good.'

'Yes, we'll be doing both of those, amongst other things.' She ran her fingers through her curly hair and stood up like a Siren, looking down at him, laying there on the parachutes, ankles crossed, arms folded behind his head, looking as if he hadn't a care in the world. He was devilishly attractive in a wicked, innocent sort of way.

She picked up her undies. A shower would have been nice but the planes needed to be checked over with the technician and there was no time.

'I feel like a real slut,' she said, hooking up her bra.

'And I feel like a reprobate. So we're a fine couple.' His eyes crinkled at the corners as he laughed, showing his stunningly white teeth. She stepped into her shocking pink flying suit and zipped it up. There was something sensuous about the feel of the fabric against her almost bare skin. She understood why Marilyn Monroe had enjoyed going without underwear.

Barefoot, she clambered back over to him and knelt down, her tousled hair falling all over his face, making for a very complicated kiss.

'Come here, you gorgeous piece of crumpet,' he murmured, nuzzling her neck.

'Get your clothes on!' she ordered, holding his wrists. 'I've got work to do.' His hands broke free and he spun over on top of her, pinning her arms to the sides so she couldn't move.

'Make me!' he said, pushing himself against her.

'I'll scream,' she threatened. 'There are two police cars outside. They'll hear and come and rescue me.'

'Ah-ah! So it's the strong arm of the law now, is it? OK. I give in,' and he released her.

The clang of the hanger's outer door stopped them in mid-banter.

'Quick,' she said. 'Make yourself decent and I'll go out and see who it is. It's probably the technician, but he's early.' She leaped up and grabbed her bag, making for the exit to the hanger.

'Is there a tap in here where I can fill this?' queried a young police officer, cap in one hand and an empty water bottle in the other.

She shut the side-room door behind her.

'No. I'm afraid not. You'll have to go into the office block next to hanger A.

'Is everything alright?'

'Yes, of course. Why shouldn't it be?'

'I just wondered what a nice-looking lady like you was doing in a deserted hanger on a lovely afternoon like this.'

'Checking parachutes. Yes, checking parachutes.' She feebly indicated behind her. 'That's the parachute room.'

There was a silence. She stepped forward.

'I'm Debbie Foxon and these are my planes.'

'Oh, I see,' he said, reluctant to go.

The side-room door opened and Roland came out, carrying his camera bag and tripod.

'Er,' said Debbie. 'This is the Show Photographer, Mr. Roland Dilger. He's been... well... photographing parachutes,' she finished hastily. 'The officer wants some water.'

'Oh. Right,' said Roland, awkwardly.

'You can get some in the office block nearby. We can walk over together.' He indicated the exit. 'Bye Miss Foxon. Thank you for your time. The parachute pictures will be just great.' Then they were gone and Debbie put her hand over her mouth and giggled. She looked down and realised that she had no shoes on.

*

AIRSHOW ILEX

Clouds restaurant had just finished lunchtime service and everything had been set up anew for tomorrow. Paula Beantree, the elegantly tall manager, surveyed the freshly equipped tables, pristine covers, sparkling cutlery and fresh flower arrangements. There would be no dinner tonight as everything had to be perfect for tomorrow's VIP luncheon. She glanced at the gilt wall-clock. It was half past two. The staff had all gone home for the rest of the afternoon and the police sniffer dog and handler would be here shortly.

Paula pulled at the cuffs of her crochet lace blouse, fingered the pearl buttons and ambled over to perch on one of the barstools. She wriggled onto it and rested her elbows on the counter, gazing at her reflection in the wide mirror that ran the whole length of it.

'Not bad,' she thought. 'Even if I say it myself.' She primped her hair and turned her head slightly in a model pose.'

'Miss Beantree?'

The police officer had entered the restaurant quietly between the blue velvet curtains, his spaniel padding softly ahead of him.

'Ah, officer. Good afternoon.' She swung down from the stool, adjusted her skirt, and shook hands with him.

'Alright to pat the dog?' The animal gave out a very low-throated, gentle growl, and backed away.

'Better not. Shall we get started? Kitchens first, I think.'

'Yes, certainly. This way please.' She gave the spaniel a wide berth.

'As you can see, we keep everything scrupulously clean and orderly.' She swept her hand in an arc that encompassed the gleaming, steel ovens, sides and walls, the kitchen machines and virginal, white floor tiles.

'Off you go,' said the officer, releasing the dog.

'What's he looking for?' Paula asked.

'Oh usual things. Drugs, explosives.'

'Oh not in my restaurant,' she protested.

'You'd be surprised what turns up in the most unlikely places.' The dog paused in front of the larder and looked back at his master.

'Found something interesting have you?'
He certainly had. A bag of aniseed balls.
'False alarm,' said the officer. They just love aniseed.'
'They must belong to one of the kitchen staff. I didn't know they were there.'
'Not to worry. We'll do the dining area now.'
The dog made its way around the perimeter of the room and then slalomed among the tables and chairs, sniffed both sides of the bar and then looked up for further orders.
'Lounge next,' said his master and all three went into the adjacent area.
'It looks clear but we'll do another sweep just before lunch tomorrow. What time do the VIPs arrive?'
'Canapés in the lounge at twelve thirty. Main service begins at one o'clock.'
'That's fine. Before I go, do you have a list of all your staff, kitchen and waiting, together with a copy of their clearance confirmations?'
'Yes, of course. Come this way.' She led him to her cubby-hole by the bar and unlocked the two-drawer filing cabinet.
'You can look at the originals of the clearance confirmations but if you want to take them away, I'll need some sort of receipt.'
'No, that's not necessary. Let me just check them against the list. Sit!' he commanded the dog and it did.
'Er, Miss Beantree.'
'Yes, officer.'
'How long have these people worked for you?'
'Oh, they're all regular employees of mine. Most have been with me for more than four years,' she said nonchalantly, adding, 'I tend to keep my staff.'
'Right. Fine. I'll leave you in peace now then. Until tomorrow. Heel!'
The dog tucked in next to his master and gave Paula a lurching kind of over-the-shoulder look, baleful and yet warning. Dogs always seemed to know.

*

AIRSHOW ILEX

Roland set up his tripod on the Press Centre balcony in the prime corner that gave him a panoramic view of the take offs and landings. It would be good to get some of the aircraft featured in the daily afternoon shows now because next week the American companies would sweep in and camp out without any regard for the other photographers. Why they needed such a large body of people was a mystery to him but they marched in each year, spread their equipment everywhere, commandeered all the red plastic chairs and talked very loudly to each other as if in a soap opera.

He could see Debbie's contingent of six *Pink Perils* taxi-ing along the side-runway in slow formation, canopies open, propellers whirring. He took off his navy-blue baseball cap, put it on backwards and looked through the viewfinder of his twenty-five million pixel digital camera, zooming in. There she was, his girl, chatting away to the control tower, the wind catching the auburn curls that frilled out from under her flying helmet. Her posture, full of anticipation, was a mixture of concentration and excitement as she leaned forward slightly at the aircraft's controls.

The twin-seater planes each sported a symbol on the side. Debbie had told him that it was better than having numbers, in case they had to use the spare and then it would look as if one was missing. She, as the lead pilot, had a white heart on each side of the fuselage and under each wing. The other five had, respectively, a diamond, club, spade, star and square. The circle was back in the hanger.

As he watched, the canopies went over simultaneously and the *heart* swung around onto the main runway. They were taking off into the sun, to the south, from which came a warm breeze. Lovely flying weather! He'd been up with her once or twice to please her but flying wasn't his favourite occupation. He heard the revs increase and then she was shooting along the tarmac, buzzing like an angry wasp, climbing steeply and banking to the left. Then the others followed, each a few seconds behind her, alternately banking to right and left as they set out on their trajectory around the perimeter.

'It's nice to see such pretty planes,' a voice beside him said. He turned to see that Eleanor Framp had joined him.

'Yes. Yes. Very attractive.' He put his eye back on the viewfinder.

'You don't mind if I take a few as well, do you?'

'Not at all,' he said without looking up. 'It's only us today. Snap away!'

She put her bag on a chair and took off the famous mackintosh. Around her neck she was already sporting a little instant camera.

'You and I are the fixtures in this place,' she said. 'I see you here at each airshow, trailing around with that tripod.'

'Ah well, the management likes me. I've done a good job for them over the past ten years.'

'It's the same with me and my newspapers. A safe pair of hands, although I don't know how much longer I want to go on doing it. March of time, you know.'

The *Pink Perils* zoomed in from six corners of the airfield, looked as if they were going to meet in the middle and then turned sharply upwards releasing trails of shocking pink and white smoke. Roland took bursts of shots while Eleanor snapped away sedately. At the top of their vertical climb, the planes opened out like a giant, pink lily and flew upside down and away, before righting themselves towards the horizon.

It wasn't long before the weaving started, a sort of aerobatic square-dance. It looked as if they flew terrifyingly near to each other.

'Amazing, isn't it?' enthused Eleanor.

Roland took another burst.

'What's that funny noise?' He turned to look at her.

'My camera goes on taking pictures as long as I keep the shutter button pressed down.'

'Why would you want so many close together?'

'Well, I look at them afterwards and choose the best arranged ones and dump the rest.'

'Oh, that is a good idea. I'd like to have a camera like that.'

He looked at the simple job she was using. One million pixels She'd never get the quality. Why would she need it?

Why would a middle-aged lady journalist want the latest technology?

'Here they come again!' he said, panning and bursting simultaneously. Indeed they did come, low and fast, streaming fuschia and purple smoke, Debbie and *square* towards each other, apparently intent on a head-on crash but at the last moment they both turned on their sides and shot away triumphantly.

'It's so thrilling!' said Eleanor. 'Such a shame it smells so awful. Is that diesel in the air?'

'I think so. They do a mixture of diesel, water and dye. It must be brilliant for the people who live around here. All that stuff landing on their gardens and being breathed in by their children.'

'I'd never thought what it was made of before,' said Eleanor. 'I suppose it's the same from all the planes that leave trails.' She reached into the pocket of her jacket and took out her little notebook. Roland, oblivious, went on capturing his images.

Suddenly, the buzz got louder and he saw Debbie coming towards the Press Centre balcony. As she went over she tipped her wings and he smiled. Eleanor said, 'I wonder who that was for?'

'Oh I expect she was just practising for tomorrow. An attempt to ingratiate herself with the... er ... here they come again.' He crouched over the tripod, realising in the nick of time that he'd nearly broken the embargo regarding the Prime Minister's visit next day.

'It's alright,' said Eleanor. 'I know about tomorrow and the *ILEX* tour.'

'Can't say anything. Sorry,' said Roland.

'Have you got a pass?'

'I'm the show photographer. It's better not to ask me anything else.'

'As you wish,' said Eleanor. They continued snapping in silence.

'Scuse me ma'am. I needs to empty that there waste-bin.'
A nearby rustling sound made Eleanor turn and look down at the cleaner who had appeared beside her. The woman was squat

and very fat, visibly perspiring in her nylon overall and flamboyant headscarf. She was dragging a big black sack over the carpet and carried a long-handled dustpan and brush.

'Yes, certainly,' said Eleanor making way.

'Don't knows what these folks is up to with all their rubbish. Jes look at dis,' and she held up a man's brown shoe. 'Why would anybody want to throws away one shoe? Where's de other one, I'm asking meself?' She tutted away. 'An' look at dis. A box of apple pies, not even opened.'

She shook her head in wonderment as she tipped the lot into her sack and then started sweeping around their feet with her long-handled brush.

'Scuse me, sah.' She elbowed in next to Roland and jolted the tripod.

'Hey! Bit more care if you don't mind. There are people working here,' he protested.

'There's other folks 'av got to do their jobs too, sah, if you don't mind me remarkin' and a fine state this place would be in without us.'

Roland and Eleanor were forced to exchange a half-smile as the cleaner went on dusting around them.

'Thank you, sah. Thank you, ma'am. That sure is a fine display those pretty pink planes is doin'. I hopes yous gets some excitin' pictures there.' Then she was gone, dragging her bag of rubbish behind her and then dumping the lot into the big, plastic, double-lidded bin on wheels.

Ten minutes later and the *Pink Perils* were coming into land, one every three seconds, touching down and swinging out of the way of the next one. Roland, now that he had his shots, panned around and zoomed in on the *ILEX*. It was a stunning-looking aircraft that somehow appeared black and sinister under the innocent blue sky. He could see four guards in helmets and leather, toting guns. It must be worth a fortune to have such tight security. From his vantage point, he watched the staircase unroll and two personnel emerge from a shutter door above it. Then the shutter closed and the steps rolled up again. The taller of the men said something to one of the guards, who saluted and let him out of the enclosure. It would be very interesting to see the inside of it tomorrow.

'Well, that's it for now,' he said, packing up his gear. 'I'm off down to the Missay building for a spot of tea.'

'Yes, I hear they are being very kind to the journalists and photographers this year. There's free hospitality all day.'

'You should try it. Lovely lounge, all the newspapers, news telly and help yourself to anything you like from the buffet and fridges. It's the place to hang out.'

'I'll come down and have a look sometime,' she said. 'Now, I've got a little business to attend to. Goodbye for now.' She gathered up her things and went inside the Press Centre as Roland continued packing away his equipment.

*

Eleanor knocked on the Press Centre Controller's door.

'Come in.' Celeste Blagden looked up at her. 'Oh, it's you.'

'I believe you wanted to see me. I picked up your SMS earlier.'

'Yes.'

Eleanor stood awkwardly by the door, clutching her belongings. Celeste surveyed the drab woman in the navy and white flower print dress, her wrinkled neck adorned by a simple silver chain and her grey mac slung over her freckled and wrinkly arm.

'Further to our altercation this morning, I would just like to say that if you act in that intimidating manner towards me again, I will have you banned from the airshow.'

Eleanor shrugged.

'However, it seems that you do indeed have friends in high places,' and she placed an *ILEX* pass on her desk. 'Please let me have your right thumb print here.' She indicated the portable electronic sensor panel. 'I should inform you also of your special password and body sign, without which you may not enter the *ILEX*.'

'Thank you,' said Eleanor, advancing towards Celeste and putting her belongings on the next desk.

'This thumb?'

'Yes.' The job was done. 'Your password is 'Shambolic' and you must remember it.

'Fine. I will. Now, what's this about a body sign?'

'Everybody coming onto the *ILEX* has a personalised body gesture as final clearance. It has been my pleasure to invent one for each visitor. This is yours. You are to scratch your right buttock with your right hand.'

'I beg your pardon?' expostulated Eleanor with eyes wide.

'You heard.'

'I utterly and categorically refuse.'

'Your choice but if you take that tack you won't get on the plane.'

'This is outrageous,' protested Eleanor, face puce with rage.

'Look, Miss Framp, you may have wangled a directive from the P.M.'s office instructing me to issue you with a pass for tomorrow... and goodness knows how you did that... but this is my party and if you want to come to it, you have to play by my rules. Now, do you want this pass or not?'

Eleanor picked up the plastic oblong with her photograph on.

'I won't forget this,' she muttered as she collected together her bag and mac and made for the door. As she went out, Gig Cattermole knocked on thin air as the door opened in front of him.

'Oh, Miss Framp. We must stop meeting like this.'

'Hello Gig,' she said, as she passed him.

'Come in,' said Celeste. 'Leave the door open. Did you get my car released?'

'All done. I've parked it in the square behind the Press Centre.' He put the keys on her desk. 'That's fifty pounds you owe me.'

'You'll have it tomorrow Gig. Thank you very much.' She paused. 'About tomorrow...'

'Something else you want to discuss?'

'Well, it's only a detail really but I was wondering whether it might be possible for me to have my photograph taken with the VIPs... a sort of publicity shot... inside the aircraft.'

'You haven't been aboard yet, have you?'

'No, I haven't.'

'Well, I think you might be in for a bit of a shock. It's what you might call… unfinished looking.'

'I thought it was state of the art.'

'The outside is but the rest is hardly photogenic. It's full of test equipment and ballast tanks.'

'That does surprise me. Well, perhaps we could do one outside instead, with the *ILEX* in the background.' She spotted Roland going past the open doorway and called him in. He stopped in his tracks, parked his folded tripod against the wall outside the door and came in.

'What can I do for you Celeste?'

*

'What the hell were you playing at?' Debbie Foxon held her flying helmet under her arm as she strode towards the hanger with the pilot of *Square* beside her.

'I was a bit close. Sorry about that. I felt the controls were on the sluggish side. Can you get the engineer to have a look for me?'

'There's nothing wrong with your plane. I took it up myself yesterday for a spin and the engineer checked it over earlier this afternoon. You showed error of judgement that could have got us both killed.'

'Be reasonable, Debbie. It wasn't that bad. Although, to be honest, I was feeling a little bit under the weather earlier.'

'Then you know jolly well you shouldn't have reported for duty.

'Probably, but I wasn't feeling too bad until I got up there. My ears weren't good. I didn't think it would affect my flying though.'

'Go over and see the medic immediately. You're grounded until further notice. I'm not having my life snuffed out by your incompetence.'

Chapter 7

Wednesday 15th June
Late Evening

Jack stepped up into the two-berth caravan which was set in the lower car park next to the three-metre high security fence at the far corner of the air-show site. He flicked on the small fluorescent lamp above the sink, filled the tin kettle, turned on the gas and lit it.

'Want a coffee too?'

Marcus kicked off his shoes and ambled through to the lounge area to flop out on the sofa that would soon become a bed.

'You bet. Lots of sugar. I worked hard in that lousy kitchen today. It's alright for you poncing about like little Lord Fauntleroy, bruv, while I was skivvying. ' He adopted a French accent and said, 'Ooo la la Miss Paula. Je suis un chef.'

'Give me a break,' grumbled Jack as he got the mugs from the hooks and spooned in the granules.

Marcus peeled off his socks and started to pick between his toes as he mused. 'I wonder what this job is really all about.'

'Don't know. We need the money though.'

'Has Paula said anything?'

'Not much.'

'So here we are, two ex-public school boys who've worked as French circus elephant scooper-uppers, recruited for... what? Something involving quick movement. That's all she told me.'

Jack snorted with laughter. 'We've done some things, haven't we? Some good scams.'

'Say,' Marcus said, rolling bits between his fingers, 'do you remember the racket we had going at that theatre up in the West End?'

'What, the coat valeting service?'

'Wicked!'

'How many did we shift?'

AIRSHOW ILEX

'Hundreds!'

'I just creased up at the thought of all those punters waving receipts about for their expensive coats when their designer clobber was tucked up safe and sound in the old warehouse waiting to be sold on the internet.'

'May I take your coat for you, sir?' you'd say, in that up-market accent of yours, looking the business with your badge and everything.'

'It's amazing what you can knock up on a PC! I think they were invented to ease our paths through life.' Marcus sat up and took the steaming mug from Jack. 'This is hot!'

'It's supposed to be,' Jack said, sitting down. 'Push over! My dogs are barking too.'

The pair of them sipped in silence.

'It's quiet here at night, isn't it?' Marcus commented.

'We were lucky to get this pitch, you know. It's really handy.

'Paula was good there. She pulled a few strings and greased a few palms. Well, she wanted us on the job.' He paused to look at his watch...

'So, what's the plan?'

'The girls will be here about ten. 'Til then we can enjoy our own company, toddle up to the bothies or, if you'd rather, go walk-about and see what we can lift. What do you fancy?'

Marcus interrupted him. 'What's all that racket?'

The sound of loud voices, revving engines and headlights glaring through the curtains heralded the arrival of something big. He peeped out. Three burger vans were being parked up around them. The quiet, dark corner of the lower car park was suddenly the hub of the universe. A camper van reversed up next to them and then another beside that. The burger-bar owners were complaining loudly at the inconvenience of it all.

Marcus opened the caravan door and stepped out onto the car-park.

'What the heck's going on? Why have you lot moved down here?'

A torrent of explanations came back at him. BurgerBaron's owner was the most vociferous.

'They've kicked us off our pitches until tomorrow afternoon. Something about security. We're stuck in this hellhole until then. Want to buy a burger?'

Blissful Burgers wasn't having any of that and, sensing customers, restarted his engine and turned on his lit-up display along the side of the van.

'Aw,' said BurgerBaron, 'if that's how you want to play it,' and he did the same.

Bappy Burgers wasn't going to be left out of it so he not only turned on his advertising but treated them all to loud music as well.

Marcus stepped back up into the caravan and shut the door quietly.

'We've got a problem,' he said.

Jack had his head stuck under a window curtain and was looking out at the impromptu jamboree that had shattered the tranquillity of the night.

'It's going to make it hard for the girls to come here unnoticed,' ahe said.

Sitting outside the bothies, the maintenance crews soon caught the drift of frying onions. Groups of them sauntered over, bored, hungry and out for a bit of a laugh.

'You should have opened up every evening,' one said loudly. 'You'd do a roaring trade. I'll give me mates working in the halls a ring,' and he took out his mobile phone.

'Hey, guess what? We're in luck. The burger-vans are open tonight. Down in the lower car park. Tell them all to come and join the party.'

Within half an hour, the place was teeming with customers. All three vans were selling their specialities, along with drinks and chips. Like some surreal refugee camp, there were men sitting in groups on the tarmac and grass verges under the summer night sky, music blaring. It wasn't long before a squad car turned up. Two officers got out, leaving their caps in the car but the blue light still flashing.

'What's going on then? You lot causing a disturbance?'

BurgerBaron beckoned one of the officers over.

AIRSHOW ILEX

'Give us a break mate. We've been turfed off our pitches up by that big, black plane. We're going lose a day's takings stuck down 'ere. Gotta make hay while the sun shines. Want a burger?'

The officer looked across at his partner who nodded and they both ordered a trio-decker hamburger with salad and anchovies and a can of cola on the side. BurgerBaron refused to take any money from them.

'Nah, nah. On the 'ouse!' He looked at the second officer who was on his walkie-talkie to the fire crew and soon they joined them too.

Jack watched all this through a slit in the curtain, with the main caravan lights now turned off.

'There must be about a hundred and fifty of them out there,' he muttered, 'plus a squad car and a fire engine, all advertising. It's like Mardi Gras. I'd better text the girls to warn them.'

*

Zelara, the cleaning lady, was putting her vacuum cleaner in the cupboard and locking it when Paula came along the corridor to the Press Centre reception area. Only the low level security lighting was now on.

'Finished for the night?'

'Yes I have. I'm fed up with this job. I want to be something better next time around.'

'That's a discussion for another day. We should be making our way down to the caravan. The boys'll be waiting for us,' Paula said.

'Well, let me just go and freshen up a bit. I'm stinking like a hog.'

'That's an insult to hogs,' Paula laughed huskily. 'I'll wait here for you,' and she sat down on one of the leather couches, rested her head against the back of it and closed her eyes.' She had a lot to think about and was deep in reverie when Gig Cattermole's voice jerked her back into the present.

'Now, now. No vagrants allowed to sleep in the Press Centre,' he joked.

'Hi. I didn't hear you coming. I'm really tired. It's been a long day. I started at six getting lots of prep done for tomorrow. You know we have VIPs?'

'Yes. I hope you're giving them something nice that I can take a bit of home in a doggy-bag afterwards.'

'Dream on! Even I'm not allowed to take anything away and it's my franchise.'

Gig rocked on his heels and surveyed her coolly. 'What are you doing here at this hour anyway?' He cast his eyes over the languid shape of the restaurant manager. Tall and slim. Long legs. Shame about the face.

'I'm waiting for Zelara. She didn't want to walk to the car park on her own.'

'Very wise. Some of those maintenance guys get sort of frisky with boredom. Can't be much of a life, stuck on site for weeks on end.'

'I bet they get paid well though.'

'Probably.'

'Here I is Miss Paula. Ready to be escorted for me own safety.'

'Evening Zelara. Long day for you too?' said Gig.

'We's all on long days Mr. Gig. We does it for de love of de work.'

Paula got up and straightened her skirt.

'Come on. Let's go. See you Gig.'

'Night ladies.'

The women walked across Press Centre Reception and made for the sliding doors.

'Some accent you turned on there,' Paula muttered, quickening her pace.

'Impressive, yes? I learned it in one of the Caribbean music clubs… sort of ethnic market research.'

'Stunning,' her companion said.

Before Paula took out her swipe card to let them both through the sliding glass doors at the top of the Press Centre staircase, she looked over towards the Press Centre Controller's office where a light still gleamed. She inserted the card in the slot.

'There's another one putting in long hours,' she said as the doors whooshed open.

*

Celeste sat at her desk cradling her abdomen with her hands. Her breasts were tingling. She looked down. Imagine, not being able to see her feet as that thing inside her grew and distorted her body until she looked like Humpty Dumpty! It was so unfair! Tears welled up again. She just wished that would stop happening. It undermined her dignity. She took out her mobile phone. No message from Rupert and there had been nothing in her mailbox from him. She picked up the landline and dialled his hotel in Hamburg.

'Hotel Weiss-Schwanbrook. Guten Abend.'

'Good evening. This is Miss Blagden calling from England. Is Mr. Skinner in please?'

As before, the woman switched to perfect English. 'I will check for you. Hold on a moment, please.'

The line went silent. There was a ringing tone, then a click. His voice came through loud and clear. 'Rupert Skinner.'

'Oh Rupert! I've been trying to get you for ages. I need to talk to you…' but he cut her off abruptly.

'Sorry. This isn't a very good time. May I call you back tomorrow morning? I'm in a meeting at present.'

'Rupert, it's me. Celeste, not some inconvenient client.'

'Yes,' he said. 'I understand. I'll call you tomorrow.' The line went dead. She replaced the receiver and sat there, astounded, unbelieving. How could he be like that to her, after everything? The beast! The utter beast! She thumped the desk with the side of her fist. He'd better ring her tomorrow!

She got up and went over to the water dispenser, filled a clear plastic cup, took it back to the desk and sat and sipped at it until calmness prevailed and she was able to consider how to tell Rupert about the baby, well, the blob really.

Her mind ricocheted between happy family scenes with her parents and their first grandchild, Rupert standing proudly with his arm around her, to the dismal prospect of a late and risky termination, alone, in a private clinic. There was the third alternative, being an unmarried mother, or even a fourth, adoption. Whatever she decided, her life would be changed forever. The options went around and around in her head. Nothing could be decided until she'd spoken to Rupert. She took an oblong eraser and started to stick multi-coloured drawing pins in it until it was completely covered. She looked at it, turning it over repeatedly.

'Nonsense!' she chided herself silently. That was thinking too far ahead. She was dealing with a collection of cells, not a real, human being. Time to go home. Ignoring the rest of the emails, she drove down her workstation and picked up her coat and bag, turning off the office light as she went out into the reception area.

'Night, Miss Blagden,' said Gig from the shadows.

'Night, Gig,' she replied and headed for the glass doors.

*

Paula and Zelara made their way along the path that followed the airshow's internal road. It was well lit but there was little traffic. Moths fluttered around the streetlights as the two women walked on the level ground towards the lower car park on this balmy summer night.

'Stop a minute,' Paula said. 'My phone's vibrating.'

'That sounds exciting,' said Zelara nudging her. A wave of the hand silenced her.

'It's a text from Jack. Look!' and she held the display out. The cleaner read aloud, '*Approach with caution. Party!*'

She looked up at her tall companion. 'What does he mean?'

'We'll soon find out. Come on.'

They stayed on the left-hand path but on the other side of the road they could see the inky silhouette of the *ILEX* with the guards' guns glinting. Dozens of planes and helicopters stood to attention in the darkness like some frozen dinosaur display.

'It looks kind of spooky over there, don't you think?' Zelara intimated.

'Nothing for us to be afraid of,' Paula replied.

As they passed the rows of entertainment chalets, sullen in the black of the moonless June night, a little breeze picked up and carried the sound of music towards them.

'There's something going on in the car park down there.'

They quickened their pace. Roars of laughter could be heard and then some impromptu drumming. They turned the corner into the dazzling light of three burger vans and a sea of men steeped in the stench of fried onions.

Using a couple of pieces of wood, a guy in a beret was sitting astride an oil drum bashing out an impromptu rhythm to the music that blared from Bappy Burgers' van. A couple of men were holding a length of steel pipe at chest height as a small queue limbo-danced its way under it, gyrating with increasing complexity as the bar was lowered and urging each other on to greater feats of ridicule.

'This is not a good idea,' Paula said. 'Let's go back,' but they were too late. They'd been spotted. The cry went up, 'The girls are here! Come on in my lovelies!'

Zelara put her hand on her companion's arm. 'What'll we do?'

'Bluff it out,' said Paula, stepping forward and waving.

'Hi fellas! Having a good time?'

'Wanna dance?' Suddenly a big, muscular man with a Pancho moustache was in front of the tall lady and had grabbed her around the waist, swinging her into a samba.

'Oh!' she said.

'Come on Miss Cuddly,' said another and seized Zelara likewise.

The women exchanged exasperated glances and jigged about as required to the sound of rhythmic clapping that had now started up. 'Show us your shimmy!' somebody called out.

Jack and Marcus watched from the darkened caravan.

'Hardly low profile is it?' muttered Jack.

'Perhaps we should go out and join them?' Marcus suggested sarcastically.

'You're joking. The less connection there is among the four of us the better.' He paused. 'Just look at the way they're throwing themselves about! It'll end in tears.'

Paula's macho-man had pulled her close to him.

'You're a right little darling' he said, putting his stubbly cheek against hers. She tried to pull away but he was strong. Was this the right moment to launch into a martial arts routine and lay him out? 'No,' she thought, 'It would draw too much attention.'

'I'm thirsty,' she said. 'How about a cola?'

'Anything you want, little lady. You and me's in for one hell of a night,' and he released her, jerking his head towards one of the food vans.

Meanwhile Zelara was in trouble. Her skinny, youthful and rather pimply dancing partner couldn't keep his hands off her rear end.

'Pack it in, saucy boy!' she said, pulling his arms away from her but he just put them straight back again.'

'I's a happily married woman, young man,' she said. 'an' ma husband's a wrestler. You jest behave or he'll sort yous out!'
He took no notice, pulling her towards him so that her ample body melted into his skeletal frame. The stink of his breath was overwhelming. He started to gyrate, pressing his pelvis against hers.

'I said pack it in!'

'Come on! Ease up a bit! Don't be a spoilsport.'

'I's telling' yous one last time,' and she put her hands on his chest and pushed.

For a normal woman that would have been a gentle rebuke but to a highly trained QR/5 agent who had already placed her left foot on his right toes and hooked her own right foot around behind his left ankle, the action was spectacular. The youth fell over backwards with a yelp of pain accompanied by the loud 'snap' of his ankle that could be heard above the sound of the drumming.

He lay on the ground wailing abuse and hugging his foot. Without any sympathy, Zelara leaned over him and said, 'Oh, I's so sorry. Clumsy ole me. Is that hurtin' you sonny?'

AIRSHOW ILEX

One of the police officers came over and knelt down beside the patient.

'Can you move it?'

The youth, face grimacing with pain, shook his head.

'She tripped me up. She tripped me up,' he complained, glaring up at the plump, black woman. 'You did it on purpose.'

'Now, now, sonny. That's not a nice thing to say to a lady. I can't help it if I's got two left feet.'

Somebody turned off the music and the drumming stopped. The plug had been pulled on the jollity and a police officer was already calling an ambulance. A crowd had gathered around the victim.

'Just stay where you are. The medics will be here soon.' The youth was shivering.

'Anybody got a blanket?' One was commandeered from a camper van and, under cover of the mêlèe, Zelara melted away quietly around the back of the vans and made her way to the rear of Jack's caravan. Out of sight of the party, she tapped lightly on the window.

Jack and Marcus who had seen the goings on, heard her. Jack put his finger to his lips and said, 'Shhhh.' He moved over to the window and peeped around the edge of the curtain.

'It's Zelara,' he said and gently undid the latch.

'What are you two girls playing at?' he hissed.

'It sort of got out of hand. Can I come in?'

'Not unless you can make it through this window and, with your size, I doubt it. You'll just have to sit out there in the dark until it quietens down. I can hear the ambulance siren coming now.'

Sure enough, the blue light was flashing as the vehicle swept into the car park. Two medics in green overalls got out and attended to the youth who was whimpering and demanding that Zelara should be arrested.

'It was just an unfortunate accident,' said the police officer in a rather off-handed fashion.

'These guys'll make you comfortable and then it's off to A and E with you,' another one said.

'I'm a carpenter. Self employed. Got no insurance. I'll lose a packet over this,' he whined.

The police officer looked around and wondered where the little, fat, black woman had gone. He turned to his partner.

'Did you see where she went?'

'Nope. Probably took off in fright.'

'Can you move it?' asked the medic, gently touching the ankle.

'No!' yelped the youth. 'It's broken. Any idiot can see that.'

'No need to be unpleasant,' said the medic producing a short board.

'Now, I'm just going to slip this under your foot.'

'Aaaaaaaah' screamed the young man, throwing back his head in agony. The stretcher arrived and he was lifted onto it, still protesting and complaining. Into the back of the ambulance he was carried, his life in ruins.

The police officer turned to his partner and said, 'Well, I suppose we'd better do a tour of the site now. Night fellas!' he called across to the fire crew who were also starting up their engine. The men from the bothies began to drift away and the burger bars knew that the bonanza was over.

Paula stood at the counter of Bappy Burgers and sipped her cola. Macho-man stroked her wrist and gazed adoringly at her.

'We're closing now,' said the boss, turning off the advertising fascia lights. Macho Man took no notice, intent only on Paula.

'You are one beautiful lady,' he said, and belched.

She turned her head and leaned away from him.

'Pardon me,' he said apologetically.

'Granted,' she replied. How was she going to get out of this one without causing more of a rumpus?

'Why don't we go on somewhere else tonight,' he said. 'You and me, we're just made for each other.'

'That sounds lovely,' she said, despair mounting. Then inspiration struck. She fluttered her eyelashes at him.

'First I just need to pop over to the little girls' room,' she said, indicating the toilet block in the other corner of the car park. 'Back in a minute. Don't go away poochy-pie,' and she flashed him one of her dazzling smiles. He simpered like a little boy about to get a birthday present. She walked away, and turned to give him a wave, aware that he was watching her accentuated wiggle as she stepped elegantly across to the toilets.

Once inside the ladies' she looked at herself in the mirror. Bit untidy but bearing up well. She had to get out of here without him seeing her. There was only one way to do it. The cubicles were all at the back of the building so she went to the end one which had a fanlight, took off her shoes and, standing on the seat, dropped them out of the top of the window onto the soft turf beneath. Then she took off her bum-bag and wig and threw them out too. After hitching her tight skirt up to her waist, she dived head-first through the narrow gap, like a baby being born, first one shoulder and then the other until she hung at the waist like a piece of drying spaghetti over the metal frame. She put her hands down trying to reach the narrow concrete window-ledge way below and realised she was stuck. Unable to go back or forward, she groaned inwardly that her mobile phone was in the bag that now lay on the ground beneath her.

With every passing minute, her erstwhile dance-partner would be getting more agitated. She wriggled, trying to go back in but it was impossible because the fanlight had dropped onto her body and stopped any reverse motion. Something rustled in the shadows by the bushes at the perimeter fence.

'Psssst. Want some help?'

'Yes. Who is it?'

'It's me. Zelara. Anybody else in there?'

'No. Stop talking and get me out of this.'

Zelara toddled over and looked up at Paula.

'Yous so ugly wivout your wig.'

'No need to be personal and drop that accent. You're fat. Want to spend all night trading insults? Bend over.'

'Charming,' said Zelara churlishly.

'Do as I say,' Paula commanded.

The cleaner did as she was bid and felt Paula's hands in the middle of her shoulders, followed by a tumbling of limbs until the restaurant manager lay in a heap on the turf.'

'Why,' said Zelara surveying Paula's concertina-ed-up skirt that exposed her from the waist downwards. 'You're rather a funny shape down there.'

Paula knelt up and struggled to tidy the skirt, scrabbling on the ground for her wig.

'Miss Paula, if I didn't know better,' observed Zelara knowingly, 'I'd say you were a fella.'

'Call me Paul,' said the restaurant manager, plonking his wig on askew

Chapter 8

Wednesday 15th June
Night

Jack sent an SMS to Paula. 'Where are you?'
Back came the reply, 'In the bushes by the fence.'
He queried, 'Is it all off for tonight?'
'Yes. Talk tomorrow.'
'Well' said Jack, putting the battery light on, 'that's it for now. How we're supposed to consolidate our plans and become the crack team Paula wants, I just don't know.'
'There's still time,' Marcus said, stripping off and getting ready for bed. 'Double or two singles?'
'It'll be more roomy if we make up the double. Hang on, I'll give you a hand with it,' and he came over and pulled out the slatted support. The pair took the duvets out of the locker and arranged the foam cushions on top of the slats to make a mattress. Jack flunked out.
'Turn the light off,' he moaned drifting off into sleep despite the noises coming in from outside as the burger vans shut up for the night.
In the bushes by the fence, Paula and Zelara sat it out on the ground, waiting for the lower car park to quieten down. They'd giggled together quietly as Macho Man had wandered about the site calling "Lovely woman! Where are you?' At last he'd realised he'd been dumped and shambled off back to the bothies, a sad individual who might have been a lot sadder if he'd tried to have his way with Paula.
'Miss Paula,' Zelara ventured in a low voice imbued with the culture of an up-market English tone.
'Whatever made you want to dress up like a woman?'
'I always enjoyed it. Even as a child. It's just wonderful to be able to be one of the girls.'

'I suppose you get the best of it, what with all the frippery and make-up and all without the bother of the other stuff we women have to put up with.'

'Don't envy you that,' Paul replied.

Zelara hesitated. 'What do I call you now, Paul or Paula?'

'You'd better stick to Paula. Try and think of me as one of the fairer sex... and you can drop the 'Miss' when it's just us.' He dragged the back of his hand over his jaw-line. 'I'm getting a bit scratchy. The hair's the difficult bit. You wouldn't believe the agonies I go through getting it off my arms and chest.'

'Why don't you try that zapping treatment?'

'I would if I could find somebody to do it for me in private. I can't face going to one of those salons full of spoilt, self-obsessed women.'

'What do you do now?'

'I use wax strips. They're excruciating.'

'I can relate to that. I use them on my legs.'

'Masochism is not my scene.'

'Try childbirth.'

'Now that's where I take my hat off to you girls. I know you've got children. Boy and girl, isn't it?'

'Yes.' Zelara looked down in the darkness and blinked a few times.

'They're in boarding school... that's what you said when we did the interview.'

'On the coast.'

'Is your husband still in the States?'

'Yes he's lecturing at his fabulous university,' Zelara replied grimly.

'I admire the way you can turn that accent on and off,' Paula smiled in the darkness.

'Well, I try to stay in character so as not to blow my cover.'

'I've been seriously impressed by the way you've taken on the persona. Nobody would think that you waddling about with a mop were part of this gang.'

'And you really had me fooled with your dressing up. Very well done. How did you get it so good?'

AIRSHOW ILEX

'I suppose I educated myself, watching women, reading their magazines, perusing the dress rails. The worst thing is the height, although keeping my voice up-range is a bit wearing on the old vocal chords.'

'That wolf tonight would have had the shock of his life, wouldn't he?' Zelara giggled quietly, then added, 'I hope you don't mind me asking, but...'

'Am I gay?'

'Well, are you?'

'No. There's an ex-wife out there who got fed up with me pillaging her wardrobe.'

'So, you were married.'

'For five years, nearly.'

'Did she know when she married you?

'No. I should have told her really.' Zelara tried to make herself more comfortable on the hard ground.

'How did she find out?'

'I laddered her tights and replaced them with the wrong brand.'

The lower car park was now in silence. All the lights had gone out on the camper vans.

Paula said, 'Time to go.'

Keeping to the perimeter fence, they made their way back to the road but instead of walking under the street-lights on the side nearest to the entertainment chalets, they crossed over and kept to the shade of the outside exhibits.

Paula whispered, 'Walk on the grass. It's quieter.'

In the distance, late traffic could be heard on the town roads but all incoming flights had long ceased for the night. As they approached the huge bulk of the *ILEX*, the lights of a police squad car came along, slowly illuminating the verges, buildings and exhibits. Paula was quick though and dragged Zelara down behind a large LPG tank that was parked on a trailer.

'Did you see them?' Zelara whispered.

'The *ILEX* guards. Yes. Still standing like dummies.'

The squad car receded into the distance but the pair had yet to get past the *ILEX* without suspicion.

Paula said, 'Let's pretend to be a couple of tarts.'

'O.K.' They immediately stepped onto the hard pavement and started laughing and telling silly stories, pushing each other in mock fun, voices disguised to sound like cheap, shrill, women.

'You never!'

'Aw, I did! I told 'im, put that thing away or else!'

'You're such a one!'

'Well, a girl's got to take care of 'erself' exclaimed Paula in a falsetto voice.

So they went on, pretending to be tipsy, two girls on their way home from a naughty night out.

If the *ILEX* guards were suspicious, they didn't move but stood there, statuesque, in the shadow of the aircraft's bulk. If they gripped the guns a little tighter or breathed a little quicker, nobody was there to notice. If the duty officer on the *ILEX* flight deck saw two women tottering home a little the worse for wear on his screen, he merely yawned and wished his shift was over. Nobody paid particular attention when Paula's car swept out of the Press Centre parking area or as she waved to the security men at Gate Alpha as she left. Nobody saw Zelara crouched down on the back seat, covered in a tartan blanket.

*

Reverend Mother Veronica was kneeling in the chapel. The rest of the sisters had gone to their cells. She folded her hands, lowered her head and closed her eyes, sincerity etched on her elderly face.

'Dear Lord,' she whispered, 'help me to deal with the crisis that threatens this convent. Tell me how to save our home and our school. You have been by my side throughout the years, your wisdom guiding me in the face of adversity. When we needed you, you never deserted us. Where are you now? What do you want me to do?'

She fumbled in the deep pocket of the navy blue serge habit for her sandalwood rosary, given to her when she had visited Lourdes many years before. The beads were worn and bore a patina testament to thousands of hours spent deep in prayer and contemplation. She kissed the silver crucifix and began to tell the decades. 'Hail Mary, full of grace...' Ten of those. Then 'Our Father who art in heaven...' Just one of that. Then, repeating the pattern, she continued around the circle of beads, praying into the night, oblivious of fatigue and age.

Somewhere at the back of the chapel a chair scraped on the polished wooden floor. Mother Veronica tilted her good ear in the direction from whence the sound came and held her breath. Then she turned stiffly and said, 'Does somebody want me? Is everything all right?' Dull silence. It must have been the wooden pew contracting with the coolness of the hour. She returned to her prayers.

Again! A scraping sound. She'd always felt safe in the convent with its barred windows and heavy, studded front door, but now she was alert and a little knot of fear took root in her ancient core. 'Is somebody there? Is that you sister?' She gathered up the rosary with a gentle patter of beads and put it back in her pocket, forgetting to kiss the crucifix. Then, painstakingly, she got up from her knees and stepped out into the aisle, holding onto the pew as she genuflected to the altar and then turned to face the back of the chapel. Only lit by candlelight, it was a beautiful but eerie place with its stations of the cross carved in niches around the walls, the statue of St. Bede on its pedestal in the corner and the velvet kneelers lovingly embroidered by the sisters down the years.

She walked carefully towards the main door, her pace slow and elderly, her hands clasped together. If this was her time to die, she was ready, but please don't let her death distress the sisters unduly. Then she saw him. He was standing under the choir loft, a man in his thirties with untidy black hair and a gold earring gleaming in his left ear. She stopped. He stepped forward.

'Remember-a me, Mudder Veronica?'

Her hand flew to her mouth. 'Brecht!' she exclaimed. 'How did you get in? What are you doing here at this time of night? What are you doing in this country?'

'I wanta to talk with you.'

'It's late. We can talk tomorrow. Do you have somewhere to stay?'

'It has-er to be now.'

'I'm very tired and I have a lot of worries at present. This isn't good, you coming here like this.'

'Pleess,' he entreated, holding his hand forth.

'How did you get into the convent?' Her voice held a tremor.

'Yourra kitchen door was notta locked. Sorry, Mudder.' He hung his head a little and tipped it to one side, looking ingratiatingly at her as she steadied herself against the pillar. She shook her head slowly in amazement.

'You have grown into a fine young man,' she said. 'The image of your father.'

'Thanka you.' He nodded with pleasure. 'I not mean to scare-a you but is terrible important I speak with-a you.'

'Very well. We'd better go up to my office, but walk softly so as not to disturb the sisters. I can't imagine what they would say. You have to be brief. Help me to extinguish the candles.'

They left the chapel together. The heavy key turned in the closed chapel door and the rough-looking man walked beside the old nun with measured consideration. Together they climbed the wide, ornate, wooden staircase and turned into the corridor that led to her office. She fumbled her way into the room.

'I have nothing in here to offer you. Are you hungry?'

'No. No tank you.'

'Please sit down. Excuse me while I drink some water.' She lowered herself into her chair, filled a glass from the carafe on her leather-topped desk and gently sipped.

What do you want, Brecht?'

'I'm-a sorry,' he said. 'I not mean to-a surprise or-a frighten you.'

'You did both.'

'Forgive-a me?'

'For your dead mother's sake, I forgive you. Now please tell me what this is all about.'

AIRSHOW ILEX

'You were so goot to my-a family in Former Kridiblikt Republic. We can-a neverra tank you enough.'

'I do not require thanks for doing God's work. In any case, I and several of the other nuns owe our lives to your poor father.' She put the glass down. 'How did you find me here in England?'

'Internet. I look up name of convent. You know there is five-a with-a same name in dis country. I telephone all. You last. I lucky.'

'Is there no privacy in this world?' she rolled her eyes ceilingward in mock exasperation, then looked at the clock above the mantle-piece. Nearly midnight. 'Go on,' she said.

'I come here on mission. My government send me.'

'What has that to do with me or my convent?'

'Nuttink. This is personal visit. I work as taxi driver for airshow.'

'This isn't making any sense, Brecht. Please get to the point. I'm very tired.'

'I come look for somebody at airshow.'

'Why?'

'I must make them return to Former Kridiblikt Republic.'

'I ask you again, why?'

'I must find woman. She work also forra my government and she in-a danger.'

'So why come here looking for me?'

'When I find woman, I need safe place to hide her for time. I want you hide her here.'

Reverend mother looked down at her folded hands.

'Out of the question, Brecht. I'm sorry. It can't be done. This convent could not be implicated in any such thing.'

'Look-a, Mudder Veronica, you very brave lady. I see what you do in my country to help us. I was only young man then, growing up in fighting zona, but you my heroine.'

'Brecht, I was twenty years younger then. It was a different world. We were trying to help the children while your country got independence. When we left we thought you were safe and able to practise our religion. We always prayed for you.'

'Thenk you but prayers not-a safe my lady.'

He sat there, looking at the nun from under his dark eyebrows, his brown eyes glinting with the passion that she had seen before in his father's eyes before he had been killed by the regime.

'It easy for you-a here in England. You have real freedom. For us, struggle goes on,' he implored. A silence. Then he said 'You leave me no-a choice. I have to play, as you say, my trump-a card.'

'Now, Brecht, I hope you're not going to do anything silly or threatening here.'

'He reached into the pocket of his brown leather jacket and she half-thought he might pull out a gun but instead he produced a screwed-up, brown envelope.'

'This-a is for-a you.' He pushed it across the table towards her.

She didn't pick it up but gazed upon the scruffy twist of paper that she knew instinctively contained something valuable.

'Put it away, Brecht,' she said. 'That won't buy my help.'

'Take eet! Take eet!' He insisted. 'It is-a my family gold ring. It genuine.' He sat back, his hands clasped across his middle, his knees open wide. He gestured, 'Take it!' and waved his hand again.

'You got in here through the unlocked kitchen door? I must have a word with the sisters about security,' she said, without moving her gaze from the envelope.

'Back door eassy.'

'Put the package away, please. Tell me more about this lady you have to find.'

He reluctantly re-pocketed the envelope and then sat up very attentively.

'She come here to learn secret technology of big *ILEX* plane. You know it?

'Yes, it came in at dawn yesterday during matins. It flew over the convent low, to avoid being seen over the main part of town, I expect. I believe it's a special aircraft.'

'Yes-a, verry special. They say it worth billions of dollars and it will-a change how aeroplanes made in future. We have big problem with energy in my country.'

'I suppose you've moved on from a rural society to a technical one nowadays.'

'Oh yes, Mudder Veronica! We have technologics, cars, aero, trains, film industry, everything, but-a energy problem. We not have natural, how you say, resoursses, coal, oil, gaz. When they give us independence they know we need them one day but they cost too much money. We want-a new technology of *ILEX* plane to make energy. We poor country. We not able buy it. My compatriot she try steal it. That is bad idea. I come save her.'

'I wish you hadn't told me that,' Reverend Mother said, shocked. Then she placed her hands palms-down on the desk and pushed herself into a standing position.

'Brecht. It is time for you to go. I'll think about what you have told me here tonight. I hope you find your colleague in time to warn her before she does anything dangerous and that you get her away safely. You are both playing a dangerous game. I thought all that sort of thing was far behind me when I became Reverend Mother of this convent. St. Bede's is a special place, you know, peaceful and proactive. We educate our girls to go out into the world and succeed. I wouldn't want anything to jeopardise what we do here... and believe me, I have enough worries in that area at the moment.

Brecht got up too and she walked with him to the door. Down two sets of stairs they paced together, past the scullery and through to the kitchen door at the back of the convent.

'You tell-a your sisters lock-a up betterer,' he smiled as he turned the handle and went out into the night.

'I telephone-a you tomorra,' he hissed and then disappeared. Reverend Mother locked the door and put the key on a shelf on the far side of the room.

'That boy,' she whispered to herself before making her way up to the stark little cell she shared with a painting of the Sacred Heart.

*

Maud had kept the sleeping pill in the cheek of her mouth and pretended to swallow it before Synth had gone off to work. She'd spat it out and rolled it up in a tissue. This evening she was going to watch late night television.

'I'm fed up with being put to bed like a kid,' she muttered. 'Come on pussies, we're going to watch telly,' and she gathered up one in each arm and, wearing her flannelette night gown and thick socks, made her way down the stairs of the little cottage into the lounge.

'Hello boys and girls.' The room, being the warmest in the house, was thoroughly decked out in cats. All available surfaces supported a feline. Every kind of breed and mixture, short and long-haired, pregnant and emaciated, had a home with Maud.

'Mummy's here my lovelies,' she crooned, pushing one aside and settling down on the hair-embossed sofa with her two favourites. She picked up the remote control and the t.v. set sprang to life with sport. 'That's no good,' she said, flicking through the channels, discarding news, football and documentaries until she found a late-night movie, sexy and steamy. 'This is more like it. Go for it fella! Give her one!' she urged.

'You want something to eat my darlings?' she crooned at the cats. 'Alright, I'll just go and get us some yummy snacks and then we'll have a lovely time.' She got up and made her way along the dark passageway into the kitchen, pausing by the coat pegs to grab a red, woolly hat and pull it on over her tangle of white hair.

Before flicking on the fluorescent light she noticed, through the open kitchen curtain, car headlamps coming down from the convent.

'I wonder who's been visiting them so late at night,' she mused. 'Tee hee! Reverend mother's got a boyfriend,' she chanted over and over as she filled the kettle, lit the gas and went to the larder to get out two large tins of best salmon which she opened with difficulty. Then she took a spoon from the drawer and clenched it in her teeth dagger-style. With a can in each hand she hit the light switch with her elbow and kicked the door to behind her.

Back in the lounge she put one of the tins on the coffee table and sat down again, saying, 'Come to Mummy,' as she dug a spoon into the salmon and ate a bit. The cats had already got the scent of the fish and were all over her, yowling and pushing.

'Alright, alright,' she said, spooning it out into their demanding, little pink mouths.

*

Reverend Mother knelt on her prie-dieu near the window of her cell. The walls were white, the counterpane on the iron bedstead was white and her face matched them both. There was no doubt about it, she was stressed. She folded her hands and closed her eyes, saying her night prayers, remembering all the poor and needy, the sisters, the pupils and her niece. Then she made the sign of the cross and rose to get into bed.

Something caught her eye through the window though, something orange and flickering along the track that led to the cottage. She rubbed the small, barred pane with the edge of her nightshift and peered out. Those were flames. The cottage was ablaze! Would this terrible night never end? She quickly put on her dressing gown and hobbled along the parquet corridor, knocking on the cell doors. 'Sisters! Sisters! Wake up! Wake up! The cottage is on fire!'

Sleepy nuns appeared at their cell doors, night-coifs over their short hair, plain brown dressing gowns over their sleeping-shifts.

'Somebody telephone the fire brigade!' she ordered and her deputy said, 'I'll do it.' The sisters milled around like bees doing a flower-dance.

One said, 'We should go down and see if we can help.'

'Yes, yes,' came the chorus and the younger nuns and novices all rushed back into their cells to put on shoes. Then, like a chattering school outing, they clattered down the stairs and out through the studded front door, waving torches and finding there way along the track that led to the blazing little house.

Because of the recent hot spell, the tinder-dry roof was well alight and smoke billowed out of the upper windows as they cracked loudly. One of the novices went to the front door and tried the knocker but pulled her hand away very fast because it was hot, so, resourcefully, she started kicking the door with her little black shoes but it did not give way. The sound of the thuds was out-shone by the crackling of timbers.

'Wake up! Come out! Your house is on fire,' they all chanted. From inside, the feint sound of cats miaowing could be heard.

Deputy Reverend Mother came and joined the sisters.

'The fire engines are on their way. Luckily there's one on stand-by at the airport. Reverend Mother is staying by the phone. Has anybody come out?'

The young nuns shook their heads sorrowfully. The Deputy went around to the rear of the house. The kitchen was well ablaze. She re-joined the others.

'Stay back! Move away!'

'The fire-engine's coming,' somebody said and suddenly it was there, spewing out hunky firemen who uncoiled hoses and kicked in the front door, two of them diving through the belching smoke wearing breathing apparatus. They reappeared after what seemed an age, carrying between them old Maud. She was covered in soot and her eyes were closed. Legions of cats shot out of the house like bats out of hell and disappeared into the night.

The ambulance arrived.

'Busy night tonight,' called one of the medics to a fireman.

'We must stop meeting like this,' he said, unrolling the hose. 'Did 'broken ankle' stop complaining?'

'Left him in A and E threatening to sue everybody,' he grinned.

'She doesn't look too good.' The fireman indicated towards Maud as the medics laid her down on her side.

'Smoke inhalation.'

Then the hiss of the water from the hoses hitting the thatched roof gave rise to clouds of steam. The oxygen mask went over Maud's face. They put her on her back and pumped away at her chest. The flashing lights from the emergency service vehicles lit

AIRSHOW ILEX

up her face in shades of blue and grey as the worried nuns looked on.

Deputy Reverend Mother said 'I'll go back and ring her daughter. I believe she does the night shift at the parts factory on the by-pass.' Waving her torch, she went off up the track to the convent with a final instruction over her shoulder, telling the young nuns to keep out of the way and stay back from the blazing cottage.

Then suddenly Maud was spluttering and spitting. 'Where's my pussies?' She demanded, coughing and wheezing as the nuns cheered. The novices in particular had taken to the eccentric old lady and waved and smiled at her as she was lifted into the ambulance.

'Let's hope the night gets quieter now,' said one of the medics.
'Dream on!' said his mate.
'I want my pussies!' Maud called as the ambulance door closed, 'and where's my lucky hat?'

*

It took until dawn to put the fire out. The building was too unsafe for an internal inspection so the firemen put up a fluorescent tape around the area, together with a sign that said 'Keep out! Danger!' Then they drove away in the early light.

Synth arrived back at about eight o'clock that morning and observed with mounting horror, as she approached her cottage, that it was a smouldering shell. She roared up to the front, leapt out of her car, leaving the engine running. Ducking under the tape, she screamed 'Mum! Mum! Where are you?' She could see along the downstairs passageway that everything was charred and black. Running around the outside of the cottage, tears streaming down her face, she peered through window frames that had no glass, into the totally burned out mess that had been their home, the upstairs completely caved into the ground floor.

'It's alright. She's quite alright,' called the figure running down the track from the convent towards her. Synth whirled around to see the Deputy Reverend Mother, flushed and breathless.

'I've been watching out for you. We're so sorry about the cottage but your mother's all right. She's in the hospital. Only smoke inhalation. They said if she had been upstairs she would have died.'

'But she was upstairs.'

'Well, they found her in the lounge on the sofa.'

'She's alive,' said Synth.

'Yes. She's alive.' The nun put her arm around Synth's shaking shoulders, the sobs of shock and relief coming in a never-ending stream.

'We tried to ring you at the factory to tell you last night but they said you didn't work there.'

Chapter 9

**Thursday 16th June.
Early morning**

Celeste Blagden was driving into work.

'*Good morning airshow addicts! This is Radio Runway broadcasting to you on your favourite frequency, reporting on all the thrills and spills of this year's Phillipstone International Airshow which opens on Monday the twentieth of June.*'

Celeste pursed her lips at the sounds that followed; first a roar and then a '*whoosh*' and '*nnnnnnneeeeyow*' which, she presumed, was an aircraft looping the loop.

'*Today's a big day at the pre-show week as members of the royal family and the Prime Minister will be taking a preview peek at the revolutionary new ILEX passenger aircraft. Experts say it will change how we fly this century.*'

She slowed down to turn into the entrance of Gate Alpha where a large crowd was gathering outside. Some were brandishing banners and she could hear chanting. Security hailed her and waved her through. She accelerated and some of the chanting turned to 'Boos'. As if it had a camera on her shoulder, the radio station continued:

'*...and demonstrators are massing outside the main gate of Phillipstone airfield, supporting the news in today's Saturnian that an application has been received by Phillipstone local council for one hundred wind generators to be built on part of the airfield by wealthy, local landowner Mr. Grant Landscar. The American is challenging the airfield's ownership of part of its land which, Mr. Landscar claims, belongs to him.*' Celeste turned off the airshow perimeter road and drove into the Press Centre car park.

'*Traffic is moving smoothly on all roads in the area. The heat wave continues and temperatures are expected to climb to thirty degrees Celsius this afternoon. With no prospect of rain in sight, people are being warned to be careful about fire and to go easy on the water. We'll have more for you on the demonstration at*

Phillipstone airfield so tune in on the hour and half-hour for news, weather and traffic updates. This is Radio Runway, your station of the stratosphere.'

'Whooosh!'

Celeste parked in the shade of the building, flicked the radio off and got out of the car. The heat haze hadn't cleared yet from the runway. The top of the control tower could be seen peeping out like a glass flying saucer. The day promised to be a scorcher. She made her way around to the front and climbed the stairs to the Press Centre. Zelara was cleaning the glass sliding doors at the top of the flight. She moved back swiftly as the doors hissed open and Celeste swept through.

'Good mornin', Miss Blagden.'

'Good morning, Zelara,' Celeste said dismissively, going across to her office, unaware that Zelara had muttered under her breath to her back as she opened the door. She went in and put her things on the desk before becoming aware of an unusual silence. Looking up at the ceiling vaguely it took her a moment to realise that the usual hum from the air conditioning was absent. It would probably come on in a minute. After all, it was only seven-thirty in the morning. She pulled the blinds across to cut out the early sun.

There was no email from Rupert. He had to ring her today. They were an hour ahead over there in Hamburg. Perhaps he'd left an SMS for her this morning? She turned on her mobile. The mailbox was empty apart from some stupid 'two calls for the price of one' offer from the network. She speed-dialled him. His voicemail was on.

'*Hi, it's me,*' she recorded. '*I'll be very busy later this morning but if you want to ring me before ten, I'll be in the office until then. Love you. Bye.*'

*

Paula Beantree surveyed her pristine restaurant. Today she was set to impress. Her outfit was chic, her coiffure avant-garde, nails and make-up perfect and her perfume expensive. She was

AIRSHOW ILEX

going to knock 'em in the aisles. She sniffed the air. It smelled kind of stale. In the stainless steel kitchen it was the same, a sort of lack of freshness. The fridges and freezers were humming, but wasn't there something else missing?

Gig Cattermole strolled in, trouser creases sharp, hair smarmed down and shoulders braced.

'Morning Paula.'

'Hi Gig. Do you think it's a bit stuffy in here?' The head of security lifted his chin and sniffed, rolling his eyes upwards to right and then left.

'Now you come to mention it, yes, but it's the same along the corridor in the Press Centre and downstairs in Hall One. I think they've got a problem with the air conditioning. Why don't you call maintenance?'

'Today of all days!' she said dramatically, waving her arms about like a prima donna.

'Have they done their sweep in here yet?' Gig asked.

'The sniffer dog and handler came yesterday but they'll come again before the VIPs arrive for luncheon. I think they're doing a tour of the halls first. Some of those stands just won't be ready you know. I heard that the men from the bothies were down at an impromptu party in the lower car park last night. Somebody told me that one of the carpenters broke his ankle.'

'Really?' said Gig. 'Poor fella. That'll make a hole in his wage packet. You know, these sub-contractors rely on the airshow to bolster their incomes.'

'I'm not surprised.'

She straightened her skirt. 'I'd better ring maintenance. I didn't really want a load of dirty workmen in here this morning but if they can't fix the air conditioning, they'll have to bring me in some portable units and that's going to spoil the look of the place.'

'I'll leave you to it then. I'm off to get final instructions from Miss Blagden about the press and VIPs. Don't say anything but we're all going over to the *ILEX* this afternoon. Doing the halls this morning.'

'Have a nice time then,' said Paula, making for her cubbyhole.

'What do you mean you can't do anything about it? We've got important visitors today coming in to *Clouds* Restaurant and it's already like an oven in here.' She transferred her weight to her other leg and wished she'd worn more comfortable shoes. 'Give me your supervisor!' A pause. 'Well if you are the supervisor, let's have some action!' She flicked her thumbnail under one of her fingernails with irritation. 'Look here my man...' Holding the receiver away from her ear she looked at it with disbelief. He'd hung up on her.

*

The royal party's entourage of limousines came in through Gate Delta at the back of the airport. When the Prince asked what was going on, for he knew the airport well, being a regular solo flier, his equerry told him that there were some demonstrators causing a few problems at the main gate but that they weren't anything to worry about. So His Royal Highness relaxed in the back of the vehicle, sighed with boredom and gave a deep sniff.

The column of cars drove slowly along the uneven dirt track causing his royal personage to be jostled around on the leather upholstery and to protest to the chauffeur, 'Steady, old chap!'

'Sorry, Sir,' said the man, 'but this is a very poor road.'

'Well, slow down. It's not a racetrack!'

'I apologise, Sir,' said the chauffeur again, glancing in the mirror at the florid-faced member of royalty whom it was his pleasure to drive today.

The car pulled up outside Hall One and delivered its exclusive contents onto the red carpet where a gaggle of airshow dignitaries was lined up to greet and faun in the traditional manner. The Prince, already suffering from hay fever, exploded into a bevy of spectacular sneezes that he captured neatly in a nappy-sized handkerchief bearing his monogram on each corner, presumably as a safeguard against mad collectors of soiled, royal nose blotters. The London photographers and Roland managed to grab shots of HRH looking like a Morris dancer.

'Delighted. Delighted. Delighted,' he said, working his way along the row and ensuring that everybody enjoyed the hand that had dabbed the royal nose.

'So, where are we going first?' he enquired.

'This way, your Royal Highness. We are entering Hall Six.'

'I thought the PM was joining us for this tour,' said the Prince, adjusting his cuffs.

'I'm here, your Royal Highness,' said the Prime Minister, falling into step beside him, adding in a low tone, 'we came in through the main gate. Taken by surprise. Crowds of demonstrators.'

'Oh, really?' said the Prince, untouched by anything that didn't interrupt the smooth conveyor belt of his life. 'What are the silly fools complaining about now?'

The royal herd made its way down the first aisle, commenting and pointing as expected.

'Something to do with a wind farm being built on this airport. They're in support of it.'

'They can't do that. I fly from here. Jolly convenient for the old country pile.'

'I'm sure it's just a rumour, Sir. The department will look into it. Some American thinks he owns the airport land.'

'Very interesting,' said the Prince, indicating a giant turbo-jet engine.

'Your Royal Highness.' A woman's piercing voice assailed the Princely ears. He stopped and turned slightly towards it, perceiving with visible distaste the gaunt and unglamorous figure of Eleanor Framp, wearing a dress that he had last seen the like of on his nanny's great aunt. An equerry stepped in between them. Eleanor leaned around him and continued:

'Eleanor Framp. The *Saturian.* As a regular flyer out of Phillipstone airport, what are your Royal Highness' views on the proposed wind farm on Phillipstone airport land?'

'Er. Er,' said the Prince, taken by surprise at the audacity of the woman. The equerry leaped to his rescue.

'His Royal Highness is unaware of any such proposals. Shall we move on?'

Eleanor was not to be brushed away so lightly. She walked sideways, keeping up with them, waving a copy of the *Saturnian*.

'Look, your Royal Highness, it's here in black and white.'
The Prince stopped. The photographers were flashing. He could see the headline, 'Woman tries to hit Prince with newspaper.' He smiled ingratiatingly at the harridan smelling of lavender water and mothballs.

'Madam, I'm sure it's all just a terrible mistake.' He gave a knowing look to the equerry who, together with two others of the party, quickly formed a wall between him and Eleanor, but Roland had got a stunning photograph of Eleanor, mouth open like a gargoyle, waving the *Saturnian* at the royal personage.

'That's one for the London papers,' he thought.

The royal group trudged on, from hall to hall, shaking hands with stand-holders, paying special court to any from the Commonwealth and graciously accepting mementoes which were passed back along the group to be carried by a servant at the rear. He discretely placed them in a black shopping bag that grew heavier by the minute. Mugs, badges, fans and mint fresheners would all find their way to the royal staff. The 'family' didn't sully their hands with such tawdry trinkets.

'Atchoo! Atchoo!' Out came the royal nappy again and the esteemed face trumpeted into the high quality, supremely soft, cotton square while those around turned unobtrusively away and pretended to be interested in the ceiling.

The entourage was standing in the open space in the centre of Hall Six, when without warning, shouting came from somewhere, growing progressively louder until, at last, a sea of demonstrators came storming in, waving banners stating: 'It's an ill wind!' 'Yes to wind farm!' and 'Save our planet! Wind generators for this generation!' they chanted repeatedly, stamping their feet in rhythm and surrounding the royal party. The Prince's security formed a ring around him, facing outwards while he kept his head down.

'Get them away from me!' he muttered in controlled rage at his entourage.
This was a well-rehearsed manoeuvre.

AIRSHOW ILEX

Gig Cattermole, who had been in a subservient place at the back of the group, next to the memento bag carrier, pushed his way forward.

'Excuse me. Head of Airport Security here.' He attempted to address the crowd but they took no notice, chanting on. Somebody was calling on a mobile phone.

'Back-up. Immediately! Back-up required!'

Roland climbed up onto a stool and then the counter of one of the stands despite the protests of the stand-holder. Today was his lucky day. Flash! Flash! He zoomed in on the top of the Prince's head, cowering within his ring of defenders.

Suddenly, a report rang out and glass tinkled down from the ceiling. The demonstrators froze as one body and the silence was deafening.

'He's got a gun!' shouted somebody.

'Police state!' called another.

The Prince's armed bodyguard, joined Roland on the counter.

'Now listen to me, you young people.' Somebody jeered. 'Get over there and turn around with your backs to me, all of you!' Nobody did. 'Do it!' He waved the gun. Mumbling and banners low, the crowd shuffled over into one of the aisles and showed their backs, every one wearing a tee-shirt bearing the words 'Yes to wind farm.'

Eleanor took the opportunity to sidle up to the Prince's cluster of bodyguards.

'There's a way out behind here, your Royal Highness,' she hissed.

'Lady says there's a way out, Sir,' one of the bodyguards said and then whispered in the royal ear conspiratorially.

'Indeed? Get me away from here.'

'Follow me,' said Eleanor and walked around the corner of the end stand, opening the door into the void where Gig had seen Roland on the previous Sunday night.

'Come along, Sir,' she said, and the Prince, Prime Minister and bodyguards went with her unquestioningly, into the low-lit world of cables and pipes that is the backbone of any exhibition.

'Atchoo! Atchoo!'

Then the howl of police cars could be heard as the Prince's group followed the unattractive, middle-aged journalist out into the sunshine.

'If we go over here, Sir, we can go quietly up the fire stairs into the Press Centre.'

The Prince's chief bodyguard nodded.

*

'Your Royal Highness.' Celeste, wearing her Press Centre Controller badge on the lapel of her sage green jacket, dropped into a deep curtsey and caught her heel slightly in the hem of her calf-length skirt. She gave a discrete kick to free it and staggered a little, rising to shake hands with the Royal personage who pointedly put his hands behind his back.

'We're very honoured that you have come to visit the Press Centre…'

She was cut short.

'His Royal Highness and the Prime Minister would like to rest somewhere privately.'

'Please, please, come into my office,' and she ushered them forward, wishing her desk was tidier.

'You may leave us now.'

'Yes, certainly.' She took up her handbag and withdrew, puzzled.

Gig came panting up the wide stairs and through the sliding glass doors.

'What's going on?' asked Celeste.

'Demonstrators. They set up a decoy crowd at Gate Alpha while a second lot hid in two delivery vans supposedly bringing in potted plants for the stands. They must have had inside information. Jumped us in Hall Six.'

'How dreadful. Lots of them?'

'About a hundred and fifty. Police have rounded them up. Mostly students from the local college.'

Celeste groaned. This didn't look good.

AIRSHOW ILEX

Eleanor sat down on one of the chairs in the reception area of the Press Centre. She felt shaky. It was hot in here. Then Celeste's office door opened and the Prince's equerry came out. Celeste went forward, sure that he wanted her but he walked straight past and went to Eleanor.

'His Royal Highness would be pleased if you would join him for a moment.'

She looked up, blinked hard, and then went with him while Celeste and Gig stared unbelievingly.

*

Paula clapped her hands smartly.

'Action stations everybody,' she said.

The maître d'hôtel threaded his way between the snowy-white tablecloths like a black swan through pond lilies, and went into the lounge. On a side trolley with raised plinth stood the brass gong with a muffled hammer beside it. This he took in his white-gloved hand and, with just the correct amount of timbre and urgency, struck the gong three times. The eloquent tone reverberated around the pale blue, leather, easy chairs, echoed off the glass coffee tables and faded in subtle splendour on the deep, cream, pile carpet of the restaurant reception area.

'Luncheon is served.' There followed an exceedingly slow-motion gravitation towards the deep blue, velvet curtains with gold swags and tassels which marked the entrance to the dining room. Politicians, actors, captains of industry, starlets, airline owners, local dignitaries and the wealthy flowed towards the free luncheon, like lava in a steady stream in a style quite in keeping with the behaviour expected of VIPs.

'I believe we are on table twelve, Mr. Landscar,' remarked Celeste to her tall escort.

'Shall I ask the waiter to take your hat to the stand over there?' she asked politely.

The man replied in his American drawl. 'No thank-you kindly, Miss Blagden. I prefer to keep it with me at all times.' He stood while the waiter pulled out Celeste's dining chair and he himself clutched the white stetson to his chest like a child refusing to part with its teddy, before deciding to place it on the empty chair next to where he sat down.

The arrangement of non-perfumed yellow roses in the centre of the table was so perfect that it looked as if the flowers were made of wax or marzipan. Matching candles embossed with gold leaf stood in gold-plated holders. Linen table napkins were arranged in orchid style. This was no economy drive. Only the best of everything had been hired for this pre-show banquet.

At the top table, the Prince held court with the Prime Minister and the defence chief. Their ladies were a credit to the fashion industry. If anybody was surprised at the Prince's insistence that Eleanor Framp join him, nothing was said and the frowsty journalist appeared thoroughly at home amid the echelons of power. The extra staff looked ready to slip their hands in their jackets at the pop of a champagne cork. Paula and the maître hovered discreetly, commanding the service with the lift of a finger or the flicker of a glance. The months of training had paid off.

'Ah, here's the menu,' remarked Celeste, settling herself comfortably and anxious to make conversation, although she was snarling inside at the sight of Eleanor in deep discussion with royalty.

'Yes,' replied Grant Landscar noncommittally. The two of them sat isolated at a table set for six. Then, bethinking himself, he enquired, 'Who else will be joining us? I seem to have come without my spectacles.'

'I believe the chief pilot of one of the aerobatic teams and the local mayor and mayoress. They are great supporters of the airshow. They know how much it does for the area, as you must too, Mr. Landscar, with your many interests in the locality.'

'Indeed,' he replied with an air of boredom as, defying convention, he placed his elbows on the pristine cloth, closed his hands together prayer-style and sighed. A shaft of sunlight glinted on his diamond cufflinks.

Paula stood to the side and discreetly watched, proud of the arrangements. She had rifled her own wallet to get some portable air-conditioners in and although they hummed, the air was cool and pleasant. Tables filled up with all the joy of a wedding reception… old friends reunited, beautiful women simpering to rich men, business people looking for the main chance and pompous stars steeped in their own glory. Finally, peeling themselves away from chatting with their local M.P. in the adjacent lounge, the Mayor and Mayoress entered, followed by Debbie Foxon. Only the observant would have seen the latter thrust her hips forward sharply and turn to hiss something over her left shoulder. Only the *very* observant would have realised that the show photographer had just pinched her bottom.

Recovering her composure, she sashayed across the floor, the Cinderella hem of her knee-length lilac chiffon gown floating seductively. Roland watched with a satisfied expression. They could all look, but he'd had her, and would do so again, wherever and whenever. Their track record of innovative love trysts was unrivalled. His mind flicked back over the list of airshows they had both attended. Mile High club? Forget it! They knew how to turn on the thrills.

Grant Landscar appeared to be delighted to find that the lead pilot of the *Pink Perils* was at his table. He had thoroughly enjoyed their recent meeting in the hotel foyer. Through the entrée of quails' eggs in aspic with caviar on the side, via the venison and chanterelle soup, through the beef Wellington followed by strawberries and fresh cream and climaxing in fine Stilton and Columbian coffee, he chatted amicably with Debbie to the almost total exclusion of the others at the table.

By limiting his part in the conversation with the rest to the employment of such exclamations as 'Really?' and 'Goodness me!' he managed to curb their attempts to speak with him. Celeste interjected banally at every opportunity but Grant studiously leaned towards Debbie so that the Press Centre Controller was reduced to discussing the weather forecast for next week with the civic pair.

They seemed more interested in gazing around them at the great and glorious rather than trying to converse with the local billionaire entrepreneur who habitually reduced the council chamber to chaos with his latest controversial schemes. After the introductions, it was if they did not exist for him. Celeste twisted her linen serviette with rage. This couldn't be happening to her. She had pressured the restaurant boss into giving her this opportunity to make a connection with the silver-haired American billionaire. She had blown it. The disgruntled manipulator saw the show photographer coming over to their table as the coffee was being served. Roland Dilger approached and sought permission to take a picture 'just for the record'. He'd done the rounds of the dining room and this would give him the full set. Such shots were an investment for the next show's brochures and advertising.

'No thank you,' said Grant firmly. Celeste looked imploringly at Deborah and then grabbed Grant's arm and leaned towards him ingratiatingly. 'Oh Mr. Landscar, it would be such a nice photograph for my album.' Grant lifted her hand away as if it were detritus.

'I said, no thank-you ma'am.' He took up his white stetson, rose from his chair, said, 'Nice meetin' you all,' and left before the speeches had even been made. The mayoress bit nervously into a silver mint.

*

Paula's bouffant hair-do had withstood the heat of the VIP luncheon service. Her scalp was itchy, her feet ached and her super-strong anti-perspirant was in danger of failure, but it had all gone perfectly. Any little cracks in the effort had been seamlessly papered over by herself or the maître d'hôtel. She bobbed down to check her appearance in the large bar mirror before going into the kitchen to compliment her staff. Like a gastronomic diva she spread her arms wide by the swing door and said, 'You were all magnificent. Utterly magnificent!' Marcus looked up from oven cleaning. 'Some tips would have been nice, Miss Paula.'

'You want tips? Go and work at the dog track!' she said. The others laughed and somebody threw a tea towel at the little kitchen hand.

AIRSHOW ILEX

'Hey!! Show some respect for a craftsman!' he protested.

'Come and see me in my cubbyhole please Marcus,' Paula said.

'Whoooooo-oo,' chorused the under-chefs, wiggling their hips.

'I'll get you later, you pimp-heads!' Marcus called, as he got to his feet and followed the restaurant manager out of the kitchen amidst the hilarity.

Paula pulled him into the niche. 'Sorry about last night. Unfortunate but these things happen. I need you tonight though. Both of you. Tell your brother. We'll come down to the caravan. When this VIP visit's over, the burger vans should be out of your car park and back up near the outside exhibits.' Then she pushed him out roughly and started to go through the menu dockets. The beef Wellington had been a triumph. She would tell chef to keep it on for next week, whatever the weather.

*

Celeste stood in front of her desk. An email or a phone call? Nobody put her down and got away with it. Her cheeks burned with the memory of the humiliation of Grant's rejection. She had spent the entire meal conversing with that mayor and mayoress about the nuances of local political life. She was too angry to compose an email and snatched up the receiver, stabbing out the number of the *Saturnian*.

'Hello. It's Celeste Blagden here. I've got a scoop for you. Put me through to the editor.' Never tolerant of being kept waiting, she drummed her fingers on the mouse mat. 'Hi! Yes, it's me. Grab your pen! Here's your headline:

'Local billionaire snubs our Mayor and Mayoress at airshow luncheon.' She paused. Should she say that he had preferred Deborah to herself? Yes, why not? Put in all the dirt!

'He flirted outrageously with *Pink Perils'* chief pilot, Deborah Foxon, turning his back on our civic representative and his wife, even refusing to have his photograph taken with them.' Had she gone too far? Why not go a bit further?

'The Mayoress was nearly in tears as Grant Landscar abruptly left before the speeches, not even waiting until he got outside to put his cowboy hat on.' She nodded her head in triumph. 'No, he wouldn't have his photo taken. You'll have to use one from your library but I'll get the show photographer to catch up with him next week, don't you worry! Bye.' She hung up with a smug and spiteful smile playing around her lips. That should teach him!

She looked up at a knock on the open door. It was Gig. She killed the screen.

'We've cleared all the demonstrators from the site and outside Gate Alpha. Security's been tripled around the *ILEX* so the tour will go ahead in half an hour. Do you want to walk over with me?'

'I wouldn't miss it for the world,' she said.

Chapter 10

**Thursday 16th June.
Afternoon.**

The four musketeers guarding the *ILEX* stood stalwartly in the baking afternoon sun. Their semi-automatics glinted. Without black leather gloves the weapons would have been too hot to handle. Their leader spoke to his group through the concealed microphone in his helmet.

'Royal party in one minute to tour. Stand by.'

The *ILEX* Captain was in on the communications loop and had heard the command. The roll-away, carbon fibre staircase started to unfold until it touched the ground where the red carpet began and its hand-rail sprang up and clicked into position. The sliding door in the fuselage above the staircase housing opened. Nobody appeared. Outside the security barrier, the carefully selected journalists and photographers waited with Celeste Blagden, Eleanor Framp and Gig Cattermole.

Two outriders on motor cycles with blue lights flashing, swept onto the tarmac ahead of the limousine bearing the Prince's standard. The Captain and his flight officer descended to greet the visitors. The barrier gate opened. The equerry leaped out smoothly from the front passenger seat of the car and walked round briskly to open the nearside rear door. The Prince stepped out, followed by the Prime Minister. Cameras flashed. Five other vehicles, including a low-level-style ambulance, zoomed in and were positioned like wagons in a wild west film, most of their occupants, wearing reflective sunglasses and marine hair-cuts, springing out to swarm towards the royal party. After this morning's fiasco, security had been upped. The gate was closed again.

The four leatherjackets stood to attention, weapons at the ready. The Captain came forward.

'Good afternoon, Your Royal Highness, Prime Minister.' He shook hands with both, nodding as he did so, and then invited them to precede him up the stairs but the Prince paused.

'I note that the aircraft has no windows,' he said, standing gazing up at the gleaming, black leviathan towering before him.

'That is correct,' replied the Captain.

The Prince groped in the flapped pocked of his suit jacket for a fresh, royal handkerchief and just managed to place it in position to catch the gigantic royal sneeze that engulfed him.

'Hayfever,' he gestured apologetically at the acres of grass around the site. 'Grass pollen allergy.'

'It must be a trial to you, Sir,' replied the Captain, suppressing a smirk.

'A trifle inconvenient.' He gave a Princely hoot, put the handkerchief away and said, 'Shall we go?' He walked forward and placed his hand on the rail, which beeped.

'Everything alright here?' asked the Prince, a little jumpy, turning to enquire over his shoulder.

'Just welcoming you, Sir,' said the Captain, knowing full-well that the royal palm and thumb prints were now safely stored in the on-board computer along with the photograph that the surveillance camera had taken through a pinhead-sized hole in the fuselage.

Once the royal party was aboard, the flight engineer beckoned to the journalists and photographers to come up and join them. One of the leatherjackets opened the barrier again and the troop of three London hacks, three major photographers, Head of Airport Security, Gig Cattermole, Roland, Eleanor and Celeste, moved towards the staircase wearing their special *ILEX* passes.

'One moment please,' said the chief leatherjacket, transferring his weapon to his left hand while, from the zipped pocket of his blouson, he produced a handtop computer that he clicked on.

'I need to see your security gestures. You first sir.'

Anybody observing the gaggle of would-be visitors would have been astounded at the absurd ritual that followed as a seemingly endless menu of bizarre bodily gestures was presented to the guard who then approved them, one by one, pressing the button on the gadget.

'Name and commissioning agency?'

'It's on my badge. Anna Divrej.   European Parliamentary Press Corps.'

'Name and commissioning agency?'

'Roland Dilger. P.I.A. Press Photographer.'

So it went on until it was Celeste's turn, second to last, and she had allocated a snapping of the fingers of the right hand to herself. Once accepted, instead of moving towards the stairs, she waited and watched with muted glee as Eleanor, the last one, stood before the guard.

'Gesture please,' he said, obviously able to read what it was supposed to be.

'It's rather embarrassing really,' said Eleanor.

'Just do it please, madam.'

'Very well, but you should be aware that this is not normally the sort of thing I would perform in public.'

'Get on with it please, madam. You're holding up the tour.'

Looking around her she was appalled to see that the entire group was waiting at the bottom of the staircase, looking at her, and that Celeste was not far from her elbow. Very slowly and reluctantly, Eleanor scratched her right buttock with her right hand.

'Thank you madam,' said the guard.

Somehow the hard stare that he gave Celeste through the slit in his visor, spoiled her joy in the spectacle. Humiliated, Eleanor shuffled over to join the rest.

The Chief leatherjacket said, 'Please proceed to the top of the staircase where you will be asked for the password before being permitted to enter the aircraft where you will receive a body-search and your belongings will also be inspected.' They all did as instructed and, once inside, found themselves in the holding area of the cabin as the roller door shut behind them. It was stiflingly hot. Through a gap in the curtain the royal party and Prime Minister could be observed, comfortably sitting on plush, ivory-coloured, airline seats to the right.

Gig muttered to Roland, 'Those fancy thrones weren't here yesterday. You should see the chaos behind the area that's been screened off.'

Roland leaned slightly towards him and whispered, 'Wouldn't mind taking the weight off. Been on my tootsies for hours.' He looked around. 'I see that the entrepreneur cowboy hasn't been invited to this then. He was at the luncheon, you know.'

'Was he? I saw him going up to the Chief Executive Officer's suite just now. Wonder what that's about?'

Two security people appeared from for'ard, one male and one female. They systematically frisked the visitors, opening their bags, checking their camera cases and asking if they were carrying anything dangerous from the list that was held before each one.

'What's in here please?' the woman asked Anna Divrej, holding up a plastic-wrapped package she had found in the girl's jacket pocket.

'That-a ees my-a sandwiches forra my-a tea.'

'Please open them.' She did so. The sardines weren't doing too well in the heat.

'Please close them.'

Everything was thoroughly scrutinised. Roland objected mildly to his tripod being confiscated.

'Sorry sir. There simply isn't enough room for you to use it in there. We'll look after it for you.' He relinquished it grudgingly. Then the curtain was drawn back and they were in the presence of higher beings again.

'Welcome aboard Your Royal Highness, Prime Minister, ladies and gentlemen of the airport staff and press,' said the Captain, his hands hanging by his side as he bent forward jerkily from the waist addressing each sector.

'Looks like a penguin,' whispered Roland.

Their host continued, 'There has been a lot of hype about the technology embodied in this unique aircraft,' he said, 'and today, we shall be unveiling some of the *ILEX*'s secrets. The amazing exterior appearance is, I'm sure you agree, impressive. Not only its size but the composition of the outer skin is unique. This will be the largest passenger aeroplane in the world and it will be made in Britain.'

A buzz of excitement emanated from the journalists and even the Prince raised his eyebrows in surprise.

Eleanor leaned wearily against the cabin wall, scribbling away on a small, spiral notepad.

The Captain continued, 'We shall be shortly touring the entire aircraft, and you should know that this is a test prototype and as such is full of experimental equipment and other paraphernalia. Try to raise your eyes beyond the apparent clutter and appreciate that history is being made. I'd like to introduce you to my flight officer who will tell you something about the amazing photovoltaic panelling that cloaks the *ILEX*'s outer skin.' He smiled encouragingly at his colleague and stepped to one side

'Thank you, Captain. Good afternoon Your Royal Highness, Prime Minister, ladies and gentlemen.' He then launched into the talk that Gig Cattermole had wanted to experience the day before. The sound of scribbling pens competed with the whirr of two electric fans trained on the royal party and the hum of various systems beyond the screen. The already stifling atmosphere grew steadily worse. Eleanor was gasping for air. She fanned herself with the note-pad. Beads of perspiration accumulated on her brow and trickled down her face, carving groove-like rivulets in her thick, powdery make-up. She licked them away as they reached her upper lip with its dark, downy layer of hair. Aware that nobody was standing near her, she wondered why. Celeste sniffed pointedly and turned her head away. The combination of lavender water and mothballs grew ever more potent in the closed, airless, cabin confines.

'... and now I would like to show you a sample of the special tiles that coat the outside of this aircraft.' The flight officer reached up into a locker and produced some bubble-wrap, carefully peeling it away to show what looked like a small, bathroom tile, its top surface coated with hard, smooth, black treacle. He handed it to the Prince who, together with the Prime Minister, examined it most carefully, marvelled at its lightness and clearly wanted to know more.

'You will observe,' said the flight officer, 'that the interior of the tile is, in fact, composed of a honeycomb type material and that the lower surface is primed with a special metal alloy that reflects the ultraviolet light passing through the outer, top, glass-like surface, into the honeycomb. If I were to shine a light through the tile, thus,' and he produced a powerful torch from his pocket, 'you would see that the interior matrix is itself transparent and capable of internally reflecting the light. The idea is that UV light comes in through the top layer and bounces about inside the matrix, unable to escape due to the alloy underneath and incapable of going back out the way it came in due to a fiendishly clever magnetic repulsion mechanism incorporated into the second layer level.'

If all this passed above the heads of the royal party and, indeed, some of the journalists, nobody was going to admit to it and they all nodded their heads knowledgeably like peasants in an amateur pantomime.

'However, you may ask, what happens to all this trapped light? Well, if we had a microscope you would see, embedded in the matrix, millions of tiny photo-receptors that turn the light into electrical energy which is transported into a new breed of lightweight, long-life batteries. It is these batteries that will power all the electrical systems on the *ILEX*.'

A stunned silence descended over his audience. 'Any questions?'

The Prince, intent on appearing intelligent, raised the first finger of one hand to gain attention.

'Most interesting. Most interesting, but might one ask the composition of the various materials contained within this tile?' He held it up by one corner and turned his wrist back and forth so that the photographers had their moment.

'Regrettably that information is not available for release at this time, Your Royal Highness.'

'Well, worth a try, eh, what?' the Prince joked to those around him, passing the tile on so that others in his party could handle it.

The Prime Minister, quick to be seen supporting the cutting edge of technology, cleared his throat and ventured, 'Why, may I

AIRSHOW ILEX

ask, is it necessary to cover the underside of the aircraft in these tiles as well as the top?' He sat back, hugely pleased with his display of acumen.

Keen on a knighthood, the Captain intervened, knowing how important it was to pump up the PM's ego.

'Well, Prime Minister,' he said, bowing slightly from the waist again, 'a very pertinent question which I will answer for you. Once up above the clouds, sunlight doesn't only come from the sun onto the top and side surfaces of the aircraft, but is also reflected onto the underside by the clouds.'

'Really?' mused the Prime Minister, settling in his chair and looking around him for approval at his perspicacity which was immediately showered on him from all sides.

'So,' ventured the Prince with another small lift of the finger, and sensing that an intelligence dual was underway, 'does the aircraft run completely on the electricity from the tiles?'

Although tempted to shout, 'Don't be so stupid, man!' the Captain smiled a tad condescendingly and waved his hand back and forth, palm upwards like a timid metronome as the flight officer received the tile back into his safe keeping, wrapped it and put it back in the locker.

'Well, Your Royal Highness, although the energy generated by the tiles is ample for all the electrical needs within the aircraft, something a little more powerful is required when it comes to lifting many thousands of kilos of fully loaded aircraft and contents into the air.'

'And that would be ... ?'

'Please Sir, if you would bear with us, we would like to take you on a tour of the *ILEX* before revealing the energy source which will power flight.'

'Very well,' said the Prince, rising to his feet. Everybody around him got up too. The modesty screen was folded aside to reveal the way through the lower cabin. Although there wasn't exactly a gasp of horror at the entanglement of wires and cables threading their way along walls, ceiling and floor, and although one or two members of the entourage smiled with slight embarrassment and looked down at their feet, on the whole the company which was used to luxury and order, took on a Dunkirk spirit and soldiered forth amid the monitors, regulators and rows of vast orange drums of ballast.

'Please mind your heads here,' said the flight officer as the crush of visitors sallied forth into the unknown. The photographers had dashed ahead to get views of the VIPs coming towards them. The journalists were craning their necks to hear the dulcet-toned comments falling from the lips of the aristocracy. Only when they had all left the holding area, did Anna Divrej, who was at the rear of the crowd, turn to look behind her and see Eleanor slumped on the floor, her head against the wall. She dashed back.

'Oh queekly! Somebody-a come here-a and-a help! Theece lady-a ees not wella!' They had all gone out of ear-shot though into the humming, buzzing area of machines that were being tested to destruction in the baking heat of the *ILEX*. Anna looked around her but she was alone with the insensible woman for only a second or two before the female security guard joined them in the holding area, alerted by her calls. Eleanor moaned as she came round.

'I'll fetch her some water,' said the lady guard, diving into the flight-deck service galley. 'Look after her for a moment please.' Then she was gone. Anna gazed down at the semi-conscious, middle-aged and oddly perfumed woman on the floor. Eleanor looked pallid and was gasping, her eyes closed and head back. Anna Divrej was at the patient's side when the female guard returned.

'What happened? Where am I?' The ageing journalist tried to get up but flopped down again.

'Let me help,' said the security woman. 'Here, sip some water. I think the heat was too much for you.' Eleanor gulped gratefully at the plastic tumbler, her trembling fingers clutching it as she breathed heavily.

'Here. Let me take that from you. If we can get you to sit over there, you can cool down by the fans.' So, with difficulty, the wilting Eleanor, supported by the two, was half-dragged to the seat previously occupied by the royal posterior.

AIRSHOW ILEX

Meanwhile the rest of the tour continued, the entourage ignorant of the fainted lady languishing by the fans in the holding area. They squeezed their way along the central aisle and then bunched together in a people jam. Roland viewed the scene with artistic horror. It looked as if the worst kind of cowboy builders had been in, ripped the place apart and then abandoned the job. Vast orange cylinders ranged along on each side of the viewing party. At least there was some colour to photograph so he set to work.

Somebody asked, 'What are the orange oil-drums for?'

'Well,' said the Captain, they are in fact ballast tanks.'

'What do you put in them?'

'It rather depends on which tests we are doing. We change the mass accordingly but we mostly use rocks or sand. When undergoing trials, they replace the weight of people, luggage and freight. We have more down in the hold.'

'How fast will the *ILEX* go?'

'I'm sorry, that is currently classified information but you may be assured that it is very fast.'

'How far can it go?'

'Again, I regret that I am not at liberty to say at this time. I'm sure you understand,' the Captain said with an air of finality. A mumble of disappointment came from the journalists.

Nervous of losing his audience's attention he smiled broadly and expounded, 'However, I can tell you about the *ILEX*'s amazing electricity production. We have some 10,000 square metres of photovoltaics capable of generating a massive kilowattage. This,' said the Captain, 'is where we monitor the power generated by the tiles.' He indicated a display. 'You can see that today, because of the clear skies, we are making in excess of what we are using. If we were flying with passengers, the demand would be more in keeping with the supply but when we're not using as much, this could be a problem. With photovoltaics on buildings, it is possible to sell the excess back to the national grid but in our case we have to find something to do with the surplus. Would anybody like to guess what we use it for?' He looked around the group.

Nobody wanted to say anything stupid. One of the male journalists said, 'I suppose you could use it in some kind of storage device, like those old off-peak radiators.'

'Not far from the truth,' said the Captain. 'The *ILEX*'s self-generated electricity can take care of all the internal systems of the aircraft, from air conditioning to flight-deck electronics, instrumentation, landing gear deployment and storage, baggage-handling conveyor belts, galley requirements, toilet flushing, hot water, in-flight entertainment, lighting, communications, both internal and external, and not forgetting the flaps. Remember that most of our flying is above the clouds and in uninterrupted sunlight.'

'How interesting,' said the Prince dutifully.

The Captain added, 'You probably know that the holds of most aircraft are minimally heated. You can tell when you collect your luggage after a long flight. So, what we do is to heat the hold.'

The Prince then volunteered, 'What happens if you are carrying perishables in the there?'

'Well, Sir, it is sectioned off into various areas, some that can take heat and some that need refrigeration. We can use the excess electricity for both.'

'What a good idea,' said the Prince.

'There is something else we can do.' This tour was becoming more interesting by the minute and people began to chat among themselves. The Captain raised his voice a little.

'Has it ever occurred to you how much water we breathe out during respiration?' There was some shaking of heads. It was difficult to believe that this had anything to do with flying.

The flight officer took over from the Captain. 'Each person exhales several litres of water vapour during a long-haul flight, depending on their bodyweight, lung capacity, activity level and relative air humidity. This varies with cabin pressure and stress. Much of this liquid finds its way between the inner and outer walls of the aircraft and accumulates there with each successive journey, adding to the payload and therefore making us use more fuel. ? Can you imagine how much liquid there might be at the end of a long-haul flight with a thousand passengers? All that would be sitting in the inter-skin space of the aircraft, ready to be hauled across the world, being added to by each subsequent flight, using up more and more fuel.'

'Yes,' said the Prime Minister, nodding sagely. 'I can see how that would happen.'

The flight officer continued. 'This moisture not only costs us more in fuel but also encourages the growth of mould on insulation and contacts contained in the inter-wall space, obviously something that could cause deterioration in the wiring and we don't want that, do we?'

The group nodded and agreed amongst themselves.

'So, the *ILEX* is the first passenger aircraft in the world to use its photovoltaically generated power to pump warm air through the aircraft's outer and inner skin, drying it out. This water vapour condenses in our state of the art moisture extraction system and is collected and recycled for use in the toilets and washbasins. Furthermore, a proportion of it is purified for drinking on board so we don't have to carry as much water and therefore again save on fuel.'

A murmur of approbation rippled through the standing audience.

The Prince, obviously very impressed, remarked enthusiastically, 'What a brilliant idea! I can see why the *ILEX* is promoted as being more environmentally friendly.'

'Indeed, Sir. However, the amount of water recaptured in this way is minuscule compared with how much is generated, so we had to find another use for it.'

'...and what might that be, may one ask?'

'If I may beg your patience, Sir, for a little longer, all will be explained,' continued his guide as they walked along the middle of the aisle, 'but the big breakthrough in environmental economy is the fuel that this aircraft is using.

'Very well, but one is most excited and eager to learn about the amazing propulsion fuel utilised by this technologically advanced aircraft.' The Royal personage looked encouragingly around the group. Everybody nodded eagerly.

The Captain, with the suppressed mirth of Father Christmas about to deliver presents, said, 'Would Your Royal Highness, Prime Minister and the rest of the ladies and gentlemen be good enough to follow me up to the floor above to view the *ILEX*'s revolutionary propulsion system?' An enthusiastic murmuring filled the space as they all climbed the curved staircase to the upper deck.

*

Eleanor rose unsteadily to her feet. The security woman activated the roll-down outside staircase and then the roller door.

'I'll come down with you,' the woman said kindly, and then, addressing Anna, 'Can you come too? I'm sure the Press Centre Controller will arrange another *ILEX* tour for you.'

'I go weeth hairr,' said Anna. 'Don't-a worry lady.'

'The taxi's on its way, Miss Framp,' the security woman said. Then the three of them went slowly down the staircase and Eleanor sat on the bottom step and waited.

*

The Captain led the party to the end of the upper deck near the rear of the plane. There he punched in a code to open a narrow, steel door.

'...and this is what you all want to know about,' he said proudly, using a diamond-shaped key on a chain around his neck to unlock what looked like a safe. The small, heavy door swung open. A steel cylinder embedded in a cornucopia of twisting pipes and dials, encased in an oily liquid, gleamed from behind very thick glass.

*

The chief leatherjacket leaned down and told the taxi driver, 'Hurry up and get away. The VIPs are about to come down the plane steps shortly.' Eleanor slumped in the back of the taxi. Anna went around and got in beside her.

The driver said, 'We must-a hurry. Where-a to, lady?' and looked in the rear-view mirror. His eyebrows shot up when he heard Anna reply, 'Theece-a lady-a is-a not verry well and has to go-a home.' Then her mouth dropped open as she realised Brecht's accent matched hers.

*

'Your Royal Highness, Prime Minister, ladies and gentleman, I present to you the first atomic hybrid fuel-cell.'
The photographers rushed forward as the royal party moved away, clearly nervous of anything with the word 'atomic' in it. Not wishing to look like a scaredy-cat, the Prime Minister enquired politely, 'Forgive me for asking, but is it safe?'

The Captain smiled knowingly. 'Prime Minister, as safe as houses. It is encased in triple-gauge lead plastiform and in the unlikely event of an air crash, the atomic hybrid cell configuration has its own orange parachute and shock deflection system for landing. It would also give out a coded signal for its recovery.'

Their guide continued, 'As I was saying just now, what to do with all this water. Well, our scientists came up with a unique way of using it in a fuel cell. Yes, this is going to be the first aircraft with integrated atomic-hybrid fuel cells. It's cutting edge technology, of course, but by the time this baby is ready for market, all the glitches will have been ironed out.' He waved his arms about excitedly. '...and this is only the beginning.'

The Prime Minster looked warily at the large radioactivity sign on the front of the unit and, with the other esteemed members of the tour, made a marginally undignified scramble down the rear staircase. Only one photographer managed to get ahead of the royal party and he positioned himself at the bottom of the outside staircase, still rolled out after Eleanor's departure in the taxi with Anna.

The Prince paused momentarily at the top of the flight of stairs to have his photograph taken shaking hands first with the Captain and then with the Prime Minister and to point to the big, old, sandstone house on the other side of the airport.

'What's that building over there?' he enquired.
'That is St. Bede's Convent, Sir,' replied the Captain.
'Atchoo!' said the Prince.

Chapter 11

Thursday 16th June.
Mid-afternoon

The whoosy lady journalist was feeling too faint to make any connection between the couple.
Anna said to her, 'Where-a you wanna go, Meece Framp?'
'Twenty-five Glade House Mansions,' she mumbled, eyes closed.
'You hear-a what-a da lady say?'
'I hear.' He took a deep breath and pointed up at the black bulk of the *ILEX*.
'Theece big-a plane, she is INGENIOUS, yes?'
Anna replied, 'More than ingenious, EXTRAORDINARY.'
Brecht smacked the dashboard with the palm of his hand. Yes! Contact! Eleanor jolted to her senses.
'What's happening? What was that noise?'
'It's-a OK lady. A fly on my-a dashboard.' He gave Anna a hard stare in the rear view mirror. She winked at him in return. He pulled away smoothly as the royal party started to descend from the *ILEX*.

Eleanor fumbled for a tissue in the brown briefcase that Anna had carried down for her. She dabbed at her forehead. She felt such a fool, collapsing like that. Nobody had warned her that the menopause would be so unpleasant. She was getting it all; night sweats, panic attacks, hot flushes and now the inconvenience of fainting.

The internal airport road was clear, ready for the departure of the Prince, Prime Minister and entourage. All other traffic had been held back by the police. Security was the highest it had ever been at such a show. The motor cycle outriders, blue lights flashing, had returned, ready to escort the VIPs to the heli-pad and were waiting in the shadow of the *ILEX*.

Brecht accelerated and took the short route to Gate Alpha. The security guards were on their walkie-talkies waiting for the non-flying VIPs to come through on their way home by car. They waved the taxi through noncommittally and it shot away to join the ring road.

'Where-a ees this-a Mansions place where-a you live-a lady?'
Eleanor waved her hand vaguely. 'Over behind those flats in Isabel Avenue.'
The taxi swung off the roundabout and into the wide, tree-lined road.

'On the right, a bit further along,' she said, struggling to sit up straighter. Brecht pulled over on the wrong side of the road across the driveway of Glade House Mansions and then leapt out to open the door for Eleanor who was gathering her things together and struggling to get out.

'Here-a lady... let me-a help-a you... hey, lady! You arrer the same wot I drove-a to the convent, no?'

'Yes, yes,' said Eleanor, 'but how much do I owe you?'

'Ow you say... on the 'ouse.'

'Thank you. You're very kind.' She stood up and swayed. Brecht's hand was under her elbow immediately and Anna slid across the back seat and got out to assist as well.

'I think-a you need-a my help to come into your-a flat, yes?' She said.

'Yes. Thank you,' replied Eleanor and the pair set off along the pink concrete path to the entrance lobby and went in.

Brecht shut the rear door, got back into the taxi and turned off the ticking indicator. What luck! He'd found her! The woman with the navy blue blazer and the white flower pinned on the lapel! That's exactly what the unattractive journalist was wearing the other day. How could he have thought that she was his contact? He pounded his temple twice with the inside of his wrist. Stupid! Stupid!

Anna came out and got into the back of the taxi and they conversed quickly in their own language.

'Is the lady alright?' Brecht asked.

'She'll have a rest. I think she was overcome by the heat. Forget her.'

'Did you get what we want?'

'I've got it,' she said.

'Where?'

'In my jacket pocket.'

'It won't be long before they realise it's missing.'

'You have to hide me somewhere.'

'I have a place for you but we can't go there until later.'

'They saw us get into your taxi. They will ask you where I went.' Brecht stroked his chin and re-started the engine.

'Where are all your things?'

'In a bed and breakfast not far from here.'

'You have to clear out of there straight away. Let's go!'

Ten minutes later he sat drumming his fingers on the wheel. She was taking too long. He glanced at his watch. Ten to four. Where could he hide her until tonight? Then she came out, carrying a hold-all, ruck-sack and handbag. She threw them all onto the back seat and got in. Where? Where? The cinema would be good later but he needed somewhere until then. He couldn't use his own place. Too risky. He pulled away, cruising the roads, looking for somewhere safe and inconspicuous. The railway station was no good. That was the first place they would look. Then they would check the hotels. If only he could dump her baggage somewhere.

The radio crackled into life. 'Taxi number thirty-two. Come in please.'

He pressed the button and activated the microphone.

'Number-a thirty-two here.'

'Where are you thirty-two?'

Playing for time, he said, 'Say again-a please. Not-a good reception here.'

'Where are you thirty-two? We've got a queue of people outside the Press Centre waiting for taxis.'

'I'm on my way-a back-a from the railway station,' he said. Arrive-a to you in seven minutes.' He turned off the microphone and reverted to his own language.

'What am I going to do with you, Anna Divrej, yes?'

'That's my name.'

'I think you should go to the cinema tonight but you have to stay somewhere until then and we must get rid of your bags.'

AIRSHOW ILEX

He turned around and glanced down briefly at what she was wearing. 'Can you change into something else as I drive?'

'Yes,' she said, unzipping the hold-all and pulling out a pair of jeans and a pale, striped, cotton top. She put the UV tile in her handbag, then, without hesitation she was ducking down, stripping and changing, adding a baseball cap as the final touch. He pulled over to a litter bin.

'Put what you were wearing in there,' he said. 'Quickly!'

'What, get rid of my clothes? she said, a little outraged.

'Yes, yes,' he replied impatiently. 'They will have you recorded on videotape wearing those.'

With a look of resentment, She rolled up her blazer and white trousers and scrambled out to put them in the bin and then threw herself into the taxi and closed the door.

'They will search my boot so I can't put anything in there for you,' he said, looking to right and left as they drove off. He made for a shopping parade outside the centre of town and veered quickly into one of the service roads behind it where a row of lock-up garages baked in the afternoon heat opposite the traders' rear entrances. It was deserted. He backed up to the last garage in the row and got out, leaving the cab ticking over.

'Quick, give those to me!' He took her hold-all and rucksack, depositing them quickly round the side of the block, where elderberry trees jostled with fire of London plants and stinging nettles. He got back in.

'We'll pick them up later. Have you got some money?'

'A little.'

'Take this.' He thrust some notes into her hand.

'If you walk through that alleyway there's a little Asian supermarket on the left. Get yourself something to eat and drink and an English magazine. Then go on down the road to the end. There's a little park. Find yourself somewhere shady to sit and eat and read. Try to look boring. Don't talk to anybody. I'll come back for you at seven o'clock. OK?'

'OK,' she said, getting out.

*

The *ILEX* visit had gone well, apart from that stupid Framp woman fainting. Sheer attention-seeking! 'Thank goodness the VIPs didn't see it,' thought Celeste, sinking into the comfort of her cream leather office chair, kicking off her shoes and switching on her mobile phone. There was an SMS. She opened it, delighted to see that it was from Rupert.

'Out of town. Return Hamburg Fri nite. R.'

'What is going on?' she said aloud, tossing the mobile onto the desk and running her hands through her hair in exasperation. Was he trying to dump her? Surely not? They'd lived together as a couple for nearly five years. Everything had been fine before he went away... or had it? She racked her brains. Had something changed? She'd been very busy with the airshow but then he was heavily involved in his career too. They had an unspoken agreement about their lifestyle. Of course a baby would change things, but they could work around it. They could afford a nanny.

She picked up the mobile again and speed-dialled his network number. Diversions were in place so she left a voice-mail.

'*Got your SMS. Please ring me. I need to talk to you. Love you.*' She switched it off. What more could she do?

Now that the VIPs had gone, the afternoon test flights had started up again, rocketing across the blue ceiling that was the celestial canopy over everything as far as the eye could see, searing vertically in a trail of white spume and punching the air with ear-drum punishing sound waves that wracked the chest and rattled the windows. Celeste wanted to scream, 'Stop it! Stop it! I'm going to have a baby and I think my partner's abandoning me! I'm scared. I'm terrified. Be quiet!'

Instead, she turned on her work station and checked the news headlines. The demonstrators from earlier had drawn the wrong sort of attention to Phillipstone Airshow. '*Students support wind-farm on airport land.*' There was a knock at her door.

'Come in,' she said.

'Local paper, Miss Blagden.'

'Thank you. Put it there.'

She didn't even take her eyes off the screen as she clicked to see what else was being said on the net about the demo.

'*Students from Phillipstone College of Further Education broke through security at the local airport this morning and demonstrated in favour of a wind-farm of one hundred generators proposed for part of the site. The students interrupted a private, pre-show tour by VIPs. Police arrested some thirty teenagers after VIPs were led to safety. It is reported that one shot was fired into the ceiling by a body-guard in order to quieten the demonstrators. Security was tightened for the royal visit to the new ILEX passenger aircraft this afternoon and there were no further incidents. The Head of Security at Phillipstone Airshow was unavailable for comment.*'

Celeste gave a long, slow blink and shook her head. This was not what was needed. Then she spotted the *Saturnian,* picked it up and gasped with annoyance at the headline:

'*American entrepreneur claims airport land for wind-farm.*' She skimmed down the page: '*Wealthy local American, Grant Landscar, is all set to shunt his planning application for one hundred wind generators through committee at Phillipstone Borough Council. Mr. Landscar says he can prove that part of the airport land belonged to his grandmother who moved to the United States upon marriage in the nineteen-twenties.*'

The article went on to detail how the Council had adopted the land and leased it to the airport authority. It also mentioned that St. Bede's Convent might be implicated in the property challenge. At the end, the by-line was 'Eleanor Framp'. Celeste skimmed through the pages. There was no mention of her own contribution about Grant Landscar at the VIP luncheon.

It was the last straw. Adverse publicity about the Phillipstone Airshow. People would think this would be the final one. Instead of a glittering career rising through the ceiling of the Press Centre to queen it in company headquarters as a top management executive, she would be joining the dole queue as an unemployed, unmarried mother... unless she could pin Rupert down on the matrimonial front. She picked up and dialled out.

*

The *ILEX* Captain was seated in the flight deck checking through some papers when his officer came and joined him.

'I think I know what blew the lights earlier after the tour, sir,' he said. 'We've run some tests and it was a simple matter of overload.'

'So we were generating too much electricity and couldn't vent it due to being stuck on the ground in full sunshine since yesterday morning. '

'Precisely sir.'

'Too much of a good thing, eh?' The Captain smiled knowingly. I think that ten seconds for the emergency lighting to come on was too long.'

'I can set that for quicker if you want, sir.'

'More to the point, we can't let it happen again. Met Office is forecasting more of the same.'

'If I might venture an idea, sir…'

'Go ahead number one.'

'Well captain, we could open the hold door at night and use the refrigeration system to blast cold air through the insulation and hold. It would only need to run for about an hour and that should do it.'

'It's a security risk.'

'There's not much going on here late, sir. You saw how it was on last night's the recording, just a couple of totties staggering home from a site workers' party. We have our special guards. '

'I'll think about it. In the meantime, I can see that we're going to overload again soon.' He indicated the panel to his left. 'We'd better use up some juice. So, off you go and turn on everything that has a plug on it. Run the vents in the loos, boil the kettle and open and shut the outside staircase and sliding door a few dozen times. I'm going to turn on the engines and work the flaps, oh, and let's have every light in the place shining brightly. That should take the edge of it.'

'Captain.'

'Yes number one?'

'I've had a thought, Sir.'

'Yes, go ahead.'

AIRSHOW ILEX

'Would it be feasible to bring along some storage batteries for outside and take a feed off the main accumulator?'

'Not a bad idea, officer. Do the sums and organise it. I leave the details to you with your physics masters degree.

'Yes sir.' He turned to leave.

'Go on ahead, number one. I want to check something myself. One of the oscillators is throwing up a duff reading on here.' The Captain got up and indicated that the officer should leave the flight deck ahead of him. They went down the stairs to the holding area.

'Just look at all this palaver with screens and fans. Didn't the idiots realise that this was a test aircraft? Get it cleared away, number one.' Then he sniffed. 'Do you smell something funny in here?'

The officer sniffed and the pair of them stood with their noses in the air like a couple of dogs trying to pick up a scent. Then they paced around the holding area, each going in the opposite direction until they were face to face again.

'It's coming from this quarter,' said the captain, neck poking forward, eyes going from side to side, nose twitching. They peered behind the seats, ran their hands along the top of the foldaway screen and crawled on the floor but couldn't pinpoint the strange odour.

'Check the lockers!'

The officer worked his way along the bank of flip-up lockers above head level. They were full of equipment and spares. When he came to the one containing the sample tile the aroma intensified.

'It's coming from here, sir.' He lifted the wrapped tile down onto the side and put his hand into the locker's recesses, feeling around. 'Nothing else in here, Captain.'

With an air of foreboding acquired through three decades of intelligence and airforce service, the Captain's face blanched. He looked down. 'Unwrap it!' he snapped. The officer did so and was greeted by an overwhelming stench. There, instead of the cutting edge, technologically revolutionary *ILEX* sample tile, lay a square package of something wrapped in cling plastic.

'Open it!' said the Captain stony-faced, but before his command was fulfilled, they both realised what was going to emerge... Anna Divrej's sardine sandwich and it was decidedly off.

*

Synth pulled the old-fashioned bell handle next to the heavily studded front door of St. Bede's Convent. Black lace-up shoes tapped along the parquet flooring inside and the face of one of the young novices appeared at the barred grill.

'It's Synth Hunt. I've come to see Reverend Mother.' The grill was closed and the door swung open.'

'Please come in, Miss Hunt.'

The casually dressed redhead stood in stark contrast next to the shiny-faced, navy-blue-clad, young nun.

'We hope you and your mother are alright after last night's fire,' said the novice with a gentle smile, leading the way to the big staircase.

'My mother's still in hospital but I hope she'll be out soon, thank you.'

Synth's stiletto heels tip-tapped sharply across the wooden floor and up the wide staircase with the ornate balustrade. If the *religieuse* was worried about the heels making dents, nothing was said. They reached Reverend Mother's office and she was on the threshold to meet them.

'Thank you sister. Do come in Miss Hunt. I want to ask you about your mother but firstly, how would you feel about a nice a cup of tea?'

'Yes. Yes please. That would be lovely,' Synth replied. Reverend Mother gave a nod to the postulant who went out and closed the door quietly behind her.

'Do sit down, dear.' Synth sank into the button-backed, very worn chair and crossed her legs elegantly. The old nun suppressed an urge to tell her to cover her knees but clasped her hands together over her stomach instead and sat down at the desk. She leaned back in her chair.

'Dreadful business, the fire last night. Was absolutely everything lost?'

'Forensics won't let me go in there to look but I should think so. We didn't have very much of value anyway, you know.'

Reverend Mother nodded sympathetically. 'Worldly goods aren't everything. It is possible to live quite reasonably without most of the things that modern society deems essential.' She paused.

'I'm sorry, Miss Hunt, I didn't mean to preach. Now, tell me how your mother is. I understand she was suffering from smoke inhalation.'

'She took in quite a lot so they're keeping her in hospital for a few days. I've just come back from there. She's very upset about the cats.'

'Naturally, naturally. She had quite a few, I believe.'

'Yes. Rather too many.' Synth smiled wryly.

'Anyway, down to brass tacks! Where are you going to stay tonight?'

'I hadn't really thought about it. Any other time I could have got a room somewhere but I expect it would be difficult with the airshow being on and everything.'

'Exactly. That is why I am very happy to offer you and your mother a temporary place here in the convent until something more permanent can be sorted out.'

'That's very kind of you, Reverend Mother, but we couldn't impose on you like that...'

'Nonsense child. You are both very welcome here. We have a small guest suite that we usually keep for visiting church officials or religious personnel. It has a twin-bedded room, a small sitting room, bathroom and kitchenette. You could manage quite well there until things are sorted out. What do you say, my dear?'

There was a light tapping at the door. 'Come.'

The young nun brought in a tray of tea and biscuits and placed it on the desk.

'Thank you sister.' The nun half-bowed and made her silent exit.

'Do say 'yes', Miss Hunt.'

'I suppose I have little choice really... sorry. I didn't mean to sound ungracious. Yes, yes please.'

'I understand,' said Reverend Mother slowly, pouring out a cup of tea, 'that you work a night shift somewhere. A parts factory, was it?'

Deep in the recesses of Synth's mind the thought flashed across that if she lied to a nun she might go to hell.

'When you're unqualified like me, you have to take work where you can get it,' she replied, avoiding the nun's gaze.

'Milk? Sugar?'

'Just a little milk please.' She reached across and took the cup and saucer, her hand trembling slightly.

'Deputy Reverend Mother tried to contact you at work last night but they said they'd never heard of you.'

Synth gazed down into the cup. Then, suddenly and without warning, the tears were plopping into the tea. If the nun had told her off for her wicked ways she could have coped but all this kindness in the face of her life-style, was just too much. If they knew what she did to earn money they would kick her out immediately.

'Sometimes,' the nun said thoughtfully, pouring her own tea, 'things happen for a reason. Perhaps losing your home and nearly losing your mother, is a sign that perhaps you need to re-think your life. Go on. Drink your tea, my dear. We'll work something out together.'

*

'Put that in a polythene bag and get it off to the lab.'

'Yes, sir.'

'I want to know everything about it. Do you hear me? Everything!'

'Yes, sir. Right away sir.' The flight officer looked down at the sardine sandwich which was now safely ensconced in a thick, plastic bag with a knot tied in the top.

'In a minute. Come with me.'

AIRSHOW ILEX

They both went up to the flight deck again. The Captain dimmed the lights and flicked on the infra-green, digital, cam play-back, running it through until he came to the moment earlier in the afternoon when the holding area was full of visitors. There was something eerily sinister in the lime green picture of the assembled gathering of VIPs, journalists and photographers, all gaping in slow-motion conversation. Some wore contact lenses that gleamed like zombies in a horror film.

The men watched carefully as the tour group slowly shambled out of the holding area and into the main cabin.

'Nothing going on here,' said the Captain.

'Wait a minute, sir. Just look. That scrawny woman journalist is sitting on the floor and that young woman is rushing to bend over her.'

'Turn up the sound.' Anna's call for help came through clearly.

'She can shout. We didn't hear her though.'

'Here comes the security guard... hold on... she's going away again.'

'Too much equipment running. That's why we didn't realise.'

'Look! That girl! She's opening the overhead locker. What's she taking out of her pocket?'

The captain gazed at the green screen, a patina of suppressed anger creeping across his face.

'A sardine sandwich, sir?'

The pair watched transfixed as Anna took the tile swiftly with her left hand and placed it in her left blazer pocket whilst simultaneously moving the plastic-packed sandwich into its place with her other hand, before quickly closing the locker door. There was a delay of a few seconds and then the female security guard returned in time to see the thief bending over the swooning Eleanor with well-acted concern.

'Who is she?' demanded the Captain, rewinding and zooming in on Anna's clip-on pass but it was hard to read as she leaned over. Then she stood up again and then her pass-badge could be read.

'Anna Divrej,' he recited slowly, with malice. 'Play the general video of the tour.'

They watched on double speed and soon realised that both Anna and the unattactive woman journalist were missing from the tour.

'Check the outside disks. When did they leave?'

Again, coldly shocked, they saw the two women get into a taxi and be driven away. The taxi's licence number showed clearly on the back. No. 32.

'We'll get him!' said the Captain grimly, opening the radio link to the Chief leatherjacket on guard outside.

Chapter 12

**Thursday 16th June.
Late Afternoon.**

As Brecht swung through Gate Alpha, aware that he had taken longer than seven minutes to get back to the airport, his heart was pounding. Had they discovered that the *ILEX* tile was missing? There had been no hint of anything in the radio taxi controller's voice. He slowed down to go through the security check but, after looking at his pass and inspecting the front of the taxi, the guard did not raise the red and white striped pole barrier. Instead, he turned away and spoke into his walkie-talkie.

'Wassa matter?' demanded Brecht through the open car window.

'Just one moment please, sir.' The man went on talking and then nodded and finished the call.

'Please pull over here.' Brecht protested. 'They are-a waiting for-a me at-a the Press-a Centre.'

'Over here please sir.' The cab driver made a gesture of exasperation and did as he was bid.

'Wassa goin' on?' he called to the back of the guard who had returned to his duties. Brecht turned off the engine and got out of the car, leaned his elbows on the roof and shaded the late afternoon sun out of his eyes with his hands. Coming down the perimeter road in a cloud of dust, hurtling towards him, was a black saloon. His stomach pitched. They knew. His mind started to race. He had to get his story straight and stick to it.

The afternoon test flights were in full swing. Two fighters were weaving around each other in teeth-rattling configurations. Should he make a run for it? Then what would happen to Anna? At this very moment she was sitting in a park, killing time, waiting for him to return. The car came nearer.

'Don't panic,' he told himself and turned around, leaned against the taxi with his arms folded and pretended to be watching the display. Any other time he would have enjoyed it. There was squeal of brakes the other side of the barrier, and he knew this was the moment. A man wearing a light grey suit got out, came towards him and leaned lightly on the horizontal red and white pole.

'Mr. Slipkopj?' He enquired congenially.

'Yes. That-a is-a me. Watta you want?'

'Oh, nothing very much really.' He produced an ID and waved it briefly before the nervous-looking cab driver. 'Just a spot check on your vehicle. Would you mind following me back to the service centre up there?'

Brecht could see another man sitting in the passenger seat. He looked like a heavy.

'There's-a nothing-a wrong with-a my-a taxi.'

'Just a formality. Shouldn't take long. Shall we go?'

Brecht got back reluctantly into the driving seat and started up. Grey suit gave the barrier guard a signal and the striped bar went up to let him through. The guard gave Brecht a cheery half-salute. The black saloon coasted away smoothly and the sound of the taxi's diesel engine throbbed loudly in comparison as he drove up the slope too.

Brecht followed into the vehicle service yard near the bothies where all the courtesy cars were logged in and out each day. There was a petrol pump near the controller's office. The grey-suited man got out and came over to Brecht.

'Just take her into the bay there and over the inspection pit. Thanks old chap.'

As Brecht reached the ramp, he heard the wide shutter door come down behind him. He knew he was trapped. He turned off the engine, leaving the key in the ignition and got out, stepping over the gap. He was alone in the dimly lit, oily-smelling, metal-roofed cavern. Gingerly, he walked over to the personnel door and rattled it but it wouldn't open. His escorts had gone. He walked back to the centre of the huge shed and, with arms spread wide, shouted, 'Watta you want? Why-a you do theece to-a me?'

He heard the sound of a spanner or some other tool being dropped on the ground behind him and turned around sharply to see two of the leatherjackets, crash-helmets and visors still in place, standing, feet apart, watching him. He looked about urgently for something to defend himself with but he knew it was no match. Waiting, like a mesmerised prey, he wondered if they would kill him. 'No, no,' he thought. 'They want me alive. They want to know where the tile is.' This thought comforted him and he stood a little more upright, lifting his chin.

Then, in unison, the pair strode slowly towards him, their heavy black boots grinding the grit on the garage floor. To resist or not? He decided not and as the taller of the two grabbed his arm and swung him around, to hold him in a neck-lock, the other put the weight of his metal-tipped boot onto Brecht's suede shoes, swivelling so that the pain was excruciating. Brecht gave a sustained yelp.

'Where is she?' hissed his captor into his ear, giving him a little head-butt with the side of his helmet for good measure. Brecht made a sort of gargling noise and tried to release the man's grip. 'I can't breathe,' he strained and spluttered.

'Let-a me go. I'll tell-a you everything I know.'

The leatherjackets released him and both stood back, the shorter one cracking his knuckles, obviously keen to inflict more pain.

Brecht rubbed his throat and undid his open collar another button, picking his feet up one by one.

'Now-a, gentlemen,' he said in a calmly controlled but slightly wavering voice, 'please-a tell me what-a I have-a done to make you-a so angry with me.'

Tall leatherjacket spat out, 'Don't play innocent with us! We know you took the two women somewhere after they came off the *ILEX*. You know it, don't you? That big, black, very, very expensive aeroplane sitting out there.'

'Yes, yes, I know it. Nice-a plane. Shiny.'

'So, where did you take them?'

'Ah, let-a me think. Ah, yes. The not very pretty lady wassa not so good, a leetle bit not well-a, so I drove her to her house in, how you say, Isabel Avenue.'

'The other one.'

'Let-a me think. Ah yes, then I deliver her to other house, not so near.'

In two strides the shorter leatherjacket was upon him and with a swipe of his gloved hand, knocked him sideways to the floor and injected the tip of his boot into Brecht's rib-cage, eliciting a howl of pain.

'Stop! Stop-a! I tell-a you. Yes, I remember now. It was-a leetle bett and breakfast near library. I take you there, yes? Then you stop-a hitting me. I am poor man. Not criminal. I come here economic migrant to send money home to my-a old-a mother in Former Kridiblikt Republic. If you make me no able to work, she starve-a.' He was now on his knees with his hands clasped together like the painting of *The Annunciation*.

'Get up!' the tall one said.

Brecht struggled to his feet. 'It-a called *Laurel House*, yes-a...' The leatherjacket took him roughly by the arm and swung him towards the personnel door and hammered on it loudly three times. Somebody opened it from outside and the captive was pushed out violently into the blinding sunlight. The door slammed behind him.

'How about some water?' said the grey-suited man. 'I'm sure they'll have finished checking your taxi shortly.'

Was the man mad? Didn't he know what had just happened to him? Couldn't he see how roughed up he was? Something instinctive made Brecht meekly accept the bottle of spring water and gulp it down.

'Ah, here's your car now,' said grey suit. 'We're very sorry to have delayed you.'

Brecht watched as the taxi backed out into the yard, driven by a dull-looking, spotty, young mechanic. The taxi driver looked into the gloom of the huge shed. The leatherjackets had vanished.

*

How did you get the key to this place?' Debbie asked, stretching out luxuriantly on the long, pale green, uncut moquette sofa. The venetian blinds were half-closed but the teatime sunlight filtered through and glistened on her white, bead embroidered underwear strewn over the back of the furniture.

AIRSHOW ILEX

'I told them I wanted some interior shots of the chalets for next year's brochure.'

'You are so wicked,' she said, pulling Roland towards her by his shirtfront. He stood there looking like a naughty little boy, no trousers and black socks.

'Why is it that you men are so reluctant to take your socks off for love-making?' she teased, tugging on the shirt.

'It's a secret society we all belong to. It's called 'The Black Sock Club' and it's a sign of weakness to bonk without them on.'

'Come here, you stud,' she said.

He knelt down on the floor beside her. 'I love you in that,' he said, picking up the bra and tracing his finger along its top edge. 'I love you more out of it though.'

'As you just proved... more than adequately,' she said, wriggling away to make room for him.

'Come on! Come back for a cuddle.'

He looked at his watch.

'I can't stop for much longer. Got a shoot with the models in Hall Two at five.'

'Casanova,' she chided, stroking his cheek. He gently pulled away from her and got to his feet. He retrieved his pale blue and navy striped trousers from the sofa, staggering around trying to get into them. She sat up.

'Well, if you're going, I suppose I'd better be making tracks too.' She looked around the well-appointed chalet, at the expensive furniture, fitted carpets, side-kitchen and viewing veranda.

'I wonder what the trade delegates would think next week if they knew what we'd been up to in their ten thousand pounds a day chalet?'

'They'd probably be jealous,' he said, turning to tidy his hair in the ornamental mirror.

'It's a shame they don't have a shower in here,' she sighed, 'I must complain.' He turned to grin ruefully at her and she was dazzled, as always, by the naughty charm of his smile.

He said, 'Look, I'd better get going, but you take your time. Just lock up when you leave and hand the key in at chalet housekeeping underneath the Press Centre.' He came back and bent over to kiss her. 'You were magnificent,' he said, holding her face in his hands and gently touching her closed eyelids with his lips.

'...and you were Mr. Magic,' she replied. He tapped her gently on the nose with one finger, then went and picked up his photographic gear from the armchair, before disappearing out into the hot afternoon, leaving behind him a very satisfied woman. Now, where were these models?

*

Brecht's toes hurt. He was lucky that none appeared to be broken. He'd driven the taxi away from the service yard and parked next to one of the buildings further up the perimeter road of the airport. There, out of sight of passers-by, he'd slid across into the passenger seat and inspected his feet. Both sets of toes were badly bruised and the skin broken in places. There was a nasty blue, raised patch where the foot met the ankle. He decided not to put his shoes back on and drove without them.

Well, he'd told them what they wanted to know. When they got there, to the bed and breakfast, they would find that Anna had already gone. Hopefully, the landlady hadn't seen his taxi or, if she had, she probably couldn't tell it from any other. He drove thoughtfully along the airport's internal perimeter road, through the tunnel and onto the ring road. Then wondered if he was being followed. Suspicious and nervous, he looked often into the rear-view mirror. It was better to leave the taxi at his digs and walk to the park to collect Anna. He did a u-turn and took the road out of town to a slightly scruffy area of big, old houses that had been divided up into flatlets. He parked on the short, front drive, limped in barefooted, cleaned himself up and changed. He put plasters on the broken skin of his toes and got out some fresh socks.

What a day! Here he was, bashed up and exhausted and there Anna was, waiting in the park for him. He hoped she was OK. Time for a snack. He took a pasty and a carton of juice from the small refrigerator and carried them across to the little table

AIRSHOW ILEX

next to the sofa. Then he flicked on the portable television. He watched the end of the children's programmes, ate his food, drank his juice and then flaked out. The theme music for the local news woke him with a start. He looked at the clock. Six-thirty. He'd be late. In the bathroom he combed his hair. Thank goodness they hadn't touched his face, although his neck still hurt and his ribs ached. He took a cotton jacket from the peg on the wall, slammed on a baseball cap and left.

Outside, he walked as fast as his bruised feet would allow to the bus stop and saw the back of the one he wanted to take him into town. Cursing under his breath, he set off after it. Two miles and he'd never be at the park in time. He decided to thumb a lift. Walking backwards and jerking his thumb, he tried to look harmless and pleasant, smiling, until, at last, a lorry driver pulled over.

'Where you want to go mate?'

'Into town. You-a going that-a way?'

'Hop in.'

Brecht was dropped off just before the ring road. He thanked the driver and gave a cheery wave as the pantechnicon pulled away with a couple of hoots. He looked around before making his way to the park. It took him about ten minutes of painful walking and when he arrived Anna was nowhere to be seen. He strolled around the duck pond, trying to look uninteresting, hands in pockets. There was nobody else about. It was too late for the bread-throwing youngsters and too early for the destructive yobs. Where on earth was she? Had they found her by chance? Remembering ruefully what they'd done to him earlier, he shuddered at the thought of what might have happened to her.

He was about to go outside the park gate and have a look up and down the road, when he heard a whistle. There she was, emerging from the bushes with a big smile. They began to converse in Krid.

'What were you doing in there? Playing hide and seek?'

'Call of nature. You could have left me in a park with a loo.' She pushed him playfully.

'Ouch! Be careful!'

'Why? What's the matter?'

'They did me over earlier. Smashed my toes and ribs about. They're onto you. I had to say where you were staying. They're going to be really mad when they find out you've left.'

She looked alarmed.

'Quick, then! Where's your taxi? Take me to the safe place now!'

'The cab's back at my flat. It's too risky to be driving around so easily identifiable and we can't go to the safe house until after dark.'

'What can we do until then? They'll be looking for us.'

'We,' he said, are going to be a loving, young couple, going to the multiplex,' and he put his arm around her shoulders.

'I hardly know you!' She pulled away.

'Want to stay alive? Believe me, these people mean business. We're going to see a nice action movie and you have to be my girl for the evening. Come on, the film starts at seven-thirty, but first I have to make a telephone call.'

'They could trace your mobile,' she said.

'That's why we are going to do it from that phone-box over there,' and he indicated outside the park and along the road. 'I passed it on the way here.'

She put her arm around the back of his waist and tucked a hand into his back pocket. He draped his arm along her shoulders, feeling the wide strap of her handbag.

'Is it still in there?' he asked.

'Yes,' she said, 'and surprisingly light.'

They walked along innocently. When they reached the telephone box he told her to sit on the wall outside while he made the call. He didn't want any arguments from her. She did as she was told and took out the magazine, pretending to read it, to cover her face from passing cars.

He put in his phone card, took a scrap of paper out of his pocket and dialled. Outside, Anna could hear his mumbled tones as he debated something with the person at the other end. Then he hung up and emerged. She stuffed the magazine in her bag.

'Let's go!' he said.

AIRSHOW ILEX

They were standing in the ticket queue in the cinema foyer.

'Act like lovers,' he hissed and she snuggled up to him, leaning her head against his shoulder and he rubbed his hand up and down the outside of her arm, very slowly.

'Two please-a,' he said, passing a twenty-pound note through.

'Nothing smaller?' said the woman. 'I'm short of change this evening. Everybody seems to have twenty pound notes.'

'Sorry,' he said.

'I'll have to go and get some silver,' she muttered, getting up. He didn't like the delay. Then Anna intervened.

'Wait-a a momenta. I have-a some money.' She paid and took the tickets but there was a queue past the sweet kiosk to get through the double doors into the auditorium.

'That man, over there. He's looking at the crowds,' she said from under the brim of the baseball cap, keeping her head down. Brecht pulled her close and wrapped his arms around her, rather enjoying the sensation.

'Talk to me like a lover,' he said, so she murmured things in his ear and they pretended to laugh together.

'I want sweets and popcorn,' she whispered, slipping some change into his hand. So he bought them.

Then they were in the hushed atmosphere of the auditorium, finding their way through the crowds, she clutching the goodies, he hanging onto her like a boyfriend should. As they pushed past to get to their seats, some wise-cracker looked up and joshed, 'Cradle-snatcher.' He ignored it. He'd forgotten how much younger Anna was.

*

Jack had put up the little table with its single supporting leg in at the end of the sitting area of the caravan. He and Marcus sat to one side of it while Paula and Zelara the other. Four mugs of coffee and a packet of ginger snaps constituted the refreshments. The restaurant manager looked down her nose at the repast but took a biscuit all the same, chewing it steadily and then taking a swig of coffee.

'Now we have important things to discuss. So let's get on with it.' She brushed crumbs from her sweater.

'What's the plan?' said Jack.

'Yes, spill the beans boss-lady,' added Marcus, grinning.

'What's about me, Miz Paula?' queried Zelara in her thick Caribbean accent.

'You can drop that spoof accent. It was beginning to get on my nerves.'

'Thank goodness for that,' the chubby, black woman replied in a cultured and educated tone that made both the boys sit up sharply.

'That's pretty upmarket,' Jack said in his best public school voice.

'Zelara, or rather Doctor Zelara Marwick, is a highly trained QR/5 operative with a gold stripe in martial arts.'

'Give us a break, Paula! With all due respect to Zelara, how can she move about and do the business with a roly-poly shape like that?'

Zelara looked at Paula who nodded sharply at her. Then, without any ado, the fat, little cleaner stood up in the cramped space and slowly unbuttoned her white overall to reveal a layer of foam rubber that completely covered her torso. She unzipped it and peeled away centimetres of pseudo-fat to reveal a slight, whispy woman whose huge breasts and ample buttocks now lay on the caravan floor.

'Sorry about the legs, guys,' she said, looking down at the pair of podgy tree-stumps. 'Would you like me to take the lagging off those too?'

The boys rolled back and clung to each other in paroxysms of mirth.

'I just don't believe it! You're brilliant! Nobody would ever guess! Fab! Fab! Fab!' cried Jack. He leaped up to hug her but Zelara wasn't having any of that and, quick as a flash, spun towards him and flipped him away with one hand so he landed on top of his brother. The pair could hardly breathe or speak for laughing. It was the best wheeze ever! Paula clapped her hands lightly together.

AIRSHOW ILEX

'OK. Enough excitement for one night. Down to business.' The boys paid attention. She moved the mugs out of the way and, from her handbag, produced a small map that she flattened out as she placed it on the table.

'The 'Target' will visit the *ILEX* during the public weekend at the end of the airshow week.'

'That's a strange thing to do,' said Jack. 'It'll be ever so busy. Lots of Joe Public about. Could get nasty. Why doesn't 'Target' have a look-see during the trade days?'

'Our information is that 'Target' will be on an official tour of South America from Monday the twentieth to Friday the twenty-fourth,' Zelara said. 'Sources report that his flight here is scheduled to land late on Saturday night the twenty-fifth ready for the *ILEX* tour on the final Sunday. It is,' she added seriously, leaning her padded elbows on the table, 'a very, very important visit with enormous implications for the British economy. They plan to place an order for four hundred of the *ILEX*.'

The boys gasped and looked at each other, open-mouthed. Then Marcus asked, 'As a matter of interest... I wanted to ask... where did its name come from?'

Zelara shrugged and replied, 'It's an acronym for 'Integrated Launchpad for Environmental Excellence.'

'Oh,' he said with an air of acceptance.

Paula, slightly irritated by this interruption, continued, 'It is therefore essential that the 'Target' does not complete business with this country by using their own nation's funds that have been accrued on the back of an appalling human rights record, massive contamination of lakes, rivers and air, Dickensian work ethics and turning a blind eye to the plight of their own starving and disabled. If Britain accepts their money in order to bolster our economy, this country is as guilty as they are.'

The boys nodded in acquescence.

'It's our job to kidnap the 'Target' so that the bid cannot take place,' said Paula. 'Security will be monumental but,' and she rotated the creased plan, 'this is how we are going to do it.'

*

As the film came to an end, the auditorium music volume rose as did the audience, trampling drink cartons and empty sweet packets underfoot, pushing their way towards the exits milling with leaving cinema goers.

'Separate!' whispered Brecht. 'Meet my around the side of the cinema away from the corner.'

He immediately excised himself from his 'girlfriend' and quickly joined a gang of equally baseball-capped lads who were jostling and shoving, breaking into song, high from the excitement of the film. He bent his knees, pushing himself into the centre of the rowdy group, chanting rubbish to fit in with them as they larked about on their way through the foyer and out into the night, past the serious-looking men who stood near the doors scrutinising them. He was out.

Anna, leaving by another aisle, saw what he did and anxiously looked for some girls to merge with but all she could grab at such short notice, were a mother with her daughter of about ten. Afraid that her accent would give her away, she attached herself to the pair and silently mouthed and waved her hands about. They clearly thought she was deaf and the mother started to talk to her very loudly, saying 'Yes, it was a terrific film. Did you enjoy it?' Anna nodded her head with alacrity, continuing to invent silent conversation and gesticulations. The child joined in and said it was her birthday. Anna mouthed 'birthday' and clapped her hands with pretend happiness. So the trio passed unchallenged and out into the warm June night. Only as they reached the corner of the building, did they wave farewell and Anna slipped into the dark alleyway at the side.

She heard a scuffle and then Brecht said, 'Well done! Down here!' Feeling their way along the wall, stumbling on the rough path, they eventually came to a car park at the rear of the cinema just as a minibus pulled in.

'Come on!' They ran towards it, he limping somewhat, and he pulled the door open.

'Get in!'

An amazed Anna clambered up the step and, eyes wide with astonishment, saw that the driver was a nun. That wasn't all, for there were a further ten nuns as passengers. The one nearest the door handed the newcomers starched, white coifs and thick, navy-blue veils. Brecht shut the door and said to Anna, 'Put it on!' He doffed his too, probably becoming the ugliest nun ever. He went and found a seat next to a novice and started talking to her about the weather. He motioned to Anna to sit down too. Then the mini-bus pulled out of the car park, turned left and left again, coasting past the cinema where four men in grey suits were gazing vacantly up and down the road.

Chapter 13

Friday 17th June
Early Morning

Grant Landscar leaned against the side of the basket and adjusted his white stetson as the pilot went for a burn and the red and white panelled, hot air balloon rose gracefully into the dawn sky. The airport fell away beneath them, the runways soon becoming miniature pathways and the exhibited planes small toys. Trees looked like lichen on a model railway layout. Suddenly there was silence. Grant gripped the lip of the basket.

'Is everything alright?'

Debbie put her hand briefly over his. 'It's OK,' she said quietly.

'Fine, sir,' said the pilot. 'Just turned the burner off. We fire as and when needed. It's a bit loud but you'll soon get used to it.'

'Great view. We were lucky you could take us up this morning,' drawled the American.

'Fridays are always quiet,' said the pilot.

Debbie, in black slacks and a pale blue sweater, seemed relaxed and thoroughly at home in the wicker basket hanging on wires from a billowing canopy full of hot air. She turned to Grant.

'Thank you for inviting me. I've been meaning to try one of these flights for ages but you know how you keep thinking that you'll get around to it one day. The moment was never right.'

'It's all about timing... life, that is. Look at us, for example. We met by chance in the hotel the other night and then a couple of days later, there we were at the pre-show luncheon, sitting at the same table.'

'Fate,' she said, laughing.

'Well, sometimes you have to give fate a helping hand,' he said.

'Like two dozen red roses delivered to my hotel and an invitation for a dawn flight?'

'Just a little gesture of admiration.'

'Women like me don't get feted much, you know,' she said a little nostalgically. 'Men see us as self-sufficient. It was very nice

AIRSHOW ILEX

of you. The rest of my team is green with envy.' She paused and then exclaimed, 'Hey, see the *ILEX* down there. It could be a giant, black moth. Doesn't it look sinister?'

'It's certainly impressive,' Grant replied noncommittally.

The balloon continued to rise steadily for a while and then seemed to come to a halt in mid-air.

'Why have we stopped?' Grant asked, looking rather concerned.

'No breeze. That's the trouble when we fly so early. Fine day. Just look at those cirrus clouds up there? They're a sign of good weather.'

Grant took his digital camera out of his pocket and focussed on St. Bedes.

'What's that blackened building near the convent?'

'Oh that's the old cottage in the grounds,' the pilot said. 'It burned down on Wednesday night.'

'Was it occupied?'

'I believe an old lady was taken to hospital with smoke inhalation,' he replied. 'They mentioned it on the radio.'

'There's another thing further over. It looks like a sort of Gothic monstrosity.'

'That's the famous Folly. It's supposed to be haunted by the ghost of a nun who was crossed in love by a local priest.'

'Sheer fantasy,' said Grant. 'Nuns are asexual.'

The pilot turned his head sharply at the comment and hit the burner control again. The canopy rocked as it filled with hot air.

Grant raised his voice. 'I didn't realise it was such a performance to get one of these things up in the sky.'

'I couldn't do it without my team, Mr. Landscar. They'll follow us in the recovery vehicle and meet us when we land.' He tapped the breast pocket of his flying suit. 'We'll be in mobile phone contact.' He killed the burner.

'I guess you would need a lot of back-up,' Grant observed.

'Oh yes. Absolutely crucial. Excuse me a moment. I have to speak to the tower.' He opened the link.

'Echo Romeo Tango four seven nine Demetri hot air balloon to Phillipstone airport control tower. Over.'

'Phillipstone control tower responding Echo Romeo Tango four seven nine. How can we be of assistance to you? Over'

'Thanks for letting us up this morning. Over.'

'Incoming civilian flights begin at nine a.m. so dawn riders no problem. Over.'

'Weather forecast looks favourable. Over.'

'Yes. South-westerly breeze of three knots expected soon. That should take you out of the area. Over.'

'Course laid in as transmitted earlier, control tower. Cruising height four thousand feet. Over.'

'Have a good flight. Over and out.'

The pilot turned and smiled at Grant.

'It's as well to keep on the right side of the airport tower. Sometimes it can be a pain when you get into the airspace of some little airport and they start cross-examining you like the Spanish Inquisition about your course and intentions.'

'I suppose it's a safety thing?'

'Maybe but I don't come up here to listen to the background chatter of the tower. I like the peace and quiet.'

'We're moving sideways,' said Debbie as a small breeze picked up.

'So we are,' said Grant, snapping away with the digital camera. 'That's all mine,' he added with a little wave of his finger.

'Really sir?' said the pilot looking surprised. 'I thought it was the airport.'

'Let's just say they are holding it for me for the time being,' Grant replied with an enigmatic look. 'Soon, though, all this plateau beneath us will be home to one hundred wind generators.' He pursed his lips and nodded his head slowly two or three times in determined contemplation. The burner roared as if in agreement.

'What'll happen to the airport if you reclaim your land?' Debbie asked in a raised tone.

'That's not my concern. The Council shouldn't have taken it in the first place.'

'And the convent?'

'You can't make an omlette without breaking a few eggs.'

AIRSHOW ILEX

'You're a hard man, Mr. Landscar,' she teased. The breeze was ruffling her curly hair as the balloon gave a little lurch and she fell against the big American.

'Call me Grant,' he said, smiling down at her.

The balloon pilot looked marginally embarrassed. It was a bit early in the morning for this sort of thing.

*

Reverend Mother Veronica rose from her pew and made her way to the front of the centre aisle, nodding in thanks to the priest as he left for the sacristy after taking early morning Mass and Matins. She genuflected to the altar and turned to face the small congregation of nuns and novices.

'Sisters,' she said in a quiet tone, almost inaudible to those sitting further back in the chapel. 'I'm sure that you have noticed that we have a guest in our midst.' She gestured towards Anna who was sitting at the far end of a pew, partly in shadow.

'This young lady is here on silent retreat at a difficult time in her life, so I am asking you all to give her plenty of space and not to engage her in conversation.' She made the point with a sharp nod of the head and folded her hands across her stomach.

'There is something else. The young lady is in some danger, as those of you who helped to rescue her last night already know, so it is important that her presence here in St. Bede's convent is kept very quiet as are the details of last night's events in town. Do I make myself clear?'

'Yes Reverend Mother,' came back in a chorus.

'We are also expecting some other guests. The tenants from our burned out cottage, Miss and Mrs. Hunt, will be staying here temporarily. So I hope you will make them welcome. They will be occupying the guest suite. That's all. Thank you my children. Go in peace. Please attend to your daily work.' She raised her hand to halt the exodus. 'Would the teaching Sisters please come and see me in the entrance hall before you get in the school bus to drive over to the school? The diocese has issued you all with new document cases in which to carry your marking.'

She turned and genuflected again and went over to Anna.

'There is no need for you to speak to me or to anybody else while you are here, dear,' she said. 'I myself will show you where the library is. It would be seen to be a good thing for you to perhaps be reading the lives of the saints. You will hear the bell sound for meals but otherwise your time is your own. We breakfast in the refectory at seven-thirty. Lunch is at noon, tea at five o'clock and there is a bed-time drink in the kitchen if you want it before retiring to bed at nine o'clock. Some of the nuns will be tired today,' she said with a rueful smile. 'They're not used to late hours and we had to keep them up especially last night.' She patted the girl's hand. 'All in a good cause though. We have to give help where it is asked for. Please come and have some breakfast now.'

*

Celeste Blagden sat reading a glossy magazine in the waiting room of the *Primrose Surgery*. She flipped through the pages, thoroughly bored and impatient, pausing now and then to look at some fashion article but all she wanted to do was get to work. Today was going to be so busy. Her glance wandered from the journal to the glass door through which she could see the path edged with bush roses. Then, to her horror, she recognised the figure coming towards the entrance. It was Eleanor Framp, grey mac and all.

The dragon came in and appeared not to see her, going immediately to the high-fronted reception desk.

'Eleanor Framp. Please can I see one of the doctors this morning?'

'Well, they're all very busy. It's always like this on Fridays but I'll see if he can fit you in. What seems to be the matter?'

Eleanor leaned forward and looked briefly to right and left.

'Women's matters,' she said.

'Oh, I see,' said the receptionist conspiratorially. 'Please take a seat and I'll see what I can do.'

Eleanor chose a high-backed chair under a painting of an orchid bearing a price of twenty-five pounds.

'For goodness sake,' she thought. 'This is supposed to be a surgery, not an art gallery. It looks like a kindergarten effort.' She sat down huffily and took out her spiral-bound pad and a pencil with a yellow eraser on the end. Then she set to, scribbling and crossing out, leafing through the pad like a rush of autumn leaves, totally unaware of her Nemesis further down the waiting room who was crossing her legs tightly and wondering whether she could make it to the ladies' and back before she was called.

'Miss Blagden,' said the receptionist loudly. Eleanor looked up suddenly. Celeste glowered at the receptionist. She wasn't showing yet but she was old-fashioned enough not to want to be addressed as 'Miss' when the pregnancy was truly in evidence.

'You can go through now.'

Celeste dropped the magazine on the table with a loud slapping sound and flounced off through the doorway to the corridor leading to the individual consulting rooms. Eleanor put her head on one side and raised a quizzical glance at the carpet. 'Wonder what that's about?' she thought, going back to her writing.

Five minutes passed, during which a steady stream of patients came in with increasing degrees of infirmity. Everything that could limp, hop, wobble or stagger accumulated in the waiting room in a cacophony of crutches, walking frames, plasters and wheelchairs. The place was cluttered with accoutrements which jousted with the inevitable pushchairs.

The telephone rang. The dyed blonde receptionist answered it and listened intently.

'Yes, Doctor. Certainly, Doctor,' she said. 'I'll tell them.'
Then she rang the little handbell on the desk and said, very loudly:

'I'm sorry to say that the physiotherapist's clinic will be running a little late this morning. If you wish to wait, that's fine, or I can give you fresh appointments.'
Nobody moved. The waiting room would be full for hours.

Celeste came out through the doorway and made for the exit without looking down. With a resounding clatter, she walked into

the side of a wheelchair as the occupant quietly moved it forward. Without a moment's hesitation, she let forth a gush of expletives and screamed, 'Can't you be more careful where you put that thing! Can't you see I'm pregnant!' Shocked, Eleanor let her spiral bound pad fall on the floor.
You could have heard a pin drop as the receptionist came flying around to help.

'Are you alright? Don't move! I'll get the doctor.'

'No thank you,' said Celeste firmly, rubbing her knee.

'Just tell your patients to park better,' and she made for the exit. Eleanor retrieved her writing pad and sat there gazing at it, pretending that she didn't know Celeste. It seemed the best thing to do.

*

'Another scorcher, by the looks of it,' said the *ILEX* Captain as he entered the flight deck, 'but it seems a bit cooler in here this morning.' The flight officer turned to greet him.

'Morning Captain. We had the hold open and extra guards on during the night, sir. It seems to have helped.'

'Yes, it does. Have you organised the external batteries?'

'They should be here this afternoon, sir. Our own engineering guys will fit us up with a bank of them in a metal portable shed. The airshow organisation office says we can put it over there by the burger bars. The arrangement should ease the over-provision of electricity somewhat.'

'Good. Good, although we'll have to unhitch before we do our display flight on Monday. Our initial demo is in the afternoon on the first trade day.'

'Well, once we can fly a bit that should use up some of the juice.'

'Presumably you'll get the batteries changed each day?'

'I'll monitor it, sir, and keep you posted.'

'Top job, number one.' The Captain made a quick optical sweep of the controls. The flight officer peered over his shoulder at the screen.

AIRSHOW ILEX

'I was watching a hot air balloon go up first thing, sir. I didn't think they allowed them near airports like this one.'

'It's OK when there's no other traffic. The natives don't like early or late flights so the aviation authority keeps it quiet around here at sensitive hours for political reasons. All hell's going to break loose when they put in their application to double the number of flight movements a year. Strictly hush-hush.'

The flight officer shut the shift log-book.

'So I've heard.' He gave a rueful grin. 'That's if the windfarm doesn't win.' He paused. 'Any news of our little thief?''

'No, she seems to have slipped the net for now, but we'll find her. Ports and airports have been alerted. I got a right rollicking for it, I can tell you.'

'What about the taxi driver?'

'He knows where she is. The boys were sent on some wild goose chase yesterday to a B and B but the bird had flown. He'll be invited in for another little conversation soon.'

'I'm really sorry, sir. Our security should have been tighter.'

'Look, number one, all those people who came in here on the VIP tour had top level security clearance. That woman journalist fainting didn't help.'

'I don't think she was really involved. From the footage she looks pretty poorly. Eleanor Framp, wasn't it? She's got a security pedegree going back decades. I suppose our thief just got very, very lucky. Opportunism is all.'

'I know, sir, but I really should have locked the security locker. Who'd have thought that she'd substitute a sardine sandwich?'

He muffled a smile.

'Don't grin, number one. It's a matter, of national importance.'

'Yes Captain.'

'I'd have preferred smoked salmon though…'

The flight officer looked up, not quite sure what was going on. Then their eyes met and the pair of them rocked with laughter.

'Shh. Mustn't laugh. Show me today's readings.'

*

Councillor Percival Springstock, chairman of the planning committee, sat with the Council solicitor in one of the Committee Rooms. They were poring over local maps spread out on the table. The solicitor, looked over the top of his horn-rimmed spectacles and said, 'The Council could be in deep trouble over this, Councillor.'

'Don't you think I know that?'

The solicitor sighed and spread his hands, face down on the table in front of him.

'As I see it, Mr. Grant Landscar has come over from America claiming that part of the land on which the airport operates belonged to his deceased grandmother and it is, by rights, now his.'

'Yes.'

'Furthermore, he has laid claim to St.Bede's Convent and its grounds which abut to the airport land.'

'Yes.'

'Additionally, he has put in a revised planning application for one hundred wind generators to be built on that part of the land which he claims is his and which currently forms part of the airport.'

'Yes.'

The solicitor leaned back in his chair. He looked very wise. Councillor Springstock hoped he was. Somebody had to dig him out of this cesspit he'd got himself into.

'So, when did the Council acquire the disputed land?' The solicitor asked.

'About twenty years ago, long before you came to work for us.'

The solicitor looked a trifle relieved.

'How was it acquired?'

'If you go down into the cellars under the town hall and have a good search around, I'm sure you'll find all the documentation relating to the acqisition in the archives. I can't recall how we did it.'

'But weren't you chairman of the Lands Committee at the time?'

'Probably.' He looked shiftily sideways.

AIRSHOW ILEX

'I've been on so many committees over the years, I start to lose track.' He leaned forward and whispered, 'I do it for the stipends you know,' and he gave a hissing kind of laugh.

'I'm sure you don't, Councillor. You've been consistently voted in, so I'm told, for over thirty years.'

'Well, I've always been good on the doorsteps,' he laughed, his shoulders shaking.

The solicitor adopted a pompous tone. 'Nevertheless, Councillor Springstock, this has got to be sorted out and fast. Airshow week is not great timing to have to announce that the lease the Council granted to the airport authority is possibly defective.'

'I know. I know. It could undermine a lot of business and, goodness, do we need it in this area.'

'Then there's the matter of the convent. If those nuns get thrown out, we'll have to house the lot of them. Can you see all those penguins in one of our temporary accommodations?'

The Councillor pondered for a moment. 'I seem to remember something about the airport land and 'Squatter's Rights' or some such expression.'

'What, you mean the land was unoccupied for an extensive period of time and the Council acquired it under the old seven year rule? That's a bit cheeky. It wouldn't stand up very well in a court of law now. Possessary Title's a very dodgy area.'

'We never dreamed this Landscar chappie would turn up years later demanding it back. The airport authority's spent a fortune developing the site, what with new runways, control tower renovation, entertainment facilities, et cetera. They'll sue us into kingdom come.' He dropped his head into his hands. '... and I'll be personally pilloried.' He shut his eyes at the horror of the thought. 'After all these years of public service. Hoist on my own petard,' he wobbled with agitation.

'Don't take on so, Councillor. I'll go down and search the archives and put in some enquiries at the Land Registry. After all, the Council must have registered it, mustn't they?'

'I suppose so,' said the Councillor, a trifle doubtfully and with an air of despair.

'Well, the Land Registry would have been pretty thorough. So just leave it with me and I'll get cracking on it. Of course, Friday afternoon isn't a great time but Ill call them on Monday.'

'You're very kind,' said Councillor Springstock, his eyes rheumy with emotion. 'I don't much like that Landscar fellow. He scares me rigid.'

'Ah well, people with money and power... they don't always win.'

'In my experience, young man, they do.'

'Well, I wasn't doing much this weekend. I'll go and ask the Chief Executive for permission to work on the premises out of hours.'

'Thank you. Oh thank you.'

'Don't mention it, but if there's a spare one of those cut crystal commemorative, anniversary vases going, my old mum would love it.'

'I'll see what I can do.'

*

Celeste sat in the departure lounge. Her flight to Hamburg was delayed. There was time to ring her parents. They'd worry otherwise. She speed-dialled on her mobile.

'Hello Daddy.'

Her father's voice was full of surprise and affection.

'Pumpkin! How are you? I can't talk for long. We're off to the concert in a moment.'

'This is just to tell you that I'm away for the weekend. I'm going to Hamburg to see Rupert.'

She could envisage his brow furrowing as he paused before replying.

'We thought you were too busy to come to the concert with us tonight.'

'Sorry Daddy. Things really are very hectic but I need to see Rupert.'

'Young love, eh?'

She ignored the sentiment.

AIRSHOW ILEX

'To be honest, I need a complete change of scene. I've been living, eating and breathing airshow for months and I deserve a little break. I'll be back on Sunday night. I have to be. The show opens on Monday.'

'OK sweety-pie. Mummy's upstairs getting ready. Do you want me to fetch her?'

'Just give her my love and say I'll ring her when I get back.'

'Will do. Have a safe flight. Say 'hello' to Rupert. You could do worse than settle for him you know.'

'Bye, Daddy.' She clicked off.

'If I could pin the blighter down,' she thought, tucking the mobile into her handbag.

'Will passengers for flight 239 please make their way to the departure gate as we are now ready to board.'

There was slow-motion scramble as the assorted medley of Germans and Brits pushed their way forward, passports and boarding cards at the ready, carrying their hand luggage nonchalantly, trying to make it look lighter than it really was. Through the doorway, down the slope, clattering along the final stretch of telescopic tunnel, and there was the aircraft, entrance gaping, ready to swallow up the next cattle-load of punters and squeeze them into cramped seats.

Celeste showed her boarding card to the slickly groomed steward. He indicated the aisle that was already crammed with passengers fighting to open lockers, nearly blacking each others' eyes in the process.

'Seat 23A,' he said, pointing.

'Thank you.'

She carried her hold-all in front of her like a baby. Perhaps it was subconscious. When she reached her seat, she put the bag under the one in front. Lockers were for tall people and she didn't want to stretch up. You just never knew. It was a window seat. Good. She could look out and not have to talk to anybody. She ignored the couple who sat next to her.

The captain's voice came over the speaker above her head. It was loud.

'We shall be leaving the stand shortly. Please make sure your seat belts are firmly fastened and that mobile telephones are switched off.'

The flight attendants passed through, checking seat-belts and luggage stowage. Television screens flapped down and the usual, boring, safety lecture was underway with a stewardess tying herself into a life-jacket, miming blowing a whistle and pretending to breathe oxygen from a drop-down mask as the aircraft trundled out backwards and swung its long wings in an arc before crawling towards the main runway. Celeste could see the plane before them taking off.

'Doors to automatic,' the pilot said.

Then the attendants belted themselves into their seats at each end of the cabin and the aircraft swung obliquely around to face the glaring, studded runway lights. The engines roared. Celeste closed her eyes. Her heart started to pump strongly as the noise reached a crescendo accompanied by a stomach-pitching sensation and a feeling as if the back of the seat was pushing her forward. She opened her eyes and looked to see the green sward beside the runway rushing past and then dropping away as they climbed steeply, leaving behind the airport buildings and radar scanners, the longterm car-parks and motor-way junctions, to find themselves floating above a candyfloss sea of fluffy white clouds with tantalising gaps showing the unreal world beneath.

Celeste took in a deep breath as the plane arched ever upwards and to the right until the seat-belt signs went off and level equilibrium reigned. The June sun was still high and behind them, glinting off the wings and lighting the clouds with a surreal glow that deepened to rose and then violet as the flight progressed towards Hamburg and the dusk of a summer evening. She felt her breasts tingle.

Chapter 14

Hamburg, Germany
Friday 17th June
Evening

Celeste re-set her watch an hour forward and looked down at the steeply sloping, red roofs of the rows of toy-town, Hamburg houses as the plane's flaps opened and the tone of the engines dropped. It was getting dark but she could still make out the suburban sprawl below, although coming in over the harbour with its myriad lights and reflections had been truly magical. A jolt. A bump. They were down. It had been a smooth flight. She just hoped the weekend would go as well.

Standing in the aisle, clasping her hand luggage, protecting the little being that was to dictate her future, all around her she could hear German voices.

'Danke schön... Vielen Dank... Danke vielmals,' as courteous passengers passed bags and briefcases down to each other. Then the hordes were on the move, running the gauntlet of the grinning flight attendants by the exit and off the aircraft, chasing up the metal walkway, through the swing doors, negotiating the long and wide concourse past the expensive snack bars.

'What is the purpose of your visit please?' asked the official in the passport control booth.

'Visiting a friend,' she replied with chagrin.

More walking, down stairs, along a skating rink of an indoor promenade, ignoring the over-priced boutiques and gift shops, down more stairs and into the baggage hall where anxious travellers stood like birds of prey, eagle-eyed, watching their cases come through the flaps on the never-ending conveyor-belt that snaked its way relentlessly around with the scent of underground stations.

Celeste had glued white, paper squares on her portmanteau to make it easier to identify. The case arrived as she did. She could see it riding along on the rubber belt, brazen and argumentative. 'Bet you can't get me before I go around again,' it seemed to say. So she elbowed her way through and just caught it, hauling it awkwardly over the side, extending the pulling handle, stacking her hand luggage on top before setting off for the E.U. customs way out. There was nothing to declare, only her love for Rupert and his precious gift to her.

She followed the signs to the taxis. Outside in the warm, summer evening air, one pulled up beside her.

'Wohin?' the driver asked.

'Hotel Weiss-Schwanbrook,' she replied, 'Aber, können Sie mir bitte helfen?' indicating the weekend case. The driver gave her a semi-snarl and got out, taking the item and hurling it into the boot. She got in the back seat. It smelled of sweat. She opened the window and did up the seatbelt, worried that the lap-strap passed across her hips. He got in, turned up some music and swung away from the taxi rank, weaving in and out of the traffic like a madman, throwing her about. Schoolgirl German had suddenly deserted her. She couldn't think of the words to ask him to go slower, so she took out her word-changer and frantically stabbed in the English for 'slow'.

'Langsam, bitte. Langsam,' she called, but his gaze refused to meet hers in the driving mirror for the entire journey of some fifteen minutes.

The vehicle screeched to a halt outside the hotel, throwing her forward and then back again. He turned around and held his hand over the back seat, palm upwards and demanded, 'Hundert Euros.'

A hundred? A hundred? Surely not. She quickly calculated the exchange rate in her head. It couldn't be right.

'Nein,' she said firmly. 'Zu viel.'

'Hundert,' he said again, jabbing his hand towards her. It was then that she realised he wasn't German. He hardly spoke or understood anything. He had to be Polish or Romanian or something like that. She took a twenty Euro note out of her wallet and gave it to him.

'Zwanzig ist genug. Meinen Koffer nun bitte.' She got out, leaving the door open, pointing towards the boot and waited. He revved up the engine and drove off, the rear passenger door flapping as he went. It was then that she realised his car bore no taxi registration plate on the back.

Starting to run after him, shouting, 'Stop! Stop!' was no use. He was off like a rocket, taking with him her case of pretty lingerie with which she had hoped to seduce Rupert into marriage and fatherhood. She'd been had.

*

Gulping back the tears, she went in through the hotel's revolving door and presented herself at the marble reception desk. She felt such a fool.

'Guten Abend. Wie kann ich Ihnen helfen?' The smart receptionist looked down on her with an air of superiority engendered by the rather high-drawn eyebrows.

'Sprechen Sie Englisch bitte?'

'Yes. Of course,' the woman replied haughtily, as if the stupid customer should be aware that every well-educated person in Germany had learned the language with their mother's milk. Celeste put her hand luggage down.

'My name is Celeste Blagden and I've come from England to see my partner Rupert Skinner. He's staying here.'

Thoroughly trained in the art of hotel discretion, the receptionist wasn't giving anything away.

'I'll just check for you,' and she flipped open the register and ran her finger down the list.

'When did Mr. Skinner arrive here please?'

'About two weeks ago.'

'This is a very large hotel. We have some two hundred beds. I am not always on duty.'

'Please.' Celeste rested the tips of her fingers on the cold marble like a child asking for alms.

'I have to see him and... and...' She suddenly burst into paroxysms of tears, her shoulders shaking with sobs and then, with a wail of a banshee, she opened her mouth like the Blackwall Tunnel and expounded, 'and my luggage has just been stolen by the taxi driver.' Then she put her head down on the counter on her elbows and snivelled uncontrollably.

The receptionist had been trained to deal with every eventuality in the hospitality industry, but not an adult woman spilling her emotions in the foyer of the Weiss-Schwanbrook Hotel. She hastily looked around. One of the bar-staff popped his head out and asked, 'Ist alles OK?'

'Gnädige Frau ist etwas bestürzt.'

'Englisch?'

'Ja. Natürlich.' She rolled her eyes and he responded with a downward jerk of the lips and a nod.

The woman came around to Celeste and put her arm across her shoulders.

'Kommen Sie mit mir meine Liebe,' and she led the blubbing Frau by the elbow into the room behind the reception desk and settled her down on a chair.

'Now,' she said, resuming her haughty tone, 'please tell me what is the matter with you and why you are so upset.'
Celeste swallowed and dabbed at her eyes, now streaked with mascara and very blood-shot.

'I've come over on a surprise visit to see my boyfriend and my case was stolen by the taxi driver.' She added hastily, 'He wasn't German...'

'I'm sure he wasn't,' the woman snapped back a trifle sharply. She had been on duty all day and it was time for her to go home.

'This hotel videos all cars coming to our frontage so we will get the number of the bad man and tell the Polizei.'

'Can you really do that?'

'Yes, we can. Now, wait there a moment and I will see if your boyfriend is staying here.'

Celeste's mobile telephone vibrated. She took it out and read the message. It said, *'Wilkommen in Deutschland'.*

*

The hotel porter carried Celeste's hand luggage into the lift which rose smoothly to the fifth floor. She felt her stomach pitch. Then he led her along a thickly carpeted and very quiet corridor to her room overlooking the Aussenalster lake. Her gratuity elicited a 'Danke schön'. He left, closing the door quietly. She crossed the room and opened the French window, then stepped out onto the iron balcony to gaze on the wide expanse of almost luminous water before her. It was a beautiful lake, surrounded by grand, stately houses and hotels, all lit up. Despite the near-darkness, a few late yachts were drifting back to the boathouse on the evening breeze and the trees were silhouetted against the street-lamps. The sound of the Friday night traffic below her was loud, so she went in again and rang room service. Hunger had set in.

She kicked off her shoes and sat on the double bed. It was very comfortable. On a table next to her she found the remote for the television which was already on standby and flicked it on, cruising from channel to channel until she found a satellite one in English. Nothing much that she hadn't heard already, so she turned it off and lay back, waiting for the food. She placed her hands on her stomach and wondered what it would be like when the baby kicked.

There was a gentle knock at the door.

'Come in!'

Room service was good. A tall, thin, young man wheeled in the gold trolley and paused.

'Would madam like to eat there or would madam prefer to sit at the table by the window?' He asked in impeccable English.

'I'll go over there. Thanks.' She eased herself off the bed and, in stocking feet, walked across the thick pile to sit at the small dining table as he moved the trolley next to it.

'Shall I serve Madam?'

'No thank you.' She gave him a smile. 'I can do it. You speak very good English.'

'I was in London for two years.' He gave a half-bow and a smile to match. 'If you need anything else, I am your room service manager for this floor. Please just press that buzzer over there for my attention.'

She nodded and smiled again at his quaintness as he left. Then she tucked into the pile of beef and tomato rye-bread sandwiches, a large serving of vanilla ice cream with a fruit salad,

177

followed by a cup of camomile tea. It was funny how she'd gone off tea and coffee lately. Happiness flooded over her. Tonight she would see Rupert. She had his room number on the floor below. Should she text him? Leave a voicemail? No, she would surprise him. Her marcasite watch showed nearly ten o'clock. He should be back from his trip by now. Into the luxurious bathroom she went, stripping off her clothes and stepping into the multi-spray shower, smothering her body in foam gel, shampooing her hair and emerging glowing and fresh.

She stood naked in front of the full-length mirror, took one of the shell-pink towels from the huge stack and dried herself. Then she styled her hair, applied fresh make-up and pillaged her hand luggage for a change of underwear. Thank goodness she hadn't put it all in the suitcase! With a dull acceptance she climbed back into the pale blue A-line skirt and matching jacket she had worn for the journey. A quick spray of *Chanson de Neuve* and she was ready. Excitedly she left her room and made her way down the stairs to the fourth floor and found his room, number 412. She patted her hair, took a deep breath and tapped lightly on the door. There was no reply, so she tapped again, a little more firmly. Still nothing. Where was he? The restaurant, of course. He would be hungry too.

The lift took her down to the foyer and she went through an archway marked *Palast Grill* into an atmosphere rich with the aroma of haute cuisine. A murmuring chatter of gourmet diners buzzed against the background of a three-piece band on a dais in the corner as the maître d'hotel came forward.

'Ein Einzeltisch, gnädige Frau?'

'Nein danke. Do you speak English?' Her eyes hungrily searched the thirty of so tables for Rupert.

'Yes, Madam.'

'I'm looking for a friend. Mr. Skinner.'

'Ah yes. I am well acquainted with Mr. Skinner and his companion.'

Celeste's head turned sharply towards him. Alarm bells rang in her mind and her heart accelerated but she deliberately forced herself to speak calmly and steadily, hoping that the imperious man wouldn't notice the waver in her voice.

'Mr Skinner...' She paused and swallowed. '... and his companion... do they dine here every night?'

'Sometimes, Madam. Now, perhaps I could conduct you personally to a charming little table near the band?' He raised his white-gloved hand.

'No. No thank you. I've already dined. Thank you.' She beat a dignified retreat. Where was he? She thought about going outside the hotel for a little air but decided it might be dangerous in a strange city alone. There was nothing to do but go back to her room. So she did. Perhaps she should ring him after all. Yes, that's what she'd do.

'Hi, it's Rupert Skinner here. I'm unable to take your call at present but please leave your number and I'll get back to you as soon as I can.' There was a beep.

'Hello Rupert. It's me. I just wanted to say that I love you and miss you. Bye.' Her eyes welled up with tears again. Why did they keep doing that? Why was she so emotional? Who the heck was his companion? Exhaustion overwhelmed her and she decided to have a little nap and try his room again later. She took a fluffy blanket from the arm of the little sofa, dimmed the main light, put on the side lamp and curled up on the bed on top of the duvet.

The sound of the telephone ringing woke Celeste from a deep sleep and, for a moment, she didn't know where she was. She reached over and picked up the receiver.

'Frau Blagden?'

'Speaking.'

'Guten Abend, Frau Blagden. It is hotel reception here...'

'Have you found my case?' she interrupted urgently.

'No. I'm sorry. The Polizei say that the registration number of that auto showed that it was stolen.'

Celeste's heart sank. 'Stolen?'

'Yes, I'm afraid so. I am very sorry. The Polizei say that if you go to the local *Polizei Revier* in the morning you can describe your case and then if they find it they will return it to you.'

'I'm only here for a short time.'

'Well, if you need anything the hotel reception will be happy to direct you to appropriate shops and we have our own boutique on the ground floor.'

'Thank you.' Celeste put the phone down and covered her face with her hands. This wasn't going well.

'Be practical!' She told herself sternly in the bathroom mirror, wiping away the smudgy mascara under her eyes. 'All you have is what you are standing up in. Wash out the used underwear. Yes. That's the most important thing.'

So, with complimentary sachets of shampoo, she laundered her bra, pants and tights, patting them dry with the towel before draping them over the warm rail. Then she combed her hair, wiped under her eyes and went back into the bedroom. The case had been a treasured eighteenth birthday present from her parents.

Once out in the corridor she became aware of how late it was. An ormolu clock on a bandy-legged side-table showed eleven-thirty. He had to be back by now. She went down the stairs quietly and arrived outside his door from where the sound of laughing emanated. Knocking sharply she heard the conversation stop. A second or two and then the door was flung open.

The look of astonishment on Rupert's face as it blanched was something to behold. Celeste froze.

'Rupert?' she said timidly. He looked a mess… short, dark, spiky hair all over the place, tie pulled loosely to one side of his open collar, no shoes on and shirt-sleeves rolled up. He blinked rapidly as if testing reality.

'Celeste?' His head jutted forward. 'What on earth are you doing here?' Then he stood aside and said, 'You'd better come in. Yes. Come in.'

Once inside the very untidy room, she realised that they were not alone. She felt rather foolish.

'This is Gunter… a business acquaintance of mine.'

A tall, fair young man got up from the easy chair and loped over towards them. He looked untidy too. She was aware of an uncomfortable atmosphere in the room.

AIRSHOW ILEX

'Freue mich sehr,' he said, extending his hand and nodding his head congenially, adding in English, 'Delighted to meet you. Rupert has told me so much about you.'

Celeste was too dumbstruck to do anything more than place her trembling, cold hand into his sweaty palm and look, mystified, from one to the other.

'Come and sit down,' Rupert said, moving his jacket from the back of the other easy chair. 'Can I get you anything?' She shook her head. This had all been a terrible mistake. Rupert started to explain, nodding his head slowly and Gunter did the same, as if corroborating the story.

'We've been out for the evening.'

'Somewhere nice?' said Celeste, voice faltering as she sat down, looking up at him.

'Yes,' said Rupert. 'We went to the...'

'The theatre,' interrupted Gunter with wide, knowing eyes. ' A very good play. We took a group of clients.' Rupert nodded in agreement.

'A very good play,' he confirmed. Both men exchanged a glance that told Celeste everything she wanted to know. They had obviously been to one of those nude shows full of glamorous and tarty-looking women in the Reeperbahn. This was Hamburg after all. Should she press them for the name of the play? She decided not to. Why make it more embarrassing for them all?

'Well,' said Gunter, picking up his jacket. 'I suppose I'd better be going. I have a busy day tomorrow.'

'Surely you don't work at the weekend?' said Celeste.

'No. I promised my sister I would help her to move to her new flat.' He went over to Rupert and they exchanged a high five, their hands slapping loudly in the air.

'Thank you for a great evening. I'll see myself out.' He went towards the door. With his hand on the handle, he turned and said, 'You two have a lovely time in Hamburg. I expect you have a lot of catching up to do.' Was Celeste mistaken or was there something of a conspiratorial look that passed between the two men? 'I'll see you on Monday. Don't do anything I wouldn't do!' Then he was gone.

Celeste looked resentfully at Rupert. 'Who is he and why didn't you answer my calls?'

The erstwhile lover threw himself down in the other chair, legs spread apart, arms dangling over the sides. Where was the passionate embrace she had expected?

'It has been so maniacally busy, you just wouldn't believe.' She didn't believe.

'It's been hectic for me too with the airshow and everything,' she said. 'I made time to try and reach you. Who was he?' she repeated, nodding towards the door.

'Oh, that's just Gunter. Take no notice of him. I need him for the contacts. He's from the agency here. He knows everybody.'

'He looked shifty.'

'No. Gunter's all right. You'd like him if you knew him better.'

'But you didn't ring me or even SMS,' she pouted.

'It's different for you, Celeste. You're your own boss there. What you say goes. I'm running around like a blue-tailed fly here trying to marry together clients, venues, products and advertising.'

She wished he hadn't used the word 'marry'. She looked down at the carpet.

'My case was stolen by a spoof taxi driver. He tried to rip me off too. All I've got with me is my hand-luggage and what I'm wearing.'

A wave of guilt and pity swept over him and he got up again and came to her, kneeling down and taking her hands in his.

'Look, it was a bit of a shock seeing you out of the blue like that. It was so unexpected.'

'I thought I'd surprise you and you'd be pleased to see me. It's been three weeks and I've missed you like crazy.'

'Me too, honeybun, me too.' He kissed the backs of her hands perfunctorily. Then he looked at her slightly worriedly and asked, 'Where are you staying?' She raised her eyes upwards.

'Here. Next floor. I tried your door earlier. I came in on the evening flight.'

He let go of her hands. She gazed at him beseechingly like a lost doe.

'Right,' he said and rubbed his chin thoughtfully. 'So, shall we spend the night together?' he added with false jollity?

'Do you want to?'

'Of course I do. You can see that I'm a bit worn out and stinky but I can freshen up and come to your room in, shall we say, twenty minutes?'

'OK.' A glimmer of a smile flickered across her face.

*

Rupert tapped on Celeste's door.

'Come in,' she called.

He entered to find the room in semi-darkness. She had wrapped her headscarf around the side-lamp to mute its brightness and was laying on her back on the double bed on lots of towels.

'What's going on?' he asked, puzzled at the sight that met his eyes. She indicated the trolley.

'Help yourself,' she said.

Only when he was nearer to her did he realise that she had perched various items of fruit all over the front of her bare body. Cherries, strawberries, grapes, slices of melon and even rounds of pineapple were in evidence.

'There's some squirty cream there,' she said, looking at the trolley. 'Why don't you get a little creative?'

*

'Maid,' said a voice that broke into Celeste's dream. She sat up suddenly. It was morning and the sunlight was streaming in through a gap in the long drapes. She looked down and realised, in horror, that she was smeared with souring cream and squashed fruits and that the towels were thoroughly juice-ridden.

'Moment please,' she called to the maid. 'Come back in ten minutes.'

'Jawohl, Madam.'

Celeste wrapped some of the stained towels around herself and shuffled to the edge of the bed.

'Rupert. Are you in there?' she called.

No reply. She walked over to the bathroom and opened the door. Empty. There was just time to take a quick shower before the maid returned. Once that was achieved, she gathered up all the sodden, juice-ridden towels and tossed them into the shower cubicle, closing the frosted glass door on the lot. Then she took her clean underwear from the warm rail, dressed and returned to survey the bed. What a mess! The juice had soaked through onto the duvets, probably ruining them. There were lumps of soggy fruit all over the place. Some had even fallen onto the carpet. She picked them up and put them on the trolley, dabbing around on the floor with tissues. There was a gentle tap on the door.

'Maid,' came the voice.

'Come in!' said Celeste. As the woman appeared, Celeste put her finger to her lips and pointed to the bed.

'Oh, du meine Güte!' said the woman, hand flying to her mouth at the sight of the mess. 'Was haben Sie hier gemacht?'

'Sprechen Sie Englisch?'

'Ein Bisschen.'

Celeste took a deep breath and spoke slowly and clearly.

'I am very sorry for the mess. If you clean for me,' and she made scrubbing motions in the air, 'I give you money.' She rubbed her thumb on her fingers in the traditional sign for cash. The woman stood with her hands on her hips, tutting and shaking her head. Eventually she said 'Ja. I do it for you because you nice lady.' Then she smiled and giggled a bit. 'You very lucky nice lady!'

Celeste left her to get on with it and went in search of her beloved Rupert.

*

She found him in the foyer talking with the receptionist.

'Hello,' said Celeste. 'Where did you disappear to this morning?'

'Entchuldigen Sie mich bitte einen Moment,' he said to the Marlene Dietrich look-alike behind the counter before leading Celeste away by the elbow.

AIRSHOW ILEX

'I thought it better to leg it back to my room before anybody was about much.' He tried to suppress a little laughing snort.

'I was too filthy to put my clothes back on so I pinched a spare duvet cover from the cupboard above your wardrobe and left in grand style looking like a sheikh.'

'Did anybody spot you?'

'Only the cleaners and I expect they've seen everything in their time in an hotel like this.'

Celeste kissed him on the cheek and sniggered.

'The bed was a real mess. I've had to pay the maid to clean it all up.'

'Well done. I'll come and get my clothes from your room later.'

He nodded towards the reception desk. 'I was just booking us an evening boat tour. It's another lovely day and I thought you might enjoy it after we've done some sight-seeing.'

'Great,' she replied, smiling. It was a good chance for a little romance.

'Why don't you pop into the hotel boutique,' he added and fit yourself up with the necessaries while I finish sorting this out. My treat.'

She beamed at him. It had been so wonderful last night, the love play. Shame it had all come to nothing, but then, she reasoned, it happens to the best of men.

Chapter 15

**Hamburg
Saturday 18th June
Morning**

Celeste came bounding out of the hotel boutique rustling two large designer carrier bags that she took to the reception desk. Rupert was no longer there.

'Oh,' she said, scanning the area. 'Where has Mr Skinner gone?'

'To collect his car,' replied the receptionist. 'He said to tell you that he will bring it around to the front shortly.'

'Thank you. Danke schön,' Celeste added, lifting the bags onto the counter. 'Please could you have these sent up to my room for me?'

'I am happy to do that for you Frau Blagden.' The woman hesitated. 'You are feeling a little better this morning I can see.'

'Yes, much.'

'I also note that our boutique has provided you with a charming outfit.'

Celeste looked down at the floating, floral skirt, skimpy white top, wrap-around long, pale blue cardigan and the comfortable sandals and thought what a waste of money it was because, if she kept the baby, none of the clothes would fit her for ages.

'Well, I had to get something decent to wear today and these will be fine.'

The sound of tooting came from outside. Rupert was waving and beckoning to her from a red, open-top sports car.

'I have to go. Wiedersehen.'

'Wiedersehen Frau Blagden.'

*

'Come on! Jump in!' He leaned across and pushed the passenger door open. It seemed strange to Celeste to be sitting

AIRSHOW ILEX

on the left. It was even stranger when he drove away on the wrong side of the road.

'How do you do this?'

'What?'

'Drive on the right.'

'You soon get used to it.' He accelerated and roared away, overtaking and weaving in and out of the Saturday morning traffic. She felt a bit precious and wished he'd slow down so she could look at everything.

'I've worked out an itinerary,' he shouted above the roar of the traffic.

'Where are we going?'

'First a little history lesson.'

'Oh.'

'I want to take you to a special church, St. Michael's. They call it the *Michel*.'

Rupert sped along the *Ost-West-Strasse* and turned right into *Englische Planke* and then left into the outside car park where coaches were already unloading hordes of Japanese tourists.

'This is one of the few free car parks and we're lucky to get a space.' He was talking to thin air because Celeste was leaning back and gazing up at the magnificent tower of the *Michel*, transfixed by its scale and beauty.

'Wakey, wakey!'

'Oh, sorry. It's really rather splendid, isn't it?'

'Just you wait 'til you see inside.

'Are those the toilets over there?'

'Yes. Why? Do you need to go?'

'I think it would be a good idea.'

'How are you off for small change?'

'I haven't had time to accumulate any.'

'The car park may be free but the loos aren't.' He jingled coins in his pocket and put some in her hand. 'My treat, again,' he said. 'I'll put the roof up while you're in there.'

She opened the car door and got out, slamming it, and made her way across the cobbles and through the turnstile. Nobody had warned her about the bladder thing.

Five minutes later they stood in the central aisle inside the *Michel*, their eyes lingering on the vast artwork of Christ above the altar. Then Celeste slowly turned around on the spot, as if in a trance, taking in the gold and white balconies, great arches, and huge pulpit reminiscent of the prow of a boat with a massive carved wooden canopy and statue above it.

'It's magnificent,' she said breathily. Rupert pulled at her arm.

'Come and sit in a pew. It's less of a strain on the neck.' So they did for about ten minutes, absorbing the atmosphere of reverential visitors speaking in low voices, on their way to light votive candles.

'We should be going,' Rupert said. There's so much more I want you to see.' As they left he put some money in the box and they made their way to the car.

'Oh, can I just pop in there again?' Celeste said.

'What again?'

'I drank a lot at breakfast.'

'Go on then. I'll put the roof down.'

With an empty-bladdered Celeste beside him, he started up the engine and turned again onto the *Ost-West-Strasse* that took them past a burned-out church. Rupert flicked a finger towards it.

'*St. Nikolai Kirche*. Commemorates the last war. They keep it to remind them.'

'They have loads of churches, a lot with green roofs.' She craned her neck to look.

'Copper roofs. That's enough of churches now, although I must say that Gunter told me that at New Year they all ring their bells at once and it's quite deafening and all the ships in the harbour hoot as well and everybody sends up fireworks and has impromptu little parties down on the quayside.'

'Sounds fun.'

'Trust me, Hamburg is fun. Now I want to show you a view.'

Up the spiral roadway they went to the top of the parking house. Round and round. Celeste shut her eyes. It didn't feel good.

'Nearly there,' said Rupert. 'You'll love it.' He parked and they got out and walked to the wall at the side of the rooftop car park.

AIRSHOW ILEX

'Look down there. That's the *Hauptbahnhof* main railway station and those tiny caterpillars are the trains. You can see miles into the distance.' She certainly could. On the horizon cranes and chimneys projected against the brilliant blue sky. She peered over the edge. Little toy cars streamed along the *Strasse* like working models and wide cohorts of motor-bikes revved at the lights so far below that the red, amber and green looked like small, round fruit drops.

She stood there, next to Rupert, who made no attempt to put his arm around her. In fact, although he had been the epitome of charm and consideration this morning, he had scarcely touched her. What if he didn't want the baby? What if he didn't want her? She looked over the wall. It was a long way down.

'How about a coffee?' he said congenially. I know a nice open-air café near the *Jungfernstieg*.'

'What's a *Jungfern* –whatever?'

'It means 'Virgin's Way'. A bit late for you old thing!' and he roared with laughter. In her maternal state, Celeste felt strangely virginal and mildly insulted.

'I'd rather have a cold drink. An orange juice would go down well.'

'OK, my little ruined virgin, we'll dump the car up here for a bit and go walk-about. Hang on while I close the roof.'

She was near to tears. Did he really think of her as sullied and easy? She was going to be a mother, if she decided to keep it.

*

The lift doors opened at street level. Celeste and Rupert jostled their way out against a small tide of people anxious to go up to the roof to collect their cars. Once into *Mönckebergstrasse* the relentless waves of humanity, out for a delightful morning's shopping in their favourite stores, swept them along past the colourfully dressed Romanian beggars sitting at the kerb, until they found the pavement café. At a table, in the welcome shade of a palm tree in a huge earthenware pot, Celeste took off her cardigan. A band of buskers was working across the *Strasse*.

'What do you want to do about your case?' Rupert asked, waving at a waitress. 'We can find a police station.'

'There wasn't much in it,' she lied. 'Just a change of clothing and a few airshow brochures for you. I can get some more if you want them.' She pondered briefly on the pale turquoise, one-piece teddy, the matching slip-on satin slippers with fluffy pom-poms, the G-string and the massage oils. It was all probably delighting some East European crook's moll by now.

'It's up to you.'

She thought about the dark, blue leather case that her parents had given her. 'I can get another case,' she said. 'Let's not bother.'

'Bitte?' said the waitress. Rupert looked up with a dazzling smile and ordered a Cappuccino for himself and a juice for Celeste. They were served promptly.

'Haben Sie einen anderen Wunsch?'

'Nein danke.' The girl tore the bill off a little pad and slapped it down on the table.

Rupert turned to Celeste.

'I've booked a dinner for two this evening on one of the restaurant boats that does a moonlight tour of the Alster and harbour.'

'That sounds nice.'

'Unfortunately there's no moonlight at the moment, but you get the idea.'

'Lovely.' She sipped from the tall, frosted glass.

'Before that, I've got one or two ideas of other places you might like to see.'

'Run them past me.'

'Well, there's the *Planten un Blomen*.'

'What's that?'

'It's a large, park with lots of features, like a lake and a rose garden... that should look pretty good at the moment. There's a Japanese teahouse too with azaleas and waterfalls and things. You'll like that. It's near the Botanical Gardens if you want to see that too. Oh, and I mustn't forget the *Fernsehturm*. Gunter said it's nearly three hundred metres high.'

AIRSHOW ILEX

He added, 'You've probably seen it in the distance.'

'That's what it was, near that skyscraper hotel.'

'Yes, that's the one. According to Gunter you used to be able to go up to the viewing gallery in a cramped cylinder of a lift and the view was spectacular. They don't allow it any more.'

'Shame,' she replied, rather relieved.

'That's for this afternoon though. We have to find something to do for the rest of the morning until I take you to lunch down by the fish market.'

She thought 'fish' and wished, rather strangely, that he hadn't mentioned it.

'I tell you what, let's go down to the water's edge and see if any big ships are in. It's always interesting there and we can walk on the floating pontoons with souvenir shops on them.'

'Whatever you like. You know it best here.' She drained her glass. He stood up.

'I'll just go and pay.' She followed him.

'I need the loo.'

'What again? That orange juice went through you quickly.'

They made their way back to the rooftop car park. The red sports car was baking in the heat, making the door handles almost too hot to touch with bare hands. Rupert lowered the car roof. A haze was shimmering on the horizon and the air was still. Down the spiral ramp they drove to street level, Celeste shutting her eyes all the way. Then it was a pattern of zooms and swerves all the way to the harbour where he found a parking place near the Youth Hostel.

He took her hand and led her to the crossing but just as they were about to step forward, a couple of hundred motor cyclists came roaring along from nowhere... all ages, helmeted, long hair flying or in plaits, beards, beads, pierced ears, studded gear, girls clinging to their backs, and throttles that reverberated along the *Strasse* so loudly that Celeste wanted to run away. They both stepped back smartly.

'It's the Bramby Trinter Motor Cycle festival!' Rupert shouted.

'There are enough of them,' she replied at the top of her voice.

'Gunter said to look out for them this weekend.'

She thought, 'Gunter, Gunter, Gunter. What's going on with this guy?' but she said steadfastly, 'Very impressive.'

They crossed safely and walked along to the *Landungsbrücken*, finding their way down the sloping, roofed-over walkway and onto the promenade pontoon. Celeste hoped it wouldn't move much but the harbour water was calm, only churned up by the double-decker water-buses and privately-owned craft that proceeded back and forth in the holiday atmosphere. The gift shops were laden with knick-knacks and the eating places smelled of herrings, onions and Bratwurst. This, coupled with the stench of diesel from the water-buses turned her stomach.

'Look, one of the big container ships is in for service on the floating dock over there.' He sounded so excited.

'It's huge,' she commented.

'Rupert! Mein Geliebter! Was machts du hier?'

A glamorous, young woman in a short skirt threw herself at Rupert, plastering lipsticky kisses on both his cheeks. He put his hands on her waist and stood her away from him.

'Was für eine Überraschung!' he replied. Then he turned to Celeste and introduced the tarty-looking individual as a business acquaintance of Gunter's. Celeste stood there like a fool whilst the pair chattered away in German. She caught the occasional word such as 'Problem' and 'Schwierigkeit' but they rattled on at such a pace that she was totally excluded. Then, as fast as she had arrived like a whirlwind, the girl was gone, waving and calling 'Tschüss!'

'What the heck was that all about?' demanded Celeste angrily.

'Just one of Gunter's crowd.'

'She kissed you.'

'Only on the cheeks. It's the continental way.'

She turned away, blazing with anger. 'I want to go back to the hotel.'

'Come on, Celeste. Don't be so touchy.'

'Don't call ME touchy! That tart was doing all the touching.' She folded her arms in rage.

He threw his hands in the air in exasperation.

AIRSHOW ILEX

'Don't spoil a lovely day by being over-sensitive. Here.' He guided her over to one of the gift boutiques. 'Let me buy you a peace offering.'

She turned her head away deliberately and gave a long, slow blink of refusal.

'Go on. Have a look. They've got some nice things.'

Reluctantly she turned and surveyed the trinkets and jewellery. Then, with cold deliberation, she sought out the most expensive item she could see, and said, 'OK. You can buy me that if you like.'

If his jaw dropped in amazement, he covered it well, coughed awkwardly and said, 'Anything that will make you happy, darling.' He told the proprietor to wrap it and paid in cash. Then, with a smear of red lipstick still on his cheek, he took his seething partner to lunch at the fish restaurant.

*

Celeste leaned back in the garden chair on the rear terrace of the Hotel Weiss-Schwanbrook. The starry skies above twinkled with promise. It had been a wonderful day, on the whole. She sighed. Rupert came out to join her.

'You were right about the *Planten un Blomen* park,' she said, extending her hand languidly towards his. He squeezed her fingers gently.

'It was absolutely lovely there and as for the moonlight tour on the Alster, it was the stuff that magic is made of, even if there was no moon!' She laughed. The little tiff earlier was forgotten.

'Good meal on the boat, don't you think?'

'Excellent. All that walking around Hamburg earlier made me hungry.'

He moved his chair nearer to hers. The traffic droned outside the front of the hotel.

'Celeste,' he said, taking her hand and holding it a little tighter, 'there's something I need to talk to you about.'

Her heart leapt. Was he going to propose? It was that sort of night and it would be the perfect end to a magical day.

She leaned towards him. 'There's something I wanted to talk to you about as well.'

'You go then,' he replied. 'Ladies first.'

She thought, 'That's a change from earlier when I was all but called the whore of Babylon,' but instead she said, 'Rupert, we've been living together for about five years now. We're a real couple. I know we are both keen on our careers but something's come up that's made me think a bit differently about our future.'

'Oh yes. What's that?'

She paused a moment. 'I'm pregnant.'

The sound of the traffic stopped as the lights changed. He let her hand go and stared down at the patio slabs, asking in a monotone, 'How far on are you?'

'About three months.' Why did she feel frightened? Her breathing quickened.

'That's what all that rushing to spend pennies was about today. Why didn't you say something before, when I was still in England?'

'You know I was on the pill, then I had that tummy bug and lost the pill without realising it and then we must have just clicked. I wanted to be certain. I thought I missed periods because of overwork on the airshow.'

He stood up and walked about slowly, plunging his hands deep into his trouser pockets.

'This has come at a really bad time, Celeste.'

With a sinking feeling in her chest she looked up at him, watching him pacing as he struggled with this sudden dilemma.

'What do you mean...?'

'Gunter's offered me a permanent position over here. I was going to tell you that I want us to break up. I didn't know quite how to do it.' He looked down at her, doubt written all over her face.

The lights changed and the sound of the traffic outside the front of the hotel roared on relentlessly again.

'You were going to dump me? Just like that?'

'I wanted us to have some nice memories, not finish with a row.'

AIRSHOW ILEX

'What? You want it all reasonable and calm? You're turning my life upside down and you expect me to be jettisoned without so much as a squawk? What about the flat and all our things?... and what about the baby?' Her voice faltered.

'I hadn't bargained on that complication.'

He sat down again and clasped his hands between his open knees.

'Try and see it from my point of view...'

'Your point of view? What about mine? How am I going to manage all this on my own? My career is going to be wrecked and what my parents are going to say, I just don't know.' She put her head in her hands and shook it woefully.

'Is it too late to have... you know...?' He indicated vaguely with one hand.

She looked up. 'How dare you! How flaming-well dare you!'

'It was only a thought.'

Without realising what she was doing, her hand smashed across his face. He recoiled. 'Ouch! There's no need for that! If you're going to start throwing tantrums, this discussion is at an end!'

He got up and started to stride towards the door into the hotel garden room but before he reached it, the receptionist accompanied by two Polizisten came through onto the terrace.

'Oh!' said Celeste shakily, starting to get up. 'Have you found my case?'

The Polizisten looked at each other in puzzlement.

The receptionist said, 'The police officers are not here to see you Miss Blagden. They are here to see Mr. Skinner.'

'Me?' said Rupert, hand to chest.

*

Sitting in the departure lounge of Hamburg airport, Celeste had never felt so alone in all her life. The English Sunday papers were on the stand but she couldn't bring herself to go over and pick one up. Then the announcement came:

'*Passagiere für Flug Nummer zwei, drei, acht kommen Sie bitte zum Ausgang zweiunddreissig um an Bord zu gehen. Bitte halten Sie Ihren Reisepass und die Bordkarte bereit,*' followed by the English translation: 'Will passengers for flight 238 please make your way to the departure gate as we are now ready to begin boarding. Please have your passports and boarding cards ready.'

She rummaged in her handbag for the items and came across Rupert's small but expensive gift from the harbour shop, still wrapped. As, carrying her bags, she trudged over to the departure desk, she dropped the silver and ruby necklace into a waste-bin.

*

The train journey from London to Phillipstone had been fast. She stepped out of the taxi, paid the driver and then looked up at the outside of the Press Centre at Phillipstone International Airshow. A lot had happened since she had gone away on Friday afternoon. There were banners hanging from the building. A pond, waterfall and exotic flowers had appeared in the downstairs foyer. She went up the staircase and put her Press Centre pass into the slot that opened the glass sliding doors at the top. 'Whoosh!' Nobody was about. It was Sunday afternoon after all. She made her way over to her office and went in, put her bags on the desk and sat down in her cream leather, executive chair, kicking her shoes off. Stacks of mail languished in her tray. She dialled her parents on the landline.

'Hi Daddy. It's me. I'm back.'

'Pumpkin! Lovely to hear you. Did you have a good time?

'Can I talk to Mummy?'

'Yes. Yes, of course sweetie-pie. Hang on a moment.'

There was a pause.

'Hello darling. Is everything alright?'

Celeste couldn't speak.

'Are you there dear?'

She swallowed.

'Yes Mummy. I'm here.'

'Did you have a lovely time in Hamburg and how is Rupert? Do tell me all about it.' Her mother's cultured tone in the safe predictability of the home counties village sounded so right and normal. Everything was fine in her world.

'Mummy, I have some a news that I think may surprise you. Are you sitting down?'

'Well, go on dear. If you don't tell me, we won't know.'

Celeste took a deep breath. 'I'm pregnant.'

'That's lovely darling. Is Rupert pleased?'

'Don't talk to me about that scumbag, Mummy. We're finished.'

'Oh, darling. No. You can't be. You're such a lovely couple. Hold on.'

Celeste heard her mother cover the mouthpiece and say to her father, 'She's pregnant.' She heard her father reply, 'Jolly good show.'

Then her mother whispered. 'She's broken up with Rupert. Some problem.'

'Oh,' said her father. 'Not so good. They'll soon sort it out. I'm just off to watch the news.'

Her mother came back on the line.

'Now tell me all about it.'

Celeste did... the whole miserable story of how Rupert was going to dump her and how the police came to arrest him at the hotel.

'They did what?' exclaimed her mother. 'What on earth for? He's a lovely man.'

'No he's not Mummy. He was working with a man called Gunter who was living off immoral earnings.'

Chapter 16

Phillipstone Airshow, England
Monday 20th June
Morning

'Springstock speaking.'

'Good morning Councillor. It's Henry Dene, the council solicitor.'

'Ah, good morning to you, Mr. Dene. Lovely day.'

'Yes it is.'

'How did you get on over the weekend hunting for those papers in the town hall cellars? I thought about you, once or twice.' The solicitor glared silently at the ceiling for a moment .

'Councillor, I spent the entire two days down there and pretty foul it was too, dusty as the desert and enough spiders to start a menagerie and charge entrance.'

'I must say it's a long time since I visited the place. Did you find what you were looking for?

'Partly. There was some documentation relating to the council taking over the airport land but no copies of anything showing absolute title.'

'Oh. That's not good.'

'It certainly isn't. Look, I'm going to ring a chum of mine at the Land Registry and see if I can get him to do an urgent search for me over the phone. It would normally take up to two weeks to get it in writing but a verbal reassurance would go a long way at this stage.'

'That's jolly decent of you.'

'Yes, it is. I'm at the Town Hall now. I'll keep you posted. Better get on with it. 'Bye for now.'

'Yes, you'd better. Goodbye Mr. Dene.'

*

Celeste hated the sound of brass bands. Yet there was one marching up and down at the near end of the runway, entertaining the crowds of visitors arriving for the first of the five

AIRSHOW ILEX

trade days. Rows of coaches and buses twinkled in the distant grass coach parks, spewing out their human cargo onto the parched field from whence they trudged cheerfully to the walkways, looking like well-dressed, escaped prisoners. For most, these few days at the Phillipstone International Airshow were a welcome holiday from real work, a merry-go-round of convivial meetings, joustings with competitors, complimentary food at every turn, relaxation on the chalet verandas watching the afternoon air display and a chance to feel free on a weekday.

'Get this pigeonhole trolley into Press Centre reception at the double or they'll all be in here demanding their mail,' Celeste barked at her assistant. The huge, grey fitment, was trundled out into the mêlée of press personnel from all over the world, conversing at the tops of their voices, waving their arms about and exchanging business cards. They fell upon the double-sided trolley like bees onto a honey-pot, elbowing and shoving, collecting their envelopes, site maps, free DVDs, brochures, press call lists, flying display schedules and press packs. It was mayhem.

Celeste appeared in her office doorway and tried to get their attention but she couldn't make herself heard. So she went back to her desk and switched on the public address system, turning it up quite loudly and placing her lips close to the microphone.

'This is Celeste Blagden, Controller of the Press Centre. Please pay attention.' She heard the clamour die down.

'Welcome to the Phillipstone International Airshow. There are plenty of press packs available. Other brochures may be found in the wall slots at the sides of the reception area. The notice board will inform you of presentations, signings and speeches so please check it several times a day. The restaurant is situated at the end of the long, curved corridor and there is a snack bar and relaxation area near reception here. You will find storage lockers for equipment next to my office and the air-conditioned computer room is at your disposal. The main radio and news-gathering rooms are out of bounds without an invitation. You may use the Press Centre balcony provided you have your Press Centre passes. Any problems, I'm sure that my team at the reception desk will be able to assist you. The opening fly-past will be at ten a.m. which is in two minutes time. So please go out onto the Press Centre balcony and enjoy the show!'

There was a click and then the buzz of vocal, press activity started up again.

'Ah Gig. I'm glad you've popped in.'

'Morning Celeste. Everything all right?'

'I just wanted to ask you to keep an eye on the balcony. I understand that every year we get people without passes coming up onto it from the fire escape and they get in the way of the professionals. Apart from anything else, they are bypassing the security check at the bottom of our main staircase and we don't want undesirables in here messing about with the computers et cetera. So, perhaps you could tell your staff to check it regularly please.'

'Will do. Coming out to see the opening fly-past?' He made for the door.'No Gig. I'm too busy,' and she shuffled a pile of papers to underline the fact as he left.

Roland Dilger, the show photographer, pushed his way through the crowd and stuck his head around Celeste's office door.

'I'm just going onto the balcony. My gear's already set up out there. Are you coming to see the *Golden Darts* fly over?'

'No thanks. Too much to do. Who's looking after your stuff for you?'

'That Eleanor Framp woman said she'd keep an eye on it. I don't think anyone would challenge her!' and he twinkled a smile before disappearing again. Celeste sighed. Would this stream of interruptions never end?

Zelara knocked on the door and entered. 'Here's another,' thought the Press Centre Controller thought.

'Can't you wait until I tell you to come in?' she barked.

'Sorry Miss Blagden, ma'am, but there's so much noise outside, ma little Caribbean ears couldn't hear yous.'

Celeste looked at her scathingly. 'What now?'

'Well. What do you want?'

AIRSHOW ILEX

Zelara raised her yellow duster. 'I jest needed to flick around in here Miss Blagden, ma'am, so's to make it all nice and shiny for yous.'

'The last thing I need is a cleaning woman under my feet in here on opening day. Go away and scrub toilets or something.' She swung her chair away and clicked on the mouse. Zelara shrugged, stuck her tongue out at the back of the cream chair and left.

Celeste called up the schedule of presentations for the day. All the lecture rooms were booked solid. Then she looked at the flying display for the afternoon. The *ILEX* was going up at three o'clock. She might go out on the balcony to see that. She checked her emails. Nothing from Rupert. No surprise there. Diary. Twelve-week scan on Friday. Well, things should have quietened down by then. It was good to be busy. It took her mind off her personal worries. Then she heard it, a low, droning.

The *Golden Darts* came in from the west, glinting and rumbling on the horizon, sweeping towards the airfield with ever-louder reverberations until the magnificence of the thirty aircraft filled the blue skies above a sea of upturned faces. Never before had the show staged such an amazing opening. Shining like something from a Pharoah's tomb, sleek as jaguars, deadly as cobras, the latest range of nuclear war-head-carrying mini-bombers passed steadily overhead, droning relentlessly and threateningly, callously impartial and a reminder that the annual airshow wasn't just a jolly week of spectacles but an advertisement to the assembled rich decision-makers of the planet that money could buy deadly power.

*

'Oh look, Synth. Look at all those planes. Dozens of them. It reminds me of the war.' On the gravel drive of St. Bede's Convent, Maud, wearing clothes provided by Social Services, stood next to her daughter's car as she gazed up at the sky. Synth shaded her eyes and watched too.

'Very pretty. Gold planes. They're still loud though. Come on Mum. Let's get you in and settled.'

'I like it out here.'

'Reverend Mother's waiting for us at the door.' Synth held up a carrier bag. 'Not much in the way of luggage, is there? Anyway, I think that's all the planes for now. It must have been the opening ceremony.' The *Golden Darts* droned away into the distance until their dazzling shimmer merged with the heat mist on the horizon. 'We can watch the afternoon display if you like.'

'Are you staying with me then?'

'Yes, you silly 'nana. Would I leave you?' She gave Maud a squeeze across the shoulders.

'In we go.' Like a lamb, she went.

'Hello, Reverend Mother.'

'Hello, Mrs. Hunt. Are you recovered?'

'They looked after me in the hospital. Coughed my lungs up but all right now, thank you for asking.' She gazed back down the slope towards the burned out cottage. '… which is more than you can say for our house. Just look at it! Where are my cats?' Synth gave Reverend Mother a meaningful look.

'Come along in and have some tea, Mrs. Hunt, but first I want to show you your quarters.'

Reverend Mother led them in across the big, oak-panelled hallway and through some double doors.

'You are completely self-contained here,' she said, going into the tiny vestibule and unlocking the internal front door of the annexe.

'Miss Hunt, you will find it a lot more comfortable than the nun's cell you have been occupying for the past few days.'

'Believe me, Reverend Mother, I was grateful to have somewhere to lay my head. It was a bit quiet though. I thought that Anna girl in the next cell might have been more chatty but she doesn't speak to me at all.'

'Anna's here on silent retreat.'

'Oh, that explains it. I thought she didn't like my perfume or something.'

Synth let out at gasp of pleasure as they entered the annexe.

AIRSHOW ILEX

'It's beautiful. Absolutely beautiful. Who did it all?'

'One of our sisters was in the interior design profession before she received the call.'

'She certainly has talent,' Synth said with admiration, putting Maud's plastic carrier bag on the sofa and gazing around the tastefully decorated sitting room. There was even a television in the corner. Maud rushed over to the window ledge.

'A *Spathyphilum*! Lovely! The friendship plant!' She picked up the pot and its contents and turned to show it to the others. Synth went over to her.

'Please put it down Mum. You'll drop it.'

'Nonsense. Tosh! After all the lovely plants I had in my cottage... my lovely cottage... that burned to the ground and turned them all to crisps.' She began to blub. Synth took the plant from her and placed it exactly over the ring it had made on the paintwork.

'I must find a saucer or something to put under that,' said Reverend Mother with a nod.

As quickly as Maud's tears had begun, they abated.

'I want to see my bedroom,' she demanded.

'Yes, yes, of course. Come through here, my dear.'

Maud followed the nun like a rich lady viewing an apartment to rent. She looked around the pale cream walls, went over and sat on the edge of one of the twin beds, felt the quality of the pale peach, floral counterpane, bounced up and down a little and said 'It'll do very nicely. Now where's the lavvy?'

Reverend Mother suppressed a smile and pointed a discrete finger in the direction of the bathroom. While Maud went to explore, she took Synth into the modern, little kitchenette and drew her confidentially to her side.

'Miss Hunt, you are both very welcome here and I hope you will be comfortable.'

'Oh, we will. You are so kind. I don't know how we would manage otherwise. I have no savings. I could sell my old car, I suppose...' She looked down dolefully at her hands.

'Don't speak about that now. I just wanted to have a word about Mrs. Hunt.' She paused. 'Your mother is a delightful lady but, and I know you understand me, she will need a certain amount of... shall we say... support while you are here?'

'The fire has shown that she can't be trusted on her own but I have to earn money somehow. I can't be with her all the time.'

'There are two issues. Firstly, how do you intend to earn money? Secondly, I can arrange shifts of two novices at a time to act as companions to your mother. The young ones have taken a real liking to her.'

'That's so good of you. Thank you, Reverend Mother'

'Now, as to how you are going to earn a living and look after your mother, I think I might have an idea. However, Miss Hunt, it will be a day job.' She gave Synth a hard stare. The old nun certainly knew how many beans made five. 'If you do feel the need to work your passage, so to speak, then there's always something to do in a house as large as this.'

'Oh, I'll do anything I can to help.'

'That's settled then. Let's go and see what your mother's up to.'

They found Maud happily drawing on the bathroom mirror with toothpaste. She'd made a great, big smiley and stuck the red lid of the tube into a blob to make a nose.

Reverend Mother said, 'That's pretty, Mrs. Hunt.'

'I had to cheer the place up. Why's this bathroom all done out in pukey pink?'

'Don't be so rude Mum,' Synth interjected hastily.

'Well, it's a terrible colour. Reminds me of the orphanage. All the carers used to wear overalls like that. The sight of it gives me the willies.' She continued with her work on the mirror. Synth whispered to Reverend Mother, 'She had a bad time as a child in the orphanage. Please forgive her. She's got a thing about not liking pale pink.'

'Don't mention it, my dear. I understand.'

'She can be a bit... quirky... sometimes. They weren't too pleased with her in the hospital, you know.'

'Oh?'

'You'll never believe what she got up to in the geriatric ward,' Synth murmured.

'Do tell me, my dear,' said Reverend Mother, turning to her with interest.

'Well, apart from tidying other people's belongings into her own bedside cabinet, she gathered up all the other patients' dentures, washed them in the basin and then redistributed them.'

'Well, she was probably only trying to be helpful...'

'But she gave them back to all the wrong people. It took the staff ages to sort them out, apparently.'

Reverend Mother chuckled. 'I can see we're in for an interesting time. Come along ladies. Elevenses.'

*

Jack and Marcus stood on either side of the entrance to one of the Conference Rooms in the Press Centre, their long, red waiters' aprons almost skimming the corridor's blue carpet.

'Good morning, sir. Good morning, madam, sir, madam, sir. Please help yourselves to refreshments,' they chanted as members of the audience filed in. The boys had worked hard setting up the midday feast on snowy-white-clad tables.

The host, the British Minister for Aviation, Space Exploration and Environmental Innovation, was already seated at one of the desks on the low stage at the back of the room with two minders behind him. A plethora of journalists surrounded him and a panoramic view of the Earth beamed onto a screen on the end wall.

'Minister,' said Eleanor, having elbowed her way to the front, 'would you be willing to comment on the future of this airshow which is so crucial in generating trade for Great Britain?'

'We'll be taking questions after the signing of the agreement,' he said with an air of finality, sorting through his papers, giving a sceptical look up to his left where Roland Dilger stood balanced on a chair with his camera at the ready.

A murmuring spread among the throng as the other party to the signing came through. He deferred to left and right, his stocky Australian build in stark contrast with the diminutive Minister whose hand he reached forward to shake and crush.

'Thrilled to make your acquaintance,' he said enthusiastically, slapping his zipped document case onto the table and beaming around him, his shining white teeth peering out of his sun-tanned face. 'What a bonza day!' With hair the colour of golden corn and expansive, water-surfing shoulders bursting through his pale blue suit jacket, he exuded star quality. The photographers loved him. A true 'Adonis'.

Somebody tapped the side of a water glass with a pencil so that it rang like a bell. The snacking audience members drifted away from the mini-quiches, vol-au-vents and coffee to find seats. The waiters stayed outside and closed the doors of the windowless, airless Conference Room as the session began.

The British Minister got up, walked across and stepped up onto the lectern dais. There was a ripple of polite applause and the cameras flashed. 'Good morning ladies and gentlemen of the press and other guests. We are here today to sign an important agreement between Great Britain and Australia. It gives me enormous pleasure to welcome the other party to the signing, the Australian Minister for Technological Export.' There was another ripple of clapping and the guest beamed until his cheeks nearly burst.

'As you came into the Phillipstone International Airshow it will not have escaped your notice that we have on display a magnificent behemoth of an aircraft in the shape of the stunning and technologically innovative black *ILEX*. You don't need me to tell you, for I'm sure that the pre-show information you received will have whetted your appetite somewhat, that the *ILEX* is the largest passenger aircraft ever to be designed and taken into prototype phase.' The reporters scribbled away.

'It is also going to change the face of flying for the future.' He paused and swivelled to right and left giving the enormity of his prediction time to sink in.

'The *ILEX*,' he continued, 'is the most economical, environmentally considerate, epoch-making aircraft ever invented.' There was a palpable silence punctured only by the avid scratching of pens. 'There will be tours for those with level one clearance only... please book through the Press Centre

AIRSHOW ILEX

reception desk... but for the rest of you, don't be downhearted, for you will be amongst the first people in the world to see the *ILEX* fly, this very afternoon.' He tapped the desk to emphasise his words... 'at three o'clock.' A buzz of interest swept around the room and the cameras flashed again.

'What, you may ask, has this to do with the Australian government?' he said as turned laconically to 'Adonis' sitting grinning.

'I now invite the Australian Minister for Technological Export to fill you in on the details.' He went back to his seat as his counterpart rose and swaggered over to the lectern, stepping up onto the stand with the same grace and ease he might display on a surfboard.

'Good day everyone. Pleasure to be here.' He nodded his head jerkily once or twice by way of homage to the attentive audience.

'How many of you guys have been to Oz?' About half of the audience put up their hands and the British Minister shaded his eyes with embarrassment. These antipodeans were so informal. Where was the man's sense of decorum?

'Well, I can see that some of you have good taste.' A wave of muted laughter went around the room drowning the sound of clicking shutters. He spread his hands on the ledge and leaned forward.

'So, let's have a little quiz.' The British Minister looked warily towards him.

'What has Australia got plenty of? Come on! Don't be shy! Let's hear it!'
Somebody called out, 'Kangaroos!' and then another said, 'Beer!' and a cheer went up. This wasn't supposed to be happening.

'Come on! Give me some more!'

'Poms!'

'Yes. We've got those.' He put his hands in his pockets and gave a wry grin. 'What else?'

'Sheep!' 'Cattle!' 'Aborigines!' The words came thick and fast from all around the room.

'Barrier Reef!' 'Ayer's Rock!'

'Got to stop you there. They've changed its name to Urulu but you're getting warmer.'

'Forest fires!'

'Could do without those. Come on somebody! Who's been to the interior or up north?' A few hands were raised.

A cultured woman's voice said loudly and clearly, 'Sand!' It was as though somebody had sworn. Everybody turned to look at her as if she'd said something stupid.

'Yes, lady. Sand.' Glances of puzzlement ricocheted around the room. Then, as if the stage manager in an amateur play had thrown a switch, the lights went out along with the projected image. The inadequate air-conditioning stopped humming.

'Stay still please, everybody. Don't move.' The British Minister's minders took out torches and shone them onto the audience. One said, 'Open the doors please.' Then a thin stream of light came into the large room.

Roland said, 'Please can I get down from this chair before I fall down?'

Nobody answered so he did. There was a flurry of footsteps on the carpeted corridor and a silhouette appeared in the doorway.

'It's me, Celeste Blagden, the Press Centre Controller,' she said. 'Please don't be alarmed. There has just been an outage due to the overload on the air-conditioning throughout the site. The unprecedented hot weather has just put too much strain on the system. I do apologise. Power should be restored shortly.' Then the silhouette disappeared to repeat its mantra in the doorways of the other lecture rooms.

'Well, I'm not afraid of the dark anyway,' came a loud Australian voice out of the rostrum corner. A titter ran around the room. 'Shall I continue Minister?'

'I don't know whether it would be better…'

'I have another torch,' said Eleanor, switching it on to illuminate Adonis's face which then appeared to hover, bodiless in the dark.

'Fame at last!' he joked.

'Well, I suppose we can manage,' came a weary voice from one of the desks, minders bristling at its owner's elbows.

'That's the spirit! To continue... before I was so rudely interrupted... the lady with the torch was quite correct. Sand.' He waited for the rustling of his darkened audience to subside into attentive silence.

'Yes, sand. In Australia over 40% of our landmass is sand. What has that got to do with Great Britain, you may ask? Well, I'll explain, ladies and gentlemen. You need our sand. Here's an exclusive for all you journalists. Only hope you can read your notes later!' A murmur of amusement went around.

'The new technology, both for your government initiative to place solar panels on every roof in your country and for the making of fibreglass for your government's proposal to super-lag every loft in Britain is going to call for a lot of sand. For those of you that didn't know it, you need sand to make glass and you need glass to make solar panels and fibreglass.'

From the darkness somebody called out, 'The Sahara's nearer!'

'A little respect for our speaker please,' came a deep, authoritative voice from somewhere.

'True, but the Sahara's not in the Commonwealth.'

A cheer went up from a group near the door and that amused the rest of the audience. The British minister groaned to himself in the inkiness and wished it were all over. It was degenerating into a comedy show.

'If Britain and Australia are to keep our historic ties we have to continue to trade. Your biggest exports to us are transport, communications, medical equipment and some pharmaceuticals. In return, apart from the other exports we send you, we are going to sell you lots of lovely, high quality sand.' He waited a moment for things to quieten down again. Eleanor's torch beam wavered on his face. She had no free hands with which to write. It would all have to be remembered.

There was the sound of a chair scraping as the British minister got up, stumbling and groping his way over to the rostrum where he stood, like a little boy in the gloom, next to Adonis who looked down on him benevolently.

'However,' the Australian continued, 'you need our sand for something else,' and he relinquished his place to his host.

Eleanor transferred her torchlight allegiance. The British Minister climbed back onto the rostrum and gestured towards the door.

'Out there on the tarmac stands the fabulous *ILEX* coated in shiny, black tiles. I have been given permission to tell you that those tiles are the first of a new generation of photovoltaics, capable of producing electricity from light in quantities never before envisaged.' A gasp of amazement filled the darkness.

'We need Australian sand to produce those too... and,' he said, raising his voice, 'we anticipate revenue totalling billions of dollars at this year's show as buyers from countries around the world place orders for the British-made *ILEX*. This aircraft is not only going to change the face of technology but generate a shower of new industries that will see all our vehicles with black tiles on their roofs and similar arrays along our motorway embankments. The sides of commercial buildings will be coated with them and outside pavements will be like black rivers of non-slip glass. This is just the start.

Where Britain once ruled the waves, she will now dominate the world with cheap energy. Yes, there's a place for solar and wave power but photovoltaics are the way forward. I now invite the Australian Minister for Export to join me in signing our agreement.'

Applause rang out and the lights came on.

Chapter 17

Monday 20th June
Noon

Roland was on the prowl. It was the first of the trade days. Loaded with photographic equipment he was looking for some good shots for next year's brochures and the national press. Exhibition Hall Two was crowded with suits. Delegates from everywhere jostled and cajoled, delighted to be out of the office. He could hear jazz playing at the far end and pushed his way along saying, 'Show Photographer coming through.' That seemed to clear his path.

He noticed that a lot of people were carrying Japanese-style paper fans on sticks, waving them energetically in front of their shiny faces in the sticky, Monday, noontide heat. The atmosphere of perspiration was almost palpable. The music got louder. The stand from which it emanated was jammed solidly with jigging, shouting men, mostly grinning lewdly. Roland elbowed his way forward to find Dixieland jazz being played by an all-girl band wearing skimpy, black corsets, shiny shorts, fishnet tights and black top hats. He'd get them posed up at the end of their set. They all had long legs, that was for sure. He would enjoy posing them. Oh yes, that was something to look forward to.

'Hello Roland,' said a cultured voice. He turned to see a beaming Eleanor Framp, for once without her perennial grey raincoat.

'No mac today, I see,' he said loudly.

'I thought I'd risk it.' She waved her spiral-bound pad about enthusiastically in an attempt to cool herself down.

'It gets worse every year,' he yelled.

'Are you coming up onto the Press Centre balcony to watch the *ILEX* fly this afternoon?' she enunciated. He looked at his watch.

'Yes. I wouldn't want to miss that. It goes up at three, doesn't it?'

'That's what it said on the board in the Centre.'

'See you later then.'

'Watch your blood pressure,' she replied with an arch look towards to the wriggling jazz musicians. He grinned back at her and shrugged. She walked off into the crowd shaking her head, leaving him wondering what she'd been like before she evolved into a hard-bitten, middle-aged journalist.

He turned away from the gyrations and went over to an East European stand to look at the model planes on clear plastic supports. There was also the front of a full-size jet sawn off just behind the flight deck. It looked incongruous near the scale models and amused him but it wasn't interesting enough for his purposes. Then something caught his eye further on. It was hanging from the ceiling, large and rotating, glinting. It turned out to be a communications satellite with extended, flat panels. He zoomed in with the long lens, hoping that the dismal background of ceiling struts would be out of focus. Not enough light. He needed to be closer with some flash, so he fought his way along. It would have been so much easier to have done this yesterday without the crowds but security wouldn't let him in. He'd pleaded but they'd refused, saying that nobody was allowed in after the dogs had done their bomb sweep.

Then he saw them, walking through the mêlée, laughing, him guiding her and she looking young and carefree, almost girl-like. What was she playing at? Debbie, with that Landscar chap in a white stetson, he who was going to build windmills everywhere. Roland gritted his teeth. He'd soon put a spoke in his wheel, or even his windmill!

He nudged his way forward.

'Debbie!'

She stopped and turned towards him.

'Roland,' she said rather formally.

'Aren't you going to introduce me to your friend?'

'Grant,' she said, 'this is a colleague of mine, Roland Dilger, the show photographer.'

AIRSHOW ILEX

'Grant Landscar. Delighted to meet you,' came the American's reply complete with warm handshake, although Roland had to juggle his camera and tripod to manage it.

'I think I saw you briefly at the luncheon the other day.' The tall American didn't rise to the bait. Roland continued, 'Pleased to meet you too.' He forced a half-smile, not caring for the way the pair was standing so close together.

'You're showing Mr. Landscar around the halls then?' he added by way of stilted conversation.

'Yes. My girls and I aren't flying until later today because of the *ILEX*.'

'Could we have a word?'

'Yes, of course. Go ahead.'

'I meant in private.'

'Well, if it's not urgent, perhaps we could talk later.' She looked up at her escort. 'Shall we go into Hall Three next and see the holograms? I hear they're very impressive.'

'Debbie...' but she was already dismissing him with a charming little wave of her pretty hand which she then tucked firmly through Grant's arm as they went off together.

'Bye, Mr. Dilger,' she said.

The photographer's face was contorted with ire. Why so formal? What happened to 'Roland'? What was she doing with this wind-powered entrepreneur? This was the man who refused to be photographed for the local paper at the luncheon last week. Well, he'd have him this time!

Out ran the fuming photographer through the side exit, clutching his equipment, panting along the paved path and in at the other end, ready to get them front-on, but they never arrived. She must have taken him to Hall Three via the inside stairs. Furious, Roland kicked the artificial rocks of a low-level flower arrangement. He'd get that stetson on legs later.

*

'*ILEX* flight Captain to special security detachment. Over.'
'Special security detachment leader to *ILEX* Captain. Over.'

'Last tour of the morning leaving now. Eight personnel.'

'Roger. Over and out.'

The Captain took off his headphones, leaned back in his seat and turned to the flight officer.

'Everything in order Number One?'

'Yes Captain.'

'You handled that well... the business about no sample UV tile.'

'I couldn't tell the visitors that it had been nicked by a slip of girl, could I?'

'Quite right.

'A new one will be here tomorrow.'

'Good.'

'By the way, what happened about that taxi driver who helped the girl get away with it?'

'Gone to ground. He hasn't reported in for work since last Thursday after the theft and a little interview.'

'Didn't the department put a radio transmitter in his taxi?'

'Yes, they did, but the vehicle's still on the front drive of his flat. It hasn't shifted and he's not there.'

'I wonder where they went?'

'We'll find them. Don't worry. He'll move that cab sooner or later.' He turned his attention to the monitor.

'Everything tied down for the flight at three?'

'Yes, sir. We leave the stand at two-thirty. They're going to take us out backwards and then tow us forwards to the holding bay next to the main runway.'

'Did they sort out the towing vehicle?'

'Yes, sir. They brought in the *Magnificotow* from Winstanton Bly. It came in yesterday on a trailer.'

'Talk about leaving things to the last minute... let's run that check through now. Take your seat. I'll just cue up the staircase. The door's already shut.'

A loud humming vibrated through the flight deck.

'That's done it. OK. Let's begin.' The flight officer put on his headset.

'*ILEX* to Control Tower. Over.'

AIRSHOW ILEX

'Control Tower.'
'Running a test. No movement from stand.'
'Roger. Over and out.'
'Batteries to on.'
The flight officer reached above to Overhead ELEC panel.
'Check,' he said.
'Yes, sir.'
'We'll get those thieving blighters,' said the Captain.

*

Councillor Springstock came into the committee room apologising for his tardiness.

'The traffic's still terrible,' he said, wiping his hand across his forehead. 'I thought it would be better after lunch but it's going to be like this all week. I shall be glad when it's over.'
Henry Dene, the council solicitor, sat at a table waiting gravely, some cardboard files before him.

'Come and sit down, Councillor. You look more than a little hot.'

'Yes, yes, Mr. Dene. Let me get myself together.' He took off his jacket and hung it on the back of the chair before collapsing onto the seat.

'What news, young man? Tell me, what news? When you rang asking me to come to the Town Hall, you frightened the life out of me. What have you found out from your friend in the Land Registry?'

Henry Dene opened a folder and spread a fax on the desk between them. Councillor Springstock reached into his top shirt pocket for his spectacles and put them on, taking the sheet into his trembling hand and skimming the print nervously, his fingers twitching.

'Is this what I think it is?'
'I'm afraid so.'
'How did it happen?'
'A clerical error at the Town Hall way back.'
'You mean, the land…'

'Well, the council assumed the land was abandoned, not owned, whatever, and was going to file for Adverse Possession with a view to gaining Possessory Title.   One could do that if they'd been using the land for more than twelve years and it was unregistered.'

'I don't recall what the council used it for.'

'Horses.'

'You don't say?'

'Yes, they used to graze some horses on there.'

'What did the council want them for?'

'Parades. Up until nineteen-fifty-nine, excluding the war years, Phillipstone Council used to have Mayor's Parade on May Day. Surely you remember?'

'Now you come to mention it, I do. I do. I always thought the beasts came from a local farm. I didn't realise the council owned them or kept them on the airport land.'

'No, the nuns owned them. The council just hired the horses from the convent for parades but they were also used for something else. Take a look at these photographs.' The solicitor spread them out on the desk.

'Well I never,' said the councillor thoughtfully, 'horse-drawn funeral carriages. That does take me back. I remember when I was a a little boy...'

'Yes, there was a family company that ran a little enterprise called 'Phillipstone Funerals' and they used to hire their horses from the nuns too. The animals were kept in the old stables behind St. Bede's Convent in the winter.'

'So the sisters were in on it?'

'More than you think. They grazed sheep on what is now the airport land too. They had quite a flock, according to these old newspaper cuttings that I found this morning at the *Saturnian* offices. Two hundred.'

'Goodness gracious!'

'Look, Councillor.' The solicitor reached again into one of the cardboard files and withdrew two flimsy faxes, placing them before the elderly man who looked sideways at him.

'Your friend has been extraordinarily helpful,' he remarked.

AIRSHOW ILEX

'He owed me a favour.'

'What?'

'I said he owed me a favour.'

'Not that! It says here that, according to the delineations on this little map, the land was registered under the Adverse Possession rule by one Reverend Mother Magdalena on behalf of the Order of the Sisters of the Holy Way in nineteen forty-six and that she was granted full Possessory Title in nineteen forty-eight.'

He looked up as the full horror of the situation sank in.

'But we've been renting that land to the airport for over fifty years. We've coined in millions from them, and, and, and...' He started to look decidedly woozy. The solicitor hastily poured him a glass of water from a carafe.

'Here, take this councillor. Breathe slowly.' He put the glass to the old man's lips.

'But, but... it can't... what?' he gibbered.

'The Reverend Mother Magdalena not only registered the airport land but all of the convent estate and buildings too. She died in nineteen-sixty. She's probably buried up there in the convent's own small cemetery, next to that folly thing.'

'The council will be ruined. Ruined. I will be pilloried. Mocked. Humiliated.' He put his head in his hands and shook.

'With all due respect, Councillor, your personal situation is the least of the worries. At this moment, there is an international airshow taking place on land that doesn't belong to us, for which we have been charging an exorbitant rent for years and which the airport authority has sub-leased to the airshow. You can add to that the claims of this American Landscar chappie, who thinks he's going to build all those wind turbines on what he believes to be his deceased grandmother's land. Let us also not forget to mention the fact that we shall probably all go to hell for having defrauded those poor nuns of vast amounts of money, plus interest, going back decades.'

A sort of howl came forth from the councillor. The solicitor thought it was grief but then realised that the elderly man had his hands in the air, fists clenched in triumph.

'What's going on?' said the solicitor, alarmed.

'He doesn't own the land. Nothing can be built there. I don't have to vote for it.'

'Surely you had a free vote anyway, Councillor.'

'No. No. You don't understand. '

'Understand what?'

The councillor waved his hands about in the air.

'He had me over a barrel, that Landscar chappie. He found out something I didn't want made public and was leaning on me to support his wind farm.'

'Was it that dreadful that he could blackmail you?

'Oh yes. It would have wrecked my career not only as a councillor but precluded me from becoming mayor or a county councillor or even an alderman later too.'

'Well, you don't have to tell me. It's obviously something long ago in the past.'

'I want to tell you. I feel I can trust you.' The Councillor's eyes flicked nervously from side to side.

'Go on then, if it makes you feel better.'

'I went to prison once.'

'You? In prison? Whatever for?'

'It was when I was living up north as a young man, renting a small flat. The local council there wouldn't fix the streetlights or pavements and I withheld payment of my rates in protest. I didn't mean it to go that far but it was a matter of principle, you see. I always cared about the local community.'

'Your secret's safe with me.' The solicitor paused. 'As a matter of interest, how long were you in for?'

'Three weeks. Then my mother paid the court. I didn't speak to her for a year, I was so cross.'

'But how did Grant Landscar learn about it?'

'Some old newspaper cutting. He found it wrapped around a piece of china he bought on the internet. It was very bad luck for me.'

Henry Dene hid a smile. 'Come on Councillor. Let's go up to your office on the fourth floor and watch the display. I believe you have a very good view.'

AIRSHOW ILEX

'Oh yes. Very good indeed.' He giggled conspiratorially. 'That took some wangling.'

The solicitor gathered up the papers.

'On second thoughts,' said the Councillor, 'I think I'd better be on my way home before the display finishes... the traffic, you know...'

'Good idea.' He paused. 'Er... I was wondering... would it be possible for me to use your office to watch the display?'

'Yes, of course, dear boy. Here. Take the spare key. Return it to me next time.'

'That's very kind of you indeed. I'm really looking forward to seeing that new *ILEX* plane flying.'

'You go up and enjoy it Mr. Dene. Be sure to keep me posted about the other matter, won't you?'

'Absolutely. I'll catch the Chief Executive of the Council before he goes home tonight. It should make his day.'

*

'We need to talk.'

'Sure Miz Paula. Hows can I help yous?'

'Turn it off, Zelara. There's nobody in here. Where've you been?'

Without so much as a blink, Zelara resumed her normal, cut crystal, up-market tone as she waddled across to Paula and heaved herself onto the pale, blue leather sofa in the restaurant lounge.

'Sorry I was late. You wouldn't believe the clearing up that's had to be done today. They must live like pigs at home. It's just as bad over in the *ILEX* crew quarters. Now, what do you want to discuss? I'm melting away inside this fat suit and my temper could be better.'

'I'm not exactly having the time of my life in this wig and suspenders.'

'OK. We're both suffering for our art. So let's get on with it.'

'The 'Target' on Sunday.'

'Go on.'

'There are things that, how shall I put it, the boys don't need to know.'

'Like what?'

'We talked about a kidnap.'

'Yes but where will we keep him?'

'It's more than that. Top Dog says he has to be executed.'

'What?' blurted Zelara. 'I didn't come into this to...'

'Hold it. I employed you to be part of this team because you have the necessary skills to work quickly, quietly, and discretely. You are also being paid an inordinately large amount of money to be placed in the foreign bank of your choice.'

'Look, Paula... Paul...'

'Stick with Paula...'

'Paula, I've got two kids.'

'... and what you are being paid will take care of their boarding school and university fees and give you enough left over to retire or set up a business anywhere in the world.' She turned towards Zelara and took her by the shoulders, bending slightly to look into her big, brown eyes.

'You were great at your silent slug routine. You came highly recommended. SG/17 didn't want you to leave.'

'I didn't have kids then. If it all goes wrong...'

'It won't. You and I can do the necessary. We can handle it... hold on. Somebody's coming.'

They got up swiftly and darted between the blue velvet curtains, into the dining room, through the door to the corridor and then into the ladies' room where Zelara had taken the sensible precaution earlier of hanging an 'Out of Order' notice on the outside of the door.

They were no sooner inside when there was a hammering on the door which then flew open.

'Can't yous read? Oh! Miss Bl...'

'Why's this ladies' rest room out of order? I've had complaints,' Celeste snapped.

'Little problem with de flushing, Miss Blagden. Water shortage. Not nice.'

'So what's Miss Paula doing in here?'

'I was just leaving to watch the display,' Paula said and swept out majestically in her red, stiletto sandals.

'Why didn't you come along and report it to me immediately?'

'I wuz on my way, Miss Blagden, ma'am, but then I thought yous might be very busy so I thinks to meself, why not report it straight to de maintenance man meself?'

'You tell me when something needs doing. I'll get on to it right away.' She stormed off.

'Somebody should get onto you right away,' Zelara hissed under her breath. 'No, sorry madam. Dis is out of order. Tries de one downstairs.' Then she shut the door and proceeded to jam reams of toilet paper down all the pans.

Paula retraced her steps to the lounge in time to see Gig waking from a nap behind the sofa where the conversation with Zelara had taken place minutes before.

'Oh, hello Paula,' he said, sitting up and peering over the back of the settee. He screwed up his eyes and blinked, then eased his shoulders. She stared at him in horror. Had he heard what they'd said?

'Gig. What on earth do you think you're doing sleeping behind the furniture?'

'I just came over so tired I couldn't go on. It's all these extra night duties. It was only forty winks.'

'You deserve forty lashes for dereliction of duty,' she retorted. 'Take your illicit snoozes somewhere else and not in my restaurant lounge.'

'Sorry Paula...'

The restaurant manager looked around the deserted room. Gig's podgy hands grasped the back of the sofa as he struggled to get up. There was no time for doubt. The rabbit punch to the Head of Security's neck swiftly laid him out cold. As he sank into oblivion, strong, masculine hands quietly throttled him, turning his pasty face to dark purple as his body slumped on the cream, pile carpet in the sofa's shadow. Paula walked briskly to the ladies' room door and walked in.

'Can't yous people read...?' Zelara started to complain, then she realised it was Paula and stopped.

'We have a problem,' said the restaurant manager sharply. 'We'll need one of those big waste containers on wheels later.'

*

The Press Centre balcony was packed. The prime position at one end, with a view of the airfield behind, had been bagged by a Canadian television company. Their presenter was smartening up his appearance in the reflection from a plate glass window. Paula sat in the air-conditioned relaxation area inside, amused, watching him although, because of the brightness outside, he couldn't see her. Fascinated, she observed as he greased his eyebrows from a little tin of cold cream, patted pressed powder onto his nose, chin and cheeks, and then dipped a comb in a plastic cup of water to get his hair under control. He straightened his tie, adjusted his cuffs and made knowledgeable faces to himself.

'Vanity,' she thought, sipping her ice-cold water. 'We're not so far apart.'

The afternoon display was well underway, following the listing given out by reception. Roland Dilger was wedged between a portly executive with beads of sweat pouring down his forehead, and a UK regional television cameraman with a massive tripod and long lens. Either way, his view wasn't great because a rowdy group of inebriated visitors insisted on waving their arms about, rolled up shirt sleeves and all, continually obscuring his field of view. What were they doing up here anyway? This was the Press Centre balcony, for the press. He looked around. Eleanor was packed in behind him. No security was in sight as still more people came trudging up the fire escape staircase to squeeze into the crowd. From the look of their cameras, they were out on a jolly and not professionals at all.

The *ILEX* had been towed to the holding position near the take-off runway, its black form sinister in the Monday afternoon sunshine. Roland zoomed in and focussed, changed the depth of field, played with the aperture. The plane's coat of glittering tiles was dazzling so he stopped down and took a burst as it taxied onto the runway. The obese man jolted his elbow forecefully.

'Hey! What are you playing at?'

'Sorry old chap.'

Then the regional news cameramen to his left, swung his long lens round at eye-height and nearly took Roland's head off with a swipe.

'Give me break!' he snapped at the man.

'Sorry. Didn't see you there.'

'This is impossible,' Roland shouted over his shoulder to Eleanor. 'A lot of them don't have passes and shouldn't be on here. How are we supposed to do our job?' He took out his mobile telephone and rang Celeste in her office. 'You've got to get some of these people off the balcony. There are tons up here with no passes, I bet. It's impossible. How do you expect us to work?'

'OK Roland. I'll get Gig Cattermole onto it. He should be somewhere about.'

'It'll be too late by then. Can't you come out here and do something? The *ILEX* will take off in a minute and I'll miss an historical shot.'

'On my way.'

In fifteen seconds the Press Centre Manager was coming out through the balcony doors but her short stature meant that she was hemmed in by a sea of giants. She stood on tiptoes. There was no way she was going to take on this crowd.

Then a loud, cultured voice could be heard asking repeatedly, 'May I see your Press Centre pass please?' Then, 'I'm sorry, but you'll have to leave the balcony. If you don't, you give me no choice but to call security.'

There were sounds of grumbling as the tall and indomitable Eleanor Framp made her way among the suspect intruders, sending them from the balcony. Celeste could hear but couldn't see where the amateur guard was because she kept moving about. However, she could sense a slow, tidal surge of people towards the fire escape, their progress causing the up-comers to turn and descend. In two minutes, Eleanor had sent half of the crowd away down the stairs and returned to stand next to Roland.

An angry female voice beside her asked, 'What on Earth do you think you're doing?'

'Your job, by the look of it,' Eleanor replied to Celeste.

'Security would have been here in a minute.'

'Probably too late. This happens every year. Didn't your predecessor tell you about the balcony fire escape problem? You should have posted a guard at the bottom of the stairs. It's impossible to work up here.'

'It's not up to you to interfere in this manner.'

'Well, somebody had to do something,' Roland said, squinting through the viewfinder at the *ILEX*.

'Too right,' said the regional cameraman, moving his tripod a bit to the left. 'There was no room to work. We've got a lot of valuable equipment here. Those guys had no respect for it.'

'The lady done good,' called the Canadian film crew gofer.

'You haven't heard the last of this,' Celeste hissed at Eleanor before storming off back inside, her voice drowned by the noise of a *Rimrad* going through the sound barrier above.

'Look,' said Roland to Eleanor. 'The *ILEX* is lining up for take-off.'

Somebody had left the balcony doors open and the commentary could just be heard outside, a garbled mixture of excited talk-over competing with the sound of the *ILEX*'s engines winding up.

'What's happened to the *Rimrad* now?' Eleanor asked. 'Won't it want to land on the same runway?'

'No. It's going back to base over at Breece Chorlton ... hey ...wow ...' His voice trailed away as he panned and zoomed.

The *ILEX* gathered speed with a surprisingly quiet humming roar and then disappeared behind the buildings, only to appear again briefly above the halls before it swept around anti-clockwise to seemingly float like a whisper above the airfield, graceful, balletic for its size, and elegant in design.

'Looks a bit menacing,' Eleanor said, snapping away with her old-fashioned, one megabyte camera.

AIRSHOW ILEX

'Beee-autifull!' said the Canadian commentator, presenting his aquiline-nosed profile for transmission to base.

'This is a moment in history, a splendid example of the technological expertise for which the UK is renowned, a foreshadow of flight to come, a pivotal transformation of aeronautics, a leap into the glorious future.' He was running out of hyperbole and looked around anxiously until he spotted Eleanor seemingly doing little. A signal to his cameraman got him out of shot and he took four paces and grabbed her by the elbow, putting his hand-held microphone behind him.

'Come and say something about the *ILEX*.'

'I'm not an expert,' she muttered. 'I'm a hack.'

'Doesn't matter. We've got another minute to fill before the satellite is gone.' He propelled her to face the camera and glanced down at the Press Pass on a cord around her neck. It stated, 'Eleanor Framp, freelance UK journalist' and '*Saturnian Special Correspondent*'

'We are lucky enough to have the great British journalist Eleanor Framp with us today at Phillipstone International Airshow. So, Eleanor, please tell Canada about your impressions of the *ILEX*?'

She wasn't used to being on the wrong end of an interview such as this.

'Well,' she said, 'it's a magnificent aeroplane which I had the pleasure of touring inside last week.'

'So, please tell us, is the inside as beautiful as the exterior?'

'It is a test plane, of course, and there was a lot of equipment in there.'

'How luxurious was it? Give us a taste of the opulence that has been promised.'

Eleanor racked her brains for one hint of anything approaching luxury that she had seen inside the black behemoth.

'They have gold taps in the toilets,' she said inventively.

The interviewer's eyebrows went up.

'...and... and seats with seventeen options for comfort.' She was really getting into the swing of it now. He nodded encouragingly.

'...but the best thing,' she said, searching frantically through her grey matter, 'is the wonderful photo-voltaic tiles that cover the outside. I actually had the pleasure of seeing one close up during the tour with royal personages and the Prime Minister last Thursday.'

'How very interesting. Well, we have to finish now from Phillipstone International Airshow in East Anglia, England, Europe. Thank you Eleanor Framp and farewell, for now, to all our viewers.'

Eleanor saw the credits go up on a nearby monitor. The *ILEX* made a swooping pass directly towards the balcony. Cameras clicked wildly and cameramen nearly fell over backwards. Hot and tired, she went and sat down on one of the red plastic chairs to check her mobile phone. There was one SMS to ring a local number. She would do it when she got home but first she wanted to say, 'See you tomorrow,' to Roland but he was showing digital images of the corseted jazz girls to the regional colleague on his camera screen.

In the distance an ant-like column of security guards could be seen slowly ambling along the concourse towards the balcony.

Chapter 18

Tuesday 21st June
Morning

'What do you mean 'he's not around'?' Celeste drummed her fingers on the desk. 'I need to speak with him urgently about security on the Press Centre balcony.' She screwed up her toes with anger. This was outrageous. Why wasn't the Head of Security there when she wanted him?

'He knows about heavy traffic,' she emphasised. 'So he avoids it by usually coming in early. Have you rung him at home?' She took a deep breath. 'Well then perhaps you had better do so. Please get back to me as soon as you can. It was chaos on the balcony here yesterday.' She put the receiver down and spread her hands in the air with exasperation.

'Morning Celeste.' Roland Dilger put his head around the door. 'Anything tasty for me today?'

'I haven't put the notices up yet,' she said, 'but there might be celebrities visiting some of the premium stands in Hall Five later.' Roland, rubbing his hands together in anticipation. 'Now, who will it be? A nice, nubile pop star? An 'A-list' racing driver? What about a foreign dignitary? Something for the big papers.'

'Let me look. Ah yes. I can help you on the last one. Prince Salaluku of Mondrahai is looking for a fleet of private jets for his extended family. They say he has quite an entourage, including his bevy of wives. It's probably worth a punt.'

'What time?'

'We're not posting that one but if you were to hang about near the premium stands next to the entrance to Hall Five at about eleven this morning, you might get something worthwhile.'

'Celeste, you're a star!'

He went over and plonked a kiss on her cheek. To his horror, she dissolved into tears.

'What did I do? Stop crying, please. I didn't mean to upset you.' He looked around in panic.

'Go! Go!' she commanded, waving her hand and shaking her head in distress.

'Sorry. Sorry,' he mumbled as he made his escape. What a strange woman!

*

'It's very good of you to see me at such short notice,' said Eleanor Framp, settling back in the deeply cushioned, aqua, suede sofa.

'My pleasure, Miss Framp.' Grant Landscar relaxed in his easy chair and sipped his coffee.

'You have a beautiful house,' she remarked, looking out through the massive patio doors at the fountains playing in the rose garden. Beyond them she could see a pool and tennis courts. She hastily turned her attention to her host.

'Thank you,' he said. 'Now what's this all about? Please enlighten me.'

'It's rather difficult...'

'Go for it,' he laughed, showing a perfect set of teeth, quite out of keeping for a man of his years. 'I don't bite... often.' Eleanor simpered a little.

'You recall our meeting at the *Old Turret Hotel* last week when you kindly granted me an interview for the *Saturnian*?'

'Yes, indeed I do.'

She smiled at his musical American drawl. He went on '... and a very nice article you wrote too, if I may say so.'

'Thank you. I try to do a good job.'

He looked at her, sitting in his morning room, her navy-blue sprigged dress at least five decades out of fashion. His gaze travelled down to what he could see of her legs, encased in milky-beige stockings ending in brown, heavyweight sandals. How could a well-boned woman like that wear her hair scraped back with a parting normally seen on a child and why that powdery make-up?

'So,' he said, 'Spill it to me... may I call you Eleanor?'

'Yes you may, Mr. Landscar.'

He noted how she still addressed him formally and felt marginally that he had been reprimanded in his own house on a sunny Tuesday morning by a scrawny matron of an uncertain age. That sort of thing didn't happen to him often and he savoured the irony.

'Go on, my dear,' he said with a hint of twinkle in his eye.

'Please don't take this the wrong way but there are many people in the Phillipstone area who are strongly for or against your wind generator plans. Indeed, the paper was inundated with calls and emails when my article was published last week.'

'So I understand but it's a very worthwhile scheme...'

'Forgive me for interrupting you, Mr. Landscar, but things may not turn out exactly as you may have hoped.' She paused and looked down at her lap. Then, in a measured tone, she enquired, 'Mr. Landscar, please may I ask you something?

'Anything you like. Do, by all means. I can't guarantee to answer it though,' he smiled.

'I hope you don't think I'm being presumptuous, but would you be so kind as to give me a little more detail about why you think the convent estate and part of the airport land belong to you? I sketched over what you told me about your grandmother owning it all in my article last week, but you didn't really tell me how water-tight it all was.'

'Fair enough,' he said. 'It's time for a little more information, I think.' He looked over the top of his coffee cup and then decided to put it down on the small table next to him.

'My grandmother Landscar, came from a wealthy English family. Indeed, they lived here in Phillipstone in what is now the old St. Bede's convent building. She was a headstrong woman, by all accounts, and fell in love with a labourer on the estate. Her family went spare and sacked him, forbidding any further communication between them. However, to cut a long story short, she eloped to the United States with him and had nothing further to do with her parents. I suspect that, as an only child, she had been spoilt.'

'How tragic,' Eleanor interjected.

'Yes, it must have been but she made a good life out there with her young husband. By selling her personal jewellery, they were able to set up a general store in a little town in New England. We're talking about the nineteen-twenties here which, you may recall, was just before the depression.'

'How did they survive those terrible years?'

'Well, they opened up a chain of soup kitchens, charging five cents a bowl, and did very nicely out of it, buying up property that had become cheap as people lost their homes.'

'I can see where your entrepreneurial streak comes from,' Eleanor said.

'Quite.' Grant Landscar stroked his chin. 'Time passed and my grandmother's parents back in England died in a bombing raid on London during the war. As their only child, despite what they considered to be her hurtful and bad behaviour, they still left her everything in their wills.'

'So she was wealthy after all?'

'Well, no, not exactly. Her first husband died and she later remarried and became untraceable for a time, name-wise, especially as she moved across country to Connecticut.'

'So she didn't know her parents had gone or that she had inherited?'

'Correct, initially, but a private detective employed by the executor found her. Do you know that danged woman was still so angry at her parents that she never came back to England again? Using an agency she leased the house and estate to the nuns for free. The agency went belly up and the nuns stayed on, not knowing who owned the convent.'

'That's quite a story,' Eleanor remarked thoughtfully, 'but what happened next?'

Grant opened his hands and went on, 'Anyway, she raised her children and lived to a ripe old age in some comfort.'

'I'm glad she had a happy ending.'

Grant shrugged.

'It was only when we were clearing out her house that I came across some of her diaries. It was in one of these that I found references to the estate over here. She also mentioned that her parents kept the deeds to everything hidden in the house because they didn't trust solicitors or banks.'

'Who can blame them?' Eleanor said with an air of knowledge, slowly nodding her head. She placed her hand carefully on the end of the arm of the chair and readjusted her posture. 'Mr. Landscar, do you know whether those deeds were registered or not?'

'Well, that's the problem. I had my lawyers do a search and there's no mention of any registration here in England at the Land Registry.

Eleanor reached into her leather briefcase and pulled out some A4 sheets.

'This hasn't been confirmed yet but we are holding the front page for when the *Saturnian* comes out on Thursday.' She got up and passed the sheets to him. He put on his gold-rimmed, half-spectacles and scrutinised the contents. Eleanor went and sat down again, hands clasped and waited. He took a deep breath.

'My goodness! This does put the cat among the pigeons!' he exclaimed, sitting more upright in his chair. 'Where on earth did you get this information from?'

'I went up to the Land Registry and did a search on Monday morning. '

'Is it right? Is it true?'

'I believe so. The property was registered under the Adverse Possession rule. As I understand it, if property is left vacant for twelve years, anybody using it for that period, could apply for Adverse Possession if the true owners can't be found.'

He looked down at the papers.

'So this long-gone Reverend Mother registered it all on behalf of the convent. Well that scuppers my wind farm plans very nicely.' He looked up, his face a picture of disappointment.

'How could the convent just take the land and property like that? It belonged to my family, after all.'

'Well, I was talking to somebody at the Land Registry about that. It seems the then Reverend Mother filed for 'Adverse Possession' for the convent building, estate and part of the airport land and then went on to get Possessory Title and registered the lot in the name of the order.

Grant Landscar sat, dumbfounded, eyes wide, staring at her and shaking his head slowly from side to side in disbelief. 'Well I'll be danged,' he said morosely.

'Furthermore,' Eleanor said, 'old Reverend Mother was able to register half of what is now the airport land on behalf of the order as it seems the nuns had a claim on it because they used to graze a large flock of sheep and some horses there for years and years.'

'Well I'll be ... but how come you could find the papers for it at the Land Registry when my lawyers couldn't?'

'I suppose your people were looking under your grandmother's married names?'

'Yes, they were.'

'No wonder they didn't find the property because, from what you say, she never formalised it. I looked under "The Order of the Nuns of the Holy Way" and there it was, registered in nineteen forty-eight by one of the previous Reverend Mothers on behalf of the order.'

'This beggars belief.'

'It was called the "Bandirron Estate", south of Phillipstone. Am I right?'

'You are correct, Eleanor. That was the name of the place. It said so in her diary.'

'Are you very disappointed?'

'Nobody likes to lose property or money.'

'They say you're a billionaire.'

'Do they indeed?'

Eleanor looked at him steadily. She leaned forward.

'Mr. Landscar, I know that you are a man of principle and that you wanted to bring modern wind technology into this area for very good and philanthropic reasons. I must be honest.'

She pushed a hair back out of her eyes.

If I weren't involved both at a business and a personal level, I'd be rooting for your plans.'

'Would you care to explain?' he asked affably.

She looked down uncomfortably at the deep pile, aqua carpet, playing with her fingers.

'It's always a little bit awkward when business and family matters collide.'

'Try me,' he said, stony-faced.

She paused and then said, 'My aunt is the Reverend Mother of St. Bede's. I'm going there this afternoon to tell her the good news.'

'Oh, I see,' he said archly.

'She's been worried to death ever since she got your solicitor's letter. Are you really going to consider taking a convent of destitute nuns to court with the intention of rendering them homeless? Have you any idea how much good they do with their school and self-sufficiency?'

'That's all very well, but who's been cleaning up all the money that's been coming in from the airport leasing?'

'I checked with the airport authority and their landlord is Phillipstone Local Council who thought they owned the land. So, a lot of rent must have come in over the years. I would have thought that the nuns would be able to arrive at some arrangement with the Council about reclaiming it, plus interest. Then, of course, something will have to be sorted out about the airport land that the convent unknowingly owns.'

'Have you ever considered a career in politics?'

'No, that's not my ambition.'

'So, Miss Eleanor Framp, what is your ambition?'

'You would laugh at me if I told you.'

'Try me.'

She blushed, or at least he thought she did. In fact it was another hot flush. She blotted her forehead with the heel of her hand.

'I'd like to edit my own magazine,' she blurted out.

'Subject matter?'

'Cross-stitch and embroidery are my passions.'

'Passions, eh?'

'I said you'd laugh at me.'

His face was kindly, not mocking.

'No, I'm not laughing. It's good to be passionate about what you believe in.' He waved his hand in a sweeping gesture that encompassed valuable antiques that decorated the opulent room.

'They are my passion.'

'You have some beautiful *objects d'art* and porcelain here,' she said appreciatively. 'I have a huge admiration for art and craft work. There are also some wonderful examples of needlecraft with very interesting histories around. I'd like to get a good camera, learn to be a better photographer and travel to capture some of the world's beautiful silk artworks. Then I want to write about them in my own magazine and inspire a new generation to take up the crafts.'

'That is ambitious.' He smiled encouragingly.

'Please don't patronise me, Mr. Landscar.'

'Far from it, Eleanor. I applaud ambition.' He put the ends of his fingers together and leaned forward.

'So why are you tipping me off about the land registration, or rather lack of it, today?' He picked the sheets up and waved them about enquiringly, looking sagely and directly at her over the top of his glasses. 'What's in it for you, Eleanor?'

'Nothing. Nothing at all. It's just that you were so courteous and forthright with me when I interviewed you last week that I didn't like the idea of you being brought down so publicly. Besides, the less stressful this whole thing is for my dear aunt, the better.'

He put the pages on the arm of his chair and stood up. With his glasses still balanced on the tip of his nose, he put his hands in the pockets of his well-cut denims and walked over to look out at his lovely garden.

'You know, Eleanor, when a man has everything, it's not often somebody does him a favour without wanting somethin' in return,' he observed.

Eleanor started to gather up her things. 'I don't want anything from you and now I must be going. I'm due to do some interviews at the airshow before I go to the convent. You may keep those copies,' she said to his back. 'I'll see myself out,' and she made for the door.

AIRSHOW ILEX

'Hold on a minute.' He turned to face her. 'Can't I tempt you to another coffee?'

'Well...' she hesitated.

He steered her towards the chair she had just vacated.

'Please sit down again. I think I can find us some fancy biscuits to go with it.'

*

Jack and Marcus swaggered along the concourse wearing matching baseball caps that proclaimed 'I'm cool.'

'What time does Paula want us back?' Marcus asked, flipping a coin in the air and slapping it on the back of his hand.

'Twelve. She said we deserved time to look around a bit.'

'Very noble of her, I'm sure.'

'It's OK here. Huge though. Where shall we start?'

'Well, I hear there are loads of freebies in the halls.'

'Do we want freebies?'

'Yes, we want freebies, lots of them.'

'Then it has to be the halls.'

They followed the signs into Hall One.

'Wow! All this for just a week!' Jack said, gazing around at the sea of well-lit stands. They systematically began to trawl up and down the aisles, their hands diving into glass bowls to grab sweets, key-rings, badges, fans and letter-openers to fill the lime green bags they got from one of the stands. When they'd scavenged Hall One, they repeated the operation in Halls Two and Three.

'Hey! Look at this!' Marcus stood mesmerised by a block of clear plastic that slowly rotated, cycling through shades from violet to rose, via blue and lemon, then back through turquoise and lilac, illuminating the small, steel parts that were embedded in its interior. 'I'd like one like that.' His brother pulled him away.

'Come on. There's a strength machine over there. Let's have a go.' They went to the stand.

'Good morning gentlemen. Would you like to pit your muscles against our magnificent contraption?' The boys looked at each other and then at the shiny steel piston.

'You bet,' they said together.

'All you have to do is push against this bar and watch the column of red liquid rise until it reaches the gold line at the top. There's a prize of a free plane ride for anyone who can do it.'

'Me first.' Marcus had his hands on the bar and began pushing. The liquid rose up the column quite readily for the first ten centimetres and then it seemed to be more difficult. He took a deep breath and renewed his effort but his face began to turn puce as he pushed with all his might. The liquid hardly budged.

'Weakling,' said his brother. Marcus let the bar go and the gauge returned to zero.

'You try. I bet you can't do better.'

Jack took over. He too ended up beetroot-faced and breathless. He said, very loudly that it was a 'con' and nobody would get a free flight.

'Don't be bad losers,' the man said. 'You've been pitting your strength against the fluid arrangement that's inside the suspension on landing gear. Here, have some badges as a consolation prize.' They reluctantly dropped them into one of their bags and walked away.

'Well, if we couldn't beat that, how are we going to overpower the leatherjackets next week?' Marcus grumbled.

'Shhhh.'

'Well, it's true. We're not heavies.'

'We'll just be using the skills we've got. Paula has it all planned. She wouldn't ask us to do anything we couldn't handle. Anyway, we're going to have a rehearsal. I meant to tell you. She's got a place for us to have a practice tomorrow night.'

'About time. There's nothing I hate more than an under-rehearsed show.'

'Come on. Let's go outside for a bit. It's sweltering in here.'

*

Eleanor came out of the Press Centre and into the mid-afternoon sun. It had been a gruelling day so far, with interviews as difficult as drawing hens' teeth. She stood on the walkway for a moment as a hot flush swept over her. She wasn't going to take the pills that the doctor had prescribed. It wasn't natural. She stepped to the kerb and hailed a taxi, half-recognising the driver.

'Where-a to, lady,' he said in a thick accent that sounded familiar.

'Is it you again?' she asked as she got in the back.

'Yess-a lady. It's me but not as-a beautiful as when-a you last see-a me.' He lowered his sun-glasses and, in the driving mirror, she saw that both eyes were nearly closed like slits.'

'Oh my goodness! Did you have an accident?'

'You could-a say that,' he laughed grimly. He pulled away smoothly.

'Where you wanna go?'

'To the convent. Where you took me before.'

'Okey dokey.'

Eleanor called over his shoulder, 'Thank you for helping me last time, when I was faint after the *ILEX* tour on Thursday. You look as if you should be home resting with those injuries.'

'I take you there. No problem.' He paused to negotiate a broken down lorry. 'I like-a to stay-a in my-a house to take-a care-a me but I need-a tha money,' he added, rubbing a thumb and forefinger together in the air.

'The other passenger was very kind to me too, when I wasn't well. I'd like to have thanked her properly.'

'He accelerated onto the ring road and took the turning that led to the narrow lane and St. Bede's.

Brecht pulled up on the gravel outside the convent's main door, put the brake on, got out, and collected some bags from the boot. These he placed by the convent porch. Then he opened Eleanor's door, waited for her to get out and, as she thrust the fare into his hand, gave her a white envelope with 'A' written on the front.

'Pleass give-a that to der Reverenda Mudder forra me and those-a bags.'

'What is it?' She asked, looking down at the envelope.

'The good-a ladee will know-a. Thanka-you verra much.'

Then he got back into the taxi and drove away very fast in a cloud of dust.

'Eleanor! How lovely to see you!' Reverend Mother Veronica embraced her niece in the convent's downstairs hallway. 'Come through and see Sister Catherine in the conservatory. You know it's in the shade at this time of day and she won't mind if we visit while she's working.'

'I rather need to talk to you privately, Auntie,' she said.

'It can wait a little, can't it Eleanor? Come on. She'll be so pleased.'

'That foreign taxi driver asked me to give you this envelope and those bags. Who's 'A'?'

'Oh, I'll explain later, dear.' She folded the envelope in half and plunged it into her voluminous skirt pocket before urging her niece along the corridor, past the guest wing, and into the glasshouse that was a jungle of home-grown produce.

Sister Catherine heard them coming, put down her things and got up to greet them.

'Good afternoon Miss Eleanor, Reverend Mother. How delightful to see you! Won't you sit down?' She drew a wicker chair forward. 'You'll forgive me if I get on with my artwork. We have a stall at the school fete and these little things I do seem to sell very well.'

'Hello Sister Catherine. I see you're busy as usual,' Eleanor said, taking a seat, adding, 'and what's that gorgeous perfume?'

'Ah, you must mean *Exacum Affine* or, as some people call it, *Persion violet*. I was given some free seeds. It's rather heady though, don't you think?'

Reluctant to appear impolite, but somewhat overwhelmed by the pungent scent, Eleanor replied 'Yes, it's very pleasant.' She looked around her in the corner of the conservatory where the old nun's small studio held court to rows of plaster statuettes, holy mementoes bearing biblical quotations, hand-made rosaries in little decorated, oval wooden boxes and embellished mugs.

'I wish I had your talent, Sister,' Eleanor said admiringly, 'Since I was a small girl you've always been painting things so beautifully.'

'Well, we're all given little gifts. You have your writing. We read everything you do, don't we Reverend Mother?'
Her superior smiled deferentially.

'Yes indeed. I own up to keeping a scrapbook. There! My secret's out! I really should have confessed it years ago, but I think I'm permitted to be a little proud of my favourite and only niece.'
She walked a few steps away from them and looked admiringly up at the bunches of purple grapes hanging from the struts. 'The produce is looking very good this year, Sister,' she said.

'We've been rather lucky with the weather, Reverend Mother, and since we've had the new collection method for rainwater, it's easier.'

'Sister had the idea of taking roof water from the convent. A very nice local builder, whose grand-daughter comes to the school, did all the piping for us, and even donated the tanks and barrels. Look, you can see them outside.'

'I really wasn't looking for...'

'No, of course you weren't sister, but it was a very good idea.' Reverend Mother clasped her hands together. 'Now, I was wondering whether we might all take a cup of tea and a slice of home-made sponge-cake out under the willow tree. What do you think?' Before Eleanor could answer, her aunt went on, 'and I've invited two more people to join us. Will you come too Sister Catherine?'

'Thank you Reverend Mother, but no. I'd really like to get on here while I'm on a roll, so to speak.' They all smiled.

'Aunty Rev,' Eleanor said, trying to take hold of the sleeve of her aunt's habit as they went out through the conservatory door and onto the lawn.

'Can't it wait dear?'

'I've really got to talk to you. It's very important.'

'Ah, there they are!'
Maud and Synth were sitting primly at a slatted wooden table under the magnificent willow tree.

*

The *ILEX* Captain strolled along the lower cabin. It was stiflingly hot and airless. The monitoring equipment hummed and flickered. He stopped to check the photovoltaic display panel.

'The amperage is still high, despite your bank of rechargeable batteries outside,' he indicated.

'I've been thinking about that, sir,' said the flight officer. 'We change the batteries out in the shed every evening and take the full ones away for discharge on the trailer, but we're fighting a losing battle really. I think we're going to have to go back to venting fresh air in through the hold overnight again.'

'I don't like it much but an aircraft like this was never intended to sit on the ground in blazing heat for days on end. She's supposed to be up there, saving the planet.' He looked at the ceiling and smiled with chagrin.

'Very well, sir. I'll arrange some extra guards.'

'Ah, talking of which, has that Head of Airport Security turned up yet? That Gig Cattermole chappie. Is it true what they say? That he's gone missing?'

'Yes, sir. He seems to do as little as possible so it shouldn't make much difference. I don't know why they still employ him.'

The Captain put his hands in his pockets and studied a taped-down cable snaking its way along the cabin. He turned his head suddenly.

'Hey-up! What's that?'

A beeping permeated through from the cabin. The pair of them rushed up the few steps onto the flight deck. The Captain turned off the beeper.

'Our taxi-driver's on the road. Look!'

'So the homing device is working after all.'

'Our people installed it under the bonnet when the vehicle went in for its 'service' last week. I thought they'd put in a duff one. He hasn't moved the taxi off his driveway since then. So what's caused our boy to go ride-about now and where is he?'

The flight officer called up the map overlay. The red dotted trail had tracked Brecht all the way from his flat on the edge of town, to a shopping parade near a park, to the airshow, and then out again on the ring-road towards a little road that ran parallel to the airfield.

'What's that big building he's approaching?'

'It's the convent, Sir. St. Bedes.'

'So what's his business there?'

'It may just be an innocent fare, Sir.'

'Who would go from the airshow to a convent? There's something going on.' He spoke into his collar-microphone.

'*ILEX* Captain to Special Security One. Over.'

'Here, Captain.'

'Our taxi-boy's on the move again. He seems to be heading towards that convent over behind the edge of the airfield. Code purple.'

Chapter 19

Tuesday 21st June
Afternoon

'It's sooo lovely up here,' Debbie said, as she lay back on the tartan blanket on the flat roof, gazing at the azure blue sky that was streaked with aircraft trails.

'I found this place the other day when I was looking for good vantage points,' Roland replied, eyes closed. 'I thought we could watch the end of the display from up here. It's nice you're not flying today.' The sun beat down on their naked bodies. It was late in the afternoon and its relentless, piercing heat had abated somewhat. She turned on her side and trailed her fingers down his face, across his chest and southwards.

'That tickles.'

'So does this.' She languidly got up on all fours and dragged her curly, auburn hair back and forth across his body, her torso swinging rhythmically from side to side. No response. So she sat up and asked, 'What's the matter?'

'I'm tired.'

'It's not like you to be off your oats.'

'I've been very busy these past few days. I'm not a machine,' he said.

'You've been overworked before. So have I. It's never stopped us.'

'Give it a rest, Debbie. Can't a man have a few moments of peace?'

'Well,' she said, reaching for her blouse, 'if that's how you feel, I'm going back down.'

He opened his eyes and caught her wrist. 'What's going on with you and that Landscar fellow?'

'We're just good friends.'

'It looked more than that yesterday in the halls.'

'Don't be so touchy. You and I never said we were exclusive.'

AIRSHOW ILEX

'Have you been sleeping with him?' Roland sat bolt upright, shaking her wrist angrily. The sound of helicopters drifted towards them.

'What do you take me for?' She retorted.

'Well, we only get together at airshows. What goes on the rest of the time, I prefer not to think about. I just don't like having it rammed down my throat.'

She jerked her hand away from his grasp. 'You can't make up rules just because it suits you,' she said. 'This is an open relationship.'

He pulled her towards him and fastened a clamp-like kiss on her lips that took her breath away but left her without feelings.

'That was anger,' she said, pushing him away. 'Don't kiss me in anger. I don't like it.'

'You always said you liked me to be strong for you.'

'Yes, but not angry. I don't buy into that.'

'OK. OK. I'm sorry. Come here gently.' He ran a caressing hand across her shoulders and stroked back her hair, planting a soft and tender kiss on her lips.

'We're so nice together,' he said. 'I don't like it when I think of you with somebody else.'

'I try not to think of you with other women,' she said.

He pushed her down onto the rug and leaned over her, gazing into her very blue eyes that reflected the sky.

'Debbie, why don't we try being together at other times, away from airshows?'

'It wouldn't work,' she said. 'It's the long gaps between meetings that make it so exciting. If I saw you every day, it wouldn't be the same.'

'It would be better. We could get to know each other. This has been going on for years. It was nice when we were younger but I'm over forty now and you...'

'Don't go there,' she said with a warning look.

'You must want to settle down,' he continued. 'All women do, don't they?'

'Perhaps your mother's generation,' she said. 'It's different for us now. We have careers. I like my flying.'

'You can't go on doing it forever. Even commercial pilots have to stop sometime. All that cavorting about the skies... it's not without danger. I saw your near-miss last week when you were practising. You nearly hit that one with the square on the side.'

'Unfortunate. She wasn't feeling too good. Anyway, what else would I do? I've been flying since I was a teenager.'

'Sell your planes and turn the troupe over to somebody else. We could go and open a little hotel in Portugal or something.'

'Together?'

'Why not? We could have a good life out there,' he said plaintively. 'Debbie, I never thought I'd hear myself saying this, but I think I'm in love with you.'

She giggled. 'In love with me?'

'Yes. When I saw you with Landscar I realised how awful I'd feel if you went off and married him.'

'He's been through a few wives already. I'm not sure I'd want to join the list.'

'Be serious.'

At that moment a set of four *Magnifo* props flew over, circled upwards and then started spewing out parachutists with flares and flags.

'Hey! Look at them!' Debbie said, pointing upwards. 'I've never seen so many coming down together before.' She started to count. 'There must be twenty.' The buzz of excitement from the trade-day visitors reached them, wafting over the metre high parapet and building to a crescendo of anxiety.

'It sounds as if something's not right,' Debbie said.

Roland grabbed his camera and stood up, moving forward swiftly to the edge of the roof.

'Two of them are tangled up together,' he said over his shoulder. She got up and joined him. He was zooming and snapping away. 'They're coming down into those trees over near the convent.'

Sure enough, the parachutists came to a sudden halt, hanging in the branches, their chutes waving in the breeze.

So intrigued by the goings on in the trees on the far side of the airport were the naked lovers, that they were oblivious to everything else until the dark shadow of a *Trepid* helicopter loomed low and loud above them from behind the roof, tilting to its side as it swept away.

'I hope they didn't see us,' said Debbie, suddenly aware of their lack of clothes.

*

Eleanor leaned back in the old-fashioned, wooden sun-chair and put her feet up.

'This is absolutely idyllic, Aunty Rev,' she said, stretching her arms and putting her head back. 'You are so lucky to live here... if it wasn't for all that.' She pointed towards the airfield where the afternoon display was underway. Her aunt flashed a warning look. Their private business was not for sharing with their guests.

'Yes, it's lovely here,' said Maud, wiping away jammy crumbs with the back of her wrist.

'Use the paper serviette Mum,' hissed Synth, pressing one into her hand.

'All right dear,' she replied, mopping around her face in an exaggerated style. 'Am I beautiful now?'

'Yes, you're perfect,' her daughter replied.

'It's very nice here,' Maud simpered. 'Like a swish hotel but without the swish.'

'Forgive my mother,' Synth said, shrugging slightly.

'It's all right, dear.' Reverend Mother moved her hand slightly in deference. 'We're very happy to have you both here and you've been such a treasure around the place, Miss Hunt... all the housework and cooking you've been helping with. The teaching Sisters are mostly involved with the school during the day, so the housekeeping gets left to the rest of us... and rightly so.'

'It's the least I can do. You've provided us with clothes and everything.'

'Oh, we've got quite a stash of those, Miss Hunt. People are very generous with donations.'

'I want more company and I miss my pussies,' Maud declared.

'It's probably a bit quiet for you but you were on your own a lot in the cottage, weren't you?' Reverend Mother said.

'Yes, but I had my pussy-cats. They were lovely company.'

' Aren't your novices taking care of you?'

'The little trainee nuns? Oh, yes. They're nice but they aren't very worldly, are they?'

'Mum!'

'Well, it's true. We've got no real conversation. Why can't I talk to that other girl, the one that won't speak?'

Eleanor looked at her aunt. Had Maud invented somebody?

'Ah,' said Reverend Mother, 'you mean the lady who's here on a retreat.'

'I didn't know you were doing retreats at the moment,' said Eleanor, puzzled.

'This is a special one. Won't you have some more tea, Mrs. Hunt?' said the nun, lifting the teapot invitingly.

'No thank you. I shall be up all night with my bladder if I do.'

'Mum!'

'We've all got bladders daughter dear. Just you wait until you're our age,' and she glanced knowingly at the old nun, adding, 'Look! Oh look! There are stunt parachutes coming down.'

Indeed there were. Floating serenely on the very gentle, afternoon breeze, trailing turquoise smoke, they drifted towards the convent grounds but, one after another, controlled their path so that they swung away in an arc.

'Those two look a bit close to each other,' Reverend Mother said, shading her eyes from the brightness of the sky. Eleanor quickly snatched up her camera from the table and zoomed in as much as she could, clicking away.

'They're getting tangled,' she said, still snapping. 'Can't you see?'

'Looks like French knitting,' Maud chortled.

'Stop it Mum. They're having an accident.' Synth stood up too. 'The parachutes are collapsing. Oh my goodness!' Her hands flew to her face in panic.

'They're falling into the oaks over there,' Eleanor said.

AIRSHOW ILEX

'They're still on the airport land,' Synth remarked.

'Yippee!' shouted Maud, waving her paper serviette triumphantly. 'They look like fairies on top of a tree!' The two parachutists were hanging like Christmas decorations, waving about somewhat. Immediately the sirens sounded as the emergency teams tore down the airport's internal perimeter road. There was so much noise that none of the ladies of the genteel afternoon tea party, heard the vehicles pull up on the gravel at the front of the convent... apart from Synth.

'Wasn't that a car?' She leaned forward to try and see around the corner of the convent building. The sound of vehicle doors slamming reached them. Reverend mother turned and took a few steps forward to have a look and then stood stock-still as Brecht came across the lawn towards her, followed by four leatherjackets in full face-masks and carrying DB/49s.

Brecht spread his hands in apology. 'I'm so-a sorry, Reverend-a Mudder. I was driving away and...'
One of the leatherjackets brought the stock of his weapon across the taxi-driver's shoulder.

'Shut up! Everybody inside.' He motioned them towards the conservatory door.

'Ooh, this is exciting!' said Maud.
Synth, grabbed her arm. 'Be quiet, Mum. This isn't a game. They've got guns.'

*

Celeste stood belligerently in her office, the telephone receiver clamped to her ear.

'It's been hell on the Press Centre balcony this afternoon. Why hasn't Gig sent his patrols up to clear away the people without passes? Worse than that, they were coming into the Press Centre lounge so that the bona fide photographers and reporters couldn't get a seat to sort out their work. It's really not good enough,' she insisted. ' Well if he can't be found, get a replacement.' She listened again. 'Is he or isn't he a missing person?' She drummed the tips of her fingers on the desk. 'Put me onto your supervisor. What do you mean he's not available? Who's running the show down there in Security?' The line went dead. She slammed down and gave a muted scream of frustration.

'Calm yourself,' she said, seeking the refuge of the big, cream leather office chair and calling up her emails. Still nothing from Rupert. They'd had such a blazing row before she'd left Hamburg... still... after all their years together... surely...? She put her hands protectively over her abdomen. 'Oh crikey! What am I going to do?' Time for the folic acid tablet. What was the point? She swallowed the pill with a gulp of tepid water from the glass on her desk and then got up and wandered out onto the balcony. A couple of photographic magazine stringers were gleaning the final thrills of the day, cameras panning and, in the corner, somebody was sitting tapping a report into a laptop balanced on one of the red plastic chairs. There were paper cups and food wrappers all over the artificial blue carpet.

The afternoon display was drawing to a close above her. She peered down. Already the trade day visitors were streaming along the concourse below, making for the exit in the heat, sleeves rolled up, jackets slung over their shoulders, plastic carrier bags full of brochures and business cards. They craned their necks to get a last look at the aerobatics of a chest-rattling *Burston Striker* as it shot across the sky, bristling with weaponry and spewing a double, white, vapour trail. The flags of many nations hung drably from their white poles along the walkway. Taxis and golf buggies vied for precedence in the stink of fumes. It was a real mêlée. She sighed and went back in.

*

Sister Catherine smiled with satisfaction as she finished painting the border on a small plaque of St. Bede holding an open book. It had been a pleasant afternoon in the conservatory. She put her brush in the white spirit and looked up to see the partakers in the little tea party marching briskly towards the building, followed by a man with tousled hair and four scary-looking fellows in black leather, helmets and face-masks. They were carrying big guns. She'd never seen Reverend Mother walking so fast. Alarm rushed through her as she got up and went quickly into the dark corridor, hoping she hadn't been seen. The police. She would ring the police but there was only one telephone and that was upstairs in Reverend Mother's office.

She heard the conservatory door crash shut and the sound of footsteps and voices approaching. Where could she hide?

'What's this all about?' asked Reverend Mother querulously.

'Move on!' commanded the chief leatherjacket, poking her in the back with the muzzle of his weapon.

'Don't you dare touch Reverend Mother!' protested Synth, putting her arm around the elderly nun.

'Yes, leave her alone!' commanded Maud imperiously.

'Be quiet, you old bat!'

'Charming!' said Maud huffily.

'Come here Mum.' Synth pulled her near.

Eleanor placed herself between the leatherjackets and her aunt and turned to face the intruders.

'Whatever you've come here for can have nothing to do with the nuns. Please let Reverend Mother and Mrs. Hunt go and sit down quietly. They are not so young and you are upsetting them dreadfully.'

'Shut up!' She received a shove that sent her reeling against the entrance hall's oak panelling.

'What's in there?'

'The parlour,' Eleanor said, massaging her painful arm.

'Open the door!'

The room was at the front of the house, its double bay windows overlooking the gravel drive. Furnished in dark brown, it would have been depressing, had it not been for the white walls, beautiful tapestries and vibrant paintings that hung from the picture rails. A small niche on the far wall contained a statue of the Virgin Mary and a vase of lilies. The shining surface of a large, oval table, reflected sunlight into a pool of gold on the embossed ceiling. In its day, it had been a very gracious room and it still retained a hint of what it had once been.

'Sit down there!' The leader gestured towards the table.

'Come on Reverend Mother,' Eleanor said shakily. 'Mrs. Hunt, please come and sit here.' She shepherded the two older women to the chairs on the other side of the table, as far away from the intruders as possible. Eleanor and Synth arranged themselves either side of the elderly ladies like sentinels. Brecht was shoved onto a button-back sofa under the window by one of the other leatherjackets. The leader thumped the table, causing a pot of African Violets to jump on the spot. The ladies jerked with fright. He leaned menacingly towards them.

'Where is she?'

'To whom are you referring?' asked Reverend Mother quietly.

'That girl. Anna Divrej. We know she's mixed up with that pig over there.' He waved his hand towards Brecht.

'She no-a here. Honestly. I tell-a you. I come-a here to bring the tall lady. Is true-a, yes?'

Eleanor nodded her head. 'It's true. He drove me here in his taxi.' Then to her aunt, 'Which girl?'

'Nobody asked you. Shut your mouth!'

Eleanor blanched.

Maud turned to Reverend Mother and said in a matter of fact voice, 'Do you think we might have some more cake?'

'Shhh Mum,' Synth hissed, and squeezed her arm.

'I don't like him,' said Maud loudly, pointing. 'He reminds me of the boss of the orphanage. He was a bully.'

'Be quiet, you old hag!'

'Really, I must protest…'

Eleanor was cut short as the leader pulled her to her feet and dragged her backwards, his arm around her throat as he brandished his weapon with the other hand.

'Tell me where she is, or Miss Po-face here is going to be taken outside.'

'Oh no. Please, don't hurt her!' Reverend Mother tried to stand up but Synth reached across and restrained the nun. Eleanor hung onto the man's arm with both hands, trying to prise it away from her neck. He shook her roughly.

'Hold still!'

AIRSHOW ILEX

Eleanor looked terrified.

'Tell me where the girl is or this one is going for a walk with one of my friends here. I'm counting to three.'

Everybody remained absolutely still.

'One!' Nobody spoke or moved.

'Two!' Silence.

'Three! OK, take her outside!' He shoved Eleanor across to one of his gang who started to pull the sobbing woman towards the door.

'Stop!' shouted Maud. 'I know where that girl is, if you mean the one that doesn't talk.'

'Really?' said the leader. 'So where might she be?' Eleanor stood, terrified, her arms pinioned behind her back, shaking.

'She not-a here!' shouted Brecht. He received a kick on the shin for his trouble.

'She's up in her room,' Maud said, pointing at the ceiling.

'Where's that?'

'It's upstairs, above here.'

'Go get her!' he commanded. Eleanor's captor pushed her away and his footsteps could be heard clattering across the parquet hall and thundering up the wooden stairs.

Maud shouted out, 'They're coming for you!' at the ceiling and started banging the plant pot up and down urgently on the polished table.

'Keep that old boot quiet or she'll be for the long walk.'

Synth wrestled Maud into silence. 'Mum, you're going to get us all killed. Please be quiet.'

Sister Catherine had stood behind the thick, brown, velvet curtain where the nuns' cloaks hung. She had held her breath as the group had gone past, only inches away. She could hear them in the parlour, raised voices, Eleanor sobbing, men shouting. She had come out of hiding and tip-toed across the hall, creeping up the stairs, hoping they wouldn't creak, until she turned right and went into Reverend Mother's study. She was barely in there, when she'd heard the man thumping up the stairs and making for the sleeping cells along the other corridor. She closed the door gently behind her and went to the telephone but she dared not lift the receiver because she could hear the intruder crashing doors and thumping about, thundering along the passageway.

His thudding footsteps approached the door so Sister Catherine crouched down behind the desk, making herself as small as her aching knees would allow. The handle was rattled and the door flew open and banged against the wall. She held her breath. The man grunted. There was a pause and then the footsteps faded away as their owner kicked open all the doors further along and then ran back the way he had come, clattering down the front stairs shouting loudly as he descended, 'She's not up here!'

Sister Catherine stayed on the floor for a moment. Who wasn't up here? They must be searching for the foreign woman on retreat, that Anna. She was clearly in danger. The nun got up painfully and tiptoed out of the room and towards the cells' corridor. All the rooms were empty, their doors standing open because the teaching Sisters were not yet back from the school and the novices were down in the basement kitchen starting preparations for the evening meal. The concealed door in the oak panelling in the upstairs corridor was closed. She pressed the centre of the wooden rose and the panel swung open and inwards to reveal the back staircase that had been used by servants in former times.

She went through and closed it gently behind her, clicking on the light and going slowly and quietly down the treads, clutching fearfully at the handrail, until she reached the ground floor back lobby next to the chapel, where a complimentary concealed door was cut into the panelling there too. She went quietly into the chapel. It was filled with the scent of lilies and the remains of incense from last evening's benediction.

'Anna,' she called softly. 'Are you in here? It's Sister Catherine.' She walked gingerly along the side aisle, looking down the rows of pews but the girl was nowhere to be seen. She heard a scuffle and looked up to see a frightened face peering over the top of the pulpit.

I'm here, Sister. Please-a help-a me.'

AIRSHOW ILEX

Back in the parlour, the trembling Eleanor was again seated at the table with the other women. The marauder had returned from his fruitless search of the upstairs rooms and was muttering something to the leader who then turned to Eleanor and said 'You. Do you know your way around this place?'

She nodded. 'I... I... was here as a child. It used to be a boarding school...' she mumbled and bit her lower lip, looking down at her lap,.

'So you have been unanimously elected to be our guide. On your feet again.'

'I need to wee,' announced Maud. Nobody took any notice so she said it louder.

'My mother needs the toilet,' Synth said.

'Tough!' replied the leader, turning his attention to Eleanor again.

Reverend Mother spoke up. 'This lady has a medical condition. I insist that she is allowed to use the bathroom. How can you be so heartless?'

'Be quiet, woman!' He looked at Eleanor. 'Show us where the girl might be. Come over here. Now!'

Without a backwards glance, the leader and his friend went out of the room, pushing Eleanor before them. The other two stood motionless, their expressionless helmet masks nightmarish in the warm afternoon room.

'This is the guest suite, where Mrs. Hunt and her daughter are staying.' The intruders pushed their way past her and inspected the bedroom with its neat twin beds, the modern bathroom, the little kitchen and the comfortable sitting room with its *Spathyphylum* burgeoning on the window-ledge and a cat on one of the beds.

'This is the library.' The men paced quickly around the free-standing, tall bookcases, threw open the stationery cupboard, and kicked the desk.

'This is the cloaks niche.' They ripped down the nuns' dark cloaks.

'This is the seminar room.' They looked into the big cupboard and pushed over the blackboard easel.

'Is this all?'

'The chapel is through there at the end of the corridor. Please don't go in the chapel.'

They went along and straight in.

Sister Catherine was kneeling in prayer in the third row from the front on the left-hand side. She turned as the trio came in.

'Why, Miss Eleanor. How nice to see you and who are these gentlemen with you?'

If she was spooked by the mirror-finish masks she didn't show it. If they thought it odd that she wasn't scared, they didn't seem to notice.

'Where's the girl?' the leader asked.

'Which girl?'

'Don't play games, lady. The one who's staying here.'

'Oh her. She went.'

'Where?'

'To catch her plane home.'

'Today?'

'Yesterday. She's long gone. Now, please forgive me, I am in the middle of a decade,' and she held up her rosary and turned away, closing her eyes as if the men weren't there.

The leader stormed over to the confessional and ripped back the curtain. Empty. He walked into the sacristy and Eleanor could hear him opening cupboards. Then he came back, climbed the shallow steps and walked all around the altar, his stag beetle-like appearance strangely incongruous against the beautiful, engraved candlesticks on either side of the tabernacle. Next, he went to the pulpit and looked. The girl clearly wasn't in the chapel. He jerked his head to his friend and beckoned Eleanor who meekly went with them out into the corridor.

'What's down those stairs?'

'The kitchen and scullery in the basement and some store rooms.'

The Filipino novices were busy preparing vegetables and making pastry at the big, scrubbed kitchen table when the men walked in. The young, student nuns let out loud squeals and fled towards the back door.

'Stop!' shouted the leader, waving his gun.

The novices clung to one another in terror.

'Where's the girl?'

'We not speak good English,' said one. 'What is word?'

'Girl. Where's the girl?'

'We not know girl. Please. Go.'

One of the intruders opened the larder and peered in the pantry and still room. Eleanor gave the girls a hard, warning look. The man swept his hand along a shelf, causing jars of preserves to shatter in a smell of vinegar on the stone floor. Then he kicked a kitchen chair and broke it before they left, taking Eleanor with them, back up to the parlour where they pushed her in roughly through the doorway.

Reverend Mother said, 'Oh Eleanor.'

She replied 'I'm alright. Don't worry,' and, white-faced, went to take her place beside the old nun, Synth and Maud at the table.

'You're a load of bullies,' said Maud, with a clenched fist stabbing the air defiantly. 'Yes you are. Nothing but big bullies.' With that she picked up the pot of African violets and hurled it at the leader. He saw it coming though and dodged to the side. It hit the wall and disintegrated on the carpet.

'Shut up! All of you!' He snapped, storming over towards Maud and thumping his black-gloved hand down on the shiny surface as he leaned across the table threateningly towards her.

'Go on! Hit me! Hit a poor old woman!'

Synth put her arms around her mother and pulled her towards her protectively.

'She doesn't mean it. She's... she's...'

The leatherjacket stood menacingly, looking down at the row of frightened women, then turned on his heels and grabbed Brecht from the sofa and hauled him to his feet.

'Outside, you!'

'Where-a you take-a me? I know nudding. I just taxi driver from Former Kridiblikt Republic.'

Then, as quickly as the raid had begun, it was over. The leatherjackets, shoving Brecht before them, strode out of the convent and into their four by four with darkened windows. They pushed the gibbering cab driver into the back seat, slammed the doors loudly and drove off at speed.

Everybody sat as if frozen to their chairs in the parlour, afraid that the men might come back. A sound in the hall alerted all four women and they stiffened with terror.

'I've shut the front door,' said Sister Catherine. 'Shall I go and put the kettle on, Reverend Mother?'

Chapter 20

Wednesday 22nd June
Morning

'Impressive, yes?' Celeste said into the telephone receiver, a look of smug satisfaction on her face. There was a knock at her office door. 'Come in,' she called, hand over the mouthpiece. 'Glad you liked it. I have to go. We'll talk later.' She hung up. 'Good morning Roland. I've got your list here. You'll love it this afternoon.'
Roland came over, placed his camera down and perched himself carefully on the edge of her desk. 'Oh?'

'Acrobatic dancers on aircraft wings... a sort of *'Flying down to Somewhere'* type thing.'

'Whose brainchild was that? Some Hollywood spin-off company trying to revive the craft of nearly killing yourself in a glamorous outfit?'

'Don't ask me. We've got to keep entertaining the troops.' She shuffled some papers and put them in her drawer. 'Did you see the runway this morning?'

'What? The protesters' slogan?'

'It was there first thing. Must have happened during the night.'

Roland plunged his hands in his pockets and tutted, 'We want wind farms!' Then he shook his head bemused. 'I took some shots of it from the control tower. How the heck are they going to get that fluorescent orange paint off the runway?'

'You can see the men are out there now but it's dried on and they don't want to use solvents in case it messes up the surface.'

'Yes, I took shots of them hosing and scrubbing away. It's not going to make a very good impression on the trade visitors.'

'I agree. I think we'll just have to paint it out tonight.' She paused. 'Is there anything else I can do for you? I'm trying to finalise the plans for tomorrow... Youth Day. I dread it. The notes from last year's effort look as if it was a shambles.'

'Of course you weren't here then, were you?' Roland said, perching on the edge of the desk. 'Yes, I'd go along with that description. The monsters were everywhere, sweaty hands all over these plate glass windows, drinks cans kicked along the corridor, snogging in the darkened lecture rooms... don't remind me!'

'Well, there's supposed to be better supervision this time.'

'Good luck with it,' Roland said, getting up, taking his camera and slinging the strap over his shoulder. 'I'll be back later.' He made for the door and then hesitated to snap his fingers. 'I know what I meant to ask you... what's happened to old Gig?'

'No idea. Personnel sent somebody round to his house because he wasn't answering the phone. I think the police forced an entry and he wasn't there.'

'You should have got Eleanor Framp to do it.'

Celeste shot him a glare.

'Oh,' he said. 'I forgot that you two don't see eye to eye.'

'Don't speak to me about that woman. She's been a thorn in my flesh from the start.'

'She's well connected though. It mightn't be a good idea to cross her.' He raised his eyebrows. 'I'd better get on. There are some models posing by the new East European Conglomerate stand.'

'You'll enjoy that,' she said straight-faced.

'What? Hairy legs and chins and farm girl ankles? I doubt it. See you.'

'That's rich, coming from the most undesirable man on the airfield.'

He pulled a face at her, went out, shut the door behind him and made for the snack bar. Neither of them had mentioned Celeste's touchiness the other day. He ambled across the relaxation area.

'Black coffee and a filled bagel,' he said, settling onto one of the high-back stools. The 'sloosh' of the machine was loud in the silence of the Press Centre relaxation area. It was still early. A few people were drifting in to pick up their mail, gather new brochures, collect the afternoon flying list and see what was on the notice board. He looked around while he waited and caught sight of Debbie making her way to the reception desk.

AIRSHOW ILEX

'Morning, Debbie,' he called across. 'Going to come and join me?'

She shook her head and started talking to the receptionist. The girl made a note and smiled. Debbie started to walk back the way she had come. Roland got up and went after her.

'Sir,' you haven't paid...'

He waved an arm at the snack-bar server and said, 'I'm coming back.'

Debbie clearly didn't want to be waylaid.

'What's the matter?'

'I'm busy today, Roland. I'm giving a talk to some people this morning about women in flying and then we're on early this afternoon.' He held her elbow but she jerked it away.

'Debbie. Have you thought about what I said? Come back to my place tonight. The landlady's out at bingo on Wednesday evenings.'

'I don't know how I stand the glamour of it all,' she said a trifle sarcastically. 'Anyway, I'm no use to you tonight. I've got my days.' Then she strode off. He threw up his hands in exasperation, the camera swinging wildly on its strap in sympathy. He turned and went back angrily to his bagel.

*

Mid-morning found Reverend Mother and Sister Catherine sitting in the conservatory, the latter carefully painting a gold border onto the plaque of St. Bede.

'We really should have summoned the police yesterday, Reverend Mother,' she said, interrupting her Superior's reading for the day.

Reverend Mother looked up at her sharply and let the book drop into her lap. 'They said they knew where Eleanor lived.'

'Nasty men... in those horrid helmets and visors. They quite gave me palpitations, I can tell you... and rampaging around our lovely chapel like that...'

'It must have been very distressing for you, Sister. Well done for keeping your calm.'

'Well, if I hadn't, they would have found her.'

'Inside the altar. What a good idea.'

'Yes. It didn't occur to them that it might be hollow. The sliding door at the front was nicely covered by the altar cloth. I only just got her in there in time, you know. There's not much room, what with all the candles and boxes of incense but there was enough air to keep her going until they marched out. Miss Eleanor looked petrified. She was with them, you know.'

'Yes. She told me all about it last night... which reminds me... she's coming over again later. You know, when they went down into the kitchen and frightened the life out of the Filipino novices, they broke some jars of pickled beetroot. What a waste!'

Sister Catherine looked up from her work. 'Do you think they'll come back?'

'I hope not. They went all over the place and seemed satisfied that Anna wasn't here.' She paused. 'By the way, Sister, have you been to confession yet?'

The other nun flashed a supressed smile at Reverend Mother. 'I'll go this evening. It was a bit naughty of me, wasn't it?'

'Disgraceful.' She snapped the book shut and then added, 'but very quick thinking. Goodness knows what they would have done to the poor girl if they had found her.' She gazed out of the conservatory window. 'I wonder why they were so angry with her? Brecht said she had outstayed her work permit but I think their behaviour was rather extreme.'

'Where is she now?'

'She went to school with the teaching sisters in the coach. She's sitting in the library there. Brecht says they have to find a way to get out of the country. I'm a little cross with him for bringing all this to our door.'

'Anna's a very frightened young lady.'

'Yes, she is.'

Reverend Mother looked admiringly at Sister Catherine's artwork. 'That's coming along very nicely. Such talent!' Her gaze ran along the shelves above. 'You have plenty for the sale.'

'Well, it all helps, doesn't it?' She reached down beside her and picked a small box from the floor.

AIRSHOW ILEX

'I've been meaning to show you my modern rosaries,' she said, taking one out and holding it up.

'Goodness! That is *avant-garde!*'

'We have to move with the times, Reverend Mother. The young people aren't content with miserable black or brown beads. They like these mock crystal ones and I've got some more here...' She rummaged in the box and unwrapped tissue paper. '...that are really jazzy.' She displayed a psychedelic concoction. 'I observed that some young ladies at church are painting little designs on their finger nails, so I had a good look and 'borrowed' the idea. It works well, don't you think?'

'Sister Catherine, your creativity knows no bounds, as does your marketing sense. I rely on your good judgement.' She stood up to go. 'I'd better look in on Mrs. Hunt. She was really shaken up yesterday.' She leaned sideways conspiratorially. 'I think that dining chair she was sitting on is beyond salvation.'

*

Debbie rubbed some more sunscreen over her arms and then lay back on the thick towel that covered the lounger on the deck of the *Lucky Lady*. The craft bobbed about gently in the noonday heat. The canopy was raised, at Grant's insistence, but the light still filtered through. He came up from the galley.

'Here we are. Lime juice with ice. Nothing more refreshing.'

She sat up again and stretched out a lazy arm to take the tall, chilled glass that sparkled with frosting and took a sip.

'Delicious,' she said.

'You can't beat it.' He sat down on a foldaway chair and tasted his drink. She surveyed his bronzed torso above the white shorts. For an older man he was in good shape. The ever-present Stetson was in place and he wore designer shades. She looked down at his feet. They were big. She tried to hide a smile of approval. She knew about men with big feet.

'What are you grinning about?'

'Nothing. I wasn't grinning.'

'Oh yes you were!'

His charming American accent enchanted her. 'Tell me or you'll get more than a taste of this.' He raised his glass menacingly and tilted it above her bare shoulder.

'OK. I give in. You have nice feet.'

He looked down at them. 'They're just regulation feet. Usual number of toes. Nothin' special. I don't believe you.'

'No. Really. I was admiring your feet.'

'Come on!' he laughed reprovingly.

'Truly.'

'Why my feet? Do you have a foot fixation or something?'

She looked coyly at him. 'Women know about men's feet.'

He looked puzzled and inspected his toes.

'I sure don't know what you mean, so tell or I shall lay awake worrying about them.'

She took a gulp from the glass and put it on the small table beside her.

'Well,' she hesitated, 'nature tends to...'

'What?'

'Match.'

'Match what?'

'Men's feet and...' She nodded meaningfully.

The penny dropped.

'Aw my gosh! You really are somethin'.' He shook his head and laughed in disbelief. She joined in and the pair of them shared a moment of conspiratorial mirth.

'Say,' he said, 'is the sun too warm for you on deck? I can move the boat under those overhanging trees if you'd like.'

'Did you say you had air-conditioning in the cabin?'

'Sure do. Wanna go down for a bit?'

'Would you care to re-phrase that?' she asked archly.

'You are one very naughty lady,' he said. 'I just thought you might like to cool off for a while. We can watch a video or play some music. It's home from home in the saloon.' He held out his hand. 'Come on. Let's take our drinks down below. We've still got a lot to talk about.'

*

AIRSHOW ILEX

Roland scanned the waiting area on the other side of Phillipstone airshow. Debbie had said they were going up early this afternoon. From his vantage point on the Press Centre balcony, the grass shimmered and reflected sunlight glinted off every metal or glass surface on the outside displays. The *ILEX* looked as if it was melting into tar, its glassy surface positively shining like black toffee as the mirage hovered above it. He took the afternoon flying programme out of the pocket of his striped trousers, scrutinised it and put it away again. The *Pink Perils* were due up fourth, after one of the leisure trainers and the *Flying down to Somewhere* plane and one other had done its stuff. There were a few stringers leaning over the rail, hands clasped in anticipation, armpits stained with perspiration. He set up the tripod. Eleanor came to his side.

'Hot enough for you?'

'Scorching and exhausting,' he replied, taking the lens cover off and turning to give her a smile. He had his baseball cap on backwards.

She was wearing a lilac check, cotton sun-hat over her straight, grey bobbed hair.

'Love the hat,' he said flippantly.

'Do you really? I got it in the market.'

'The colours suit you.'

'Why, thank-you Roland. How very nice of you to say so.'

'We photographers are artists,' he said. 'We know about colour.'

The trade days' visitors started to troop up the fire exit staircase and pile in behind them.

'Here come the hordes again,' she said. 'Where on Earth is Gig?'

'Somebody said he was off ill. His deputy should be here though.' She looked around. Not a security guard in sight. The crush got worse. Somebody shoved Roland in the back. He responded angrily.

'Give me a break. I'm trying to work here. It's not a jolly day out for some of us.'

'Sorry. Sorry. Somebody pushed me.'

Roland turned away and zoomed in on the waiting area. Yes, Debbie's *Pink Perils* were snaking along. He panned, looking for her sign on the side of the planes. Six aircraft were there. *Circle, Triangle, Diamond* and so on but no *Heart*. Was she OK? The lead was being taken by *Circle*. He took his mobile phone out and speed-dialled her number. It was on voicemail.

From the east a low droning gradually increased in volume. Perhaps the show was starting early. A buzz of excitement spread around the balcony and was taken up by the crowds next to the runway, grandstand and those standing on the concourse as their eyes turned upwards to scan the dazzling blue sky. The small, yellow aircraft was trailing a banner reading 'NO TO WINDFARM.' Then, as they watched, myriad yellow leaflets were released and fluttered down like brimstone butterflies, peppering the airfield in a paper-chase, pursued by breezy eddies, slamming against the static aircraft, flying in the faces of the golf-buggy drivers and coming to rest in the hands of the astounded watchers. Roland zoomed in on the offending aircraft and saw that it was a stunt-plane, obviously hired for the occasion. Celeste watched from her office window.

'Well,' said Eleanor. 'That's a turn-up for the books.'

'Do you know something?' asked Roland, squinting through the view-finder.

'My lips are sealed,' she said. 'Just wait until the *Saturnian* comes out later this afternoon.' and she pursed her mouth firmly.

'We didn't get any leaflets up on here,' Roland said. 'Probably just 'No to Windfarm' again.'

The little yellow plane droned off into the distance, its slow-motion raid safely accomplished. The airshow commentator took up the baton.

'Good afternoon ladies and gentlemen. We apologise for that unexpected interruption. Please make yourselves comfortable for the Phillipstone Airshow daily display. Now, if you look over beyond the control tower, you will see the Strimper two-seater trainer approaching...'

AIRSHOW ILEX

The commentary was underway and the afternoon rolled on.

'That looks rather obscene,' observed Eleanor gazing up distastefully but fascinated as the huge *Drock-Nater* air-to-air refueller passed across their view, trailing its penis-style refuelling hose like some randy airborne whale. Roland shot her a sideways grin and said, 'It's enough to make a man jealous.'

'Really Roland!' she replied outraged.

'Sorry. No offence meant.'

'None taken,' she said crisply and paused. 'But I could see what you mean.' She stifled a girlish giggle. He chuckled, then said, 'Hey! Look! Here come the *'Flying Down to Somewhere'* look-a-likes.'

Sure enough, a low-cruising, loudly droning *Plinger* sauntered across the sky, heaving with girlish glamour. Feet firmly strapped down to the wings, four nubile lovelies in silver swim-suits and cloche hats dripping with sequins, sparkled as they gyrated in a series of movements that drew a roar from the crowds below. Roland was loving it and took burst after burst of shots.

'Your film will run out in a minute,' Eleanor remarked.

'It's digital, remember? He corrected her. She nodded wisely in agreement. 'Yes. Of course.'

'Don't miss this!' He said, pointing upwards. Two of the acrobats had unfastened their foot straps and had climbed down to hang by their teeth, spinning like tops under each wing.

'A tribute to our NHS dentistry,' Eleanor said.

'As long as it's their own teeth and not dentures,' he laughed back at her. '*Gummy-grip* was never so important.'

More and more trade day visitors were climbing the fire escape staircase to the balcony, pushing and shoving, jostling for the best view of the nineteen-twenties style airborne lovelies.

'Where's security when you need them?' Roland asked grimly, sticking his elbows out to maintain his space. 'Hey, stop waving your hand about in the middle of my picture!' He protested angrily at a massive man in a broad check, tan suit.

'Sorry old chap.'

'Don't you 'old chap' me. Have you got a pass for the Press Centre balcony?'

The visitor held up his palms dismissively. Eleanor pitched in, unable to contain her colleague-supporting anger. 'Can't you see that this photographer is a professional and you are interrupting his work? If you haven't got a pass, I'm calling security to have you removed.'

'We'll see,' said the man, making for the interior lounge area.

The sparkling, silver-clad acrobats swung back to their places on top of the wings, helped up by willing hands.

'Now,' said the commentator, *'for your entertainment, the Plinger will perform a centrifugal, horizontal loop. Hold on tightly ladies!'* With that, the biplane gathered speed and climbed steadily towards the west, the crowd gasping with dismay as the acrobats clung to their safety bars until the aircraft was on its side, inscribing a vast invisible curve against the cerulean sky. Then, as one, the girls all let go and hung upside down, arms thrown wide, entirely dependent on the grip of their foot and ankle clamps.

'What a way to earn a living,' Eleanor said.

'I hope it doesn't go to their heads,' Roland smirked as the *Plinger* regained equilibrium and cruised past, its glittering passengers climbing back into position, waving enthusiastically at the cheering crowds below.

'May I have a word please, Miss Framp?'

Eleanor turned to see Celeste Blagden, face like thunder.

'I'd like to introduce you to Lord Jolian St.John-Fawcett-Blythe, deputy chair of the Phillipstone Airshow board,' she said. 'I understand that you insulted him just now.'

The big man in the check suit stood pompously beside her. Eleanor was quick to see the danger in the situation. She could be told to leave, making reporting on tomorrow's Youth Day impossible, and she was commissioned to do that.

'Why, Lord Jolian,' said Eleanor, mustering up all the charm that the stickily hot afternoon permitted. 'I didn't realise it was you. Do forgive me. I think we actually met about ten years ago when I interviewed you about fox hunting. Do you recall?' She ploughed on. 'You are looking so much more well, nowadays.' She looked with feigned approbation at his massive girth, tiers of chins and podgy fingers clutching the programme. She continued. 'We've had such a lot of trouble with interlopers on the Press Centre balcony that we are all getting a little tetchy about it, aren't we Mr. Dilger?'

Roland turned and said flatly, 'Yes,' then returned to his viewfinder. Celeste glared up at Eleanor who glared back.

'Miss Framp, I have warned you before about challenging the visitors to this balcony. You do not know who they are or how important…'

Out of the corner of her eye, Eleanor saw Lord Jolian swell with pride, his ginger moustache vibrating with the timbre of his nasal intake of air.

'And what is more,' Celeste added 'if you presume to talk to any other visitors to this balcony, Miss Framp, it is you who will be removed by security. Do I make myself clear?'

'Yes, you do, Miss Blagden. I apologise most sincerely and it won't happen again.'

Celeste was in her stride now. 'What is more, I must ask you not to stand here near the front of the balcony because that is only giving you another opportunity to challenge people coming up.'

'I prefer to stand here. The view is better.'

'I am asking you to move.'

'I have given you my word that I won't ask anybody else for their passes. Now, can we end this conversation please? You have made your point.'

'Don't let it happen again,' Celeste said, turning her back on Eleanor. 'Now, Lord Jolian, how about a nice cup of tea in my private office?'

Then she linked her arm into his and steered him like a ship through the melêe.

Roland turned to Eleanor. 'You were magnificent. I'd have floored the woman.'

'Oh,' she said. 'I've been insulted by better people than her. Besides,' she added, tapping the side of her nose knowingly, 'as we speak, Lord Grope-Worthy will be chasing her around the desk.'

Chapter 21

Wednesday 22nd June
Late Afternoon

Paula draped one elegant leg over the other and tapped the pointed toe of her court shoe impatiently in the air. She had plans for a busy evening ahead and could have done without this interview with the Press Centre Controller at the end of the hot Wednesday afternoon. Celeste Blagden shuffled through the menus and accounts sheets, spreading them out on her desk. The air conditioning struggled loudly.

'Mmmm,' she said, poring over them. 'You've done well, Paula.'

'Thank you.' Paula patted her bouffant, blonde hair and blinked rapidly, her long, black lashes batting the air like dragonfly wings.

'I see the lemon chicken flew out of the kitchen.'

Paula half-smiled at the weak joke. 'Hot weather. Refreshing.'

'...and the salads.'

'Ditto.'

Celeste looked up. 'There are only four more days to go and I can see that you have prepared varied menus for the remaining time.'

'Yes. So what did you want to see me for?' Paula asked nonchalantly.

'We need to discuss the catering arrangements for Sunday's important guest.'

'They are all in hand. Special security came up to see me after luncheon service. They're taking the visitor for a trip on the *ILEX*... something about a barbecue before they go?'

'Yes. We thought it would be a good photo opportunity to put up an open-sided marquee over by the take-off waiting area. They're moving the *ILEX* over earlier and we can get some groups enjoying the barbecue with the plane in the background.'

AIRSHOW ILEX

'Won't it be a bit noisy with all the display aircraft taking off and landing?'

'No. It'll all be over. With the public days only being Saturday and Sunday, they aren't going to fly the *ILEX* for the masses on the last day. They're keeping it for the visitor at the end of Sunday afternoon before it goes on a long-haul test flight to the U.S. and then Australia.'

'So what time do you want them to eat?'

'Maintenance will put up the big green and white striped marquee overnight, together with a smaller white one for your catering purposes. Let's say, seven o'clock?'

Paula took a notepad and pen from the jacket pocket of her pastel pink two-piece suit.

'What about the barbecues? Charcoal or gas?'

'Whichever is more convenient for you. Tell Airshow Services.'

'Gas would be more reliable.'

'Fine.'

'How many people?'

Celeste looked at her screen.

'You'll have to be a bit flexible, I'm afraid, but there will be six in the visitor's party, plus Lord Jolian St.John-Fawcett-Blythe, representing Phillipstone Airshow board, the *ILEX* pilot, half a dozen of the airshow brass and my good-self, of course. Special security will be in operation from our side and the visitor will have his own bodyguards. I believe there will be about ten of them, but they won't be eating. So that's fifteen needing feeding but allow for twenty just in case.'

'Seated or standing?'

'Seated in the marquee... plush chairs, white cloths, floral arrangements and a string quartet.'

Paula scribbled away. 'I'll also need a fridge over there.'

'Again, tell Services. They'll see to it all.' She slowly swung her cream leather executive chair around to face Paula. 'So, what are you going to give them?'

'Well, as there are no special dietary needs, I'm going for barbecued king prawns with a variety of side-dressings, freshly baked garlic bread, cold collation of meats, smoked salmon and salads, followed by fresh fruit in own juice jelly with cream or a choice of mini-trifles and cheesecakes.'

Celeste felt a wave of nausea sweep over her at the thought of all that food.

'Are you OK?' Paula asked huskily. 'You've gone pale.'

'The heat. It doesn't suit me.' She took a deep breath. 'I think that's all. I leave it to you. Thank you Paula.' She swung her chair back towards the monitor and started tapping away.

Paula said, 'OK. I'll be going then,' and left, feeling slighted.

*

'Here kitty, kitty.' Maud crouched down awkwardly and twiddled her fingers, enticing the cat towards her. It looked in a bad way, tail blackened and whiskers shrivelled. 'It's all right my darling,' she cooed. 'Look, I've got something nice for you.' With head down, the bedraggled moggie padded slowly towards her, and sniffed delicately at the proffered saucer of sardines. It looked up nervously. 'Go on. They're for you.' It tucked in and the purring started.

Reverend Mother came out via the conservatory door.

'Mrs. Hunt...'

Maud turned her head and staggered as she got up, putting her finger to her lips.

'Oh, I see,' said the nun smiling. 'Another one come home to roost.'

'They know where their Mummy is,' Maud said with a satisfied smirk.

'So how many does that make now?'

'I believe twelve of them have found me, your Reverendship.'

'The stable's getting a bit full, you know.'

'Well, they have to sleep somewhere.'

'They cost money to feed, Mrs. Hunt.'

'My rescue pussies need looking after. I hope you're not suggesting I get rid of them?' She gave a haughty sniff and looked away.

AIRSHOW ILEX

The stray scoffed the meal urgently and then sat down and gazed up at Maud.

'Just look at her little face.'

'Yes, a very pretty cat... when its fur grows back.'

'She's been *traumaticised*, haven't you my sweet?'

'Mioaw.'

'Ah, bless her little heart.' Maud bent over rather creakily to stroke the cat.

A car door slammed. The cat jumped and ran into the bushes at the edge of the lawn. Women's voices grew louder as Sister Catherine came around the corner of the convent accompanied by a small, sun-tanned woman with short, dark hair streaked with grey.

'Ah, Mrs. Upton. How good of you to come.' Sister Catherine melted away into the conservatory. The visitor smiled toothily and put down her heavy bag as she shook hands.

'Very pleased to help, Reverend Mother.'

The nun leaned towards her and said confidentially, 'This is the lady I was telling you about.'

'Why are you whispering?' demanded Maud. 'Has she come to take me to an old people's home?'

The little lady gave a girlish laugh and stepped forward to shake hands with her accuser.

'No. Nothing like that. I'm Mrs. Upton from Phillipstone Animal Rescue.'

'Well!' Exclaimed Maud. 'I never thought a nunship could be so deceitful!'

Reverend Mother hastened to intervene. 'You've got the wrong end of the stick, Mrs. Hunt. This kind lady has come to help you with the cats, haven't you Mrs. Upton?'

'Oh yes, indeed.'

'Shall we go into the conservatory and tell Mrs. Hunt what we have in mind?'

Maud looked suspiciously at the other two women.

'It's a trick. You're going to put a bag over my head and take me away.'

The little lady held up her hands.

'No head bag. Just lots of tins of cat food.' She picked up the hold-all and shook it.

'Shall we go inside?' said Reverend Mother. Maud followed them in reluctantly.

*

'Well, I must say you did me proud, Miss Framp.' Grant Landscar waved the *Saturnian* at Eleanor as the pair of them sat out on his terrace, cold drinks at their elbow, in the comparative cool of the evening.

'Just doing my job, Mr. Landscar, but thank you anyway.' She sipped her lime-juice gratefully.

'How on earth did you manage to get that on the front page?' He asked in his charming American drawl, dropping the paper on the coffee table.

'Oh, when one has been in the business as long as I have, one has, shall we say, connections?'

'You took the picture yourself.'

'Yes, on my little *Brownset* digital camera.'

'What a brilliant ploy!'

'Oh, just a little luck, I think.'

'You know, she spent this afternoon with me on my boat. I had no idea …' and he collapsed with laughter.

'Well,' said Eleanor, starting to get up and firmly believing that something was going on between Grant and Debbie and she ought to be on her way. 'It's been a long day…'

'Oh please don't go, Miss Framp… Eleanor. I assure you there's nothing of any importance between Debbie Foxon and myself. She's giving up flying and wants me to go into partnership with her to open an hotel in the Balearics'

'Oh, I see.' Eleanor settled down again. 'Very well, Mr. Landscar. I could stay a little longer.'

'You must call me Grant.'

'If you insist.'

'I do.'

Eleanor sank back into her comfortable lounger. Again the scent of roses was heavy in the air. Some late goldfinches were

AIRSHOW ILEX

feeding from a seed container in the apple tree nearby. The garden was subtly floodlit.

'It's idyllic here,' she sighed.

'You are more than welcome to visit me as often as you please... Eleanor.'

He looked at her flushed face, the crepe floral dress with the nineteen-forties neckline, the lisle stockings and the heavy sandals.

'Eleanor, do you mind if I ask you something?'

She shrugged.

'Tell me about your life. How did you get to this point?'

'Oh, I'm not very interesting. Really.'

'Just humour me.'

'Very well. My parents died in a jeep crash in Africa when I was nine. So I was brought up by my mother's sister, my aunt, Reverend Mother Veronica at St. Bede's. It used to be a boarding school. My aunt's a very kind woman and has been extremely good to me, within the limits of her calling. My parents left some money so my education and keep weren't a drain on the order.'

'That's very sad. I'm sorry you lost your parents.' He paused. 'Well, I suppose you had the company of the other pupils in term-time, but what did you do in the holidays?'

'I mostly hung around the convent, helping out, but sometimes I'd be invited to stay for a while with one of my friends. That was nice, to be in a proper, family home.'

'Poor Eleanor.'

'There's no need to patronise me,' she retorted gently.

'Sorry.'

'It wasn't so bad. I always had my writing.'

'When did that start?'

'It was always there. I've got a room-full of files and boxes of it. Nothing creative published but lots of factual stuff, especially since I've worked for the papers.'

'I thought you wrote for the *Saturnian*.'

'Oh no. That's comparatively recent... only about ten years.'

Her grey-green eyes looked candidly into his with a hint of pride.

'I used to be a correspondent in high places for one of the broadsheets.'

'A woman of great talent.'

'I don't think so but I scrape a living.'

'You have a place of your own?'

'Yes, a little flat in Isabel Avenue. It's quite pleasant there and I have space for my hobby.'

'Ah, the fabled embroidery...'

'I do have a quite a large collection. I also like to do embroidery myself.'

'You must invite me over sometime to see it.'

'Oh... Grant... you wouldn't find it very interesting.'

'Let me be the judge of that.' He picked up the *Saturnian* again and waved it about triumphantly.

'First, I want to take you out to dinner to celebrate your digging me out of a hole. What a strategist! Not only do you get my withdrawal from the wind farm project downgraded to the second to last page in a minute square under the planning applications, but you engineer a stunning, diversional, front-page photograph which will have tongues wagging for weeks!'

Eleanor put her glass down and studied him carefully.

'Mr Landscar ... Grant ... I'm not the sort of woman who gets wined and dined. Men don't find me attractive and I've never been taken out to dinner *à deux* in my life.'

'It's time you were, then.'

'I don't even possess a pretty pair of shoes or anything in the way of an evening gown. As you can see, I dress for work, which is mostly my life.'

'Come with me.' He held out his hand.

She looked up at him and his kind, creased face. Something stirred in her that spoke of distant longings for a tall man who would take her by the hand and be kind to her, perhaps a substitute for the father she had lost.

'Come on,' he said again and went over and pulled her out of the chair.

The feel of a strong man's hand in hers and the power with which he had seemingly easily extracted her from her seat, sent

AIRSHOW ILEX

a kind of thrill through the middle-aged spinster's frame as he led her from the room.

Growing up in a convent hadn't been a great preparation for real life. Indeed, men were something to be feared. Dreadful things could happen to a girl who allowed herself to be led astray. The nuns had drummed home the purity message.

At the bottom of the huge, sweeping staircase that grew from its carved roots in the large marble hall and climbed ever upwards until it split into two balconies that ran all around the first floor landing, she hesitated.

'I don't think I should go up there,' she said.

'Why ever not?'

She looked embarrassed.

'What do you take me for Eleanor? Some kind of monster?"

'No. No.' She stepped away from him. 'I think I should go home now.'

His voice softened. 'Eleanor, Eleanor, there's a magic room up there that I know you will enjoy.'

'I told you I'm not worldly like those glamorous women you are used to.'

'Eleanor. Listen to me. I bought this house from a pop star. There is a wardrobe room upstairs full of his wife's beautiful clothes that they simply abandoned when they left. You have a good shape and I bet my bottom dollar that you could have real fun with a free shopping spree up there.'

She looked at him. 'You weren't going to try to...?' Her lower lip quivered.

He rolled his eyes in desperation. 'Look, you frightened little lamb, I'm going to go and sit out on the terrace and finish my juice. You go up those stairs, turn to the left and go along until you see the door marked 'wardrobe'. Don't you dare to come down until you've changed into a princess!'

Then he walked away, leaving her standing like a lost child at the door of a sweet shop.

He went back to the terrace and sat down, picking up the newspaper. Then he roared with laughter at the front page. It was a picture of Roland and Debbie, stark naked, on the roof of the Phillipstone Airport, their naughty bits covered by labels that said 'his' and 'hers'.

*

'Right guys,' said Paula. 'I've got the numbers for Sunday's visit by the 'Target'. Pay attention!'
Zelara leaned back on the caravan settee and picked at her fingernails. Marcus and Jack were having an elbow-nudging competition on the other side of the table.

'Are you lot listening?' Paula barked.

'Yes, yes,' Marcus said dismissively.

'Then concentrate!'

The boys stopped messing about and sat still.

'Now, we've had our rehearsal so here's the scenario. The Target is flying in to Phillipstone airfield on Saturday night. The main object of his visit is to place a very large *ILEX* order for his corrupt regime. *Amalgamated British Ilex* is keen to sell. There's talk of four hundred units at one hundred million dollars each with the possibility of more to follow.'

'So, what's that got to do with us then?' Jack asked sulkily, rather fed up that his evening of fun at the bothies had been interrupted.

'Everything. The whole purpose of setting up this little team of the four of us is, shall we say, to remove the 'Target' so he can't place the order.'

Jack said, 'A kidnapping?'

'Yes,' Paula replied, carefully avoiding Zelara's hard stare. 'There will be a lot of people around at the barbecue. It's being held on the grass next to the waiting area... you know, where the planes line up before take-off. The *ILEX* will be parked there ready to give our man a test flight. There'll be about sixteen security staff from both sides, various top brass, that snotty Celeste Blagden from the Press Centre and a few select photographers. Oh, and a four-piece band.'

Marcus put his elbows on the table and gave the matter in hand his full attention.

AIRSHOW ILEX

'So how are we going to do it Paula? There aren't many of us.' The leader peeled off her blonde wig to display short-cropped hair. Then she reached down into her sweater and pulled out two silicone breasts. She dumped them on the table. A dumbfounded moment from the boys was replaced by hysterical laughter.

'I told you she was a tranny,' Jack screamed, drumming his hands on the table in triumph.

Marcus sat, mouth slightly open, eyes popping. 'Why? Why dress up like that?' He queried, shaking his head in a mystified manner.

'I had to establish a strong alias.'

'You've been looking like a tart.'

'Enough!' interjected Zelara, still sweating in her fat suit, but the boys knew about that already. 'Think of it from Joe Public's point of view. Without our disguises, the tall, blonde, restaurant manager, and the short, fat, Caribbean cleaner, look like totally different people. Nobody would suspect that I worked for the secret service and that Paul ... but you'd better go on calling him Paula... is a highly decorated ex-commando.'

'There are still a lot of people to deal with though,' Marcus said doubtfully.

Paula reached into his trouser pocket and took out a sketch map of the marquee arrangements for the barbecue. He put it on the table and stabbed at it with his now strangely incongruous pink-varnished fingernail.

'There will be one large, open-fronted marquee with proper dining tables and full service staff from our very own *Clouds* restaurant. Next to it will be our kitchen marquee also with the front wall open. Within it will be a screened preparation area where we can stash dirty crocks et cetera. The barbecues and oven will be just outside. In front of their marquee will be a small dais with a microphone. We'll be serving a very nice seafood and general spread.'

'When do we take him?'

'When I accidentally tip a tray of puddings into his lap.'

'Then what?'

'Security will be all over us like a rash, but I'll have him hostage with a knife to his throat.'

'Then what do you do with him?'

'Drag him backwards towards our catering van parked there. Zelara will have the engine started and the side sliding door open. I'll throw us both in and away we go.'

'What about us?'

'What about you? You're just innocent cook-waiters. Nobody's going to suspect you of anything.'

'Then why do you need us on the gang at all?'

'To create a diversion.'

'You only need one of us to do that and what sort of a diversion anyway?'

'A fire. You have to start a kitchen fire in the cooking marquee. Pouring fat onto a hotplate should do it. I need the other to cue the rest of us via a radio link to our button ear-pieces so that we are fully co-ordinated.'

'Right,' said Marcus.

'We need split second timing. There'll be a code word for when the action must begin,' Paula said.

'When do we get that?' Jack asked.

'You can have it now. It's '*Airshow ILEX*'.'

'There's one other thing,' Paula said. 'We're going to blow up the *ILEX*.'

AIRSHOW ILEX

Chapter 22

Thursday 23rd June
Morning

Celeste Blagden glared up at Roland 'What on earth were you thinking of?' she raved, clasping the arms of her cream, executive chair.
He waved his hands vaguely in the air and looked pseudo-innocently at the Press Centre Office ceiling.
'Stark naked on the roof with some floozie.'
'She's not a floozie. We're almost engaged,' he muttered.
'That,' she said firmly, 'is beside the point. You have made a laughing stock of the entire airshow. They even had the photograph on the regional television news.' She slapped the local paper down on her desk with such force that the crack it emitted made Roland jump slightly but he said, 'It should certainly generate some fan-mail for me.'
'Don't be flippant, Roland. This is serious. I've had an email from above demanding that you make a public apology and then resign.'
'That's a bit extreme. It was a hot day.'
'This is an international airshow. Where's our credibility in the world aeronautical market now? I don't need this. You know it's the Youth Forum today, don't you?'
'I know. I've got to follow them about.'
'Within half an hour the entire site will be crawling with errant teenagers bent on a chewing, can-swigging and larking about extravaganza. I'm out first thing tomorrow morning, then we've got that mega-VIP flying in on Saturday night, not to mention the weekend public days. I don't have time for your shenanigans.'
He plunged his hands into the pockets of his landmark, royal blue, striped trousers and whistled gently through his teeth, starting to pace. He stopped and turned.
'Celeste.'
'What?'
'I'm a good photographer. You know I am.'

'That's not in dispute.'

'Couldn't we come to some arrangement?'

'Try me.'

Keeping his chin down, he looked at her from beneath his wicked eyebrows, took a deep breath and said, 'You're a gorgeous-looking woman. I could take some model-style photographs of you and maybe get you into one of the glossies.'

'You are joking.'

'Deadly serious. You seem to be, shall I say, quite well endowed...' He looked knowingly at her chest.

'Roland! You are utterly exasperating. What makes you think I would even contemplate such a thing?'

'Vanity?'

She placed her wrists against her temples, shut her eyes and said, 'Get out!'

'It was only a thought... if you could have a word with on high...'

'Out!' She threw the newspaper at him and it hit him on his shoulder as he went. He popped his head back in again, grinning and added, ' Perhaps you'd like a little time...'

'Out!' she roared, pointing her finger at him like a witch casting a spell.

*

'Good morning airshow addicts! You're tuned into Radio Runway bringing you all the news and views about Phillipstone International Airshow.' There followed the usual, *'Neeeee-oooow'* and *'Whooooooosh'*. The presenter continued, *'We're all ready for today's big event which is,* (sound of fanfare,*) Youth Day!'* (Sound of cheering, probably lifted from a football match.)

'Yes, we're ready and waiting for an exciting day for our young people. Some two hundred local youngsters, aged fifteen to eighteen, will be the guests of Phillipstone International Airshow. (More cheering.) *To tell us all about it, we have in the studio Councillor Percival Springstock. Good morning Councillor.'*

'Er, good morning, er, yes.'

AIRSHOW ILEX

'Now, Councillor, I believe you've been really instrumental in getting this Youth Day organised.'

'Well, I've done a bit to help it along, yes.'

'So, what has the airshow got in store for the cream of the borough?'

'Oh, lots of exciting things.'

'Would you care to share some of them with us?'

'Er. Um. Yes, yes. Of course. Just a moment.'

The listeners were treated to the sound of rustling paper.

'Ah. Here we are. Hold on please.'

More rustling and then the sound of a nose being heartily blown.

'Sorry. Sorry.'

The exasperated presenter jollied the Councillor along by saying, *'No rush. We have all the time in the world.'*

'Here we are then. Ah yes. They're going to have tours and things.'

'Would you like to tell us what of?'

'Aeroplanes. Stands. That sort of idea.'

'It sounds very interesting.'

'Oh, it will be. Then they'll have some food... oh yes... and a talk by a test pilot.'

Eleanor sat in the traffic jam that snaked its way to the external parking. She hit the radio 'off' button. Only four more days of it and then this annual fiasco would be over. After all the excitement of dinner last night with Grant Landscar, the wretched Youth Day had quite slipped her mind. If it was anything like last year, it would be mayhem. She selected neutral, put on the handbrake and took out the information sheet. Perhaps it had been a mistake to bring her car in this morning. Walking to the park-and-ride each day had worked reasonably well, although it was getting increasingly exhausting as the hot spell continued. She hoped it would soon cool down.

She looked sceptically at the sheet of paper and read, *'Improvements have been made to this year's Youth Day event based on the experiences of last year.'* She scanned the list quickly.

1. All young people will wear their passes at all times and be supervised in groups of ten by airshow personnel.
2. No food or drink will be brought into the halls, lecture rooms or Press Centre.
3. No mobile telephones will be used in the Press Centre.
4. Young people will be allowed on display aircraft in groups of five.
5. Any young person not complying will be escorted from the airshow site.'

Eleanor tossed it onto the passenger seat. 'Utter nonsense,' she thought. ' It will be chaos. Whose stupid idea was it anyway? That daft old Councillor.' The traffic started to move and she was soon into the off-site parking. She found a good place in the shade and, taking her brown briefcase and mac, got out, locked the car and trudged over to the free bus.

Even at this hour of the morning it was stuffy in there and, after showing her pass, she took a seat near the door. The vehicle slowly filled with disenchanted media people who were tired of aircraft and crowds, bored with press releases and seminars, stuffed full of information, bloated with free food and exhausted from looking. The magic had definitely worn off. Eleanor's gaze calmly flowed from one passenger to the next, taking in the air of desperation as she silently empathised and longed to be back in her little office at the the *Saturnian*, sifting through and rewriting news stories.

The bus jerked into throttling action, throwing her sideways as it swung over the bumpy ground making for the link road that led to the airport access tunnel. Panting like an unfit athlete, it crawled along in short bursts of acceleration followed by sharp braking. Passengers lurched about as they determinedly perused their morning papers. Eleanor peered out of the murky windows as the vehicle burst from the tunnel entrance into a sea of sunlight and made for the setting down point. It ground to a halt and the pneumatic doors opened with an explosive hiss to welcome in the stench of hot diesel mixed with *Planefuel Five*. Eleanor gathered up her things and got off, making for the security gate where she showed her press pass again. Then it

AIRSHOW ILEX

was a slog up the hill, past the coach park where charabancs were spewing out hordes of blazered teenage boys with cloned rucksacks and hairstyles like hedgehogs.

As she made for the boardwalk that led to the Press Centre building, a group of lads came running along, jostling past her, whooping with the joy that only a day off school can bring. She smiled grimly and wondered what it would have been like to have lived a normal youth. Then, along came the girls, hips swaying with confidence, hair like mermaids, lip-gloss shining in the early morning light... a far cry from the gawky, shy, young thing she had been.

'Welcome to Phillipstone International Airshow students. This way!' commanded a senior airshow steward. 'Please gather over here in your colour badge sets and your group leader will guide you to your first appointment.

Eleanor skirted around them, crossed the concourse, narrowly missed being hit by an enthusiastic golf buggy, and went into the building.

*

In response to the insistent ringing, Sister Catherine went to the convent's main door, opened the grill and peered out. A dishevelled Brecht looked back at her.

'Oh!' she said.

'Don't-a be afrrraid-a, Shistaire. I am peasheful. Pleashe-a tell-a tha Reverend-a Mudder that I am here-a.'

The nun looked at the state of him, hesitated for a moment, nodded and shut the grill. He paced about nervously in the tiled, oak-framed porch, glancing furtively back over his hunched shoulders, hands thrust deep into the pockets of his denim blouson.

After a few minutes he heard the heavy bolts being drawn and the studded door swung open.

'Please come in Mr. Slipkopj.'

The nun stood well back from the bedraggled, limping, bruised foreigner as he shambled past her with a grateful and obviously painful smile of thanks.

'Reverend Mother will see you in the parlour... you remember it from the other day...' her voiced trailed away. He grunted a nod, made for the door and turned the handle.

Reverend Mother was sorting holy pictures at the dining table. She rose to greet him.

'Brecht! What on earth has happened to you? Ever since those dreadful men took you away I've been beside myself with worry. As for that poor little Anna, she's been in a terrible state.'

'Shorry,' he lisped.

'What's wrong with your mouth, dear child?'

'Losht-a some-a teeth.' He grinned ruefully through swollen lips and pointed to the gaps.

'That's dreadful. Sit down. Where have you been since Tuesday?'

'Shleeping in the park-a. I could-a get-a water from-a the drink-fountain. No food for two daysh though.'

'Here. Sit down on the sofa. Let me get you something.' She went over to the door. 'Sister Catherine,' she called after the retreating nun. 'Some porridge and a glass of milk for Mr. Slipkopj, please.' She came back into the room.

'We did as you asked on the telephone last night. Come to think of it, I thought your speech sounded odd.'

'It was rishkee to telephone-a you... I realishe-a that... they know everrything. I afraid-a that they come-a back and shcare you again-a.'

'I must admit it was a traumatic experience. Why on earth were those men after you?'

'They think-a I know-a where Anna is.'

'They want to arrest her? Are they police-men?'

'No. They not polishe-a. They sheecret men from...' he waved his hands expressively, 'from shumwhere.' He struggled to speak clearly with his lack of teeth.

Reverend Mother walked over to the window, the swish of her long skirt suddenly loud in the muffled atmosphere of the salon. 'I hope they didn't follow you here.'

'No. No. I come across fieldshsh, hiding by-a hedshes.' He coughed weakly.

'You are in a lot of pain. I can see that.'
'They kick-a my ribsh verry hard.'
'You poor boy.'
'You should-a see what-a they did to-a my taxshi. Ruined! They slash-a the tyresh, break-a tha windshcreen, cut-a the shteering wheel cablesh. I don't worrrk no more.'

He hung his head in misery, then looked up suddenly. 'Anna. Ish she oky-doky?'

'Apart from worrying herself to a shadow, she's fine. We've kept her tucked away.'

'Where-a you hide herr when black beetle men come to convent?'

'It's better you don't know.'

Reverend Mother came back from the window and sat down gently beside him.

There was a tap at the door.

'Come!' she said.

The door opened slowly and then Anna stood before them. Sister Catherine was behind her, bearing the tray of food.

'Anna! Anna!'

Oblivious of his pain, he stood up and rushed over to her. She buried her head in his chest and he winced but held her to him.

'My Anna.'

Then the pair exchanged a rapid stream of words in their own language, gripping hands and looking into each other's faces.

'I am sorry to interrupt this reunion, Brecht, but we got the tickets for you. I'm just wondering if you are in a fit state to travel though.'

He held the girl by the shoulders. 'We leave. Tomorrow. Fly. We go-a home. She-a has-a ticketsh?'

Anna nodded.

The nun said, 'Our Sister who looks after the computer printed them out but won't they be watching the airports for you?' Reverend Mother asked.

'We musht-a go. We OK if my plan worksh.'

*

'Jes yous listens to me, you young hussies.'

The group of teenage girls totally ignored Zelara's attempt at restoring order in the Press Centre ladies' cloakroom. Beauty makeovers on a grand scale were in full swing. Hairspray and perfume fizzed out of spray-cans, creating a choking haze. The toilets were blocked with unmentionables, the basins strewn with hair and tissues and one girl was studiously popping her spots so that they splatted on the mirror.

Zelara tried again. 'Girls. Girls. This aint good. Yous destroying ma nice clean arrangements here.'

She might not have existed. The prattle and primping went on unabated. Putting her hands on her ample hips, the nylon-coated cleaning lady took a deep breath and bellowed, 'SILENCE!'

Fifteen pairs of eyes turned towards her as one, rather like cows in a field quietly observing a passing rambler.

'That's better ladies. Nows, would you, missie, take your hair out of my sink this minute and you, madam, wipe your pus off my nice mirror please?' She handed the girl a tissue. 'As for the rest of yous, I thinks we has enough of them spraying cans to give us all lung disease. So put them away before I take them from you.'

A mixture of disbelief and sardonic amusement filtered through the crowd. They clearly thought she was mad.

Eleanor chose that moment to enter the cloakroom. She paused in the doorway, greeted by a slow-motion tableau of young, female icons laconically putting away their instruments of titivation. Zelara stood with her arms folded, glaring at the gaggle.

'Is everything alright in here?' Eleanor queried.

'These young ladies wuz jest leavin' right this minute,' Zelara said firmly, lifting her chin and folding her arms more purposefully. Eleanor stood aside as the smirking teenagers sauntered out, one hesitating to blow a large, pink bubble-gum orb close to Zelara's face as she passed by. Eleanor waved her hand about.

'It's dreadful in here,' she said. 'The place reeks like a lady of the night's boudoir.'

'How does yous know about that?' Zelara chuckled.

AIRSHOW ILEX

'I was just speaking figuratively,' Eleanor said nonchalantly, making for one of the toilet cubicles.

'Don't even bother, Miss Framp. They is all blocked up. Here, let me unlock the executive one for you.' She produced a key. 'I got to get Miss Blagden to send for the engineer.'

'Thank you. You're very kind.'

'Don't mention it ma'am. I was real glad to see you. Thought them girls might turn nasty. There was a lot of them.'

'Won't be a moment,' said Eleanor.

Zelara took her rubber gloves out of her pocket, put them on and started picking up reams of paper towelling from the puddled floor. She stuffed the wet débris into a black sack and stood it beside the over-flowing waste-bin. Then she started cleaning the sinks. The toilet flushed and Eleanor came over to wash her hands.

'I dread Youth Day,' she said, looking at Zelara's reflection in the mirror.

'Me too, lady. These youngsters jest don't know hows to behave.'

'True.' She dried her hands.

'Have a nice day, Miss Framp,' Zelara called after her as she left.

'You too, Zelara.' The cleaner took her mop from the bucket in the corner and started to wipe the floor.

Wearing her leather, buckled sandals, Eleanor strode along the curved, Press Centre corridor, her navy-blue and white sprigged crepe dress too hot for the gathering heat. She stopped momentarily to look out through the plate glass windows at the static displays. The *ILEX* crouched like a liquid, black panther, shimmering in the morning sun and the military helicopter engines were winding up for demonstrations for important customers. The flags hung limply on their avenue of white poles and the gangs of youngsters trailed behind their group leaders, making for the aircraft tours.

She went back into the computer room. Teenage boys were everywhere, lazing in the chairs, feet on the desks, swigging from cans, throwing paper darts, arm-wrestling and filling the air with unmistakable stench of unwashed, male puberty. In the far corner a large group stood with their backs to her, giving out gasps of appreciation, gathered around a terminal. There were no other journalists in here this morning. She walked over to see what was going on. Her jaw dropped. She turned on her heel, walked briskly to Celeste's office and marched straight in.

The Press Centre Controller looked up, surprised and not at all happy.

'Would you please knock before coming into my office?' she said tartly.

'Miss Blagden, you have to come now. The Youth visitors are watching unsuitable material in the computer room.'

Celeste stood up and went silently to the scene of the crime, followed by Eleanor. As they came into the room, they heard, 'Core! What a pair! Come on! Move for us!'

The amateur nude model on the web-cam in some pokey bed-sit, wriggled and posed to the unheard cheers from not long broken voices.

'What's going on here?' Celeste demanded.

'Clear off lady! What's it got to do with you?'

'I'm the Controller of the Press Centre and you are out of line.' The diminutive woman struggled to appear taller as the group rose to their full height and looked down at her with disdain. Somebody turned off the monitor.

'Shouldn't you boys be at a lecture now?' she said, trying to control the nervousness in her tone.

'Boring,' said a voice from the back of the crowd. There was a murmur of agreement. 'Boys,' sneered another. 'We're not boys.'

'Whatever you are, you have no right to be in this computer room. Didn't you see the notice on the door?'

'This one?' said a ginger-haired youth, throwing a paper plane at her.'

'It's nice and cool in here.'

'Yeah. Cool.' The rest sniggered meaningfully.

Eleanor came and stood next to Celeste as the latter unclipped her mobile phone from her belt and pressed for Security.

AIRSHOW ILEX

'Let's go,' Eleanor muttered.

'I have the matter under control, Miss Framp,' Celeste said imperiously.

Eleanor had seen enough and strode across the floor, arms flailing. She called out into the corridor.

'Security! We need some assistance in here. Will somebody please help?'

A couple of reps waiting outside one of the seminar rooms came swiftly over.

'Got a problem, Miss?'

Eleanor indicated into the computer room where Celeste stood surrounded by teenage boys making jibes at her. The more well built of the reps went in and Eleanor followed.

'Come on fellas. Leave the lady alone. Outside.'

The other man jerked his thumb and made encouraging gestures to vacate the room. Grumbling, the youths picked up their rucksacks and blazers and shuffled out into the corridor.

'Let's go down the caff,' one said.

'Good idea.'

Two group leaders suddenly appeared, nearly getting knocked over in the exodus. The reps withdrew, smiling.

'Where have you lot been?' One of them demanded. 'You were supposed to wait for us by the bus stop for the trip down to the Planet Future hall.'

'Sorry, sir,' a plump lad replied mischievously. 'We got lost.' The others guffawed. The crowd moved off.

Eleanor went back to her workstation to find that her brown leather briefcase was open and full of crisp packets and disposable cups. She turned to Celeste to complain but the latter sat down at one of the terminals, blanched, shut her eyes and said, 'I don't feel well.' Then she put her head down on the desk.

Chapter 23

Friday 24th June
Dawn

'I don't know what the mother house would say if they knew we'd had a man sleeping on the sofa last night,' Reverend Mother said, clasping both of Brecht's hands in hers as the group stood on the convent's gravel drive in the quiet, chilly dawn.

'I don't-a tell them if you don't-a, eh?'
She nodded slightly and gave a slow blink of acquiescence.

'Sister will bring the mini-bus 'round in a moment.' She looked across at the airfield's heat haze. 'It's going to be another hot day.'

'We get-a nice view when we-a fly from London then,' he grinned painfully. '...but first we must catch-a our-a train.'

'I'm sorry you have to leave so early but we need the vehicle back to take the teaching sisters over to the school. In any case, it's better that you go from here while not many people are about.' She turned to Anna. 'We wish you both an uneventful journey. Write and let us know that you are safely home... and don't forget to post the...' She nodded her head knowingly, 'back to us.'

'We-a will do it, Reverrrend Mudder and thank-a you so much-a for these.' She indicated the two battered old suitcases. 'Our village will be-a so verrry pleazed to have some warm clothes. You are verrrry kind.'

'Don't mention it. The things were all donated for a good cause. Have you got your hand-luggage safely labelled?'

'Yes thank-a you. Here comes-a the bus.'

'Tickets?'

'Yes. I have-a them here.'

The gravel crunched as the vehicle drew up beside them. Anna looked up and received a reassuring smile from the nun at the wheel.

'Goodbye my children,' said Reverend Mother.

She took Anna into her arms and pecked a continental style kiss on each of her cheeks. Then she turned to Brecht as the girl climbed aboard with her bags.

'You were a harum-scarum little boy and I don't think you will change now but be careful what you do in life.'

'Yesh-a Reverend Mudder. I hear-a you. You have-a been verrry good to ush and I am so shorrry about the bad men.'

'So you should be. Our poor novices may never get over it.' She patted his arm as she steered him towards the bus. 'Your father saved my life during the revolution in your country. I owed you a debt of gratitude.'

'My father would-a be grateful that you-a helped-a ush. May he resht-a in peashe.'

She held out her arms and embraced him until he winced but he didn't complain.

'Away with you now!'

He bent over and kissed her on the cheek before picking up the cases and hauling them aboard. Then he turned and paused for a moment on the bus step. She looked at him standing there, his black, curly hair tousled and the single gold earring glinting. She knew they would never meet again. He gave her one, quick, tooth-gapped smile and the door hissed to behind him. He went and sat next to Anna and the vehicle drew away.

*

'Is Miss Blagden in this morning?' Eleanor put her elbow on the Press Centre reception counter. The receptionist set down the pile of flying schedules, rolled the mouse wheel and looked at her screen.

'No. I'm sorry, she's off-site until later this morning. I believe she has an appointment somewhere.'

'That follows,' said Eleanor knowingly. 'She wasn't very well yesterday.'

'The heat's getting to everybody,' said the girl wearily. 'They say the warm spell will break tomorrow.'

'It can't be too soon for my liking,' said the journalist grimly.

The receptionist waited patiently.

'Now, what was it I wanted to ask you?' Eleanor rummaged in her briefcase. 'Ah, yes. Please can you give this to Miss Blagden when she comes in? It's a letter of complaint about the behaviour of the Youth Day visitors yesterday. Will you see that she gets it?'

'Yes. I will, as soon as she arrives.'

Eleanor's mobile phone rang. 'Excuse me,' she said and turned away to take it out of her jacket pocket.

'Grant. How nice to hear from you! I would have rung if you hadn't called me first. Good news... well partly! I got a letter this morning from the Land Registry confirming what I told you. The convent is registered in the name of the order. I'll ring my aunt shortly to tell her. She'll be so relieved.' Her face creased with pleasure at the sound of his voice. 'Yes, I'd love to have dinner with you but it had better be here. This is the last trade day. The public will be in tomorrow and Sunday.' She studied her sandalled feet, aware of how ungainly they looked. 'Fine. Fine. I'll meet you in *Clouds* restaurant upstairs here at six thirty. Yes, I look forward to it too. 'Bye.'

She put the mobile in her pocket and went over to study the notice board. As the week had worn on, many of the trade visitors and London press had melted away so the seminars were getting thinner on the ground. Anybody who was anybody had come and gone.

The hospitality chalet invitations for presentations and lunches were diminishing by the day. There was to be an open lecture in the communications pavilion later. Another notice promised a history of flight film. Some author or other was doing a signing in Hall Five after lunch.

She stooped to read a small card advertising a vacancy for a features editor at a rival local paper. Into her pocket it went. After checking her pigeonhole and finding nothing in it, she went through the open sliding glass doors at the top of the Press Centre staircase, on her way to the exhibition halls.

*

AIRSHOW ILEX

'Debbie! Debbie!' Roland ran along the concourse, followed the spiral ramp and caught up with his co-stripper at the miniature aircraft stall. She pretended not to hear him as his feet thudded on the walkway and he skidded to a halt beside her, wheezing.

'Didn't you hear me calling?'

'Oh, hello Roland,' she said nonchalantly, continuing to pick through the model planes as if she had all the time in the world.

'I need to see you.'

'Thought you and the rest of the county had seen enough of me.'

'Debbie,' he hissed, 'come away from here and talk to me.'

'I'm a bit busy at the moment,' she said carelessly, walking further along the stand. He grasped her arm and tried to pull her away. Her cold stare of indifference made him release her.

'Debbie. We've got to discuss this.'

'Why?'

'Well, we just must. That's all.'

She turned her back to the stall. 'I don't think there's anything to say, do you? My entire team has seen me showing my all with you on the roof. How do you think that makes me feel?'

'How was I to know a helicopter with a photographer on board would fly over and snap us? It makes my blood boil!'

'Oh, I know all about your boiling blood,' Debbie said sarcastically. She turned back to the stall, picked up two miniature model helicopters and paid for them. Roland lingered not knowing what to do.

He followed her along to the ice-cream stand. 'A double-top cornet please,' she said.

'I'll have one too,' said Roland, rummaging for change. The vendor asked, 'Syrup? Chocolate sprinkles?' She shook her head. 'No thanks.'

'Here. Let me pay.' Roland thrust the money into the man's hand. 'Keep the change. Now, come on Debbie. Let's go and sit on the grass in the shade at the back of the stands.'

She shrugged moodily and walked sulkily beside him until they found a quiet patch where the guy ropes were skewered into the lush turf. He took off his jacket and spread it on the ground.

Without invitation, she sat down on it. There was a loud crunch. She'd broken his sunglasses in the top pocket.

'Sorry,' she said unconvincingly.

'It doesn't matter.'

She licked away at the ice cream, curling her tongue tantalisingly around the smoothness. She knew how to drive him wild.

'Stop doing that. You're doing it deliberately.'

'What?'

'You know what.'

She pushed her tongue deep into the middle of the cone, closed her eyes and sucked hard.

'You're just taunting me.'

'No. Really?' She turned her crystal blue eyes towards him. He licked his lips. Then, without warning, he swiped the cone away from her, threw his own on the ground and pressed his lips to her very ice-creamy ones. He drew back and looked at her. She was speechless with mirth.

'You've got a white ring around your mouth... like a clown!' she chortled.

'So have you,' he laughed as he unbuttoned her blouse. She didn't object.

*

It was hot in the departure lounge. Anna sat reading her prayer book while Brecht perused his broadsheet copy of *Religious Times and Mail*. The dog collar was too small for him and he longed to take it off. Anna perspired under the white, starched coif.

'It's enough to put you off a life of piety,' she said in their own language, looking down at her long, dark blue, habit and his black trousers, shirt and jacket.

'If it getsh ush out of the country without inshident, it's worth the inconveniensh,' he lisped and went on pretending to read.

'Just remember not to smile,' she added quietly, hardly moving her lips and not looking at him. Anybody watching would have thought she was praying. She glanced at the wall clock.

AIRSHOW ILEX

'It's only one and I'm so fed up and bored with waiting. We've been hanging around this airport for hours. I'm hungry.'

'Shorry I forgot to ask for shum money. I haven't been able to earn much thish week. When I changed into thish rig-out, I left what I had in my other trousersh. We'll get food on the plane. What time's departure?'

Anna looked at the boarding cards.

'Two thirty-five.'

Without taking his eyes off the paper he said, 'It'sh already five o'clock at home. It'll be at leasht eleven by the time we land.'

'A long day. I need to spend a penny.'

'Go on then.'

'Do nuns do it?'

'Of coursh they do. Go on. Over there.'

'OK, but don't let my hand-luggage out of your sight.'

She got up as gracefully as she could, placed her prayer book on the seat and walked with downcast eyes and folded hands to the last-minute loo. Nobody else was waiting to go. Once inside, she surveyed herself in the mirror. How innocent the coif made her look.

A woman came and knelt down in front of Brecht.

'Excuse me, Father,' she said in an Irish brogue. 'I was wondering whether you would be good enough to give me a blessing before I fly.' She piously folded her hands, closed her eyes and bowed her head.

Brecht lowered the newspaper. Oh crikey! This he did not need. It was years since he'd been to church. How did it go now? He'd try and bluff it out in his own language, taking the chance that she wouldn't speak any. He rattled off something about the price of fish, trying to keep a straight face as he struggled to deal with his toothless pronunciation. Internally hysterical at the absurdity of the situation, he gritted his remaining teeth and waved his hand about above her red hair, muttering something about the weather forecast in a singsong voice.

'Oh,' she said. 'I'm sorry. I didn't realise that you didn't speak English. Forgive me.'

He smiled benignly and apologetically at her as if blessing anxious passengers was a daily routine. She got up, looking duly holy, thanked him profusely and went back to her place.

Anna emerged from the toilet just in time to see the end of the blessing. She came towards Brecht smoothly, as if on roller-skates, picked up her book and sat down. She opened it and pretended to read.

'What on earth were you playing at?' she murmured.

'The lady wanted a bleshing. I had to perform one or she'd have called my bluff. I did it in Krid. She didn't understand a word. Don't worry. Nobody elsh heard. I mumbled it.'

'It's a good job you took that gold earring of yours out then. A gipsy priest would not have been convincing or even got you through passport control.'

'True.' He paused. 'I musht shay that you make a very good nun.'

'I can't believe Reverend Mother lent me that teaching sister's passport and her own ring. She's an amazing woman.'

'I'd never under-eshtimate her. You really do look like the parshport picture, eshpecially with the darkened eyebrowsh.'

'Well, I suppose one nun looks very much like another, 'she murmured, hiding a smile.

The loudspeaker crackled. 'Will passengers boarding flight number ZB988 for the Former Kridiblikt Republic please come to the desk. Please have your passport and boarding cards ready. Thank you.'

'Thish ish it,' said Brecht, folding away the broadsheet and dumping it on the empty chair next to him. He grabbed his hand luggage.

'Keep the newspaper with the title outwards. Walk calmly,' said Anna, picking up her bag. He did as she said and the pair proceeded to boarding.

*

Eleanor sat on one of the leather sofas, crossed her feet as elegantly as the sandals would allow and arranged the folds of her lilac crêpe dress so that they hung artistically. She touched the silk scarf around her neck. In the lounge area of *Clouds* restaurant, it was still early. Dinner service had just begun. She could smell tempting aromas wafting through from the dining area. She gazed at her hands. No rings. No nail polish. White moons to the oval nails. She looked up. Grant was standing in the doorway, his silver hair shining and the white stetson in his hand. He was wearing a pale, grey-blue suit and black chukka boots. Her heart skipped a beat. Then he saw her and came across the deep pile carpet with his hand out in greeting.

'My dear Eleanor! I'm not late, am I?'
She turned and patted the seat.

'No. I was early. It's good to see you.'

He put his hat on the side-table. She observed his black, string tie pierced at the throat by a diamond stud. He sat down. They were an unlikely pair, the dapper billionaire and the mundane, middle-aged journalist. People passing through looked at them unbelievingly. Eleanor didn't care. She felt like a child again, riding on her father's shoulders in the park... a surge of never-ending joy unlike anything she had ever experienced before. She smiled. He smiled.

'I've booked the table so they should be calling us through shortly,' he said. 'What have you been up to today?'
Her gaunt face creased up with pleasure.

'Oh just going around the halls collecting brochures and leaflets. I'll put them away for next year so that I can write a retrospective when the time comes. Some of the stands are already deserted.'

'Why are they going so soon? The public will be in over the weekend, won't they?'

'Yes. That's why. They don't want the unwashed masses spoiling their merchandise, I suppose. On the other hand, there are stands here that probably won't interest people unconnected with the industry. This is a trade show, after all. I think they only let the public in at the end of the fortnight to assuage their curiosity and pour entertainment oil on the disgruntled local proles,' she laughed.

'You have such a way with words,' he said admiringly in his seductive American drawl.

'You have a beautiful voice,' she replied. 'I love your accent.'

'Really? Now, there's a thing.'

The maître d'hotel approached them and bowed slightly from the waist. 'Your table is ready, madam, sir.'

'Thank you. Shall we go in?'

Grant took up his hat and they both rose and followed through but before they reached their table for two in the alcove on the far side of the room, Paula came over.

'I'm sorry to interrupt, Miss Framp, Mr. Landscar, but I wondered whether you, Miss Framp, will be attending the special VIP barbecue for the foreign dignitary on Sunday after the show closes. I'm just looking at the list and you don't seem to be on it. I know you usually get included in these events.'

'I don't know anything about it,' Eleanor replied.

'Do you want to go?' Grant asked.

'I don't know. It's been a long fortnight.'

Grant turned to Paula. 'Miss Framp will be absolutely delighted to attend.'

'Sure?' asked Paula.

'Yes. Alright. Thank you for telling me.'

'Do enjoy your meal. The saddle of lamb is particularly good.'

Then she went over to the bar, her silk skirt rustling and her hips swinging in an exaggerated fashion.

'She's a type,' Grant whispered to Eleanor.

'It takes all sorts,' she replied quietly.

Once settled on their dining chairs, Grant ordered two spring waters. Eleanor knew he would remember. The menus came and went.

'So,' he said, placing the tips of the fingers of both hands together. 'This is by way of a celebration, on two counts.'

'A celebration? Is it your birthday or something?'

'No. That's in the fall. I want to thank you.'

'You already did that with dinner last night.'

'Ah, but that was for reducing my humiliation over withdrawing from the wind farm idea.'

AIRSHOW ILEX

'You more than spoiled me, what with the loan of that beautiful red, velvet dress and the wonderful dinner at *La Raducette*. The dress is still back at my flat. I meant to return it to you today...'
He waved his hand dismissively. 'Pleasure. Pleasure. Please keep the dress.'

'I couldn't possibly accept such an expensive gift.'

'Well, just borrow it on long-term loan then.'

'Very well. If you insist. Thank you, but I won't forget it belongs to you.' She paused. 'Now, please tell me what we are celebrating. Mid-summer's day, a bit late?'

'Eleanor.' He reached across and took her hand away from where it was playing with the edge of folded, linen napkin. 'You saved me a heck of a lot of money.'

'It won't last if you keep taking me out for meals.' She withdrew her hand gently.

'Dining out is small fry compared with the enormous cost of the hundred wind turbines that I nearly signed a contract for. If you hadn't warned me about the land title, I'd have squandered away a large fraction of my fortune on them.'

'Happy to have helped,' she said with the merest shrug of her narrow shoulders.

The starters arrived. They'd both ordered sautéed wild mushrooms on a bed of rocket salad with ricotta cheese and black olives.

'This looks good,' she said.

'So do you,' he replied.

'Now, now... Grant. Don't tease me. I told you I'm not your kind of lady.'

'Oh Eleanor, I think you are.'

She put down her knife and fork and swallowed. The colour rushed to her face. Now was not a good time for a hot flush. She fought it, sipped some water and then took a deep breath to compose herself.

'Don't worry,' he said. 'We're going to take this thing nice and steady, you and I. First we are going to be friends, good friends. Then we are going to be even better friends and then we'll see where it goes from there, but only if you want to.'

'Grant. You've been married before, several times, you said. I have no experience whatsoever of men. Look at me. I'm a plain Jane. I'm gawky and awkward and I grew up in a convent. I wouldn't fit into your world at any level.'

'I think that's for me to decide.'

'It's my life too.'

'Don't you ever get lonely, Eleanor?'

'I'm used to it.'

'That doesn't make it right. Look,' he said, 'what I intend to do is to worm my way into your affections, trick you into spending some time with me, and hopefully make myself indispensable to you. What do you say?' He reached into his inside pocket and brought out two tickets.

'How about a concert tonight? Wagner? Car into town and back. Deliver you safely to Eleanor's Nook by midnight so your reputation will be untarnished.'

'You're impossible,' she said, intent on carrying on with the meal. She hesitated and looked up at him. It was a stand off.

'Very well, but only if I can wear that red dress again.'

'Done,' he said and the corners of his eyes wrinkled up in that kindly way that made her heart turn over.

'There's something else.'

'I don't think I can take much more. I'm used to a dull life,' she said with chagrin, the horror of the convent raid still fresh in her mind. She put down her fork.

'Time for change,' he said, producing an envelope from his other inside pocket. He passed it to her.

'Go on. Open it.' She put down her knife and gingerly did so.

Dear Miss Framp,

As per Mr. Grant Landscar's instructions, I hereby grant you one year's lease from 1st July on the fully serviced first floor office at Curtis House, The Circle, Phillipstone, for the purposes of starting up your magazine.
Yours Truly,
Smoggs, Boggs and Sillitoe,
Solicitors.

AIRSHOW ILEX

Grant reached across and dropped a set of keys onto the snowy, white tablecloth next to her plate.

'See how you get on. If you like it, we can extend the lease indefinitely. If you don't, no harm done but at least you will have had a crack at your dream.'

'I can't accept this.'

'I think you can.'

'No. It's wrong. Fairy tales don't happen to people like me.'

'I can make them happen for you, Eleanor.'

'I don't want charity.'

'OK. OK. If it'll make you feel better, we'll share the profits.'

'I'm too old to start something new like this.'

'Hey! Stop making excuses. You know you'll love it... and we could go looking for interesting old embroideries together... I might even like some to go on my walls... to compliment all my collectables. What do you say?'

Her eyes were shining with tears.

'Take a chance,' he said. 'This isn't the dress rehearsal. It's the show.'

'Let me think about it,' she said, and knocked over her glass of water.

*

'The sheatbelt shigns have gone off now,' Brecht said in Krid.

'Good. I can looshen my collar for a bit. You roashting too?'

'Yes. This habit is hot and scratchy. How they put up with it I will never know.' Anna looked out of the window. Through the intermittent, fluffy, white clouds she caught glimpses of the river below. 'It looks like a model from up here,' she said. They had two seats together in the same row but as nobody had taken the third one, they had left it vacant between them. Possibly the booking clerk at check-in had done it on purpose.

'Itsh been quite an adventure,' the fake priest said.

'You bet, but I've never been so scared in all my life,' the spoof nun replied. Then she giggled. 'You do sound funny with your front teeth missing.'

' I hope I can put it down to exshpenshes.'

He touched his face ruefully. 'Anyway, our people will be delighted that we got what we went for,' Brecht said with satisfaction. 'A job well done.'

'It's a good thing Reverend Mother had no idea or she wouldn't have helped us to escape.'

'Can I get you anything, Father? Sister?' The steward enquired.

'No. We arr-a fine, thank you,' Brecht said.

Anna leaned over sideways and said 'Well, pleass, I would-a quite-a like my hand-a luggage down.'

'Certainly Sister. Which locker is it in?'

'That-a one up therr, thank you.'

The flap went up, the bag came down and Brecht put it on the seat between them. He looked at her and then at the bag.

'I wonder what itsh worth?'

'Priceless,' Anna said with a hint of avarice in her tone.

The hours ticked by. The drop-down monitor showed that they were over the mountainous region. The lights were low. Most of the other passengers slept. The plane droned on. Anna turned her head sideways so she could see Brecht from the confines of her white coif. He looked so innocent asleep like that. She moved her hand towards the hold-all between them and slowly and gently unzipped it, her fingers plunging down inside, feeling for the *ILEX* tile. She slid it out and unwrapped it.

'Brecht! Brecht! Wake up!'

'What? Whatsh going on?' He looked around him panicking and sat up more in his seat.

'Look! Look!'

He rubbed his eyes and, as they came into focus, saw what lay in Anna's hand, a beautifully embellished, small, square tablet bearing the words *A Memento from St. Bede's*, carefully decorated by Sister Catherine's artistic hand.

'Thish can't be right. Turn it over!' Brecht said.

There was a sticky, white label affixed crookedly to the back. They read the small, wobbly writing. It said:

I thought you would like a prettier one. Love Maud Hunt.

Chapter 24

Saturday 25th June
Morning

'You're late,' said Celeste impatiently as she stood on the boardwalk that led to the static outside exhibition. 'I'm not sure I should be speaking to you anyway after your rooftop nude show.'

'Sorry,' Roland replied. 'I had to discuss something with Press Centre Reception.'

'Come on then. I haven't got all day. The public will be flooding through the tunnel in half an hour and it's going to be one very frantic weekend.'

'Don't remind me. OK. Where shall we start?'

'Let's walk while we talk. Well, you know that the airshow is not as popular as it might be with the locals.'

'I had heard.'

'So we need a strong public relations exercise to show the yokels that we are really the good guys, that the traffic disruption, air pollution and general chaos is all worth while. I mean, they receive lots of revenue into the shops and businesses, there are loads of temporary jobs, their under-twelves will get free rides on everything today and tomorrow, there will be special kiddies' snack boxes, face painting... oh why do they enjoy that so much?... and, best of all, an appearance by a couple of children's comedians.'

'I suppose you want me to just follow the little blighters around like last year, trying to get endearing shots of the face-stuffing monsters.'

'That's the idea but try and get some of wholesome looking kids and not... how shall I put it?... the verminous type. We are trying to keep up our world image here.'

'Ah,' said Roland, stopping with a slightly worried expression. 'The world image and my contribution to it.'

'You have struck lucky. 'On high' has gone down with a bug and won't be in until next week. Hopefully, by then, the memory of your Adonis-type body will have faded somewhat. It was a very unwise caper, you silly man.'

He attempted to look shame-faced but the mischievous grin that continually erupted without warning, burst through and Celeste couldn't keep a straight face either. Quite out of character, she punched him on the arm and declared vehemently, 'You are utterly impossible! Let's go and look at the fairground.'

*

'Eleanor, my dear, how lovely to see you again!' Reverend Mother Veronica embraced her niece heartily on the lawn at the side of the convent. 'Come and walk with me. I'm going up to the folly for my constitutional. Are you well? How are the bruises on your neck?'

'Very well, thank-you Aunty Rev. They aren't too bad. I've been wearing a chiffon scarf over them. Look! Not very nice in this heat but needs must. How are you? I can't stop for too long. I've got to get back to the airshow later this morning. Thank goodness it finishes tomorrow.'

'Yes, it must get a bit tedious. Oh, I'm a survivor. I've just about got over the shock of those dreadful men the other day.'

'It was pretty scary. I still wonder whether we should have called the police.'

'No. That wouldn't have been wise. They said they knew where you lived and we had to hide Anna for a little longer as well and there would have been too much explaining to do. Anyway, there's something more important worrying me.'

'What might that be? Please tell me and I'll see if I can help. Is something wrong?'

'Yes, there is. I'm deeply troubled about the state of Sister Catherine's soul. Do you know, she told a blatant lie to those unpleasant intruders? She hid that young girl Anna inside the altar and told a barefaced untruth about her having left the convent already.'

'Anna was doing some kind of retreat here, wasn't she?' Reverend Mother looked a little perturbed.

AIRSHOW ILEX

'Well, that was just to stop the others talking to her. No, the men in black leather jackets who herded us all into the parlour, rampaged through the convent looking for her and scared the wits out of our Filipino novices down in the kitchen... they were after her for more than an over-run work permit in my opinion. Anyway, she and Brecht flew out yesterday, home to the Former Kridiblikt Republic. I shouldn't think we'll hear from them again.'

'You had a special bond with Brecht, I think.'

'His father rescued four of us sisters when we were out there on a missionary tour over twenty years ago. On looking back, it was a bad time to attempt such a thing but the mother house was keen to get a foot in the door there. I suppose you don't remember that, do you?'

'Yes, of course I do. I was working up in Fleet Street then. We ran the story.'

'It seems like only yesterday. He was such a delightful, intelligent child. I hope he doesn't go wrong in life.'

The ground sloped up a little and the nun stopped to catch her breath. 'I love this walk. I take it every day to contemplate and ask for guidance. I've been so concerned about our tenure here. Thank goodness you managed to sort it out for us. When you rang yesterday with the good news I could hardly believe it. Fancy that! Registering the property in the order's name! Old Reverend Mother was indeed a resourceful woman! So we won't be turned out onto the streets after all!'

'I'm so glad for you. Look,' Eleanor said, struggling to unbuckle the briefcase as they walked along together, 'here's the proof.' She waved a sheaf of papers about.

'Wonderful,' said the elderly nun. 'When we're back in my office and I've got my glasses on, I'll have a proper look. Thank you, dear, for all your detective work.'

'After all you've done for me throughout my life, Aunty Rev, I had to try and help. It's good it's turned out well. There's more, though. I'd just prefer you to be sitting down when I tell.'

Eleanor smiled enigmatically and put the papers away. The pair linked arms and set forth once more.

'I've made a new friend.'

'Oh yes?'

'A man.'

'Really?'

'You might not be pleased when I tell you who he is.'

'Try me, my dear.'

'Grant Landscar, the American who wanted to take the convent and make a wind farm on the airport.'

'Goodness, Eleanor!' She stopped, shocked.

'I want you to meet him. He's really nice. He took me to the theatre last night. He's not a tyrant at all.'

'I'll take some convincing.'

'He's offered me the editorship of my own magazine.'

'Can you trust him?'

'Yes. I believe I can.'

'Well, I won't make a judgement until I've clapped eyes on him and cross-examined him as to his intentions,' she said with a twinkle.

'Oh Aunty!'

'I'm happy for you dear, if it pleases you. You're an adult and have to make your own choices.'

'Thank you. I knew you'd understand.' They walked in silence for a few moments.

'Doesn't the folly look lovely in the morning sun?' Reverend Mother said.

'It always intrigued me,' Eleanor replied. 'I used to make up stories in my head about a princess who lived in it.'

'Did you dear? You never said.'

'Well, just silly, girlish fantasies.' They walked a few paces and then the nun said, 'It must have been a strange life for you here at the convent when all your friends had proper homes and families.'

'It was perfectly good, Aunty, really it was. Don't forget I had the run of this beautiful old house and grounds and the kindness of all the sisters. Just a different kind of childhood, that's all.'

Reverend Mother stopped and turned to her niece. 'Did I tell you about old Maud Hunt and the cats?'

'I think you're going to,' Eleanor replied with a smile.

AIRSHOW ILEX

'Well, since the cottage burned down, her strays have been gradually coming back to the convent to find her. She really loves them, you know, but it was getting a bit out of hand with them mewing at the kitchen door all the time and one or two of them got in and we can't have that.'

'So what's going to happen?'

'I found this nice lady from the animal rescue place and she's coming in with her helpers to convert the old stables into a temporary cattery for them all. It will be properly sectioned off and made hygienic. Over time, we hope to persuade Maud to let some of them go to good homes but, in the meantime, it's nice for the old lady to have some pleasure in life.'

'You're too kind but the Hunts can't stay here forever, you know.'

'That's already in hand. The buildings insurance will pay for one of those new prefabricated bungalows with solar panels and things. It'll go up on the old cottage site. Look. Turn around.'

The charred cottage remains sat there in the morning sun, its stout chimney pointing skywards.

'It's a real mess,' said Eleanor.

'It'll be demolished and the débris removed. Work should start in about eight weeks. Until then, the Hunts will stay with us.'

'The daughter? She doesn't have a job now, does she?'

'Well,' said the nun meaningfully, 'she had some kind of profession but I think she's given it up. I'm hoping to persuade her to go on a cookery course. She likes doing that. Then maybe when school cook retires later this year, Miss Hunt can take over. She's quite keen.'

'You're a living saint, Aunty.'

'I don't know about that,' she replied. 'Here we are, at old Reverend Mother's grave. I don't know what we would have done without her resourcefulness.' She stopped and looked down at the simple monument engraved with the words:

God helps those who help themselves.

*

Roland unfolded his tripod to the side of the boardwalk where it forked, one way leading to the statics and the other to the fairground and children's amusements. He fixed the digital camera, set it to wide angle, clicked it on and looked through to check the aperture and speed. Although it was a bright, sunny morning, he noted that the readings had changed from the other days, probably due to a slight haziness over the sun. He used the pan and tilt mechanism to swing around and capture a panoramic view of the rides and take a few establishing shots.

The sound of the gallopers' merry-go-round organ dominated. The owner was already doing a roaring trade as his horses relentlessly pursued their interminably boring race around the limited circumference of the mechanism, children clinging either gleefully or woefully to the painted ponies' necks. Roland zoomed in and captured the moment as parents stood waving cheerfully at bewildered youngsters gradually being overcome with terror at the increasing speed with which mummy came and went. Wails of misery started to compete with the organ but a quick tweak of the volume soon overcame that little problem.

The photographer panned across to the kangaroo ride. Big, multicoloured, grinning marsupials perched on their hind legs, sat with individual children lashed into their voluminous pouches as they continually changed direction with an unnerving jolt that elicited screams each time. He zoomed in for thrills and terror pictures.

The Ferris wheel was painted bright red and he took a long shot of it against the hazy blue sky. Luckily a couple of children were waving and that was good. The stink of burgers and onions pervaded the area and the public queued eagerly for their fix of fries. He wondered how they could stomach them so early. Then a slight breeze wafted the aroma of candyfloss towards him and he sniffed the air. The mixture of smells together was utterly disgusting.

He picked up his rig and walked further along to where the *ILEX* sat baking in the sun, its staircase unrolled. As usual, the special guards were standing there motionless. A little boy was hanging onto the barrier, sucking the grey aluminium, gazing with

AIRSHOW ILEX

wide eyes at the rather scary men in black leather. His big sister was talking to her friend and noticed too late that he had decided to go over the barrier to try and touch the plane.

'Come back here at once!' she yelled but the lad was on his way, dodging past the leatherjackets, making for the stairs up to the plane. One guard suddenly swung into rugby tackle mode and brought the child down onto the tarmac with a thud. The boy gave a wail of pain as a trickle of blood spurted from a cut on his forehead and his big sister started to climb the barrier too.

'Stay back miss,' said one of the guards, placing himself firmly in front of her as she straddled the barrier, his reflective eye-mask fixing her with a blank gaze. She got down again and backed off slightly. 'Give me back my brother!' she said, waving her free arm about. Her friend came to join her. 'Yeah, give her back her brother!'

Zelara drew up on the tarmac in her golf cart, buckets and mops stashed beside her. She got out next to the barrier, unloaded her gear and waddled over to the guard who put his hands on his hips.

'Excuse me if it pleases you sir, I needs to goes and do ma usual cleanin' chores' She held her pass at him in a slow swinging motion. He stepped aside and waved her through. On the first step of the *ILEX* staircase, a loud beep came. She stopped. A guard went over to her. 'Special personal signal please,' he said, taking out a palm computer and stabbing in the pass code from her badge. She put down the cleaning gear.

'I's been in an' out of this monster all week. Surely you knows me by now?'

'Special sign please,' he repeated in a monotone.

Wearily she put down her things, crossed her arms and took her opposite ear lobes between first fingers and thumbs.

'Pass through,' he said. She collected her gear together again and climbed the staircase of the *ILEX* with an air of resentment.

One of the other guards picked the child up and delivered him, flailing and squirming back to his sister.

'He's bleeding,' she complained loudly. 'You shouldn't be treating a little boy like that.'

'I suggest you take him to the first aid point next to the Press Centre building over there,' the man replied coldly. 'Keep him under control in future.' Then he turned his back on her and strode over to his former position where he resumed his leather statue stance next to the liquorice coloured *ILEX*. Roland got it all on his digital camera.

'What do you think you're doing?' said an irate woman beside him.

'Taking photographs of the airshow,' he replied without removing his eye from the viewfinder.

'I've been watching you. You're taking pictures of children. Aren't you that pervert who was in the paper?'

He stood up, turned his baseball cap around the right way and looked down at her. She was short and plump with a bird's nest hairstyle and wrists of bangles. Standing a few feet away was her husband keeping an eye on their gaggle of subdued children, all studiously sucking ice lollies. He nodded encouragingly at her.

Roland reached into the back pocket of his red and blue striped trousers and produced his card.

'Take this, madam, and if you would care to arrange a session of glamour photography with me, don't hesitate to call.' Her shoulders went back and her chest moved up, as did her chins.

'How dare you!' she said pompously, placing her hands across her ample stomach. The husband, realising that matters were escalating, pointed a finger at his bunch of offspring and came over.

'Is something the matter darling?' he asked affably.

'This man wants to take glamour pictures of me,' she said imperiously.

'Does he now?' The man put his head on one side and looked enquiringly at Roland who, guessing that the pair was out for a fight, used his wits and pointed at one of the children.

'I think your little girl is choking on her lolly.'

The parents turned quickly to look and Roland seized the moment to pick up his equipment and run with the tripod still open. Shouts of, 'We're going to report you!' rang after him as he panted up the slope and into Hall One. Inside, he folded away the tripod and put it over his shoulder with the camera still attached. He looked at the site plan on the wall beside him. It was time to have a look at the Space Exhibition.

He cut across the hall and went out of the far exit, taking the brick-paved walkway to his quarry. As soon as he entered the large, separate building, he felt the call of deep space. There was a low, humming sound and the dark interior ceiling was studded with pseudo-stars and planets. The attendants were clad in one-piece suits of royal blue, speckled with silver. He pointed to his press pass as he went in.

'Would you like an information sheet, sir?'

'Yes, thank you.'

'May I recommend the *Psillent Space Capsule* through there and to the right. It's a scale model of the one to be used in the *Uranus Venture Spacecraft*.'

Roland nodded and went the way indicated. As he arrived at the exhibit he could see that a little girl with bunches had somehow got through and into the craft. She was peering out of the thick, hexagonal, murky window. Her trail of footprints was clearly visible in the formerly pristine, smooth sand around the exhibit.

'Come out! The man will see you and tell you off!' hissed her mother frantically. The child stuck her tongue out and ducked down. The woman turned to Roland.

'She won't come out. Somehow she's managed to shut the door.'

'It seems to be steaming up in there,' Roland said. 'I think we'd better call somebody.' He beckoned to a sparkly-suited, female attendant and she came over.

Muffled cries could now be heard and the child's face was contorted with misery as she squirted tears and drummed her little fists against the thick glass. Roland propped his gear up against the wall and stepped into the sandy area with the attendant. They both tried to force the door open but it appeared to be locked. Their efforts only distressed the child further.

'Emergency,' said the attendant into her walky-talky. 'Child trapped in exhibit. Space Exhibition.' She listened for a moment and then said, 'Roger. Over and out,' before she turned to Roland again.

'The fire brigade is on its way. They'll be a few minutes because they're over at the far side by the hangers checking hydrants. We're going to have to have another go ourselves.'

A crowd had started to gather and the mother too had stepped onto the sand and was kissing the glass window frantically, peppering it with lipsticky blobs that made the child's already puce face look as if she had the plague.

'Hang on,' said Roland to the female attendant. He stepped out of the area and got his folded tripod with the camera still on top. 'Stand clear!' Then with brutal swipes and no care for his equipment, he bashed repeatedly at the edge of the door with the feet of the tripod until their rubber bits fell off but still he kept on going, alternating between the lock side and the hinges. Thud, thud, thud. The child's wails grew louder.

'You're terrifying her!' screamed the mother in between kisses.

"Do you want her out, alive and terrified or not?' said Roland, keeping up his tirade of blows to the door. Suddenly the lock fell off. The attendant tried to prise it with her fingers but to no avail.

'Keep clear!' said Roland as he renewed his attack, this time concentrating on the hinges. The crashing noises drew even more crowds who encouraged him with, 'Go for it!' and 'Give it some welly!' Two other attendants joined them.

Then, suddenly, the top hinge broke and clattered down, landing on the sand. Roland dropped his tripod and got his hands in to wrench at the door until it hung on its twisted lower hinge. Out of the corner of his eye he saw a flash. The rush of incoming air revitalised the child's yelling ability and she gave out an ear-piercing scream. The crowd applauded and the mother ran around to the door to pull her daughter out.

'You naughty, naughty girl!' she chided, plonking real kisses all over the turkey-cock-faced child, who, realising that she had an audience, opened her mouth wide and hooted with all the power of a beached whale.

Roland surveyed his ruined equipment. He'd have to go back to the locker room for his spare set.

AIRSHOW ILEX

'Well done, Roland!' a woman's voice said enthusiastically. He looked up to see Eleanor Framp standing there and rolled his eyes upwards in utter exasperation before leaving the Space Exhibition to the sound of the recently released child yelling her head off. He felt like doing the same.

*

A roll of thunder shook the Press Centre building.

'Just look at it out there,' said Celeste to Roland as they both stood in her office gazing out at the sodden show ground and the teeming rain. The concourse was running like a river, people were making for the exits like disgruntled lemmings and the flags of many nations hung like rags on their poles.

'A fine public relations day this has turned out to be. We've had to cancel the helicopter rescue from the inflated swimming pool. Just look at it overflowing and some joker's put washing up liquid in the water. The runway's getting covered in foam. All this, on top of everything else.'

She gave a sort of gulp.

'You alright?' Roland asked.

'Perfectly,' she retorted, turning away.

'I got a few good shots before the downpour started. Do you want to see them?' He indicated his wrecked equipment propped up by the door.

'That lot looks as if it's been through the mincer. Whatever happened to it? Surely your pictures will be ruined?'

'It met with a little accident. I got the digital card all right though.' He took it out and held it up. 'I'll just get my card reader and spare gear from the locker room, although it looks as if today's display is off.

'Continual storms are forecast until evening. I must say it's been building up all week. Hopefully it'll clear the air for tomorrow. Go and get your stuff.'

She sniffed as he left and she went to her desk, blinking rapidly,

*

The girl giggled. Roland knew what he was doing. 'You're gorgeous,' he said, pressing his lips against her bare shoulder. She squirmed and he held her close.

'I've been admiring you all week.'

'Have you?' she simpered, batting her eyelids with mock amazement.

'You know I have. Every time I walked past reception. Couldn't take my eyes off you.'

'I've got a boyfriend,' she said, wriggling against him.

'So?'

'He might get jealous.'

'Only if you tell him.' He took the locker room key out of her hand and put it on the shelf next to them. 'I want your body,' he said in a low voice.

*

Debbie knocked on Celeste's office door. There was no reply. She tried again and then paused. There was a funny noise coming from inside so she turned the handle and peeped in. Celeste was sitting at her desk, head down on her arms, sobbing her heart out. Debbie quietly shut the door and went over to her.

'Celeste. What on earth's the matter?'

A flash of lightening lit up the room and was followed by a deep and resounding roll of thunder that rattled the windows. Celeste shook her head and muttered a muffled, 'Nothing.'

'Of course there's something wrong. Would it help to tell me about it? Are you upset because this afternoon's display's been cancelled?'

'Don't be so stupid!' Celeste barked, lifting her tear-stained face and dabbing at it with a tissue. Her mascara had run down her cheeks in a blobby mess.

'I'm only trying to help,' Debbie said sympathetically. 'Is there anybody I can get for you?'

'Go away.'

'You don't mean that.' She went to the water dispenser and filled a plastic cup. 'Here. Drink this. It'll calm you down.' The hysterical Press Centre Controller took it and sipped, punctuated by sobs. There was a knock at the door.

'Don't let anyone else in,' Celeste hissed, but it was too late and Eleanor Framp appeared, her famous mackintosh dripping and her short grey hair plastered to her head like wet cement. She stopped in her tracks.

'What's going on?'

Debbie gave a gesture of despair. 'She won't say.'

Eleanor said, 'There's a television crew outside in reception wanting to know whether the flying display will go on later.'

'Tell them it's cancelled for today,' Debbie said.

'Since when were you speaking on my behalf?' barked Celeste with a dramatic and drippy sniff.

'Well you go and tell them yourself then,' Debbie snapped back.

'How can I?'

Debbie turned to Eleanor. 'Miss Framp, please can you go and tell them? She's in no state to see anybody.'

'Very well,' replied the mackintosh lady and withdrew.

'Now,' said Debbie, 'tell me what's the matter.'

'I can't.'

'Yes you can.'

'It's too awful.' There followed another bout of hysterical sobbing.

The telephone rang. Debbie answered.

'No, I'm sorry. Miss Blagden is in a meeting. Yes, I'll tell her you called.' She put the receiver down.

Celeste raised her head from her muted bawling session and asked calmly, 'Who was it?'

'It was your father.'

This set her off again.

'Ring him later when you're less upset.'

'I'm never going to be less upset,' she blubbed.

There was a tap at the door and Eleanor came in again.

'They'll be back tomorrow morning at ten. What's the matter with her?'

'She still won't say.'

Eleanor took a deep breath.

'I saw you in the doctor's surgery last week. I heard what you said.'

'You know then. You've known for days. How could you understand how I feel, you dried up old spinster.'

'Hey! No need for that!' said Debbie.

'I'm not so easily offended,' said Eleanor with an air of superiority. 'Anyway, she's pregnant.'

Celeste let out a roar of rage and started tearing tissues wildly from the box, tossing them around randomly.

'How dare you give away my personal business!' she screamed, throwing the box on the floor and standing up to stamp on it repeatedly like a demented flamenco dancer.

Debbie stepped back in disbelief. Eleanor calmly slapped Celeste around the face. That stopped her yelling. With her breath taken away she gasped, 'You... you... you...' and for the first time in her life was quite speechless.

'Sit down!' Eleanor commanded. 'I did that for your own good. You were hysterical.'

'You just don't get it, do you?'

'What?' said the other two in chorus.

Celeste threw her arms open wide in a melodramatic gesture, took a deep breath and wailed, 'Triplets! I'm going to have triplets!'

Chapter 25

Sunday 26th June
Early Morning

'Debbie! Please listen! The girl meant nothing to me!' Roland hammered on the door of the *Pink Perils'* room in the outside extension of the *Old Turret Hotel.* 'Let me in! I can explain!'
There was no reply. His eyes scanned the ornate rock garden around him.
'I know you're there. Please give me back my lucky trousers.'
'Can I be of assistance, sir?' said a passing member of staff.
'No. No thank you. I just can't get my girlfriend to hear me.'
'Might I suggest telephoning the room, sir?' The man took out his mobile and offered it to Roland.
'She won't answer. I tried earlier.'
'Ah,' said the man, putting it away again. 'These affairs of the heart!' He paused. 'Forgive me for saying so, sir, but in my limited experience of such matters, I have often found that a large bunch of red roses usually assuages the offended lady.'
'It'll take a whole rose garden to get me out of this one,' Roland said grimly.
'Oh,' said the man, 'a truly grave transgression.'
'The worst kind.'
'Leaving out grand larceny, murder and treason, one must suppose that we are treading into the realms of infidelity. A truly heinous offence.'
'Got it in one.'
'Well, sir, may I respectfully suggest that a discrete time lapse generally reduces the acrimony?'
'I don't have time.'
'Then, sir, we only have one solution to your problem.' He held out his hand, palm upwards, and bestowed upon Roland a meaningful gaze that sent the latter scrabbling for his wallet.

'Thank you, sir,' said the man, folding away the proffered notes and tucking them into his burgundy waistcoat pocket. Then, without hesitation, he stooped and picked up an ornamental rock and smashed it hard against the glass face of an external fire alarm.

The shrill ringing had guests flying out of doorways, many in disarray, disturbed from their morning lie-in or worse.

'Where's the fire?' somebody said. 'I can't see any smoke.'

Suddenly Debbie was there, standing in her pink negligée, hair tousled, brush in hand. The moment she saw Roland she went to go back in again but the member of staff said, 'Is this the lady, sir?'

The penitent lover gabbled, 'Yes. Yes, of course it is.'

'I'm sorry, madam, but I can't allow you to go back inside until the premises has been checked,' said the other man.

'Debbie! Debbie! Let me explain.'

The alarm continued to ring loudly throughout the hotel as guests poured out from the main building and gathered at assembly points.

Roland went over to her and got down on both knees, clasping at her hem. 'Marry me, Debbie. I love you. You are everything to me.'

A group of guests broke into a ripple of applause and a couple of ladies urged her to say, 'Yes'.

'Go away, you snivelling little man,' said the star-crossed lady pilot.

'Oh!' moaned the audience and looked at each other in amazement.

'...but I love you.'

'No you don't. You're a common philanderer.'

'Ooooh,' said the crowd.

'I'll change. I'll be faithful to you forever.'

'Give him a chance dear,' a guest in a bathrobe called out.

Debbie, aware that she had a dramatic moment in hand, exclaimed, 'Chance? Do you know where I found him? In a locker room with a tarty receptionist and,' she paused for effect, 'without his trousers on!'

AIRSHOW ILEX

Now she had the crowd on her side and there was a general groan of disapproval.

'Dump him!' called the ladies who had previously been so keen on matrimony.

'Castrate him!' called another. It was getting rather ugly.

'Time to leave, sir,' said the member of staff, touching Roland gently on the shoulder but he wasn't going without a fight.

'You're my everything. I'll die without you,' he continued, looking beseechingly up into Debbie's face.

She wacked him across the cheek with the back of her hairbrush and he recoiled. As he recovered, she brought her fluffily slippered foot neatly into his groin. The audience cheered and he rolled onto his side with a moan.

'Ready to go now, sir?' The member of staff said, helping Roland to his unsteady feet. The sound of fire engines could be heard in the distance.

*

'Yes, it's the horns and halo effect,' guffawed the Sunday morning presenter on Radio Runway, followed by the trademark *'Neeee-ooooow'* and *'Frooooooooom'*. He was in full over-jolly mode, trying to make the best of his final day on trial.

'Remember that rascally airshow photographer caught with his pants down during the flying display last Tuesday? Well, guys and dolls, he's certainly come up trumps by rescuing a little local girl when she became trapped in one of the exhibits in the Space Centre yesterday on the first of the two public days at Phillipstone International Airshow,'

There followed the stock recording of football crowds cheering.

'We'll be having that little girl and her mother into the studio later this morning. In the meantime, this station is proclaiming Roland Dilger, show photographer extraordinaire, our hero of the week.'

Then came the trumpet fanfare.

'If you want to see action pictures of the rescue, then take a look at our website www.radiorunwayontheair.gop. Another item of news is just coming in. Demonstrators are again massing

outside the main gates of Phillipstone Airport. Their grievance this time seems to be that they've got wind of the nuclear element in the new ILEX passenger aircraft. Now here's a little music to take you up to the traffic report.'

The radio was on in the kitchen of *Clouds* restaurant where Paula was helping chef prepare for the end of show VIP barbecue. It was all hands on deck as canapés were arranged with artistic flair, freshly delivered seafood was hauled in plastic crates into the big refrigerator and feather-light pastry cases constructed for the cheesecakes. The entire team was rushing about with the calm, purposefulness that only a well-run professional kitchen engenders.

'Turn that wretched radio off please,' Paula said. 'That presenter's just too much at this time of the morning.'

'Did you hear what he said about Roland?' Jack asked.

'Yes I did. Stupid man trying to make amends I suppose. Right. Put these trays in the fridge on the middle shelf. There should be room.'

'Yes, Jack. Do that,' said chef meaningfully. It was his kitchen and he held rank. Paula gave him a look.

'Chef, could you please ask the sous-chef to see me about his missing whites?'

'Yes Paula,' he replied, face deadpan. Then he stopped, rolling pin in hand and asked: 'What's this barbecue for anyway? We've got enough to do with the final restaurant luncheon.'

'A VIP flew in late last night. I was still here. Saw the private jet land. Police cars everywhere. The fire brigade had cleared up all the suds and pumped away the floodwater. That was a terrible downpour yesterday,' she said, thumping her bread dough so that a cloud of flour flew up in a haze.

'So we've all got to work late on this the last day,' grumbled chef. 'Why couldn't they have done this during normal show hours?'

'He's too important. Rumour has it he's going to order four hundred of the *ILEX* for his...' she paused and thumped the dough viciously with her plastic gloved hands, 'regime.'

AIRSHOW ILEX

'I suppose the aircraft industry could use the work,' chef said, resuming his pastry trimming. Paula looked stony-faced. Why wouldn't he leave it alone?

'... and,' he added, cutting out pastry flowers freehand, 'they said on the radio just now that its got a nuclear bit in it.' No response. 'Those demonstrators just have to have something else to complain about now the wind-farm thing's been sorted,' he persevered. 'They'll always find a reason to demonstrate, students mostly. It's part of their job description.'

Paula turned the dough over and punched it. 'I'll leave you to finish that, chef. I'm just going to freshen up.' She peeled off her plastic gloves and whites. 'See you later over at the *ILEX*.'

*

Zelara was polishing the chromium plated mixer taps in the ladies' cloakroom when Paula came in.

'Where is everybody? It's like the grave in the Press Centre this morning.'

'Mornin', Miz Paula. How's yous today?' She jerked her head knowingly towards the cubicles.

'Very well, thank you,' came the nodding minimal response. There was a sound of flushing and an ashen-faced Celeste came out, ignored them both, rinsed her hands, shook them and went out without drying them.

'She looks ghastly. End of show exhaustion?'

'Certainly looks bad.'

'Anybody else in?' Paula whispered.

'No. We have the place to ourselves now.' Zelara hung 'CLEANING IN PROGRESS' on the outside of the door and locked it.

'How did it go yesterday?'

'It's in place.'

'Toilet cistern?'

'Yes. No problems. It's in the third one along in the crew's quarters. I took the precaution of super-gluing the cistern lid on.'

'Good thinking.'

'I was lucky.'

'Yes?'

'Some kid got over the barrier and they were too busy dealing with that to body-search me. I can tell you Paula, walking around on a hot day with a Fremdex bomb in my left bra cup was not good for my nerves.'

'You padded out again afterwards?'

'Oh yes. I had the silicon boob in my bucket under the rest of the stuff. I didn't want to draw attention by looking uni-chested!' She giggled.

'Well done, anyway.' She turned and looked at herself in the mirror.

'I've got flour all over my face. Why didn't you tell me?'

'I thought it was your new Geisha look,' Zelara said archly and smiled that big Caribbean smile that was all teeth and goodwill. 'Is everything OK for the barbecue?'

'Yes, it's all in order. The boys have their hidden ear-pieces and microphones. Here are yours. Just click that little button to switch it on. I tested them all last night. I'll have the knife in a sheath up my sleeve. You keep your accelerator foot perky.'

'Will do.'

'We'll load the refrigerated van at four o'clock and you can drive it around the perimeter road as discussed. Here's your new pass.' She reached into her skirt pocket and took it out. 'Obviously you won't need your fat suit for the event. Come to the service entrance at five to six wearing it. You can leave it with your nylon overall in the bin inside the entrance. I'll kit you out with whites, lensless spectacles and a kitchen hat. Clear?'

'Yes Paula.' She paused. 'Paula.'

'Yes Zelara?'

'You have a five o'clock shadow.'

*

'Come in,' said Maud. The old lady was sitting in the little easy chair in the bedroom of the convent annexe. The sun was streaming through the window and she had her favourite cat on

AIRSHOW ILEX

her lap. Reverend Mother appeared, a mug of coffee in her hand.

'I thought you might like this,' she said, setting it down on the little side-table and pretending not to see the forbidden cat.

'That's very kind of you, your Reverendship,' she said graciously. The shaggy moggy with the singed whiskers looked adoringly up at her.

'There, there my darling,' Maud said, stroking her firmly and encouraging the crescendo of purring.

'I just came to tell you the good news,' said the nun as she perched on the edge of one of the single beds.

'Oh yes?' said Maud, half-interested.

'Your new bungalow will be ready in about 12 weeks time.'

'You mean we have to leave here?'

'You can still come up to visit and don't forget the nice new quarters we are making in the stables for your strays. So I expect we'll see a lot of you.'

Maud looked a bit worried. 'Do I have to see to all the cats myself?' she asked tremulously.

'No you don't. One of the Filipino novices will help you and that nice lady from the animal rescue place will come in once a week to see everything's in order.'

'I miss that girl who stayed here. Where is she?'

'She's gone back to her home country. She flew away on Friday. Her name was Anna.'

'She didn't talk much.'

'No, she didn't.'

'Do you think she liked my present?'

A tingle of alarm ran up Reverend Mother's spine. She clasped her hands together and leaned forward in the knowledge that Maud had temporarily misappropriated several items while she had been staying in the convent.

'So, Mrs. Hunt, what did you give her?'

'Well, not so much as give, but swap.'

'Do tell me,' said the Reverend Mother encouragingly.

Maud lifted the cat onto the floor. Then she got up and went over to the window ledge and moved the plant from its stand.

'I was awake early the other morning, you see. I couldn't sleep... wretched pigeons cooing. So I went into her room to see if she wanted to talk but she wasn't there. Her travel bag was on the bed, so I thought I'd check to see that she had everything she needed and I found this.' Maud held up a square, black tile. 'I think it's one of Sister Catherine's blank plaques. I don't know why the girl didn't buy a pretty one.'

Reverend Mother looked puzzled. It was a very boring-looking tile.

'So,' continued Maud, 'I took it away and went and got one of Sister Catherine's decorated ones from the conservatory and put that in instead. I'll pay for it, your Reverendship, really I will. You won't put me in a home, will you?'

*

Celeste Blagden stood alone on the Press Centre balcony in the late afternoon sunshine. It had been another, hot summer's day. The carpet under her feet was still damp and squidgy from Saturday's storm. Not many members of the press had been in today, indeed, it had mostly been staff and their families. The public had now left. Outside exhibits were already on the move, being manoeuvred to their take-off positions at the end of the runway. Gaps were appearing on the tarmac aprons. She could see helicopters being lifted onto long-loaders and maintenance crews were bringing in ladders and scaffolding ready to dismember hoardings.

She leaned over to look down at the sound of cheerful chattering. A group of cafeteria servers had got lucky in the halls and been given loads of plants and floral arrangements. They staggered along under the weight, laughing at their luck, looking like a mobile flower shop, awash with blooms.

'Turn the main off!' an electrician called to his mate. 'Let's get that fountain disconnected.' Celeste guessed they must be talking about the water feature down in the foyer. It was amazing how quickly everything had been put together and must now be dismantled.

AIRSHOW ILEX

'Alright if I clear these chairs Miss?'

Celeste turned. A youth in overalls had come through pushing a trolley.

'Yes. It's fine. Take them away.'

He stacked the red plastic chairs and loaded them.

'Carpet rippers'll be up later,' he said.

She nodded and smiled in acquiescence. Her world was systematically being destroyed. Tomorrow the contents of her office would be back in company headquarters. Within a couple of weeks, all trace of the temporary buildings would be gone, save for their foundations.

Over beyond the boardwalk, the funfair rides were being taken apart, folded and hauled onto their transporters, ready to grace some other major event. Golf buggies were still buzzing about, ferrying hall staff to the car parks. The pick-up truck was working its way along the concourse, taking down the flags of many nations.

Vans were pulling up to take away the contents of exhibition halls. The cleaning machines were out, stripping the site of its coating of litter. The *ILEX* was already in place over by the hangers and, near them, she could see the green and white marquees set up for the end of show barbecue for the special guest.

Celeste wandered back into the relaxation area, so recently crammed with reporters and television crews, now completely empty. Even the snack bar had been dismantled. It had been a successful fortnight though, she mused, despite the heat, the storm, the power cut, that irritating Eleanor Framp, the ghastly Youth Day and Roland's nude escapade. A smile erupted despite everything. It would be her first and last job of such responsibility. What would her parents say when she told them about the triplets? She'd hardly slept last night and felt like death. It was probably only going to get worse, this pregnancy thing. Placing her hands over her abdomen, imagining her tiny offspring suspended there, her future in waiting, she knew she would keep them. It didn't matter that Rupert had dumped her. She was made of tough stuff and would manage it all somehow.

She shaded her eyes and watched the white catering van snake its way along the perimeter road. Would they miss her if she didn't go and join the wrap-up party? She ought to be there really, when the Minister for Defence of the foreign power took his test flight on the *ILEX*. It was to be the climax of the show's marketing strategy and mooted to draw in a massive final order. With a sigh, she locked the balcony doors behind her. On a hook in the corner of the office, hung her change of clothes.

*

Paula was wearing a cream trouser suit and pink, sling-back sandals. She had lacquered her hair stiff and applied her make-up with great care. It was almost as if she was preparing a body for burial. Indeed, this would be 'her' final appearance. She stood supervising the last culinary items as they came off the van that was parked behind the white marquee that stood a few yards from the green and white striped one which was the venue for the finale barbecue.

Approaching along the perimeter road from the west, came a slow cortège of large, black limousines with outriders flashing blue lights. It was early evening but the sun was still high and the airport field glistened. The *ILEX*, standing like a bird of prey, was in dark, stark contrast to the jollity of the marquees, awnings and bunting.

The ovens in the kitchen tent had been on for some time so that the garlic bread would be presented to perfection. The three, super-size barbecues were well alight and attended by sous-chefs in crisp whites and hats. The technicians had tested the amplification system and left. One remained behind just in case. The string quartet, consisting of three lady violinists and one man on cello, struck up Vivaldi as the cars drew to a halt nearby.

Lord Jolian St.John-Fawcett-Blythe, representing Phillipstone airshow board, stood with Celeste Blagden in line with five other show top brass and the plane's captain. The leatherjackets were on guard around the *ILEX* where a red carpet ran from the podium in front of the marquee to the plane's unrolled staircase.

AIRSHOW ILEX

Two Fleet Street photographers were in evidence.

'Where's your own show photographer?' queried Lord Jolian quietly.

'He's still in A and E. He met with a slight accident this morning,' Celeste replied. 'That Fleet Street chappie over there will let us have copies of his photographs for our records.' Lord Jolian nodded in approval.

All four doors of the first and third limousines flew open simultaneously and six men in combat gear leaped out of each. Four had XJ250s and took up positions by the second car. The other eight shielded the exit of the foreign Sinchurian Defence Minister as his diminutive form emerged with what appeared to be a duplicate of himself. The soldiers then escorted the pair in a ring of steel to meet the dignitaries. The doppelgänger was only distinguished from his master by his humble posture. Both wore maroon suits with stand-up collars and gold epaulettes. They looked like brothers.

The more humble of the two shook hands with Lord Jolian and said, 'Permit me to introduce myself. I am Jingh-du Hongwei, official interpreter to our esteemed Minister of Defence of Sinchuria, Mr. Altszung Shlei.' He bowed from the waist. His master gave an effusive and complex greeting in his own language which involved much showing of teeth that were narrow near their roots. The Lord looked down on the Minister with a benign, nodding grin. Any onlooker could see that he was twice his size.

Then the rest of the introductions took place with much bowing and interpreting. Celeste felt that her presence wasn't approved of as the Minister's perfunctory handshake bore all the sincerity of a defrosting Dover sole as it grazed her palm.

It had been decided that the speeches would take place before the meal after which a tour of the *ILEX* and a short flight in it would follow. The Minister was ushered to the podium along with his twin and there followed a torturously translated speech about the regime's interest in improving life for its people and the environment. He explained how the purchase of four hundred *ILEX*es would ensure a vibrant tourist trade to their country, as well as enhancing communications generally.

Some polite clapping followed. The photographers flashed. The scent of garlic bread wafted. The guests were conducted to their tables by Paula and the Maître d'Hotel. The Minister gave Paula a very circumspect look before he sat down. The barbecue began.

If Zelara could have seen the guests from her place in the driver's seat of the kitchen delivery van, she would have viewed a tableau of surreal magnitude as the foreign dignitaries ate rhythmically, and with no apparent pleasure, in the middle of a circle of stony-faced bodyguards. Jack and Marcus in the kitchen tent spoke in low tones into the microphones concealed in the yellow flowers on the chests of their whites.

'Just checking.'

'All OK.'

'Zelara. Check.'

Paula turned away and spoke briefly into her microphone. 'Stand by.'

*

'Over 'ere. More ter the left. That's it, you great git!'

The forklift truck driver worked his way to the side and deposited one more drum on the pile in the maintenance yard. He called down to his mate 'Easy peasy. Like stacking kids' bricks. No bovver!'

The last of the orange drums was in place. He switched off and climbed down.

'Where'd this lot come from?'

'Off that ruddy, great, black plane over the far side there... where they're 'aving the barbecue. Can smell them king prawns from 'ere.'

His mate leaned on the truck. 'Why we got them drums over 'ere then?'

'Guv says plane's going long-'aul. Took 'em off to save fuel.'

'Flipping 'eavy.'

'Got rocks in, 'e said. They use 'em fer ballast.'

There was a sudden grating noise. He looked up.

AIRSHOW ILEX

'Hey! Watch out!'

Both men dived out of the way as one of the top drums came bouncing down the stack, hit the side of the truck and burst open with an unbelievably, noxious stench as its lid flew off.

They both picked themselves up, coughing and sticking their tongues out at the disgusting smell. The drum lay dented on its side with a gooey mass oozing out of it. The forklift driver grabbed his mate's arm.

'That don't look like rocks.' Holding their collars over their mouths they approached the mess. A man's putrefying head lolled out.

'Don't look mate! I think we've found that missing security chief.'

*

Paula was on the point of giving the code words into the microphone embedded in her flower when a chant of, 'No nuclear-fuelled planes! No nuclear-fuelled planes!' started up from behind the hangers. She looked to see a couple of hundred demonstrators with radioactivity warning signs on their tee-shirts, rattling the four metre high fence that kept them out. She walked calmly over to the quartet.

'Play loudly!' she commanded and they, realising the urgency of the request, followed their leader into Khatchaturian's Fire Dance at high volume.

The guards started to bristle slightly and all turned to face the demonstrators. Lord Jolian's joke about high-spirited youngsters lost something in translation. However, help was at hand as the fire appliance, still on duty to the side of the main hanger, appeared. A couple of the crew rolled out a hose and within thirty seconds were spraying the demonstrators with water from their tank while the rest of them set up a second hose from the fire hydrant nearby.

Paula was quick to see how this diversion could be useful and she started to clap, giving encouraging looks to all her staff to do the same until eventually the guests joined in and one or two of the foreign guards tucked their semi-automatics under their arms, laughing and clapping too. The tension was gone. It was a good time for action. The clapping died away. The demonstrators fell back.

'AIRSHOW *ILEX*!' Paula commanded into her microphone, picking up a tray of puddings which she carried over to the main table. Jack poured oil on the hot griddle plate. It smouldered.

'I can offer you trifle, cheesecake, or jellied fruits in their own juices,' she said graciously, fluttering her long, artificial eyelashes, the action of which caused the 'Target' to look up at her in a rather mesmerised state. His interpreter rattled off the list in their language. The 'Target' pointed to a mini-cheesecake garnished with strawberries. As he withdrew his hand, Paula let the tray slip and the entire consignment fell into his lap in a welter of fruit, cream, crumbled pastry and multi-coloured juices. He leapt to his feet but she already had him, her knife held neatly to his wrinkled neck. The griddle plate burst into flames and copious smoke.

Somebody barked out an incomprehensible command. Somebody else countermanded it. The music stopped abruptly. There was a squeal. Paula drew the 'Target' towards the rear of the marquee. Jack hissed into his microphone, 'Now Zelara!'

The kitchen van reversed with a roar and screeched to a halt, its loading door open. With all the skill of a high-jumper performing a perfect western roll, Paula threw herself backwards into the van which then jolted forward to the sound of its tyres being shot out. Zelara struggled to keep it going but one of the limousines revved up and roared alongside her, curving in to cut off her escape path so that the van ground to a halt, its bonnet excruciatingly crumpled against the car's reinforced wing in a hiss of steam.

Paula tried to hold onto her victim but the sudden jolt sent her skidding on her back along the inside length of the van and out of the flapping back doors onto the dust of the perimeter road. The 'Target', his throat bleeding superficially, had thrown himself at Zelara's back and was hanging onto her like a monkey, calling for assistance. The fire crew, realising that there was an incident taking place, took shelter behind their appliance and radioed for

AIRSHOW ILEX

police assistance. Griddle flames licked at the marquee roof. At the first sound of shots, the sodden demonstrators behind the fence took flight. The fire crew crouched powerlessly.

'Target' bodyguards picked Paula up, dragging her along, ripping her clothes, taking her back to the marquee. Zelara was carried, struggling, behind her. Once there, both were pushed onto chairs. One of the foreign guards pulled Paula's hair back to question her but her wig came off, revealing a man in drag.

'Peverted personage!' spat the interpreter who had been joined by the Sinchurian Minister for Defence sporting a blood-soaked, linen napkin around his neck.

In the marquee, the hosts were lined up against the flapping side-wall at gun-point, except Celeste who was on the carpet in a dead faint. The kitchen staff crouched down behind the ovens, hoping they had been forgotten. The string quartet acquiesced to the command to put down their instruments and join the others. One woman took her violin with her but didn't keep it for long. A guard dashed it to the ground and trod on it. The sound of the instrument being crunched flat elicited a wail from its owner.

Orders were barked out and the interpreter said, 'The Sinchurian Minister for Defence would be obliged if you would all please go aboard the *ILEX*.'

Paula and Zelara exchanged looks of terror.

'What shall we do?' Zelara screamed. 'Tell them! Tell them there's a bomb on the plane!'

'There's a bomb on the plane!' Paula shouted.

'That won't work, pervert!' sneered the interpreter.

'This is preposterous!' spluttered the lord, only to receive a butt in the stomach for his trouble.

'The Sinchurian Minister for Defence would be pleased if you would do as you are told and then no more people will be hurt.'

'Drop your weapons!' barked the interpreter to the captive leatherjackets who had been herded together near the marquee by the Sinchurian bodyguards. As one man, the entire troop of leatherjackets reached for their guns but instead of dropping them, went as if to fire. As crack shots they should have been quicker but the would-be hijackers mowed them down as if they were fairground toys and they lay on the grass like dying stag beetles, thrashing and groaning away their last seconds, anonymous behind their reflective face-masks beneath black helmets.

The sound of the shots roused Celeste from her faint on the carpet. All eyes were turned towards the leather-clad bloodbath or the flaming kitchen marquee, so she chose that moment of supreme self-preservation to quietly roll under the floor-length white tablecloth covering the buffet serving table and out of sight. She curled up, head shielded with hands and hoped they couldn't hear her heart pounding as she fought breath-strangling panic.

Like sheep, the terrified hostages climbed the *ILEX* staircase, looking back at the blood-strewn, smoking shambles beneath them. Jack and Marcus hoped that they would be spared.

'Get the kitchen staff!' commanded the interpreter. The terrified boys shambled forward in their whites, past the Sinchurian Defence Minister, sitting soaked in pudding and blood.

'Paula…' said Jack imploringly towards his boss who was sitting, shoeless, the designer cream trouser-suit streaked with blood from a huge gash across the forehead.

'Do as they say,' said Paul hopelessly before a fist smashed across his face and he was hauled to his feet to be propelled towards the aircraft that he knew contained a ticking time bomb. Zelara was weeping copiously. 'I've got children. What's going to happen to my children?'

'Get up those stairs!' She received a shove in the back.

'You! Captain!'

'Yes?'

'You will call me 'Sir', if you please.'

'Yes, Sir,' he replied with slow deliberation.

'You will fly us to our country.'

'There won't be enough fuel.'

The interpreter gave a look to one of the foreign guards who kicked the pilot in the knee.

'Don't lie. We know that the *ILEX* is fuelled up for a long test tour. Get to the flight deck but first please tell me why some men's, striped, trousers are flying on the airport windsock pole?'

AIRSHOW ILEX

The captain, first foot on the *ILEX* staircase, turned and looked, replying sardonically, 'I expect somebody is drying their washing,'

'Ha! I see your English sense of humour does not desert you.'
The captain replied, 'My first officer's been on board the whole time. He will have told the control tower what's going on. '

'Good. Then they will know that we are taking the *ILEX*.'

'They'll scramble the airforce to intercept us.'

'What, and risk a nuclear disaster over your suburbia? I don't think so. Get aboard!'

*

Eleanor reclined in the sun chair on the deck of the *Lucky Lady*.

'This is so lovely,' she remarked appreciatively.

'You deserve it,' Grant said, looking up from his newspaper. 'I'm glad you decided to skip the airshow barbecue and spend the afternoon on the Broads with me.'

'So am I. It's much more relaxing here. I think I did more than my duty this past fortnight, although I would have liked to have seen the *ILEX* one more time before it flies to America and then onto Australia. They say it's going to do it in one hop in future.'

'Seems like your wish is to be granted,' he said. 'Look!'
The distinctive profile of the *ILEX* rose in the western sky and passed above them, heading east.

'That's funny,' said Eleanor. 'I thought it would have been going the other way.'

'So did I,' he replied, looking over the top of his glasses at her. 'By the way, I've been meaning to ask you, have you thought any more about my magazine proposal?'

'The editorship?'

'What else?'
She sat up straighter and leaned forward,

'I'd like to accept your kind offer on a fifty-fifty split of the profits basis,' she said, extending her hand.

'It's a deal,' he replied and kissed the back of her fingers.

*

333

By a fishing shack at Lake Ustelsk, an old man in waders was hauling in his nets. He paused to shade his eyes against the setting sun as a dull 'boom' reached his ears. He just saw the burning fragments of an exploding aircraft spiralling out of the sky along the length of the lake towards him. He staggered backwards in his haste to get out of the water as the myriad particles hissed and splashed, peppering the surface and sinking without trace. It was over in seconds apart from a small orange parachute, bearing what looked like a large, metal safe with a radioactivity sign on the side, drifting down and landing in the lake's central deeps with a large splash. He didn't care. As an escaped prisoner, living in the wilderness for the past ten years, he minded his own business.

AIRSHOW ILEX

Appendix

The Hamburg streets in Chapter 15 exist but the story taking place there and in Chapter 14 is fictitious. The German/ English translations below may enhance your enjoyment of *AIRSHOW ILEX*. Grateful thanks to my husband Pitt for his assistance. MBL

Page
5   *Guten Abend.* Good evening.

173 *Danke schön. Vielen Dank. Danke vielmals.* : Thank you

174
Aber, können Sie mir bitte helfen? But can you help me please?
Langsam, bitte. : Slowly, please.
Hundert : hundred   *Nein* : No.   *Zu viel* : Too much.
Zwanzig ist genug. Meinen Koffer nun bitte. : Twenty is enough. My case now please.

175
Wie kann ich Ihnen helfen? : How can I help you?
Sprechen Sie Englisch bitte? : Do you speak English please?
Gnädige Frau ist etwas bestürzt. : Madam is a little upset.
Ja. Natürlich. : Yes. Of course.
Kommen Sie mit mir meine Liebe. : Come with me, my dear.
Wilkommen in Deutschland. : Welcome to Germany.

178
Ein Einzeltisch, gnädige Frau? : A table for one, madam?
Polizei : Police. *Polizei Revier* : Police Station.

183 *Jawohl* : Yes. (Strongly)

184 *Oh, du meine Güte!* : Goodness gracious me!
   Ein bisschen : A little.
   Entchuldigen Sie mich bitte einen Moment. : Excuse me a moment, please.

AIRSHOW ILEX

188 *Kirche* : church.

189 *Strasse* : street.

190 *Haben Sie einen anderen Wunsch?* : Do you have another wish? (Anything else?)

192
Mein Geliebter! Was machts du hier? : My darling! What are you doing here?
Was für eine Überraschung! : What a surprise!
Schwierigkeit : Difficulty.
Tschüss! : See you later/ 'Bye for now. (Colloquial)

195
polizisten : policemen

Note. Nouns in German begin with a capital letter.

AIRSHOW ILEX

Song of the Ilex

© Mary B. Lyons 2010

Here comes the Ilex, soaring through the skies,
The twilight's shimmer, tracks her as she flies.
Her silhouette so sinister and stark,
Elusive as the evening's cloak of dark,
Glides through clouds above the city's pall.
The Ilex is the blackest bird, the blackest bird of all.

Chorus

So close your eyes and dream of distant parts.
When Ilex flies, her beauty touches hearts.

Throughout the history and magic of manned flight,
The Ilex thunders like velvet in the night.
The leading edge of wings that cut the air,
Ebony profile shines in moonlight there,
Swooping with a silent, muted call,
The Ilex is the blackest bird, the blackest bird, of all.

Here comes the Ilex, spanning time and space,
The finest aircraft to serve the human race.
Leviathan of power and secrets deep,
She haunts the skies above the Earth in sleep,
Captured in the future's unseen thrall,
The Ilex is the blackest bird, the blackest bird, of all.

The sheet music SONG OF THE ILEX by Mary B. Lyons
will be available, with guitar chords, from
www.wordpower.u-net.com later in 2010.

The Lonely Shade

by Mary B. Lyons BSc(Hons)

The Lonely Shade is a sensitively written booklet of original poetry that fills a long-felt need in times of bereavement. The contents are suitable for reading aloud at funeral and remembrance services or for the quiet comfort of the bereaved. This publication is presented in large print so that at the difficult time of loss, when tears are often near, reading is easier.

The companion CD *(The Lonely Shade-CD)* contains numbered tracks ideal for peaceful, personal listening or for playing through the funeral venue's compatible system, when care should be taken in selecting just the right poem or poems suitable for the occasion.

To order "*The Lonely Shade*" booklet and CD please visit our web-site:

www.wordpower.u-net.com

The Lonely Shade booklet
ISBN 978-0950821214

The Lonely Shade – CD
ISBN 978-0950821221

The Lonely Shade
by
Mary B. Lyons BSc(Hons)

**Original
Sympathetic Poetry and Words
For Funerals and for the Bereaved**

48 page large-print booklet and a CD spoken
by the author, both available from
www.wordpower.u-net.com

MARY B. LYONS

Mary B. Lyons is a freelance writer, photographer, artist and cartoonist who has had her work published in the following:

The Times Educational Supplement
The Lancet
Hampshire the County Magazine
Police Gazette
Surrey Monocle
Mail on Sunday (financial pages)
Omega
Machine Knitting Monthly
Hampshire Now
Royal Photographic Society Journal
Pilot
Funeral Director Monthly
Funeral Service Journal
Antiques magazine
SAIFinsight
Business Digest
Local and National papers

Mary has had her own magazine and newspaper columns and broadcast on BBC local radio and appeared on BBC television.